Acknowledgements

Firstly Janners, for planting that seed in Gibraltar and then constantly watering it ever since; you are an incredible inspiration and a trusted sounding board. Andy, for your sage advice and honest feedback, all in spite of your immense literary snobbery. And Hilary, for your constant and unwavering belief in me, and for leaving me alone for long enough to get this done!

Creeping Sands

Chapter One

It was only five in the morning but already the temperature was in the thirties, and the humidity in the nineties. The sun's first rays were starting to penetrate the canopy and dissipate the dark gloom. Jerry squirmed and carefully shifted his position, feeling the sweat roll down his neck, across his shoulders and onto his chest. The sensation was quite tolerable, but the whine from the millions of mosquitoes dancing around his head, in his ears, up his nose, and on his eyelids was not. Fuckers.

The infiltration had progressed as planned. After parting with Bravo Team at the force separation point shortly into the patrol, he had led Alpha Team towards their laying up point. The four man-team was dressed in dark combat fatigues and wearing night-vision goggles, allowing them to slowly pick their way through the pitch black along the forest floor - a mass of dense undergrowth with spikes and barbs on every branch, sitting atop ankle-grabbing grasses, roots and vines. The vicious undergrowth was interspersed with small open areas where the ground was covered with a thick layer of decaying leaves and rotting branches dropped from the canopy above. The team had used these open areas where possible to minimise their signature, all the time ensuring they continued on the correct bearing to the target, which was displayed on the lens of his goggles, giving him a constant direction and range to the target. There was nothing easier, or more disheartening, than getting lost in the jungle at night. Stick to the bearing, count your paces, and most importantly hope the GPS signal doesn't drop out.

The GPS hadn't dropped out, so they had arrived at the laying up point eight minutes early, giving them a chance to rest, take on some water and check their weapons and equipment. The four men moved silently, each conducting his own final battle preparation with a well-practiced confidence and smoothness. As he worked, Jerry had eyed each member of his team, noting the calm look of concentration on each face as they stowed away NVGs, checked weapon sights and double-checked ammunition. Their calmness was testament to their professionalism and experience, but belied the gravity of the mission they were about to undertake. When it was time Jerry had given a hand signal and they had silently moved towards the target, each man knowing his role, as well as those of his team.

Now they were each laid silent and still in position, on a springy soft bed of leaves if they were lucky; on a hard root or spiked branch if they weren't. Each man mentally rehearsed his role as the seconds ticked towards H-hour - the start of the raid.

In the gloomy first light of day Jerry regarded the target from his position, laying on his stomach on the edge of a clearing in the jungle. The circular clearing was 150 metres across, with a single access track from the south, a black hole in the tree line. Three large troop trucks were parked near the entry point. A short burst of the radio in Jerry's ear told him the track was now being covered by Bravo team, who having already silently disabled the trucks were laying in wait 100m down the track to ambush any squirters trying to escape.

The clearing contained twenty large military accommodation tents, and six smaller storage tents. The tents were arranged in rows, each with the opening facing towards the centre of the clearing. In the centre of the clearing was another accommodation tent and a large square tent, its flaps open, exposing the tables and chairs of the dining facility within. The remains of last night's fire smouldered on the ground outside the mess tent, surrounded by scattered chairs.

On the eastern side of the mess tent was a smaller tent with a large HF radio antenna and a satellite dish adjacent. It was the only tent with a light showing. Jerry could vaguely identify a single figure seated inside the tent with his feet up on a table. Jerry guessed that this was the radio picquet, monitoring the security sensors around the camp, and most likely sleeping on the job. Rag-tag forces wouldn't have a watchkeeper.

Jerry reached into a pouch on his front and extracted the hornet - a small drone which looked and sounded exactly like its deadly namesake. He launched it into the air and set it off on its flight path, to sweep around the camp at twenty feet, looking for hidden dangers and unexpected enemy. Jerry watched the images being streamed to the lens in his left eye. As he moved his eye left and right the hornet banked and swooped, allowing him to explore any areas he chose. He steered the hornet to the command tent and hovered outside, confirming the presence of the sole occupant, before releasing it to swoop away to its pre-programmed path.

Satisfied that all was as expected, and after another check of his watch, Jerry looked up to the sky. It was now a slightly lighter shade of grey, giving them just enough light to move silently through the camp, without hitting unexpected obstructions. He looked to his left and then his right, gave a slow, deliberate hand signal, and as one they silently rose from their final assault position and stalked out of the tree line, into the camp, weapons raised to their shoulders.

The team moved carefully yet deliberately, ensuring their footsteps were silent yet swift as they made their way towards the lines of tents. They knew their targets, which tents they would be in, how many there would be, and what weapons they would have. The target had been reconnoitred extensively over the last two days, using the hornet, and its big brother the parrot - an actual African gray parrot which could be controlled by a tiny chip in its brain, providing video images from the tiny camera mounted on its chest.

The team split into pairs as they approached the first tent. Jerry and Al moved to the opening of the second tent, where Jerry lowered his weapon and slowly drew open the tent flap. Satisfied that they had not been compromised, Al lowered his rifle and drew his K-Bar fighting knife as he crept into the tent, heading for the nearest target who lay sleeping in a cot by the door. In one smooth movement he clamped his hand over the sleeping man's mouth and thrust his dagger into the side of his throat. The man jerked awake, his eyes opening wide and hands raising to free himself, but as blood gushed from his neck in powerful spurts he weakened and eventually slumped dead, his arms splayed and eyes staring.

Al exited the tent after a cursory glance at the ten or so other sleeping figures and with weapons raised they moved together to the next tent. Jerry noted the progress of the other pair, Nat and Yash as they exited and moved stealthily to their next target.

The team worked methodically and clinically, dispatching the sleeping guards in each tent without fuss or noise, moving on swiftly each time, aware that their work was far from over. After a few minutes the accommodation tents had been cleared and they moved towards the tents in the centre of the camp, weapons raised, alert to any movement or noise.

From one of the accommodation tents came a terrified scream. Jerry and the team halted, and turned their heads towards the sound. A girl's voice shrieked and wailed, presumably as she discovered the bloodied corpse of the guard sprawled on the cot. Jerry's mind raced as he quickly weighed the options. It would be too late to silence the girl, not to mention the others she would wake. Instead they should push on to the central tents and complete the mission as fast as possible.

There were shouts from within the central tents as the rest of the sleeping men woke and began to hurriedly organise themselves. Shouts of confusion and barked orders competed with each other as the as yet unseen men struggled to find weapons and clothes. Tent flaps were being wildly thrown open, and men starting to emerge into the early morning light, rifle barrels leading the way.

Jerry did not need to issue any orders now, the plan had been briefed and the men were well drilled. The team separated into their pairs; Nat and Yash quickly headed for the command tent to eliminate the signaller, who would no doubt be calling for reinforcements already. Jerry and Al continued their advance towards the tent, weapons raised to their shoulders, issuing short bursts of automatic fire. Two enemy soldiers fell as they emerged from the tent, not having any chance to return fire. Jerry knew there should be three more hostiles in the tent who needed to be quickly neutralised before they could endanger the team. Al raked the side of the tent with a long burst of fire, hoping to force the hostiles to the ground where they would not be able to fire effectively. From the command tent came the sound of more automatic fire, not only Nat and Yash's P12s but also some AK47 fire from the hostile. It ended as quickly as it started. Aware that they could be fragged with their own grenade, Jerry tossed a flashbang through the opening. After a short pause there was a chain of flashes and a deafening blast causing the sides of the tent to billow out and release a cloud of smoke and dust. Al was already there at the opening of the tent, weapon poised, spitting fire into the tent in short bursts. There was no return fire.

The screams and yells from the accommodation tents continued, though their tone had changed from horror and shock to fear and panic. Girls were emerging from the tents now, unsure of what was happening, but sure they didn't want to stay trapped inside a tent. The team quickly confirmed all hostiles were dead and the team were unhurt, at which time Jerry called the Bravo team into the camp via his radio. He turned to look at the girls, who were now streaming from the tents into the central open area. They were a sorry sight, and Jerry felt his chest tighten as he beheld them. Dozens of girls were emerging from the tents, crying and wailing, holding their faces in their hands and staring, wide-eyed with shock at what had happened. Some were dressed in traditional long abayas, some only in torn dresses, looking ragged and abused. Many fell to their knees and prayed when they realised what had happened, some hugged each other, many stood silent with their arms wrapped around them looking terrified. There were 58 girls, aged between nine and nineteen. They had been taken two weeks ago from a school some two hundred kilometres away in Gabon. They were being held for ransom by the group of militants, and Jerry judged from the look of many of them that they had not only been held, but also subjected to terrible cruelty and most likely sexual assault. He recognised the hollow look in the faces of the girls, as though they were so beaten and subjugated that they didn't dare feel relief or joy. The usual reaction of such victims was uncertainty of whether Jerry and his team were their saviours, or just a new set of captors. The team had seen it before in the faces of hostages, and they knew they had to treat them carefully in case any should panic and try to run for the trees. An authoritative tone and clear instructions were needed to manage the situation effectively.

'Tout le monde s'asseoir ensemble' shouted Jerry, instructing the women to sit down together in the central area. The ambush team were approaching and began assisting Jerry's team in corralling the girls together. The girls moved slowly and warily, looking nervously at the troops and their dark-haired leader. His thin face looked authoritative yet kind, his dark eyes glistened and his thin lips turned up in a reassuring smile. Even though he brandished a number of weapons, he had a non-threatening posture and they instinctively trusted him.

'Nous sommes là pour vous aider' he said, reassuring them that the teams were there to help the girls. He went on to explain that they were going to take the girls home to their families, and that they would be safe now. There were cautious expressions of relief and celebration from the girls - they had been lied to and thoroughly manipulated in the last fortnight and their instinctive self protection was warning them to be wary. Jerry and the teams were reassuring in their tone of voice and body language, deliberately lowering their weapons and moving slowly so as not to alarm the girls. He went on to explain that they would be transporting the girls away from the camp very soon and they should stay where they are until then.

With Bravo team now co-located, Jerry turned to Al, 'Checked in with HQ?'

'Yep, helos are in-bound, five minutes'.

'Okay, let's get the landing site marked. Nat, Yash - strip out that end tent to make some more room'. The men moved away towards the disabled trucks and got to work. Jerry turned back to Al, 'Not exactly how I hoped it would go down. Did the signaller manage to get the word out?'

'Yep, Yash said he was putting down the handset when they got to the tent' replied Al, 'it'll be a nice surprise for them when the gunship greets them'. He chuckled and reached into his webbing pouch for his water bottle. Jerry smiled and looked at his partner and friend as he drank. Al Van de Berg was a bear of a man, only just over six feet tall but weighing a hefty 230 pounds, with heavy broad shoulders, a heaving chest and arms as thick as most people's legs. He was a pretty fair boxer, but a great rugby player, having played in the scrum for the Australian Commando Regiment. His massive head bore several fearsome scars and he looked every bit the soldier, but that huge head also housed a formidable brain, as Al also had a Master's Degree in Political Science and had finished top of his class at the Royal Military College Duntroon. He was a great team-mate, and he and Jerry had done a lot of shit together since they'd met, just over two years ago, when they were both recruited into the Task Force.

'Another great story of the cavalry getting there too late and getting slaughtered. Like Gettysburg, but with helicopter gunships' joked Jerry.

'And sweaty dudes in the jungle' laughed Al.

'You'd think they'd have learned by now' said Jerry, reaching for his own water bottle. 'There's no point trying to pull this kind of shit any more. We're just gonna kick their asses every time'.

'Yep, but these guys are dumb and desperate. They're hurting, they don't have many choices and this is an easy way out of the shit hole they're in. Until they all die of course'.

'Well, death is a choice. They made that one' said Jerry.

'Just like they did in Sierra Leone, Congo, Mali and all the others'. Al put back his water bottle and grasped his weapon. He turned his head to the sound of choppers approaching. 'I'll get these girls ready for the coolest school-bus journey of their lives!' He grinned and stalked away towards the seated crowd.

As Jerry watched him walk away he reflected on the operations he and Al had been involved in over the last two years. They had been most active in Central and Western Africa, flying in for short missions, usually straightforward kill or capture, sometimes a bit more sophisticated counter-insurgency, but always with a full mandate to destroy the enemy with extreme prejudice. Was it right? Was it the best way to deal with Africa's many regional and tribal disputes? Probably not, but there weren't any better options on the table at the moment, and there were plenty of customers lining up for their services as resources grew shorter and humans inevitably resorted to more brutal and greedy methods of profiting from others' misery.

As the first wave of choppers landed Al and the team began to shepherd the girls onboard, while Jerry conducted a search of the command tent, looking for any intelligence which may prove useful in the fight against the militants. The group was known as La Fraternite, meaning The Brotherhood, who were operating in the Mahongue tribal region which bridged the north east of Gabon and the west of Congo. The aims of the Brotherhood were little known, except for the obvious collection of money from ransoms and extortion, and occasional bloody attacks on villages. Their operations had remained fairly small-scale, but were sufficient to cause a concern to both governments, particularly the Gabonese government as they seemed to suffer most of La Fraternite's attacks. Task Force analysts had suggested it was actually a proxy guerrilla force, acting in Congo's interests to destabilise the eastern tribal regions of Gabon. It was this analysis which had prompted the government of Gabon to request that the Task Force neutralise La Fraternite as quickly as possible. Jerry, as head of operations of the West Africa Division of the Task Force, had been instrumental in the planning and execution of the missions. During his days with US Special Forces he would have adopted a much more considered and measured approach to planning operations, taking into account not only the desired endstate but also the effect on regional politics, the management of media reaction, and on minimising the loss of life. The Task Force had a very different mandate - the destruction of specified targets in the most expedient manner. Such was the appetite of the international community for swift resolutions, effectively they were given a blank cheque to make it happen. It was certainly more satisfying than diplomatically tip-toeing his way through operations - something Jerry had never really enjoyed.

Jerry recovered some paper documents and a notebook computer from the command tent and headed out to the waiting choppers. The combined downdraught from the rotor blades was whipping dust and loose grass into the air, and blowing the tents as if in a hurricane. Jerry boarded the aircraft, and as it lifted above the canopy he surveyed the camp below, empty of all life and with bodies of militants sprawled where they had fallen. Another target neutralised. Another serial on the long list of bad guys taking a shot against the established order. Another crime against humanity swiftly resolved, and the execution carried out. As he, the executioner, looked down on the camp fading into the distance, he had mixed emotions. Part of him was satisfied that they had completed the mission with no casualties, and that the girls would be returned to their families safely. But part of him also deeply regretted that any of this shit was even necessary. All the pain and suffering, death and destruction, what was it really for? He thought about the hopelessness of Africa, the endless cycle of hatred, violence and retribution, and he wished it didn't have to be that way. He wished for a world where people co-existed in relative harmony. He looked around the helicopter, at the faces of the school girls and of his team, each dreaming their own personal futile daydream of an unrealistic utopia, and he felt a sadness surround him. How was the world so fucked?

Chapter Two

Joseph Ayatumbe, President of the Republic of Chad, stood by the window, looking over the palace grounds. The flowing stream, lush green grass, bright flowers and thick trees looked like a vision of paradise. A gardener tended to a bush in the thick heat of the day, not daring to pause from his work to mop his brow, nor to regard the beautiful butterfly flitting by. Ayatumbe could feel the heat of the sun radiating through the window, warming his face and chest. It was a strange contrast to the air conditioned chill he felt on his back. He shrugged off the cold and continued his gaze out of the window, regarding the gardener again, a small insignificant speck in the vast grounds of the Presidential Palace. He breathed a deep satisfied sigh as he surveyed his dominion, reflecting on the pleasure it gave him to see such a great swathe of greenery. It hadn't been so in his youth, when he had lived in the desert of Darfur, in Western Sudan. Greenery had been exceedingly sparse then, and was often torched by the militias driving him and his family from their villages, raping, pillaging and murdering as they went. He remembered the screams of the unfortunate victims as they fell under the tracks of the tanks, or worse, the swinging machetes of the frenzied attackers. He shuddered and turned away from the window, turning his back on the images that still haunted him.

He rested on one of two large couches in the room - his private office on the first floor of the palace. The office was large, perhaps 50 feet across, and 20 feet high, with high windows on one wall. The walls were clad in dark wooden panelling, with a Chadian flag hanging on each wall, giving the office the look and feel of a courtroom rather than a workplace. On the floor was a sumptuous thick rug, flowing between gratuitously large and extravagant furniture. The couches were covered with silk, the tables and desk made from the finest walnut, and the water jug and glasses on the table from thick crystal. He reclined on the couch and closed his eyes, trying to

14

soothe his mind and his aching brain. He had had a taxing morning, and his afternoon wasn't looking much brighter.

There was a soft knock at the door. 'President Al Quraysh will arrive in five minutes, Sir.'

'Okay' murmured Ayatumbe in response, neither opening his eyes nor lifting his head. He wished he could sleep. He didn't have the energy for this particular meeting and it was sure to be a long one, and unpleasant to boot.

After another few moments he hauled himself up from the couch, rubbed his eyes and yawned. He straightened his jalabiya - his long white robe, and quickly inspected it for any specks or stains. Even though there would be no photos today it was important he looked good - in this game appearances always mattered. He poured a glass of water and drank it down in one go, feeling the cold liquid shock his system into life. He strode towards the door, picking up his tagiya from his desk and placing it on his head as he went. This bastard, he thought, he was a prickly customer, and a tough negotiator, as well as a terrible conversationalist. This was not going to be a good afternoon.

As he exited the main door of the palace, Ayatumbe felt the blast of heat hit him in the face. The desert heat still pervaded, despite the green defences he had constructed in his grounds. And it was only March! This was sure to be a long uncomfortable summer, as it was once again predicted to be the hottest on record. Even though he had lived in these conditions his whole life it was still a shock to feel the blast of the heat in contrast to the building's cool air. He squinted at the bright sunlight and turned to face his advisers, who were lined up to his right.

'Is everything ready?' he demanded.

'Yes sir' replied the closest adviser. 'All is prepared.'

A convoy of black SUVs swept along the drive, through the trees. At its head and its tail were heavily armoured cars, each bristling with powerful-looking remote weapons stations.

Out on the city streets the message was clear - get out of our way or face destruction - Ayatumbe noted that this was also the foreign policy stance of the convoy's occupants.

President Al Quraysh exited the SUV unhurriedly, regarding the beautiful surroundings before turning towards Ayatumbe. He was an unusually tall man for an arab, around 6 foot 2; he even towered above his security detail as they surrounded him. He was dressed in the traditional thobe - the long white robe worn by arab men across the Middle East. On his head he wore the keffiyeh, a red and white chequered headscarf, held in place by the black rope-like agal. His face was long and thin, and appeared almost hidden behind his perfectly sculpted beard and black sunglasses perched on top of his long hooked nose. He removed his glasses as he slowly walked towards Ayatumbe, revealing deep dark eyes. He parted his thick lips to issue the traditional greeting of 'As-Salaam Alaikum', as he stretched out his hand.

'Wa Alaikum-Salaam' replied Ayatumbe as he stepped forward to greet the President. 'Kaif Halak?' he enquired after his guest's health.

'Al hamdu lillah' *Praise be to God* replied the President, 'Kaif Halak?'.

'Al hamdu lillah. Shu Akbarak?' *What's your news?*

'Al hamdu lillah. Shu Akbarak?' replied the President, such was the custom of greetings in the Arabic language, every question was answered and returned. Ayatumbe was not Muslim, nor was Arabic his first language, but he had found it advantageous to learn at least a minimal amount of Arabic custom, particularly given the way Africa was these days.

'Al hamdu lillah. Please, come inside, it is hot today. I have some refreshment ready for us.'

Ayatumbe led the President through the high open doorway, into the cool of the palace. They entered the salon - a cavernous, double-storey room, furnished lightly yet opulently, with dark furniture sitting atop thick rich rugs. The smooth white walls were adorned with several tall portraits of the President in varying orders of dress, as well as a Chadian flag hanging from each wall. An enormous marble staircase curved its way from the centre of the far wall to an unseen upper floor. There were doors at either end of the salon. The two men walked towards the door to the left. They walked in silence. This was not an official state visit, hence there was no need for the usual strained civilities. Each man was occupied with his thoughts about the tactics he was about to employ during the afternoon's discussion.

Ayatumbe was dreading this meeting. It had been preceded by many others like it, as well as by hundreds of hours of negotiation by his ministers and diplomatic staff. Al Quraysh was pushing hard, and he was pushing back as hard as he could, but the arab's diplomatic and economic weight was considerable, and he had been struggling to resist his demands. However resist him he must, his country's very existence depended on it.

Ayatumbe guided his guest to a smaller, yet still lavishly decorated, meeting room. Its style was that of a traditional arabic majlis, with the walls painted orange on the top half, and covered in ornate mosaic tiles on the bottom half. There were sumptuous rugs on the floor, heavy wooden furniture around the walls, with scattered urns and tall ceramic pots. In the centre of the room were three luxurious red couches, to which they headed. As they sat, servants appeared with dates and coffee. Even though this was no social gathering it was still an important element of a meeting, and Ayatumbe saw no harm in smoothing the process as much as possible before the unpleasantness began.

Although he was quite sure the President could not be flattered or bribed into changing his course of action, Ayatumbe had few options left. He regarded the President as he sipped his coffee. Mohammed Rashed Al Quraysh was a cold man, who rarely smiled or indeed showed any emotion. He had been appointed President of the Islamic Republic of North Africa when it had been formed three years before. Before that he had served as the head of the Council of Senior Scholars in Saudi Arabia, and had established himself as a truly pious man, beyond personal or professional reproach. He had led the first Islamic Republic to be newly created in nearly fifty years with skill, with unfaltering support and with an iron fist. As the head of nearly two hundred million citizens from the former states of Libya, Egypt and Sudan, and with control of the largest economy in Africa he was formidably powerful, and so commanded enormous respect.

After a few more salutations and health enquiries the President abruptly turned the conversation to the topic of the day. 'So Mr President, have you reached a decision yet? My position has not changed since we last met, and time is pressing, the attacks have worsened.'

'Nor has my position changed Ameer. It is inconceivable that I cede power of my own land. I have made this clear from the start and will not change my mind.'

'This is an unwise decision Mr President, the borderlands are in great peril, there is a real danger they will be lost to you anyway. The flow of refugees in both directions is not abating. I know you are ill-equipped to cope with those coming south. Furthermore your militias are suffering such heavy casualties, it just cannot continue this way. Will you not let me help you resolve this trouble? It has been two months now and it shows no sign of ceasing.'

Ayatumbe swallowed hard, pushing down his rising anger. The fucking President was playing a clever game, pretending to be offering assistance when everyone knew it was him that was sponsoring the violence in the borderlands. Who else would be interested in so viciously attacking the Chadian minorities and driving them from their homes and tribal lands? The brutality was shocking, and reminded him only too clearly of that which he had witnessed and experienced first-hand, fleeing from his home as a child. His mother and father had both

18

been taken by that wicked act, as the Janjaweed militia committed such atrocities across Darfur, while the Sudanese government played their own evil political games.

'Ameer, I am well aware of the suffering of my people, both Muslim and non-Muslim. My government and I are exploring every option to resolve this crisis quickly and with the minimum of suffering. It is in no-one's interest [*except yours you bastard*] for this to continue, but I do not see how ceding power to the Republic will resolve this issue. It is my land, and I will seek my own solutions.'

'But your problem is affecting my people, Mr President. I am not asking you to cede power of the borderlands to the Republic, only to accept my help. Am I to continue absorbing the flow of Muslim refugees, forced from their homes by your troops? As their closest spiritual leader, I cannot stand by and watch my subjects being killed and driven from their villages. It is my duty to protect their lives and their faith, and both are being threatened by this action. This could be easily resolved by a limited deployment of my troops, which would…'

'Ameer, my own troops have been deployed, and I will deploy more if necessary, I do not require any assistance from your troops.' Ayatumbe was well aware of the President's intentions. A deployment of Republic troops was the beginning of the end for his land. He had been resisting it since the Republic had formed, although their methods had not been so obviously direct until now. Their offers of aid, development projects, mutual border patrolling, shared use of regional natural resources, they had been such transparent moves. If he began to accept these measures, then the creep of the Republic's influence would be continuous, stealing his land village by village, plain by plain. He could not afford to lose his control, particularly of the mountains, they were vital to the future of Chad. If only the President knew just how vital, he would no doubt be pushing much harder.

'Look my friend,' President Al Quraysh was changing tack, almost cracking a smile as he uttered the civility. 'These are difficult times for us all. Africa has never before seen such hardship. We are all suffering. This drought is literally killing us. How long has it been since we saw rain in the borderlands? Five years? More I think. People are starving and desperate, and not just in our countries, look at Guinea; look at Niger; look at our neighbour Ethiopia! Once the breadbasket of North Africa, so prosperous and so promising, struck down by this tragedy we all suffer. How its people suffered. Al hamdu lillah I was able to extend my hand to them, and they wisely took it. You would be well-advised to show similar wisdom, such as you showed in the routing of your oil pipeline through our territory? Partnership benefits us all, let us form such a partnership and end this suffering.'

He was right in that respect, thought Ayatumbe, the oil pipeline had been a wise decision. He had reluctantly agreed to a deal with the Republic, in order to gain easy access to the Suez Canal in order to supply his oil in place of the faltering supplies from the Middle East. Although the value of that agreement was nothing compared to the importance of keeping those northern borderlands. He could not afford to re-draw the boundaries, as seemed so common these days in Africa. Borders were shifting daily it seemed, as tribal tensions fuelled by famine and drought sparked unrest and uprisings, tribes and regions railing against the arbitrary straight-line borders created by the colonial powers a hundred years ago. Mali had been racked by such terrible ethnic conflict that it was almost a relief when it split apart and the regions had been left to self-govern. Whilst they certainly had not prospered - these were very tough times for Africa - at least they had achieved a level of peace never seen before, at least not since colonisation had brought plunder and rape to the continent.

However, re-drawing borders was not an option for Ayatumbe. 'Ameer,' he began, not accepting the change of tone the President was attempting, 'economic partnership is one thing, but defence partnership is something quite different. I have the resources and the will to do this alone, and I will not be swayed from this position.'

'That is foolish!' snapped Al Quraysh, leaning forwards. His dark eyes grew even darker as he frowned. 'People are dying needlessly. You cannot control your own lands. I will not stand by and watch my subjects being murdered. If you do not accept my offer then I will be forced to act in the interests of the Republic and its people. You know my resources are considerable, you do not want to force me into this course of action President Ayatumbe. You will live to regret it.'

'I will not have you come into my own palace and threaten me!' growled Ayatumbe, gripping the armrest of the couch. 'You have no right here. Do not be fooled by your own rhetoric. Just because you have a large country, it does not make you powerful. What resources do you actually own? that are not given to you? They are declining faster than you let on. Controlling the Red Sea ports and the Suez Canal, and presiding over a dwindling supply of oil isn't much of a weapon to wield. If I had rich benefactors as you do then I suppose I might feel a similar false confidence, but instead I make my own way, and fight my own battles. And that is exactly what I will do. I will fight the militias in the borderlands, and I will fight any attempt to interfere in my country's affairs.'

Ayatumbe had escalated the argument faster than he had intended, but he was not going to be pushed around by the bully with some big brothers. He knew he was taking a huge risk, but it had to be worth it.

Al Quraysh stood. He glared at Ayatumbe, his eyes wide and his lips tight. Ayatumbe rose too, standing shorter than his counterpart, but equal in determination. He met the President's stare with a cold expression, showing his firm resolution. He had chosen his path and now he must walk it.

'Be careful with your threats Mr President'. Al Quraysh spoke in a low menacing tone, his eyes fixed on Ayatumbe's. 'Or you will know the full force of my resources. And you will regret your show of bravado. Remember the people I command, the power I wield. You can choose to benefit from it, or to suffer from it.'

'People?' spat Ayatumbe. 'What use are people when they are starving and thirsty? If anything, your *people* are more of a burden than a boon. You know as well as I do that people are not a weapon. Look at China - the growing superpower, with 1.3 billion people back in the early 2000s, and see how it fared in a collapsing economy, when all those people needed food and water. Did it manage to mobilise all 1.3 billion of those people in its war with the US and its allies? No, they were too busy trying to survive. Their empty tanks and empty threats spoke much louder than the brief missile barrage. Do not try to threaten me with people Ameer. I wield a far greater weapon - legitimacy.'

'Legitimacy? You fool. I stand elected by two hundred million, who will all obey my command.'

'Obey, perhaps. But you will find my people have a stronger motivation than obeying orders. Like all defenders throughout history, we will fight much harder than any invader. Any attack by you will smash on the rocks of my mountains and my troops, just as China's miserable defence was smashed.'

Al Quraysh turned and headed for the door. As he reached it, he turned and fixed Ayatumbe with one last stare. His fists were clenched and he was gritting his teeth with rage. 'Do not hold such sway in the lessons of history Mr President. It is littered with myths and fables written by those watching it unfold. I, however, am writing the future, and yours looks bleak. I will give you twenty four hours to change your mind before I take action. Think carefully about your future, before you and your nation become history.'

He strode out of the door, followed by his entourage. Ayatumbe watched him go. His blood was boiling in his veins as the adrenaline pumped through him. He was furious, jubilant and terrified all at once. He had not expected to stand up to him so forcefully, but it had been unavoidable. Now he would have to follow through on his threats, and face up to the greatest challenge of his presidency.

Chapter Three

Hassan Fourani scanned the horizon, his eyes narrowed against the fierce wind, swirling and blowing dust into every gap it could find. The sinking sun would soon disappear behind the distant hills. He tightened his cheche around his nose and mouth and tucked it in securely, keeping out the dust. His dark eyes with their long thick lashes looked tired, and if his face had been visible his downturned mouth would have shown a look of fear and desperation. The landscape below him was desolate - sand and scrub as far as the eye could see, interspersed with small rocky outcrops and small dunes. This land had changed so much in his lifetime. When he had been a boy this had been a fertile plain, rich with palm trees and savannah grasses. His clan had farmed this land and grazed their goats for generations, living in peace with their neighbours and the land. He did not recognise it now. Those days were gone.

He turned from the vista and regarded his clan, or what was left of it. A group of Toubou families sat amongst the rocks, looking exhausted. A small herd of goats stood nearby, nosing around for any food they could find. His heart sank even further as he regarded the sorry group. Their energy had entirely run out during their long journey from the plains up to the foothills of the mountains, literally running for their lives. As head of the clan he was responsible for saving them and he had made this choice - the mountains seemed the safest place for them in light of the threats below, but he wondered if it would yield the food and water they so badly needed. He looked at his own family; at his wife comforting their three remaining children, too exhausted to speak, too dehydrated to shed tears anymore. Too many tears for their dead children had already been shed during their week-long flight from the plains, as they ran scared from the attackers that had so brutally invaded their oasis, and destroyed their lives with their guns and their blades.

He shook himself. He had to get the clan to a safe place for the night, somewhere to rest and seek refuge from the wind, and most of all to find water, though that seemed increasingly unlikely up here in the mountains. His bet that the rocky heights would have a greater chance of yielding water than the arid plains below had so far not paid off, as they had passed several dry wadis on their climb. In years gone by these wadis would not have flowed, but at least trickled with cool water from their sources within the mountains. But now in them they found nothing but more dust and dry rocks, and desperation.

He took a deep breath and searched in himself for the energy to rouse his clan once more. The collection of five families had come so far, and had endured so much hardship these last few days, it seemed cruel to force them on even further. But he knew it must be done. They could not sit and perish quietly on this mountain side, they must go on and find salvation. Allah would protect them, and would provide all they needed. They just needed to continue their journey and believe in his justice. He approached his wife and touched her shoulder.

'Jamelia, we must go on. Night will come soon and we are too exposed here.'

'Yes my love, but just a little longer. The children are exhausted.'

'We are all exhausted my love, we have come so far, but we have far to go yet.' He left her and walked slowly to another family. 'Hissene, we must go on. Night is approaching.'

'I agree Hassan. This is no place for us to shelter from this wind. Do you see anyone below?'

'No, all is clear. But we must not rest. They could come again. They will destroy us.'

'I fear so my friend. But Allah will protect us.'

'Insha'allah,' agreed Hassan, 'let us continue our climb. I believe we will find our refuge just over the next ridge.' He held out his hand to help his friend up.

'Insha'allah. Let's go.' Hissene grasped his hand and struggled to his feet. The families started to murmur and rouse themselves.

'My friends,' Hassan addressed the group, 'we must go on. It has been a long day, but al hamdu lillah we have not seen our attackers today, and I believe we are close to our refuge. Insha'allah we will find water and shelter further up this mountain.'

'Insha'allah' they echoed, and began to rise to their feet and gather their few possessions.

An hour later, as they reached the top of a steep slope, which they had struggled up, each footstep heavier and slower than the last, they were met with a spectacular sight. They stood atop a ridge running east to west, and looked down to the south. The land fell away below them more gently than behind them, down towards a shallow valley, perhaps 300 metres long, sitting nestled under an even greater peak. It towered above them, its sides stretching out wide like huge shoulders. They continued around in a horseshoe shape, providing a protective bowl around the short valley. At its western end the ridge dropped into a deep saddle, allowing the deep red sun to throw the last of its rays into this haven, as it finally finished its day's journey across the sky. Hassan breathed deeply and praised Allah for the beautiful sight below.

The glow of the early evening sun bathed the valley in a deep red hue, which seemed to light up the valley like a fire. Its stark rocky sides glowed red. But down in the bottom of the short valley, at the eastern end, was a much more glorious sight. A small group of palm trees grew beside a pool of water, which looked dark and cool in the shadow of the trees. Around the pool and stretching down the valley was a swathe of green ficus bushes, perhaps two hundred of them. It was a miracle to see such richness after so long seeing nothing.

'Al hamdu lillah! God is Great!' Cries of thanks and relief rang out as the Toubous reached the top of the ridge and beheld the sight below them. They were suddenly energised by the discovery, and wasted no time before beginning their descent into the valley. Hassan felt uplifted, almost euphoric. They had so badly needed some good fortune, and Allah had delivered them to paradise on earth. His instinct had been right. He looked up and to the south, past the great mountain two kilometres away and over the peaks he could see beyond. Who knew what other treasures lay within those deep valleys he thought. He looked up to the sky above the horseshoe ridge, at the darkening sky. He saw a bird soaring above the distant ridge, perhaps an eagle judging by its great wingspan. *If there is an eagle then there is life* he thought. He thanked Allah again and followed the group as they raced down the slope.

As they sat around the fire later that evening there was an air of optimism among the clan. The jubilism had grown as they reached the pool, and had all sank to their knees and drank deeply from the pool. They had eaten goat, roasted over the fire, washed down with more sweet cold water. The children had quickly sunk into their parents' laps and found comfortable deep sleep, feeling safer and more secure than at any time in their lives.

'Al hamdu lillah' praised Hissene, 'God has delivered us to salvation. We are saved and have found a home!'

'Al hamdu lillah' agreed Hassan, 'He has rewarded us. However I do not believe we can stay here for long. We may still be being pursued, and even though this is indeed more of a home than we have seen in some time, we cannot stay still.'

'Brother we have been moving for so long, do you not long to rest?' pleaded Hissene, 'We have not seen the attackers in two days now, and we have found the refuge we sought. Can we not stop and enjoy what this magical valley has to offer us?'

'We are a nomadic people brother. The Toubou have wandered this region for centuries. It is in our blood to move on, to seek the next refuge.'

'It is in our blood to walk this land, I agree. But it is also in our blood to make our home where we find it. Too much of that blood was spilled when those demons chased us from our last home. I long to stay here awhile, and to enjoy this while we can.'

'Perhaps for a few days' conceded Hassan, 'but we must look to the south. The further into the mountains we go, the less likely it is we will be pursued.'

'I agree' said his wife, 'those beasts were determined to kill us, and I do not wish to give them another chance.'

'Yes,' agreed Hassan, 'they will come, seeking more blood.'

'Why us?' asked Hissene, 'what did we do to them? And who were they? They spoke Arabic but looked like they came from the south.'

'Yes, their faces were darker than we usually see in this region' agreed Hassan. 'It doesn't make sense that they would be there on our plains.'

'It's not like there's anything there for them to take either. They only wanted to kill us, or to drive us away.' said Hissene.

'Well they did both' said Hassan. 'We all lost family to those demons. And I do not want us to lose any more, so we will move on. We can stay here for two nights at the most and then we must continue our journey into the mountains. We will not find any answers there, but we may find our destiny, and that will have to be enough.'

Chapter Four

Jerry was sat in the debrief room with Al and the rest of the assault force waiting for the meeting to begin. His deep dark eyes regarded the men sat around a large oval table, with the chair at one end empty. The assembled men spoke in murmurs to their neighbours, occasionally breaking out into cross-table conversations. He studied the group around the table, each man a former special forces operator, either from the US, UK, Australia, South Africa, France or Germany. They were all here due to their extensive experience of special operations, and thus had no need to prove themselves with unnecessary bulllshit stories or locker room banter. Jerry had always hated the archetypal special operations alpha-male, wearing an enormous watch and telling everyone how great he was, and he was pleased to note that none of them had found their way into this unit, where reputation and recommendation were the two most important selection attributes. He felt very comfortable in such professional company.

The door opened and through it came Lionel Caplin, the head of Task Force Africa - a white haired man, stocky in frame, and evidently rounder than he had been in years gone by. He stood at a little under six feet in height, but had the stature of a man used to authority; indeed he had served for thirty years in the US Marine Corps, commanding troops in combat operations around the globe. As a former Lieutenant Colonel he was accustomed to command, and he strode into the room as if he owned it.

'Gentlemen. Good morning.' he announced loudly. The crowd murmured their greeting. 'Thanks for waiting, my apologies for keeping you, as usual a crisis is brewing.'

There was always a crisis somewhere in Africa, and it was usually just a question of time until the Task Force were deployed to avert or end it. He took his seat at the head of the table.

'Now, Gabon. A great success. All the girls returned to their families, and a very grateful government. Good job!' He used the Americanism freely, despite knowing how it irked his British colleagues. 'That's the headline, but let's talk details. What can we learn from the operation? What goals did we kick, and which did we miss? Jerry, you wanna lead off on this?'

Jerry was well prepared for his speaking part, as head of operations of the unit and the leader of the mission he knew the drill. Post operational analysis, or a wash-up, was standard practice for all missions, in order to identify areas of strength and weakness, to ensure good practice was shared and to ensure mistakes were not repeated.

'Sure boss. Everyone has a copy of the report in front of them. So all hostages were recovered successfully, with zero friendly casualties. In the follow-up operation their relief force was destroyed by our attack helicopter - four vehicles containing 15 militants. Site exploitation revealed that Vincent Ugaru, their second in command, was among the dead. Our team also recovered some data on their funding streams, which has been passed on to the Intelligence guys. Now, if you turn to page one-of the report, we'll begin. Personnel...'

An hour later the debrief was complete and the teams drifted out of the room, chatting and joking as they went. Jerry stayed seated at the table with Lionel.

'Again, great job Jerry. Now when are you gonna hang up your boots and run these missions from the ops room? You're too god damn valuable to me to be getting shot or blown up by some punk.' The operations room was the usual place the head of operations would be found, coordinating resources and taking an oversight role on all elements of the operation.

'Not yet Lionel, I'm still feeling good. And I think there are three or four countries I haven't seen yet!' joked Jerry.

'Jeez, those days are behind me - my knees can't take it anymore. But you do have ten years on me so I guess you should enjoy it while you can.'

'I think it's closer to fifteen years actually, and you did your fair share of ops boss. Plenty of trigger time.'

'Well anyway, you're doing a great job, and it's great to have you onboard. I knew it was a good call recruiting you.' Lionel had personally head-hunted Jerry when he took over as head of the Task Force, refusing to take no for an answer when Jerry had asserted his loyalty to the Marine Corps. Jerry had served as one of Lionel's most trusted company commanders and had been genuinely torn between his duty to the US and his respect for his former commander.

'I'm glad you did. It's been a great opportunity. The Corps was good to me and I had lots of good times, but this has been something else.'

'Sure, it's like soldiering used to be, before we were too afraid to shoot anyone. Those god damn UN missions in the twenties were a pain in the ass, and a waste of time to boot. I was on the recon team for the peacekeeping mission in Venezuela in '29. Jeez that was a fuck up. Standing by watching innocent people being massacred, waiting for the UN to pass a god damn resolution while Caracas turned into a morgue. Crazy waste.'

'I remember seeing it on the TV, and then we studied it at the Academy. It was a key case study in the story of the UN's demise.'

'Yeah, well thank god we don't have to jump through those hoops anymore. We got a lean system that actually works now. But hey, come on to my office, have a coffee with me.'

They left the meeting room and made their way through the main atrium of the building - a huge open area, perhaps one hundred metres long and five storeys high, with walkways circling it on each floor. The distant ceiling was glass, and flooded the atrium with bright morning light. The temperature was a pleasant air-conditioned twenty three degrees, a stark contrast to the high thirties with high humidity outside in the city. The atrium was quiet, except for a few small groups of people sitting chatting in easy chairs, and the sound of unseen footsteps echoing from one of the walkways above. It looked more like a corporate headquarters than the hub of a rapid response military force; there wasn't a uniform in sight.

'Senegal is looking fragile' began Lionel as they headed for the elevator. 'Mauritania is protesting over the border incursions in the north around Lake Aleg. And a company of government troops have just been ambushed north of Dakar, no survivors according to Porter. It's a shit storm waiting to happen, turning back the clock eighty years.'

'Any request from President Kama yet?' asked Jerry. He made a mental note to get an update from Porter, their head of intelligence, after the coffee

'No, that asshole wants to do it all himself. Fucking Africans and their goddamn pride. I guess he doesn't want any scrutiny of last year's election result. That mother fucker is lucky to be in office again, and he knows it. He's just like all the rest of them, corrupt as shit and keeping control through oppression and threats.'

'In the interest of balance, Ivory Coast have been doing well I gather, and Porter was telling me that Liberia is right back on track now' said Jerry. He pressed the button for the elevator.

'Ah who gives a fuck about Ivory Coast? They've got a half decent soccer team and that's about it. And Liberia, sure, they've made some progress, but they can't wipe out generations of corruption and abuse just by being the current chair of the African Union. I still wouldn't trust them. Just apply my test - would you send your kids to school there?'

'I don't have kids' smiled Jerry as they entered the elevator. He had heard Lionel's 'school test' being applied to every country in Africa before. The only country that passed was Nigeria, and that was probably only because that was where the Task Force was based in West Africa. 'And yours have already finished school...in San Diego'

The elevator door opened. Inside was a woman, looking at an electronic reader. She looked up and smiled, and stepped out of the door. Jerry quickly noted her slim figure and shoulder-length black hair, framing her pretty face. He guessed she was Indian, judging by her large almond-shaped eyes and long nose.

'Hi Ananya, how are you?' said Lionel.

'I'm well thank you Lionel, how about you?' she replied.

'I'm just great thanks. Ananya have you met Jerry yet? Jerry Vasquez, this is Ananya Devi. Ananya heads up our genetic research program here. Her team have been working on a vaccine for the Remi virus. Jerry is head of operations here in the headquarters, but spends most of his time out, doing the operations!'

'Pleasure to meet you Ananya' said Jerry as they shook hands. Her long fingers gave an impressively firm grip.

'You too Jerry' she smiled.

'It's odd we haven't met before' said Jerry.

'Ananya has been based out at the field research station in CAR. But now she's here to finish up the project' explained Lionel.

'Ahh, I see. Well it was good to meet you' said Jerry with a smile, as they entered the elevator. 'I didn't know we did genetic research too now' he remarked to Lionel as the doors closed.

'Hey, we don't only battle bad guys! Africa has all sorts of problems. They're not limited to drought, famine and corruption. Just add it to the list of things they're not equipped to deal with, and so we have to come and do it for them. Goddamn it. I'm tired of that political bullshit people spin about not measuring African nations by western standards...their tribal culture isn't compatible with our values..yada yada yada. We *should* be judging them by our standards if they want to trade with us, and be taken seriously.'

The doors opened and they turned left towards Lionel's office.

'Well I think that's what we *are* seeing' countered Jerry. 'The fracturing of states and removal of old borders is a sign that progress is being made. Countries are finally waking up to the notion that their destiny is in their hands, they can be prosperous, and they're taking bold steps to find a form of government that works for them, whatever it is.'

'I admire your optimism Jerry, I really do, but wake up and smell the fucking coffee' chided Lionel. As they walked through his outer office he ordered coffee. 'This continent is not so much a breadbasket as a basket case. Most of their wealth has been stolen, either by their own corrupt officials, or by the colonial powers last century. Now they're really fucked. The population is two billion, global warming has raised the temperature two degrees, most of the savannah has turned to desert, lakes have been sucked dry. How the hell will they get themselves out of this mess?'

'Well they shouldn't have to do it alone. It's still in our interest to help them out isn't it?' countered Jerry. He approached the huge window which covered a whole wall of Lionel's office, and looked out at the view. The Task Force headquarters was located on Lagos Island in Nigeria's largest city Lagos. Lionel's office looked out on the Lagos Lagoon - a great expanse of polluted water, filled with barges and small boats transporting people and goods from one side of the city to the other. An ugly road bridge, a kilometre long, also stretched across the lagoon, linking Lagos Island with the Apapa Port, and then the huge desalination plant ten kilometres beyond. It was a fairly dismal sight, but it was busy with traffic, coming and going from the busy port. 'And look, they seem to be doing pretty well here. Trade is pretty healthy.'

'Why do you think we're here?' urged Lionel. 'This is the only goddamn country in the whole continent that can get it's shit together, and even then we have to turn a blind eye to the occasional bit of embezzlement or theft. We can't go busting heads everywhere we see it going on or we'd never get anywhere. Nigeria is a friend in protecting our interests, and we enjoy a mutually protective relationship. Olatomi gets it. He makes sure the right laws get passed and he has consensus. *And* it helps that they still have some oil left!'

The coffee arrived. They took a seat in soft leather armchairs and took a sip. Jerry sat back and regarded the view some more. Even though it wasn't very pretty, he wished his office had a view like this. His was on the other side of the building, with a view of a street and some depressing high-rises. 'I guess you're right' he sighed. 'I just like to think that there's a point to all this. That we're more than just mercenaries. That we're actually helping them to develop.'

'That sounds like the UN mantra from years ago. It's a great idea, but it just doesn't survive contact with the reality of Africa. You can't be a doctor and a cop. We're not really here to help them. We're here to kick their asses when they screw up, or to kick asses for them, and all in order to ensure they don't fuck it up for the rest of the world by doing something stupid, like breeding terrorists, trying to build new weapons, or anything else we disagree with.'

'Well, you're the politician, I'm just a shooter' conceded Jerry.

'I'm no politician, I'm a Marine!' laughed Lionel. 'I just see the world the way it is. And you my friend are way more than a shooter. You're one of the smartest guys I know. A degree in Robotics, first in your class at the Academy, the brightest Lieutenant in my company, and then promoted to Captain before any of your peers. You got a brain Jerry, and you're good on the tools too. That's why I brought you on board. You're the kinda guy that can really get shit done without me needing to nursemaid you. *And* you're the kinda guy that *gets it*. Am I right?'

'Sure. I get it. Kick their asses until they agree with us.'

'Basically, yes. But also make out like we're holding their hands too. It's complicated.'

'Life always is' mused Jerry.

Later, sat in his office, Jerry reflected on Lionel's words. The UN's history was rich with examples of failure, but it had been particularly ineffective in Africa, where it had failed to exert any sort of authority during mass genocides in Rwanda at the end of the last century, and Darfur in the early 2000s. The Task Force had grown out of a frustration with the UN's inability to exert the world's will by any other means than economic sanctions, as well as a growing concern over increasingly savage outrages against humanity, which the UN wasn't structured to deal with. Its embarrassingly creaky and impotent response to the Syrian regime's use of torture, execution, indiscriminate bombing and mass murder during the brutal civil war had highlighted the limits of an organisation relying on global consensus. Like any 70 year-old, it struggled to move quickly enough, and was very much stuck in its ways. From that point the writing had been on the wall, so when it once again failed to act decisively in Egypt and Libya during the early 2020s, which saw muslim extremism sweeping across North Africa, the world finally retired its aged sherriff, and recruited a young, agile force, able to meet the security challenges of the post-globalisation world.

The Task Force had been established five years ago in 2025, as a response to the ever increasing number of small-scale disputes, kidnappings and insurgency activities around the world, all of which needed more than sanctions to be applied. Its resources were significant, with a Division of troops on every continent, comprising regular infantry, combat support troops such as engineers and logistics, marines, and special forces. Each Division was supported by highly mobile armoured vehicles - modern replacements for the traditional main battle tank, which had ceased to be versatile enough to support modern-day operations; a battalion of drones, which were able to conduct long-range extended reconnaissance, as well as perform a lethal bombing campaign due to their increased endurance and load-carrying capability; a fleet of fast offshore patrol vessels and battle cruisers, able to patrol coastal waters and out to several hundred miles offshore, designed specifically for the increased number of anti-piracy operations required; and finally a wing of medium and heavy lift helicopters, used to move troops and equipment around regions as part of air assault operations. It was a significant, agile multi-operational force, capable of reacting at high speed in all environments.

Initially there had been widespread concern about the formation of what effectively amounted to a mercenary force, employed by 'concerned nations' to take swift and decisive action against any party threatening regional or international stability. But this concern had faded once the world saw the benefit of such a force, particularly as it had freed up UN resources to focus on the distribution of aid to the developing world, as well as to be the lead on international cooperation on prevention of human trafficking. The UN had found an equilibrium which everyone could agree on, and the Task Force had a solid, agreed place as the new global stabilisation force.

He understood the history of Africa; all its problems with implementing democracy in a tribal system; its critical shortage of natural resources and the resultant droughts and famines, and in particular the recent spate of conflicts over access to natural water sources; but he couldn't shake the feeling that Lionel was over-simplifying a hugely complex problem, and furthermore that his 'ass-kicking' approach had some serious limitations. Lionel had been a great commander in the Corps, but things were different out here, there were some more complex politics at work. Jerry wondered if it was actually he or Lionel that didn't get it. He then wondered if he was over-thinking it and decided to go home.

As he left his office he bumped into Simon Crossey, his second in command, striding purposefully down the corridor, carrying a thick buff-coloured file.

'Simon! Hey, how are you? It's been a while.' They shook hands warmly.

'Hi Jerry, welcome back. I hear Gabon was a success, congratulations!'

'One hundred percent successful, mostly thanks to you and your excellent planning Simon. Good job.'

'Thanks, but it was a fairly straightforward one. Mostly thanks to Porter and his intelligence gathering. Are you heading home? You must be shattered'

Yeah, I'm beat. How about you? You look like you're in a hurry.'

'Oh no, I'm fine, just been working on that research.'

'Yes, the ethno-linguistic study of CAR?' said Jerry, 'When will I get to read it? You've been working on it for months now haven't you?'

'Yes, not long now until it's ready' answered Simon. 'I need to get on though, I'll see you tomorrow.' He headed to his office, next to Jerry's, giving him one final nod as he opened the door and disappeared inside, closing it firmly behind him.

That's odd thought Jerry. Simon had seemed more distant than usual, particularly as they hadn't crossed paths in over a week now. It was as if he was keen to get away from him. But he shook his head and headed for the elevator. He'd done enough thinking for today, it was time for a cold beer.

Chapter Five

President Al Quraysh sat deep in thought, his steepled fingers resting on his lips, staring into space. He sat at the head of a long dark wood table. Ten men dressed in white thobes also sat at the table, each of them either looking awkwardly at the President, or inquiringly at each other. This was the President's shura - his consultative group of advisors. There had been silence in the room for about a minute, since he had learned that there had been no communication from the Chadian government. Not unexpected news, but certainly unwelcome.

Finally the President lowered his hands and looked around the table. He regarded his advisors, each of them now looking expectantly at him, awaiting his decree. He sighed inwardly. Why must he have to make every tough decision? Such was the price of leadership, he was expected to know the best course of action at all times. Mostly it was easy, as invariably his advisors and followers unanimously agreed that whatever he decided was of course the best course of action. However that was for mere domestic issues, such as laws and judgements. When it came to foreign policy, things were a little more complex. Other important players were involved and must be considered. Unilateral decisions had proven in the past to be very unwise, so instead he chose to ask a question.

'Tell me, what are the options we have?'

His advisors were silent. They had of course anticipated this question, but there were few viable options to consider, particularly as he had taken such a tough stance with President Ayatumbe during their meeting. His uncharacteristic outburst had surprised many of them when they had heard of it. The calm and measured manner of Al Quraysh was one of his key strengths, and was certainly a key factor during his selection as President. Hot-headed radicalists were not at all required or encouraged in these modern times, making his diplomatic slip all the more surprising. The silence dragged on, broken only by the sound of people shifting uneasily in their chairs.

'Abu Khalid' the President turned to his deputy, sitting on his right. He used the familiar address, which literally meant *Father of Khalid*, his first-born son. 'Tell me, what am I to do? President Ayatumbe refused to accept any terms, which was most unexpected. Am I really to order a deployment of our troops into Chad? An action of this magnitude has not occurred in the history of this Republic.'

'Ameer' began Abu Khalid, clearing his throat and stroking his beard nervously. He was only forty five, but looked much older due to the enormous bags under his eyes and the grey hair in his beard. 'If you believe that God wills you to order an invasion then I cannot offer any contrary counsel. It is God's will. Allahu Akbar, God is Great'

Al Quraysh inwardly sighed. Supreme command was indeed a double edged sword - very gratifying to have absolute authority, but very frustrating to have everyone agree with you all of the time. 'Allahu Akbar. However, I did not threaten an invasion, merely a deployment of troops to protect our people. Now we are faced with that as a real option I want to know the price of such a move. Is this likely to provoke a reaction from the international community?'

'Ameer, may I offer an observation?' The question had come from Abu Rashed, Minister of Foreign Affairs, on the left side of the President. He was an altogether different looking man, having the appearance of a hawk, with narrow dark eyes and a sharp nose. His features were angular, including his beard, which was pointed, jet black and perfectly trimmed.

'Of course Abu Rashed, what is your counsel?'

'Ameer, I would urge great caution in this matter. Every international border incursion in the last hundred years, probably longer, has been met with great resistance, and has resulted in dire consequences for all involved, both politically and economically. Do we really need to extend our borders for such a high price?'

'Ameer' retorted Abu Khalid, warming to the discussion. 'As President you have been chosen by Allah to command all citizens of our great country. Through you, God's words are communicated. You alone can decide if such an action is God's will.' He cast a sideways glance at Abu Rashed.

'Ameer, what is the will of the people?' asked a third man, Abu Hamed. 'Is it in the interest of your people to extend the borders?'

'This is no matter for the people' rebuked Abu Khalid. 'It is haram to consider such prejudice.' He turned to the President again. 'Such a judgement can only come from you Ameer, in accordance with what is written in the Qur'an.'

'That is true, Abu Khalid' said the President. 'I was elected by the shura to follow God's will and speak on his behalf. I will not commit an unlawful act according to what is written in the Qur'an. But there are Muslim people being killed and displaced by non-believers, and this is just cause for me to act in their defence. My people need me.'

'This is true Ameer, but such an act would be regarded as an invasion of a country' said Abu Rashed. 'And whilst there may be just cause, it is hard to defend such an action, particularly now as we do not have the UN at which to plead our case.'

'As I said, this is hardly an invasion' argued the President, 'more of a defence in fact.'

'I fear the Chadian government may have a different view' countered Abu Rashed.

'This is ridiculous!' said the President, his exasperation clear. 'I am having to balance the will of the world against the lives of my people. And I do not even understand how this has come about. We have ordered no attacks on anyone in the borderlands, neither Muslim or non-Muslim. What is my way through this?'

'There are no reports of any proxy involvement of any other countries Ameer' answered Abu Rashed. 'Our intelligence agency has not detected any unusual activity by agents of any of the main players in the region. Nothing from India, or the US. My best assessment is that non-Muslim groups in northern Chad are competing with the local Muslim clans for scarce resources, and it has escalated into violence. The non-Muslims do not appear to be sponsored by Chad'

'But there were no claims for help from our people. Why did they not seek our assistance rather than resort to fighting and unnecessary bloodshed?'

'That is hard to say Ameer. They do not have any formal governing structure, and so perhaps were not able to organise themselves sufficiently to request our support. But now they really do need help.' Abu Rashed paused before delivering his next line, 'May I suggest a different approach to the problem?'

'Of course, I welcome all suggestions.'

'Perhaps there is a way out of this without provoking any unnecessary tension between us and our neighbours, which will also allow us to get much needed support to our people.'

'Insha'allah there is' agreed the President. 'Tell me your idea Abu Rashed.'

'What if we were to request the assistance of the African Union. We could maintain our non-combatant approach, invite the legitimacy of the AU, and get the much-needed aid to our people in a short time.'

'The AU have been nearly as ineffective as the UN in the past' countered the President. 'I am not sure I have any faith in their legitimacy or their reliability. They were a disaster in Somalia, and in the Central African Republic, and I fear they would be a disaster here too. The problem with them is that even when deployed as a combined multi-national peacekeeping force, they are still tribal Africans, and so still have preferences and motivations which may be contrary to their mission. I wish we could rely on them but history has proven otherwise.'

'I agree Ameer' said Abu Khalid. 'The record of the AU is unimpressive, mostly because they are unable to exert any real authority in what are mostly tribal conflicts.'

'But this is not a tribal matter' argued Abu Rashed. 'This conflict is based on religious beliefs. But that is not the point Ameer. The important thing that the AU would bring is scrutiny. They would uncover the truth, which is that we are not responsible for this matter, and that action must be taken.'

'I see your point Abu Rashed' agreed the President, pausing to gather his thoughts. His advisors sat back in their seats and reflected on the proposal.

'It is true that with the AU comes the media, and that will certainly highlight the issue. However it will also take time, which is not something our people have a lot of at the moment. Finally, I have never felt that the AU fully supports our right to legitimate nation status. I fear they are biased.'

No-one was going to argue with the President on that point. The AU had not been a great friend to the Republic since its creation. The traditional African nation bloc had been formed in a generation before the re-drawing of international borders in Africa had become commonplace, and it was struggling to keep pace with the changes. Just like the European Union's massive size and inherent inflexibility had caused it to fail in the early 2020s, as it failed to hold together its increasingly disparate member states, the AU had also become too bureaucratic and cumbersome, and unable to accept change. This was mostly due to the conservative and protectionist nature of its member states, who themselves had difficulty accepting the legitimacy of the new Republic.

'Ameer, there is another option.' Abu Khalid broke the silence. 'The Task Force is now very active in West Africa, and has proven to be very effective. Their methods are unconventional but their success rate is reputed to be exceptional.'

'I am reluctant to invite mercenaries to fight on our behalf, particularly on the Chadian side of the border' replied the President. 'The size of our armed forces is considerable - easily big enough to complete this mission.'

'But the problem we face is perception' countered Abu Rashed. 'If the media reports a deployment of our troops across the border, without the consent of the Chadian government, then we ourselves will become the target. I agree with Abu Khalid. If we cannot trust the AU then another independent force would be better than troops in uniforms of the Republic.'

'But they would not be independent - they would be there at our behest. That makes it a proxy invasion force, which is little better than we ourselves doing it' said the President. He sighed and rubbed his eyes. He felt trapped by all the things he couldn't do, and hugely frustrated that they didn't even know why this was happening.

'Ameer, may I offer an insight?' The request had come from Abu Habis, the President's Minister of the Interior.

'Please Abu Habis, share your thoughts'. *What do I have to lose at this stage?*

'Ameer, the options we have discussed so far are great deliberate gestures, which deliberately or not will inflame the situation. I would suggest a more subtle approach, which does not require great risk. That is to seek to further the negotiations between us and Chad, again privately, in order that we can find a diplomatic way through this situation.'

'I fear it may be too late for further negotiation' said the President quietly. His shame at his outburst returned to him like a cold blast.

'Insha'allah it is not too late Ameer' Abu Habis reassured him. 'The negotiating table is always an option. No-one wants this to escalate. It has no benefit to President Ayatumbe either. He is no authoritarian, he rules a peaceful country, and he does not engage in political showmanship. Furthermore they are a desperately poor country, with no natural resources other than a shrinking supply of oil, and can not afford a war over a trivial matter such as this.'

'You speak wisely Abu Habis' said the President. 'Insha'allah you are right. I do not wish this to escalate either. No-one will win from such an action. What can we say now?'

'That we are keen to support the efforts of the government of Chad' suggested Abu Habis.

'That we will provide materiel support, perhaps humanitarian aid to distribute' offered Abu Khalid.

'And perhaps some military hardware, such as surveillance equipment' suggested Abu Rashed.

'Brothers...' the President addressed the group. 'This issue must not grow beyond what it ought to be - a small regional matter which requires water rather than oil to be thrown on the fire. Go now and sit together. Come up with a proposal I can take to President Ayatumbe, and help me to resolve this situation peacefully, insha'allah.'

'Insha'allah' they chimed in response, rising to their feet as the President stood. After he had left the room they sat down and began their work.

In his personal chambers, the President reclined on a couch and reflected on the situation. This approach seemed to him to be the best way through what had been a rapidly deteriorating situation. Thanks to God for his wise counsellors. He had acted poorly in his meeting with President Ayatumbe, and had almost blown the problem up. Again thanks to God for his counsellors for not making an issue of his slip. They were loyal and good men.

He thought deeply about what was happening in the borderlands. How could something like this have happened without any warning? There were always some signs that a problem was coming, but this had come from nowhere. The

Chadian government had claimed it was a disaffected Muslim group, who had taken up arms to take a water source from an ethnic Chadian clan, brutally forcing them from their homes. This seemed quite plausible, given the terrible shortage of water across the continent. Why wouldn't people fight over water? His own country was suffering too, both in the west, where the Sahara had extended deep into the state of Libya, and in the east, where it was now engulfing the southern half of the state of Sudan.

It was only the enormous coastline the Republic now controlled, and thus the access to seawater to desalinate, that saved them. But this was such an energy intense process, and their supply of oil now so dangerously low, that they were reaching crisis point. All natural fresh water sources were now depleted, sucked up and used by the surge of agriculture and industrial activity, by dredging for sand for the endless construction, or dried up by the rising temperature. If there had been enough water in the borderlands then it would certainly be worth risking a war to take it, but Chad was as dry as the Republic. In fact, even more so, as it did not even have a coastline from which to drag water. Chad was truly in a sorry state, at the bottom ebb of its luck.

But did this desperate situation mean that it was worth the risk for the Chadian government to orchestrate this whole crisis? What did they possibly have to gain from it? There was nothing of any value in those borderlands, and they certainly would not be a good start point for a full-scale land grab, which Chad was not equipped to carry out anyway. It just didn't make sense for Chad to start and foment these problems. With God's will they would be able to successfully negotiate a way out of this situation, and avoid the need for expensive deployments or conflicts. God knew his armed forces were in no fit state to fight any battles just now, despite what he might claim in public.

He rubbed his eyes again and stretched his limbs. It had been an exhausting day, and his brain was tired. He needed some distraction from his thoughts. He knew just what he needed. He called to an aide.

'Inform my wife that I will call on her shortly.'

The aide hurried away to deliver the message. His third wife Aishah knew just how to please him, such was her duty. She would prepare a hot bath for him, and joining him in it she would take away all his stress, with her smooth hands and soft lips. She had been particularly distracting lately, hence he had arranged quarters for her in his palace. He thought he had better be careful to also share his time with his other two wives, but then at half the age of his other wives she seemed to have twice their enthusiasm. He gave a satisfied sigh as he rose and left the room, smoothing his beard.

Chapter Six

Jerry was sitting in his office, hunched forward with his head in his hands. He felt as if he had been punched in the stomach and couldn't breathe. He had dropped his phone having just had news that his second in command, Simon had been killed in a car crash that morning. His mind swirled with memories of time spent with Simon, flicking to imagining his death as the oncoming bus swerved into his lane and crushed his vehicle. He felt nauseous and hung his head. Simon's legs had been crushed, his ribs broken and he had suffered a major head trauma, which he succumbed to before any emergency services could reach him in the rush hour traffic. It was so needless and random that it had struck everyone badly. Jerry sat and thought of the fragility of life and its paradoxical nature. How easily Simon had been senselessly killed by a bus, despite having served so many years in the British military, and deploying to some nasty conflict zones. At least he wasn't a family man, which would have made it even worse.

Jerry suddenly felt a long way from San Diego, with its palm trees, wide roads and cool Pacific breeze. He had grown up happily in that beautiful city, with his parents and two older brothers, living on the Marine base during his father's service, and then in the suburbs after his retirement. They were happy American days. Well, happy compared to Africa anyway. In truth they were fairly desperate times, with the American economy waning, creaking under the pressure of the global financial crisis which defined the second decade of the 21st century, and then rocked by the great political scandals which undermined the entire democratic process on which America had been built. He remembered the great depression of the early '20s, when he had been finishing up high school and going on to university in Los Angeles, while so many of his classmates had signed up for the military, eager to defend America against the rising power of China. But what he remembered most about that period was how his father and brother Raymond were both taken from the family too early, and how that had shaped his life, and had ultimately brought him here to Nigeria, putting himself in harm's way too, in search of what? He wasn't sure if he was running away or chasing something, but he was sure that Simon's death was a tragedy; a sudden end to a bright life, and he did not want to go that same way.

He stood up slowly, shaking off the sadness that had engulfed him. He should sort out Simon's affairs, and get his things together from his office. It was quite different from the ordered, minimalist space of Jerry's office. There were books, journals and piles of paper stacked on his desk, and on his conference table. One wall was full of maps, planning charts, and a large whiteboard with diagrams and lists all over it. The other wall, next to Simon's desk, was his memory wall, full of framed photographs. Jerry stepped closer and studied the photographs. A photo of Simon in uniform, with his arm around a man who must have been his father. A photo of an Air Assault platoon, lined up in front of a Chinook helicopter, with Simon at the centre as its commander. A photo of Simon stood beside a huge UAV; its missile-laden wings standing taller than his head. He had spent some time working with drones, Jerry remembered.

He moved from the wall to the desk, and sat down in the chair, regarding the mess laid out before him. Simon certainly had a busy mind if this desk was anything to go by. He picked up some reports and looked at the covers - 'Insurgency campaigns of the Niger Delta 2020-2025', and 'A Review of Task Force Direct Action Procedures - Nov 2029', both had Simon's name on them as the author. Gripping stuff he smiled, but Simon was forever the details man, and therefore a great planner. He had masterminded, and overseen a great number of the operations that Jerry had commanded. He dropped them on the desk and looked around at the other papers, wondering if there was anything here he could send to Simon's family. He opened the top desk drawer and looked inside. Pens, various bits of stationery, a cheap-looking watch, some boarding card stubs. Jerry picked up the stubs and read the destinations - Bangui in CAR, N'Djamena in Chad, Yaounde in Cameroon, Khartoum in the Islamic Republic. Simon was a busy man. He was certainly committed to the research he had been conducting. That reminded Jerry that he had never got to read Simon's research on the CAR. He thought of the buff-coloured file and searched the desktop for it, lifting up all the reports and books, to no avail. He had seen Simon with it just yesterday, it must be here, unless he had taken it home with him. He opened the bottom drawer of the desk, and there was the file. He lifted it out and put it on the desk, taking care not to drop any of the many documents inside.

He opened the file and took out the first page, which was covered in what looked like a set of notes in Simon's characteristic blue scrawl. He scanned the first few lines and frowned.

Update - 6 Mar 30

1.   Chad - pol conditions approaching readiness. A under pressure. Bardai plant 40%.
2.   Republic - progressing well, RAQ under pressure, tensions high. Meeting RAQ/A 4 Mar perfect. Shipment delivered.
3.   Aouzou field test complete. 100% success. AD ready.

This didn't look familiar, he thought. It didn't seem to be relevant to an ethno-linguistic study. What had Simon been working on? He read on.

4.   Aircraft 94% ready - est 2 days FOC
5.   Div 85% CE -   Inf 80   Air 90
6.   Media plan ready

Jerry sat back and frowned. He held the sheet of paper in his hand and read it again. This was written yesterday. As far as he knew, and as the head of operations he should know, they had no ongoing or planned operations in either Chad or the Republic. Both countries were relatively stable and content, notwithstanding the obvious ongoing issues of drought and famine. Points 4-6 looked like regular briefing stats, but 1-3 were strange - what field test? Something wasn't right about this file. He put the sheet on the desk and reached for the next page to find out more.

At that moment there were quiet voices outside Simon's door and the door suddenly swung open. Two TF agents came through the door, carrying empty cardboard boxes. They stopped suddenly, and looked at Jerry with surprise.

'Hello sir' one of the agents said. 'Sorry, we're supposed to be clearing out Mr Crossey's office. I don't know if you heard but he was killed this morning.'

Jerry stood up and closed the file in front of him on the desk. 'Yes, I did hear. I'm Jerry Vasquez, head of operations. Simon was my deputy.'

'Oh I'm sorry Mr Vasquez' said the agent. 'We weren't told there'd be anyone here. We were just told to clear out all of Mr Crossey's documents.' He looked down at the file on the desk.

Jerry put his hand on the file and picked it up. 'This one is mine. I was just retrieving it from Simon's desk. He has been doing some work for me on Chad.' He stepped away from the desk, file in hand, and made to leave the office. 'I'll let you get on with your work' he smiled.

'I'm sorry sir, you'll have to let us have that file' said the agent. 'We were told to recover everything in the office.'

'I can assure you, this file is mine, and is not part of your task' replied Jerry. He was feeling uneasy about this situation. There was a tension in the air which did not feel natural. The second agent put down the empty boxes and shifted his position slightly, as if covering the door.

'Mr Vasquez Sir, I must insist that we take all the documents that are in this office, including that one in your hand. Our orders came direct from Mr Caplin.' The agent was polite, but very firm in his tone.

Why did Lionel give that order? he wondered. This wasn't standard protocol for when someone died in service, not even when it was a senior officer like Simon. He could always call Lionel and ask him what the hell was going on, but that wouldn't help him right now - Lionel had given the order. This guy was going to take the file whatever happened. Jerry could tell he was a good agent - resolute and firm, following orders to the letter. His mind was racing, were these guys a threat? They looked neutral enough, but their tone was firm, and they clearly weren't going to be intimidated. He would have to talk to Lionel about it, and then Lionel would let him see the file again.

'Fine' he said, 'you can take the file, but I will expect to have it back.' He handed over the file and left the office as the agents set to work, closing the door behind him. *That was weird* he thought. He headed directly to Lionel's office, only to discover he was out at a meeting and would be gone all morning. He called Lionel's number, hoping to catch him before the agents left the office. He could always take back the file before they left. Voicemail. He hung up and thought for a moment. His brain was fuzzy. The shock of Simon's death, his own musings on mortality, the strange notes in Simon's file, and then the strange office-clearing agents. It had been a hell of a weird morning, and he could really use a beer now. His favourite bar was only ten minutes away.

Chez Chay was empty, except for a lone tourist sitting in the corner reading a book. Situated at the popular Bar Beach, it was generally packed with punters day and night, sipping cold beer and cocktails, pretending there wasn't so much poverty and deprivation going on just a few kilometres down the coast to the west. Jerry came here most days when he was in country, to enjoy some ice cold Heineken, to scout for girls, and to listen to the world according to Chay - the bar's owner and head bartender. Chay was nowhere to be seen though. The sea breeze blew off the Atlantic, across the sandy beach, and through the open shutters. The bar had been built from wood, deliberately in a traditional shack style in order to look authentic, Jerry assumed, and to maintain a cool temperature inside while it soared to the mid-thirties outside. The ceiling was low, with fans spinning lazily, to match the lazy reggae music playing.

'Hey Chay' he called as he approached the long wooden bar, which had been carved out of one of the many pieces of driftwood found around Lagos. The lagoon was full of loose planks and spars, drifting with the tide, and causing a hazard to shipping. This was no plank though, it was eight inches thick, twenty inches wide and twenty feet long. It had been hewn from a tree taken from the rapidly receding rainforests in the south of Nigeria. He leaned on the bar and looked out of the window at the beach. It was a quiet day, not many beachgoers or swimmers braving the fierce currents and tides. He peered around the side of the bar, looked down and saw Chay on the ground in the push-up position, supporting himself on his hands and toes, his face staring down at the ground in quiet concentration. 'Going for a new record?' he asked.

Chay looked up and smiled. 'Four minutes so far. My core is so unbelievably strong thanks to yoga.' He rested on his knees and slowly stood up, rising to his 6'2' and towering over Jerry. He was dressed in his usual board shorts and loose vest, to disguise the inevitable spread which comes from being a 39 year-old bartender and bon-vivant who thinks that yoga is a suitable alternative to physical exercise. 'Hello mate' he said as he dusted off his hands and offered a firm handshake. 'Everything okay? What's been happening? You haven't been around for a while. Been anywhere nice?'

'All good thanks, just been to Gabon for a few days on some business. No beach bars there though!'

'The trips you take mate, you must have a million air miles by now' said Chay, reaching for a glass. 'The usual?'

'Please,' answered Jerry. 'You don't earn air miles the way I fly, buddy. And let me tell you, the flight crew aren't all that pretty either! It's a different story from when you were flying.'

'Yeah, those were good days. Business class everywhere, swanky hotels, free food and booze. But ultimately it was all empty and hollow. What was it all for?'

'Money I guess. You were selling the dream man, very successfully too. As we can see.' He gestured to indicate Chay's prime beachfront location.

'Well beer pretty much sells itself mate, especially Heineken, and this was my way out of the rat race mate.' Chay filled the glass and placed it on the bar. 'What's been happening then Jezzer? What's new?'

Jerry took a sip of the ice cold beer, held it in his mouth for a moment, and let it slide down his throat, savouring the taste as it fizzed in the back of his mouth. He told Chay about Simon's death, and about the mysterious agents clearing out his office. He did not mention the cryptic notes he had read - operational security was always at the forefront of his mind, even if he didn't know what the operation was. Loose tongues cost lives, especially in today's world where enemies were non-traditional and often unseen. Chay was a good man and a good friend, but as a bartender he spoke to a lot of people, and Jerry would never entrust secrets to him.

'Oh God, that's awful about Simon, but that sounds a bit weird' said Chay absently, whilst leaning on the bar and closely studying his right tricep as he bent and straightened his arm. 'It sounds to me like someone's trying to hide something. Or do you think Simon was killed deliberately?'

'I hadn't thought of that' said Jerry, 'but who would do that?'

'Dunno mate. That's your field. I just do beer' his voice trailed off as he walked down the bar to greet a customer.

Jerry sat at the bar, holding the cold glass in his hand and thought deeply about the morning's events. What had Simon been up to? He hadn't seen much of him over the last few months as they had both been busy with planning and conducting operations, and Simon spent lots of time in the operations room, planning and monitoring operations. The notes had suggested there was some sort of operation in the offing, but it was unfathomable that Jerry wouldn't know about an official op. So it must have been some sort of private venture of Simon's. What was the Bardai Plant that was at Initial Operating Capability? Was it something to do with the field test? A test of what? As it was a plant, that suggested some sort of manufactured product, and it was 100% successful. Could it be a new weapon system? Why didn't he know about it?

The agents collecting all Simon's documents bugged him. Did Lionel know that Simon was doing some unofficial research? Why else would he order the documents to be recovered without telling Jerry? Why wouldn't he tell Jerry what was going on? Did he not trust him? If he had doubts about Simon then he would surely have shared his concerns with Jerry, as his direct boss. There was only one course of action open to Jerry. He had to speak with Lionel, and get some answers to all these questions. He didn't have enough information to answer them himself. He'd just finish this beer and then head straight back. Lionel's meeting must have finished by now.

His phone rang. He looked at the screen and saw it was Lionel calling. *Maybe his ears were burning* thought Jerry. He answered. 'Hey Lionel. How's it going?'

'Jerry, where are you?' replied Lionel curtly. Jerry was taken aback. Lionel was always direct but never blunt.

'I'm just grabbing some lunch. What's up?' Something he couldn't put his finger on told him not to reveal where he actually was. Perhaps shame, or perhaps a nagging thought in the back of his mind that he should be careful what he said to Lionel. The morning's events didn't make sense.

'This thing in Senegal has flared up and we need someone to do a recce. I know it's shitty timing, with Simon, but I'm thinking you're the man for the job. We need our very best man on it. Come on in and Porter will brief you. I need you to fly out tonight.'

'Oh.... right' stammered Jerry. He hadn't been expecting that. 'Sure, give me ten minutes and I'll be there. Also Lionel...' he quickly added, 'there's something else I need to talk about...with you.'

'What is it?'

'Well, I don't want to do it over the phone, it's sensitive'

'It's not about Simon is it?' asked Lionel, almost immediately.

'Well yes, it is actually.' Jerry was surprised at Lionel's directness, and also that he seemed to know what he wanted to talk about.

'Look, it was shitty bad luck, and Simon was a good man, but shit happens and we need to move the fuck on.'

'Right, sure, but it's not about his death, it's something else.'

Well can it wait until you get back? I need to be in Abuja this afternoon.'

He paused. *Should I bring it up now? Over the phone? Maybe this is too important to wait. No, it needed to be done face to face.* 'Sure, that'll be okay.'

'Okay, good luck in Senegal.' Lionel hung up abruptly.

Clearly Simon's death wasn't slowing the pace of work at the Task Force, or softening Lionel's manner. He wasn't known for his sensitivity or emotion, which some said made him the outstanding military commander he had been, but Jerry wasn't a fan of such directness. Lionel was dealing with people, not robots. Jerry wondered how Lionel had become so callous. He had also served in the Corps, and had managed to retain most of his humanity. But that was Lionel, love him or hate him he was the boss, and he would get his chance to discuss the mystery eventually, but first there was work to do. He finished his drink, bid farewell to Chay, and strode out of the bar.

Chapter Seven

The convoy of four black SUVs sped along the road in close formation, cars and bikes spilling out of their way as they hurtled along. An ox being led alongside the road by a small boy pulled at its rope in surprise. A woman sitting in the shade of a small stall, selling sad-looking fruits and vegetables, sat up and looked hopefully down the road as the cars approached, but slumped her shoulders as they sped past. Women dressed in faded dresses and children dressed in dirty torn clothes stopped what they were doing to watch them pass, staring in wonder at the rare sight. A man emerged from a ramshackle wooden hut by the side of the road just in time to see the convoy disappear over the brow of a hill. As quickly as it had appeared the convoy was gone, and the people went back to their routine, not even bothering to wonder who was in the vehicles and where they were going.

President Ayatumbe sat in the back of the SUV and watched the Chadian countryside flash by. He was an hour south of N'Djamena, and the landscape had changed during his journey. The rich red Sahara desert plains of N'Djamena were far behind them, having been replaced by the dusty savanna of the Sahel. The once lush grasslands and rolling hills were now instead dusty expanses of land, interspersed with the occasional acacia tree huddling below rocky outcrops. The grasslands were now arid, having been deprived of life-giving water for so long. Such a precious resource. There was occasionally a patchy blanket of dead and drying grass, but mostly wide open dusty spaces being beaten by the cruel sun.

'Sir, Minister Al Salmi is asking for a decision on the offer from the Republic.' The request came from the aide sitting beside Ayatumbe. 'He recommends that we accept the offer of humanitarian assistance in the northeast, as a gesture of compromise, but refuse the military hardware.'

Ayatumbe considered the suggestion. *Humanitarian assistance will still most likely come in the form of troops with trucks, but at least in the northeast they will be out of the way.* 'I agree, tell him to accept that the humanitarian assistance be delivered to the refugee sites, where our own troops will receive it from them. There is to be a hard line no more than ten kilometres from the border, which Republic troops may not cross under any circumstances. I want that line under constant surveillance. Also tell him I agree with his suggestion on the hardware. I do not want any Republic military equipment on our soil, under any circumstances. Ensure he communicates those orders to General Akweli also.'

'Yes Sir.' The aide turned away and got to work. Ayatumbe thought for a moment and then closed that book in his mind. He looked out over the landscape with an unpleasant familiarity. When he had first come to Chad, and had made his way west to the capital and then south to the Sahel region, he had noted the abundance of nomadic agriculture - small farms and grazing areas were all around during the wet season. The Darfur landscape had been dominated by the Sahara weather patterns, and so was dry and dusty, with small tough bushes and an unforgiving constant wind. The Sahel had seemed like paradise to him. Over the following years he realised that it was a pitiful child's paradise, and its future was the same as that of the Sahara to the north. The rising temperatures and over-grazing of the land, interspersed with some punishingly long periods of drought had reduced the area to little more than a dustbowl, whipped by fierce winds and baked by constant hot sun.

Ayatumbe remembered the long journey he had made with his aunt and his brother out of Darfur, across the border and into the huge refugee camps. Four million people had fled the violence in Darfur, and 260,000 of them had become refugees in eastern Chad. They were kept in one of the twelve refugee camps established in Chad, where they huddled together, terrified for their lives and unsure of how they would get either food or water. The aid agencies had provided basic food and water, as well as limited shelter, but there was not enough to go round the thousands of starving victims. He remembered seeing the brutal fights break out every time a UN convoy delivered aid to the camp, with desperate men and women literally stamping others to death to get a few grains of rice and drops of water for their families.

He and his brother Yabo were both aged less than ten and his aunt only in her teens, so they stood little chance in the fights for supplies at the back of the trucks. Instead his aunt had relied on the only asset she had available to provide for her nephews, and she had sold her body to the troops protecting the camp. The African UN troops were there to protect the camps from the marauding troops of militia, but instead spent their time corrupting and stealing as much as they could from the already destitute refugees. She gave in to countless abuses in exchange for what morsels they would throw her way.

One day his aunt did not come back from her daily visit to the troops quarters. He and Yabo had sat together waiting for her return for two days and two nights. They had no idea at the time why she wouldn't return, but he assumed later that she had been killed by one or many of the troops, perhaps over a disagreement about payment, and her body discarded with the hundreds of others that had succumbed to disease or illness.

He and Yabo eventually had to go in search of food and water, and so they had wandered hand in hand until they saw a group of soldiers stood under a tree smoking. Yabo had begun to plead with them for some food or water. They had pushed him away but he had begged them, screaming in desperation. Then he had watched in horror as one of the soldiers turned his rifle on Yabo and pulled the trigger. His big brother's body had been thrown back by the force of the bullet, which tore a hole through his chest. He had fallen on his big brother's body and clawed at his face in desperation. The soldiers did nothing.

They just went back to their cigarettes and stood by as he sobbed over his brother's body. Ayatumbe shifted in his seat and winced at the painful memory. He had tried to forget that pain but it came rushing back as he remembered the events.

Eventually he had gone to find help. He wandered through the vast camp, not knowing what he was looking for, for what seemed like days, he couldn't remember. But he did remember the moment he met Celine, the aid worker from France, who was processing patients at the medical facility. Hers was the first white face he had ever seen, and she was smiling at him. She wrapped him up in her arms and took care of him, giving him food and water, and shelter, and love. He didn't remember much of the next year, until the time that Celine left. She had finished her time in the camp and was returning to France. Obviously she could not take young Joseph with her, despite them both wanting that very much, so instead she had arranged his relocation.

There had been an agreement at the time between the Chadian and Sudanese governments that Sudanese refugees could not be relocated anywhere other than Sudan, but Celine had somehow managed to arrange for him to be taken to southern Chad. A new life in a new place with a new name, he supposed. After a tearful goodbye he was taken away in a truck and never saw her again. That french angel had saved his life and given him a new one, in the safety of the Sahel.

He thought of the modern-day version of his birthplace in Darfur, which was now within the borders of the Republic. Darfur still did not enjoy prosperity, even after more than twenty years of conflict had ceded to a reluctant peace under the command of the Republic. Darfur was still desperately under-developed and as prone to ethnic violence as ever. The aid agencies had lost interest in Africa long ago, too concerned with shrinking budgets and return on investment. Their projects were replaced by speculative efforts by China and then India to find some value for themselves. But they too had given up on Africa as a lost cause, leaving millions of people starving and fighting for survival. He shuddered when he thought of what would have become of him if Celine had not saved him. He may have now been a citizen of the Republic! If the President had his way then he still may be. As the Sahel landscape continued to rush by he turned his thoughts to the business of the day. He picked up the file from the seat next to him and began to read its contents.

An hour later the landscape had still not changed, but ahead of them he could see the outline of an industrial complex on the horizon. The distinctive towers, chimneys and pipes of an oil refinery dominated the scenery now, as around the approach road there was increased evidence of industrialisation and pollution. Chad's oil production had been going for over 30 years, and oil revenue represented a massive proportion of the country's GDP, with the rest coming from the gold and uranium mining operations. Middle East and Russian oil production had sharply declined as they had reached the end of their reserves, leaving a clear opportunity for Chad to sweep in and make a killing, profiting from the continent's continuing, and actually increasing, dependency on a diminishing resource which only pushed the price higher.

He had enjoyed enormous profits in the early years, when they literally could not refine enough oil to keep up with demand despite having thousands of wells all across the Doba basin in the south. Now those days were gone. There was perhaps four or five years of supply left at the best estimate. Oil had all but had its day, and he now had to take action to recoup his lost profits before they disappeared for ever. After that he would be able to draw equal if not greater profits from his next project.

The convoy came to a stop outside a two-storey metallic-looking building at the front of the refinery, the logo emblazoned on the building, AMAPEC, represented the Amazon Petroleum Corporation. This was Chad's chosen partner in their oil production since the forced removal of Esso in 2019, after claims by the government that Esso was pumping more oil than they claimed, and therefore stealing billions of dollars every year. The deal the Chadian government had brokered with AMAPEC had been much tighter, as had been the monitoring of their production.

As he stepped out of the SUV he was greeted by Eduardo Sousa, CEO of AMAPEC's production in Chad. He was a short and stocky man with jet black hair, dark eyes and a thick black moustache over his white teeth. He was dressed smartly in a grey suit and pale tie, and gave a wide smile as he shook Ayatumbe's hand.

After the greetings Sousa ushered Ayatumbe into the building, engaging him in polite small talk until they reached a meeting room. The room was not big, but was comfortably furnished with leather couches at the near end and a meeting table at the other. They sat and enjoyed some cold water.

'Mr President, may I say it is wonderful to see you here, and that it will be my pleasure to give you a tour of the facility today." Sousa was turning up the charm dial to ten, over-compensating for the panic he was feeling inside at this unplanned visit. He had flown in at short notice when the visit had been announced, cutting short a trip to India. He didn't know the purpose of this visit, but he certainly wanted to start it on his terms.

'No tour will be necessary Mr Sousa. I have come to discuss the terms of our contract. There will be some changes.'

'Mr President...the contract still has five more years to run...'

'The terms are no longer acceptable' Ayatumbe cut in. 'I will present you with the new terms and the new contract.' An aide passed him a file, which he coolly opened and took out the documents within.

'Err, Sir, this is not what we agreed...' Sousa was reeling from the shock. He didn't imagine this was what the President wanted to discuss. His mind raced as he tried to think of a position to adopt against such a stonewall bargaining position. Africans were notoriously hard to deal with, but this was something else.

'I have reason to believe that AMAPEC are defrauding my government, and stealing my oil, which is in clear breach of our contract. As such I judge that the contract is void.'

'Mr President, no-one is stealing oil, and there is certainly no fraud taking place at all. This is a very open and transparent organisation, as proven by our continued compliance with the regulation conditions stipulated in the contract.'

'Mr Sousa, we have evidence of your deception. Your company has been stealing from the Chad government for years, profiting from our resource and cheating my country out of billions of dollars of revenue.'

'Sir, that is simply not true.' *What evidence?* 'AMAPEC and the government of Chad have been in a mutually profitable relationship for twenty years now. The profit-share of the revenue is clearly agreed, and every cent of that profit is accounted for.'

'Oh come on, we know that you falsify your accounts to show greater costs than you actually have. You are raping and pillaging my country while you can, stealing our money from in front of our noses'

'Sir, I can assure you that is not the case. We have always maintained an open approach to our accounting.' *What was he doing? Didn't everyone understand this was one of the overlooked elements of the relationship. There was always a margin added, and no-one ever mentioned it.* 'My team routinely shares production and profit figures with your minister, at quarterly meetings…'

'Fabricated figures Mr Sousa!' the President raised his voice. 'Your figures are lies, and you are now lying to me.'

Sousa did not like the direction this meeting was going at all. Time to slow it down and divert it to safer territory. 'Mr President, I am an honest man, and have enjoyed a strong relationship with your government since I took over this position. I have had many meetings with your Minister for Energy, Mr Okeke. He tells me that you enjoy the finer distractions in life. Scotch whiskey for instance…?' He beckoned to a waiter.

'Mr Sousa, I cannot be bought off with expensive whiskey, and cars and girls like my minister. You insult me.'

If rumours were true, he most certainly could be bought, but the price was clearly much higher. 'I apologise Mr President, I did not mean to suggest that I am offering you a bribe.' *Of course I am, just get round to naming your price. You corrupt bastards all have one. Your minister certainly did - luxury foreign holidays and young girls for starters.*

'Good, because I will accept no such thing. The years of graft are behind us now Mr Sousa, in the dark murky days of the oil boom when you and your weasel colleagues could flash a smile, grease a palm and walk away with billions. You should know this is a much changed country now.'

Sousa paused, waiting for an opening from Ayatumbe. His tone and words were certainly not indicating that he was preparing to put a price on the table. He couldn't actually be serious about changing the contract. That was unprecedented. *No*, he decided, *wait for his next move, it is sure to be a bargaining position.*

Ayatumbe again picked up the piece of paper from the file and proffered it. 'These are the new terms of the contract. The Chadian government will receive eighty percent of the revenue profits, AMAPEC twenty percent, and you will continue to contribute one billion dollars per year to the ongoing program of development in southern Chad. You have also been failing to meet those terms, as is evidenced by the worsening environmental conditions and living standards in communities surrounding the oil wells.'

Is he serious? AMAPEC had made the required compensation and development payments, but they never reached the intended recipients due to the many thieving hands the money had to pass through on the way down. *The goddamn hypocrisy of this guy! His hands were probably the first ones on that money.*

'Now look here' Sousa had a more urgent tone to his voice. He sat forward, and held out his hands in a pleading gesture. 'AMAPEC takes its commitment to supporting the local communities and the development of infrastructure very seriously. We can very clearly demonstrate our compliance with the terms, based on the receipted payments we have made.'

'Mr Sousa, do you accept the terms of the contract?' Ayatumbe was tiring of the discussion. 'This can be easily resolved with an agreement today. It would be a great shame if it was necessary to take this to the courts to resolve. I fear for you that the evidence we have gathered would not reflect well on you or your corporation.'

That was the first threat, albeit a veiled one, Sousa noted. He was being boxed into a corner, with very few punches left to throw. The threat of courts was worrying as Ayatumbe would clearly exert his influence on their proceedings. His mind again raced with thoughts of how to extract himself from this nightmare. *Best come out punching then.*

'Mr President' he retorted confidently, 'that will absolutely not be necessary. If any court is to be consulted, it will not be a Chadian court. AMAPEC is a Brazilian corporation, so it will be taken to a Brazilian court, where you can present any evidence of wrongdoing you think you may have, and they can decide the outcome.'

'The affairs of *my* country will be decided in *my* courts!' Ayatumbe was becoming agitated now. 'Do not think I will allow this to drag on in your legal system, with your lawyers slowing it at every turn. No Mr Sousa, you will answer for it right now!'

'I think we have said enough Sir' said Sousa, getting to his feet. 'This nonsense is going nowhere. Have your legal representative present your case to my lawyers in N'Djamena and we will discuss it appropriately. I will not sit here, listen to lies and be threatened...'

Ayatumbe slowly rose to his feet. He spoke calmly and in a decidedly menacing tone. 'Mr Sousa, you have misjudged me. Don't for one moment think that just because we have allowed you to suck the milk from our teat for so long, that you have any authority over me. I have made you and your board incredibly wealthy. It is with my permission that you continue to enjoy such wealth. And it is my decision what happens next.' His voice grew louder. 'You are a guest in my country. You do not instruct me what to do, and you certainly do not dismiss me from this meeting!'

Sousa was silent, numb, and not at all liking the tone of the conversation now. His gamble to come out punching had not paid off, and now he was the one being punched. He had nowhere to go now. He couldn't possibly agree to the terms of the new contract, not without admitting liability and giving up more of the profit share, which would cost AMAPEC billions. He could not plead for reason as Ayatumbe did not appear to be in a conciliatory mood now. His final option would have to be to request time to review the new terms, and therefore buy some time and space.

'Mr President, I am not a lawyer. I cannot review a contract and its thousands of clauses right now. Allow me to take this to my legal team, review the implications and table a discussion in a week or two...'

'You will accept the terms of the contract now!' shouted Ayatumbe. 'There is no discussion Mr Sousa. I am telling you!'

'I'm afraid that isn't possible Sir. That is not how we do business.'

Ayatumbe looked over his shoulder at the security detail waiting behind him. 'Very well Mr Sousa, I have given you every opportunity to comply.' Two of the three security men approached Sousa. He backed away, edging down the couch towards the door.

'Stop!' called Sousa. His own security detail reacted to his raised voice and burst in through the door, pistols drawn, but before they could make it through the door Ayatumbe's third guard had raised his pistol and blasted the leading man in the chest. The sound was deafening in the small room and Ayatumbe instinctively ducked down by the couch, fearful of any stray bullets that may come his way. The first man fell backwards, propelled by the force of the bullet at such short range. The second man had his pistol hand obstructed by his colleague falling back into him. The half second delay was fatal, the shooter was already moving towards the door with his pistol raised and ready to fire again. He squeezed the trigger and the pistol spat its bullet into the man's chest from five feet away, sending him spinning backwards with a grunt. He bent down to check the status of his two victims, removed their pistols from their death grips, and stood guard at the door, standing by for any reinforcements that may arrive.

Sousa looked on in horror. He couldn't believe what had just happened, and all in the space of about five seconds. His ears were ringing from the two shots, and he was trembling. The two security men seized him and pulled his arms behind his back, clamping handcuffs on his wrists. 'What are you doing? This is madness!' he shouted at Ayatumbe. 'You cannot do this!'

Ayatumbe laughed. "Mr Sousa, this is my country. I can do anything I want. I can have your men shot and you thrown into jail, and who is going to stop me? You think you can threaten me with your bullshit courts and legal team? You and your fancy suits just don't get it Mr Sousa. You think that because you make billions from this deal and others like it across Africa that you can call the shots? You think that you have some sort of authority? I am the President! I make the law here, and I have the authority. You will be taken to one of our facilities where you will have the opportunity to rethink your position, *without* your legal team. How long you spend there, and whether you ever come out again, is entirely up to you. Take him away!' he barked.

'You can't do this!' shouted Sousa as the security men hustled him out of the room. 'My company will protest this!'

Ayatumbe laughed, and said to no-one, 'Of course they will.' He finished his glass of water and followed the men out of the door, stepping over the sprawled bodies.

Chapter Eight

Hassan and his clan finished their Fajr prayer and rolled up their prayer mats. He stood in silence and regarded the beautiful golden sunrise breaking over the mountains. They had prayed and given thanks to Allah for this beautiful oasis where they had slept for two nights now. But it was now time to move on, further into the mountains and further from their attackers. There had been no sign of them anywhere below on the plains to the north. A sentry had been posted day and night to monitor that approach, but there had been nothing moving below but sand and wind. He felt they had stayed long enough, and to stay any longer would be complacent. Of course if it was Allah's will that the attackers had come sooner they would have faced it, but they had been protected, and given the opportunity to continue their journey.

He turned to see the clan packing up their few belongings and preparing to move, filling waterskins and taking a last deep drink from the oasis; they did not know when they would next find such a source of fresh water. He had already called the sentry down from the ridge, and so began the final checks. Had they left any sign of having come this way? There were some fire remnants that they had buried and covered as well as possible, and all collected branches and stones were distributed around the site in order to look natural again. Finally they used fallen palm fronds to clear any footprints from the dust and sand. It wasn't perfect, but it may fool the casual observer looking from a distance.

He looked to the east. The sun was slowly climbing in the sky and in an hour or so would break over the top of the ridge, flooding them in its light and heat. They should move now he decided, no more lingering and worrying.

'Come my people, let us begin our journey again.' He stepped off to the south east, heading to the left of the large mountain dominating the valley. He and Hissene had debated whether to head to the low saddle to the west and so avoid a climb at the start of their journey, but they concluded that south was their preferred direction, moving away from danger.

The clan shuffled off behind him, leaving behind the haven they hadn't dreamed possible, and optimistically continuing on into the unknown in search of some other impossible haven. The goats too bleated as they set off, their bellies full of green grass and fresh water, and their legs rested. Even they seemed optimistic.

The initial climb was tough and steep, but they were well rested, and the sun was not yet shining on them, so they made it without too much strain. When they reached the top of the ridge they discovered that in fact it was not a ridge but a long plateau, stretching away several hundred metres to the south. It was featureless, except for a few small mounds of grass and of course the large mountain to the west, which now towered over them as they were closer to it. The early morning sun bathed the plateau in a golden light, and they felt warm and happy as they crossed the plateau. Hassan glanced up at the mountain as he detected movement in his peripheral vision, and it was strange to have seen anything outside their own clan move in the last week. Sure enough there was movement - in the air - the eagle he had seen on that first day and regularly since then, was circling high above, perhaps three hundred metres up, gliding on the thermals from the mountain. Its path was circular, high above them in a wide arc, almost as if it was regarding them as potential prey. Perhaps it was contemplating taking one of the goats?

When they reached the end of the plateau they stopped and looked at the scene below. It was breathtaking. The mountains stretched out before them as far as they could see, deep into what must be Chadian territory - perhaps fifty kilometres or more. The peaks were tall, shooting straight up out of the red sand in towers and buttresses. Some were flat topped, some jagged and forbidding. Between them were flat expanses of red sand, giving way to a lighter dusty-looking sand further to the south. The light blue sky above contrasted with the brown-red rock in a stunning contrast, making them look even more severe and dramatic.

Hassan's face lit up in wonder at the sight, but it soon gave way to a concerned look as he assessed the terrain for possible routes for them to take, and possible water sources. To the east he could see sheer vertical mountains with wide red sandy plains beneath them. It did not look like much water sprang forth there, and there were no likely hidden valleys where they might discover another surprise oasis. Looking further south the mountains became more densely concentrated, and he could see what looked like valleys and ridges running in a northwest to southeast direction. He couldn't see what lay behind those mountains, but that was potential enough for him.

They set off down the side of the mountain, carefully picking their way down the rocky slope, avoiding loose stones and rocks. The goats kept pace beside them as they descended. As he walked Hassan kept glancing to the distant mountains, attempting to calculate an approximate distance and therefore journey time. He guessed the first slope was five kilometres away, so they should reach it by mid-morning, before the sun was too high in the sky. However they were still very exposed on this slope and the sand below. Exposed to the sun, and also to any attackers, but this was the only route they could consider. No doubts now.

Hours later they had reached the first slope without incident. The sun was now high in the sky, beating down on the clan on the hot sand. They paused for a rest and to sip some water. Hassan looked back to where they had come from as Hissene joined him.

'We have come far Hassan. The people are tired. We should rest.'

'Not here Hissene. We are too exposed. We should climb this slope and see what lies beyond. We may find some shelter there.'

'Insha'allah. You see no sign of anyone following us?' Hissene indicated back to their start point.

'Nothing at all, al hamdu lillah' He looked up at the sun to check its position, he guessed it would soon be noon. They should get going. He noticed the eagle circling above again. *Is that eagle following us? He must really think he has a meal coming. Not today.* 'Come, let's go.'

They turned and joined the clan, rallying them to begin the climb. Small children cried, but their mothers swept them up in their arms and began the ascent. It was long slow work, and the slope had no shade from the sun, making it even more draining. Finally they reached the top of the slope and looked down a long valley stretching away from them to the south for perhaps eight kilometres or more. Hassan felt the sweat running down his neck and adjusted his headscarf, which was now drenched in sweat but at least provided some cooling effect. There was also a slight breeze up on the slope, which provided some relief.

The clan stood and looked down the valley, their eyes searching for signs of water or vegetation. They found none, only a long dusty valley a few hundred metres wide with steep rocky sides. Hassan's heart sank, he had been counting on something positive. He looked to the west beyond the ridge, and saw more peaks. More peaks meant more troughs, and valleys, and potential sources of water and shelter. This valley didn't look like it would yield any comfort. If they walked to the west, they could stay on this high ground for as long as possible. It even swept slightly round to the south where it met another slope. Then they could climb that slope and drop down into the next valley and hope to find something more encouraging.

Jamelia approached him. 'Hassan, this is hopeless, look at this.' She gestured down the dry valley. Her voice was pleading, 'Please Hassan, let us return to the oasis. We can be safe there for a while longer.'

'We cannot turn back Jamelia, we may be followed. We must keep moving away from the attackers.'

'Hassan, you are a good man, and you are a good leader for our clan.' she began. He could see a 'but' coming now. 'But..' she continued, 'this may be the wrong decision. The attackers had vehicles. If they were chasing us then they would surely have caught us long ago, no?'

He felt especially responsible for the decisions he was making now, as he had insisted they move from the oasis. He had heard the frustration in the people's voices when they saw this valley was dry too. It was understandable that they would want to return to the oasis. They hadn't seen any sign of their attackers in nearly a week now, and Jamelia was right, they would have caught up to them if they had wanted to. Maybe she was right, and they should turn back, but they had been going forwards for so long now it didn't seem right to stop. Moving was in their nature as a nomadic people, so even though it would be unpopular just now they had to keep going. He was sure there would be salvation for them if they kept moving.

'Jamelia my wife, you are a great woman, and your wisdom is a great strength to us. You know I never make a decision without first consulting you, but I must make this decision, and I say we must keep moving forward. Look over there.' he pointed to the ridge to the west. 'We will follow this high ground we are on, all the way around to that slope, where we can climb a short distance over and find another beautiful oasis.'

She sighed. 'Alright my love, I trust you and your leadership, but I pray to Allah that we find something soon. The children are tiring.'

'Insha'allah' he replied, and they rejoined the group, where he explained his plan, while looking at some despondent faces. 'We must move forward into the future' he said, 'and discover what awaits us.'

They moved off again, stumbling over the rocks as they attempted to pick their way across the downward slope, trying not to lose height too much. It would certainly be shorter to drop down and walk across to the slope, but going around meant less climbing, and he judged that was better for all. He hoped.

Eventually they reached the slope and made the climb, which was considerably shorter because of their detour around the slope. As a result they made the climb quicker than they thought, and reached the top in good order. But their good spirits soon sank again as they saw what lay below them. A long dry valley, just like the one to the east, ran southwards and curled round out of sight to the west. Further to the west there were more peaks, more ridges, and more climbs. Some of the clan cried out in despair. They had all been counting on some good signs.

Hassan stared at the scene before him in disbelief. *What have I done?* His people had trusted him to lead them to salvation, and instead he had delivered hopelessness. He closed his eyes and prayed to God for some help. He heard the people calling out and crying, venting their frustration and fear. He once again regarded the scene, and scanned the horizon for any sign of life, straining his eyes to pick out details in the distance. *Is that some smoke in the distance to the southwest? It's hard to see, the haze is making it blurry.* He called over Hissene and pointed.

'It's hard to see Hassan, but it could be smoke, or it could be the heat of the day playing tricks on our eyes.'

'Well it's something' replied Hassan. 'But why would there be smoke in the mountains? It must be people, but how do we know they will be friendly? It could be more men with guns.'

'Perhaps' agreed Hissene. 'And who makes a fire during the day?'

'I don't know, but at least there's a chance it may be something good. I think we should go and see what is there.'

'Agreed, but we should be careful. I don't like the idea of stumbling on a whole camp of those attackers.'

'It doesn't seem likely this far south, but I agree, let's be careful about our approach. It looks like this valley will turn right around onto the source of the smoke, so we can follow it down and have a look when we get to the turn without exposing ourselves.'

They showed the clan the smoke and explained the plan. There was a noticeable uplift in the mood of the group as people saw the potential for something life-giving. At least it was a sign of life, which was a lot better than nothing. There must be something there to sustain life, whether natural or artificial. And they could be there before nightfall if they made good time.

They stepped off down the slope with renewed energy and enthusiasm; the children even ran down some of the way. They walked throughout the afternoon, down the long valley, sticking to the west side so they were protected from the sun as it continued its arc across the sky. Initially they made faster strides, eager to get to the end of the valley and discover what it held. But as the afternoon wore on they slowed their pace as they tired, and also as they began to wonder what was the source of the smoke. Wild fantasies ran through their heads as they walked, flitting between finding heaven and finding hell. Due to being in the valley they could no longer see the smoke, and Hassan even began to wonder if it hadn't been smoke, and was actually just a trick of the light. But they continued on, and eventually came to the beginning of the turn in the valley.

The valley was particularly deep here, with the sides stretching up above them so steeply it would require climbing rather than scrambling to reach the top. It was in shade, with the sunlight just hitting the top of the valley on the east side as the sun was finishing its daily journey. The shade made everything seem more forbidding, and the Toubou people began to worry about what lay around the corner. They huddled together, speaking in low voices, sitting on their haunches and resting after the long walk.

Hassan had already thought about what to do. He and Hissene would make their way around the valley, sticking closely to the west side, and attempt to get a view on what was there. They would stay as high as possible in order to get a good perspective on the valley floor. It was not ideal to be doing it so close to sunset, but they were too close now to not take a look. He looked at Hissene and nodded. He nodded back. They had agreed the plan and were ready. He approached Jamelia and took her by the shoulders.

'Jamelia my wife, Hissene and I will discover what lies around the valley and will come back to you. Everyone is to stay here and stay together. We will be back as soon as possible.'

'Okay my husband' replied Jamelia, taking his face in her hands. 'Be careful my love. Come back soon.'

'We will. Do not light a fire yet. We cannot expose ourselves.' One of his sons approached him.

'Father I will come with you.' 8 year-old Wahali was a strong boy and loved an adventure.

'Wahali my son' Hassan lifted him up into his arms. 'This is a job for adults only, and I need you to stand guard for the clan here. You must look after our people and our goats. Can you do that?'

'I can father, but I want to be with you, Fadyaa can look after the goats, she is big enough.'

'Wahali, Fadyaa must stay with your mother, she is too small for this great task. Don't worry, I will return soon and we will be together then.' He kissed the boy and held him close. They had lost two of their sons in the attack last week, and he did not want to jeopardise the lives of the remaining three children. He released him and Wahali shuffled away with his head down, kicking stones as he went.

'Come Hissene, we must leave' They set off together, carefully picking their way along the edge of the valley floor among the boulders and rocks. They would begin to climb up the western slope soon, when they saw an easing in the slope. They jumped and scrambled their way around the corner for several hundred metres, going desperately slowly. It would certainly be faster to walk along the valley floor but they would be too exposed out in the open. The sun had now cleared the top of the valley and it was darkening as nightfall approached. Hassan looked up into the sky to judge how much light they had left; darkness may actually be an asset for their reconnaissance mission. As he glanced up he again saw an eagle circling several hundred metres above. *Not again! Surely it can't be the same eagle? It would not stray this far from its nest. It must be another. Maybe this is a good sign? He may be showing us the way.*

They continued on, scrambling and struggling their way along the side of the slope as it arced its way around. They stopped every minute or so to check for any signs of life beyond. And suddenly they saw it. There was the edge of a building, perhaps a kilometre away on the valley floor. Hassan grabbed Hissene's arm and they edged closer to get a better look in the fading light. It was lighter around the building as the sun had not yet set on that part of the valley. They could see the whole building now, it was tall, and long but had no windows, only some large doors around the bottom. Its walls and roof were made from light green metal. Around the building were several vehicles - pickup trucks, a bus, and some construction vehicles. They couldn't yet see the source of the smoke so they edged closer. Hassan felt sure they couldn't be seen here as this part of the valley was now too shaded to see any detail from the site.

As they moved forwards, more of the site came into view. Beside the building was a collection of buildings, walkways, railings, and some sort of metallic installation with four enormous pipes coming out of the ground and into a building. There were cranes and construction vehicles moving around, and four tall towers with what looked like lights on top of them. Behind the installation was an opening in the valley which looked like it had been blasted away by explosives. There were people moving around the installation, Hassan estimated about a hundred. Just then Hassan froze and again gripped Hissene's arm. On the valley floor in front of the pipes he saw three open top vehicles, with camouflage markings, and heavy machine guns mounted on top. They were most certainly military vehicles, and not dissimilar to those that had routed their village last week. A group of soldiers were emerging from a building and heading for the vehicles. They were running. Hassan could not see what lay further round the valley as it continued to stretch off to the west, but it didn't matter now, the soldiers were in the vehicles, and they were beginning to move, up the valley and towards the clan!

'Wallah! They're coming this way!' whispered Hissene urgently.

'Yes, we must get back to the clan quickly.' But they both knew they couldn't make it back in time before the vehicles got there; it had taken them at least thirty minutes to walk here, and this was not good terrain for running.

'Who are they?' stammered Hissene as they began to pick their way through the boulders. It was harder now that the light was fading; they could not see well enough to find their footing.

'I don't know, but I don't think they're friendly' replied Hassan, breathing heavily as he leapt over a small boulder.

'They couldn't have seen us, we're too far away. Are you sure they're coming for us?' Hissene gasped hopefully.

Hassan glanced quickly back over his shoulder. The vehicles were coming fast up the valley floor, kicking up a trail of dust behind them. They were only five hundred metres away now. At this rate they would be on them in under a minute. There was no chance of escape. *The only chance now is to hide, but what about the clan? Will the soldiers stop if they find us and not go further up the valley?* He stopped. Hissene stumbled on a few more steps and then stopped too. He looked back, confused.

'What is it Hassan? Why are you stopping?'

'We need to distract them Hissene. To stop them from going up the valley and finding the clan. They don't know there's anyone else here.'

Hissene stared at him, thinking. His chest heaved as he panted. They both knew there would be little chance of escape for them, but there was a chance the clan could be saved if they played it convincingly. Hissene nodded.

'I wish I had told them what to do if we don't return' said Hassan, 'they would know to flee.'

'Too late now brother' said Hissene. 'Let's get down there and stop them.'

They turned down the slope and began to walk as quickly as they could. They were about a hundred metres from the valley floor, they could almost make it to the bottom by the time the vehicles reached them. They watched the vehicles approach as they descended, now with their hands in the air, looking as innocent as they could. The vehicles were about a hundred metres away now, the soldiers had seen them. They could hear shouting between the vehicles and one of the men pointed at them. The men looked different from their attackers. Their skin was lighter and they looked more like a proper military unit. Hassan's heart leapt. Perhaps these were Chadian government troops, and they would protect them. He smiled and thanked God, holding up his hands higher, and waving to the vehicles as they approached. He had been right, they had found their salvation.

The lead vehicle began to slow slightly as it approached them, it was now fifty metres away. The two soldiers stood in the back of the vehicle looked at them and exchanged some words. *Why are the other two vehicles not slowing down?* Hassan and Hissene waved again and shouted, stumbling over rocks as they hurried to the foot of the valley. Hassan froze in horror as the lead vehicle's machine gun turned towards them. *What are they doing?* He held out his hands now, trying to stop them, but it was a useless gesture. The heavy machine gun lit up, firing two hundred rounds a minute. The bullets ripped through their bodies at over two thousand metres per second, tearing flesh and shattering bone. They fell to the ground without a sound as the two other vehicles sped by on their way up the valley.

Hassan lay with his eyes half open, trying to pant but unable to. His lungs had been torn apart and he was losing blood fast. Through his half-open eyes he thought he could make out the shape of the eagle again, circling high above. As his vision darkened he thought of his family, and of his clan, and of how he had failed them. He had led them away from the safety of the oasis into a valley of death. What was this place the soldiers were protecting? But it did not matter now, they would meet again in heaven and would know salvation.

'La ilaha illallah - There is nothing worthy of worship except Allah' he managed to mumble Shahadah, thereby securing his place in heaven. He hoped his family would have time to say it too. As his eyes finally closed he thought he could hear the sound of machine guns again, and then he heard nothing.

Chapter Nine

President Al Quraysh lay in bed and sighed with contentment. The morning sun glowed behind the drapes, and he listened to the sound of birds outside. Aishah lay beside him, her arm and leg draped over him in post-coital repose, and her head on his chest, her long dark hair falling around her back and his chest. He could feel his heart beating under the weight of her head. She kissed his chest and stroked his stomach with her soft hands.

'Do I please you my husband?' she purred softly, in the gentle timbre of the Middle East.

'You know you do Aishah. You please me greatly. More than I ever thought possible. Tell me, would you like me to divorce my wives? I will do that for you.'

'My love, I cannot ask you to do that for me.'

'You're not asking. I am' he replied.

'No my love. They have done nothing wrong except to be old.'

'But I never see them any more' he said. 'I spend all my time in your bed. You may as well be my only wife.'

She propped herself up on an elbow and looked at him. 'Darling you have children with those wives. Think of your sons. They need you to be there too.'

'I will still see them, and their mothers will still be provided for, very comfortably. That is the law and I will of course follow it'

'My love, that is your choice' she said, laying back down. 'But you have more important matters to deal with just now. What of the offer from the president? Do you think he is insulting you?'

'No, I think he is protecting his borders. I would do the same. These are hard times for our countries, people are starving and water is incredibly scarce. I think he sees me as a threat to his sovereignty, and he thinks I will try to take land from him a piece at a time, and keep going until I hit his oilfields and uranium mines. He is protecting his land.'

'Are they not your people in his land? Firstly they are Muslim, and secondly they are nomadic and wander across the border routinely anyway.'

'The people are mine, but the border is his.'

'But is the will of the people not important? Isn't that why they are fighting the government? Don't they want to be all yours?'

He thought for a moment. The nomadic people of the Sahara were mostly Muslim, but he hadn't thought that they would want to be considered part of the Republic. No-one had ever declared that. 'Hmmm' he murmured.

'I am all yours my love. I have no borders when it comes to you. You can take all of me, just like you can take anything you want from anyone.' She slid her arm and leg over him and raised herself up so she was kneeling over him. Her long hair fell onto his face. She looked at him through the tunnel of hair she had created, her big eyes with long lashes were beautiful, and her full lips parted in a smile. 'You are the President. The ruler of the great Islamic Republic. I am your wife. You own me just as you own your two hundred million subjects. No-one can deny you what you want, so what do you desire my Ameer? What do you want to take now?' She leaned down and kissed him softly, her breasts delicately brushing his chest. He lifted up his hands and ran them down her back and over her buttocks. She moaned as they kissed deeply, and he decided where he wanted to go.

The President strode into the majlis, where his shura council was waiting for him. He greeted them warmly. They rose as he entered and returned his greeting, followed by a selection of pleasant enquiries about their health and families. They all sat down on couches, with the President in a large leather armchair at the head of the horseshoe shaped seating area.

'Gentlemen, what is the latest situation with Chad? What is President Ayatumbe saying?' He wanted to get straight to business this morning, all other matters could wait.

'Ameer' began Abu Khalid, 'there has been no further contact with the Chadian government since their communication yesterday. President Ayatumbe has accepted our offer of humanitarian assistance, but refused our offer of military hardware to combat the militants.'

'Furthermore Ameer,' added Abu Rashed 'I have just learned that there have been further attacks on our people in the west of Sudan State this very morning. It seems the militants have crossed our border and have killed fleeing refugees. The death toll is not yet known, but it is estimated to be at least fifty.'

The President was aghast. *They are now crossing into our land and killing our people? This is too much.*

'They were chased from their grazing lands over the border and forced to enter our territory for protection. Before they could reach the safety of our troops they were cut down it seems. There could be many more in that same area.' added Abu Rashed, his face grim.

In MY land! His militants cross into MY land and kill MY people! I will not have this!

'Right, then I will need to provide a response to President Ayatumbe's demand' said the President, clasping the arms of the chair in a majestic pose. 'I, Mohammed Rashed Al Quraysh, President and ruler of the Islamic Republic, will not tolerate the killing of muslims, whichever side of a border they happen to be. Inform President Ayatumbe that I will be deploying troops into the borderlands area, and they will take all necessary steps to protect the muslim people there. I will not stand by and watch while his weak leadership allows his militias to destroy my people.'

'Ameer, may I urge caution before we escalate this too far' said Abu Khalid. 'Such a move is impossible to come back from without great cost, politically, militarily and economically.'

'I will not hear it!' snapped the President. 'I have had enough of his arrogance and his posturing.'

'Forgive me Ameer, but as your deputy I must advise you to step back from this and think of other options. Perhaps we could adopt a more aggressive stance on our side of the border? Make it clear to President Ayatumbe that we are ready for action without crossing into Chad? A show of force.'

'He is too arrogant to be intimidated by a show of force, and he clearly thinks we are toothless, just because we have been a peaceful nation so far. In Africa, perceived strength is everything. I can not be seen to be weak, and allow his proxies to do as they like in my country.'

'Perhaps Abu Khalid may have a point Ameer, interjected Abu Rashed. 'This is a very aggressive action. Perhaps we could consider a more threatening approach without the commitment of troops across the border?'

The President took his hands off the arms of the chair and put them in his lap. 'What do you mean Abu Rashed?'

'Well Ameer, I think I am correct in stating that we have recently procured a UAV surveillance system, which as well as having a very sophisticated camera system on board also has the capability to carry a number of missiles.'

'Drones are not new technology. We have had them for many years. Why is this important?'

'Because these drones have a much greater range than previous models Ameer. They have the capability to overfly the border, *and beyond,* to monitor movement of people, to find targets and destroy them all in one platform.'

'That is a tempting idea' the President conceded, as his rage began to recede. 'How many do we have?'

'We have recently received eight I believe, that may be enough to patrol the entire border' said Abu Rashed. 'They also have the benefit of being a lot more deniable, whereas boots on the ground on the wrong side of the border is much more obvious.'

'I agree with Abu Rashed, Ameer' said Abu Khalid. 'We can maintain a strong front, without having to move many troops to the borderlands.'

'...and one or two missile strikes on their militia will send a very clear message that we are prepared to do whatever is necessary' added Abu Rashed.

'Fine, that is a good plan, make the arrangements. In future I also want General Al Buraimi to attend the shura so he can brief me on developments. And I want to know how much of the border we can patrol with the drones, and where we should position troops.'

'As you wish Ameer' said Abu Khalid. 'That just leaves the statement we are to deliver to President Ayatumbe...'

'Yes, I want him to be very clear that we will not tolerate any more cross-border attacks. Tell him we will deliver the aid he wants, and make it clear that we will be aggressively patrolling the border...'

'May I suggest 'robustly' patrolling the border Ameer?' suggested Abu Rashed. 'It gives the impression of a determined defence rather than threatening an attack.'

'Fine, robustly will do. But make it clear that there will be no more gamesmanship. This is now a matter of life and death, and I will take any necessary measures to protect my people and the Republic.'

"Yes Ameer, as you wish' replied Abu Khalid.

'Good, Now what of the trade deal with the EAC? Are they in agreement with our terms?'

'No Ameer, there appears to be some division amongst its member states. Tanzania and Uganda are currently in dispute over access to Lake Victoria. I believe Tanzania is accusing Uganda of drawing out more than their allotted amount of water. Added to that they claim that the outflow from the Ugandan mineral mine on the border is polluting a water source which runs directly into the lake. They can not reach agreement on their own issues, let alone our proposals.'

'This is the problem with trading blocs' said the President. 'They really can't get anything done outside their own areas, which only limits them and their development. If they keep looking inside their bloc for the answers then they will never see the obvious benefits of trading with regional partners, like us. Can we apply some pressure to them? We have been waiting for quite some time now.'

'They are stalling Ameer. There is also a suggestion that they may be attempting to negotiate a free trade deal with Mozambique, in order to increase their supply of aluminium and steel for their automotive industry.'

'Wallah! This is outrageous. We have been offering them aluminium for years now. What is this? Protectionism? Why are our products not good enough for them?'

'I think they may have doubts about the quality of our production Ameer, as well as our capacity to produce enough goods. Our industrial base is still relatively small, whereas Mozambique's aluminium production is now the largest in Africa.'

The President sighed. 'We must find a new trade partner in the region. The collapse of the EU and the decline of the US has been painful for us.'

'It is true Ameer, we were very reliant on our trade deals with them, but we have also seen a fall in our mining production, and obviously the oil and gas sector…'

'Yes, yes, I know' he paused and thought for a moment. 'How do we turn this around?'

'Well, our trade deficit is still huge Ameer. If we were able to increase the flow of foreign direct investment for our manufacturing industry, and perhaps look to our neighbours in the Maghreb.'

'We may also look to the east, and consider the failing economy of Saudi Arabia' suggested Abu Rashed. 'Their heavy reliance on oil has now left them exposed. We could seek to trade with them on good terms.'

'Yes, like us they relied on oil for too long, and some might say became complacent' agreed the President. 'Okay, here is what we will do…'

An hour later the shura broke and the men emerged from the majlis, speaking quietly in pairs as they dispersed to their various tasks and duties. Abu Khalid and Abu Rashed walked together.

'The President seems resurgent' said Abu Khalid. 'I have not seen him this animated in some months now.'

'Yes, this crisis is igniting a fire inside him it seems. We see his true character emerge at such a time - see what his values are' agreed Abu Rashed.

'Yes, he is showing great strength, but also great restraint. He is a wise leader.'

'Indeed, very wise. I must return to my chambers Abu Khalid, a salaam alaykum'

'Wa alaykum salaam Abu Rashed. I will see you tomorrow.'

Abu Rashed turned and headed down the corridor towards the exit from the palace. He made his way through the great halls, gazing at the splendid mosaics and paintings on the walls as he went. The size of the palace was incredible, the largest palace ever constructed, covering an area of 150,000 square metres, decorated lavishly and furnished luxuriously. It was an incredible statement of power, for the most powerful man in Africa. He exited the building and headed for his waiting car. He reached into the pocket of his thobe and pulled out his phone. He selected a number and dialled it.

'Wa alaykum salaam...Yes I have just sat with him...Yes, exactly as planned...Exactly, go ahead and make the arrangements. And keep up the attacks, they're having exactly the desired effect.'

Chapter Ten

Jerry entered the Task Force headquarters and passed through security. It had been a long and tiring 36 hours, meeting key ministers and military commanders, travelling around the country and conducting recces of the target sites. He had written most of the report in the airport lounge and on the plane journey, but he needed to tidy it up now before submitting it to Porter. It would normally be Simon's job, as he always had such a great appetite and aptitude for planning. He hadn't thought much about Simon or the mystery notes when he was away as he was so busy, but now walking back in the building and seeing Simon's office door brought it crashing back into his mind.

He tried the handle of Simon's door, curious to have another look for any signs of Simon's mysterious work. Perhaps in their haste to take the documents away the agents may have left some tasty piece of intelligence behind. But as he opened the door Jerry instead saw nothing but empty office furniture. Every piece of paper, poster, map, book, journal and report had been removed, as well as all of Simon's photographs from the wall. The office looked as though Simon had never existed, and certainly wasn't going to reveal any more secrets.

He stepped inside, and closed the door behind him, putting his bags on the floor. He started to look in any hidden places he could think of for any clues - behind the bookshelf, under the bookshelf, inside the lining of the chair, under the drawers. He laughed at himself. *I've watched too many spy movies, people don't really do that.* He sat back in Simon's desk chair and looked at the blank walls. Even the whiteboard had been cleaned off. There was nothing here to give him any more clues. Disappointed, he picked up his bags and retired to his own office to finish the report.

Two hours later he knocked on the door of Porter Fogle, the Task Force's head of intelligence. He didn't wait for an answer, but just let himself straight in, as was customary between department heads in the headquarters. Porter looked up quickly from the document he was reading at his desk, and closed the file. He took off his glasses and stood up, stretching to his full height of 6 ft 5. He was lean verging on thin, dressed in a shirt and slacks, and his big eyes and shaggy light-coloured hair conveyed the look of a mad scientist. In fact he was a brilliant intelligence analyst, having come from a glistening career at MI6, heading up the Africa Branch.

'Jerry, how delightful to see you! Come on in, how was Senegal?' They shook hands.

'Hot. And sweaty' smiled Jerry. 'But good, and very productive. I've written the report' he held up the report and placed it on Porter's desk. 'It's not quite the standard of Simon's work, but should be enough to get us going.'

'Ahh, poor old Simon, such a tragedy' said Porter. 'His body was repatriated yesterday.'

'That was fast work. Didn't they want to do an autopsy?'

'No. No need for it really - just a tragic accident. We managed to pull a few strings to get the repatriation process speeded up. No point having the poor guy hanging around here.'

That is crazy fast for a repatriation. 'What about his stuff? All his belongings, his photographs, clothes, books?'

'They were sent back too. His family will receive it all today I expect. You'll have to find a new deputy in due course.'

'Yes, eventually. I can't do two people's work.'

Here's an opportunity. 'Speaking of which Porter, what's going on in future ops just now? After being away in Gabon and then yesterday I don't feel like I'm fully up to speed on developments.'

'Well, it's the usual water-based disputes. Uganda and Tanzania are in dispute over access to Lake Victoria, there's a potential coup brewing in Sierra Leone, and Niger is having increasing problems with the tribal north, which may spill over the border into the Islamic Republic.'

'The Republic? I thought it was quite stable these days.'

'Well for the most part it is, politically it seems very stable, with the President uniting the fairly disparate states quite effectively, and actually being moderate in his stance on Shariah. His human rights record is good, with the obvious exception of the failed insurrection in Sudan; he definitely put his foot down on that one.'

'I'd say five thousand dead was a bit more than putting a foot down. It's like stamping it down again and again.'

'Yes, quite. Well things seem to have settled down a bit now in that respect, but there are some worrying indications of increased aggression due to their dwindling economy.'

'Oh yeah, like what?'

'Well there have been fairly extensive attacks in recent weeks on the Toubou, the main ethnic group in Chad's north. They mostly graze what little grassland there is all along the borderlands between Libya State and Chad. Intelligence reports indicate that the Republic is conducting these attacks by proxy in order to extend its borders south, with the intention of conducting a land-grab. Analysis suggests it may intend to expand its mining operations throughout the Sahara region, as there is no other reason those borderlands would be of interest.'

'Attacks? What sort of attacks are we talking about? And where?'

'Oh, the usual brand of militia violence - burnings, dismemberment, rape, displacement. Anything to get the people moving and cause instability in the area. Totally typical of

African tribalism. It has mostly been in the northeast and east of Chad, all along here.' Porter indicated the borderlands between Chad and the former countries of Libya and Sudan on a large wall map.

Jerry raised his eyebrows. 'Still, it seems a bit extreme just to secure some land for mining.' He searched the borderlands for the area of Bardai. He saw it way up in the northwest, deep in the Tibesti mountains. *Here's my chance to do a bit of probing, to see what he knows.* 'What does Chad have going on up here in the Tibesti mountains?'

'Nothing at all, they're just a rocky wasteland. Why do you ask?'

'Oh, just wondering why the attacks hadn't been focused up there too.'

'Yes, well there appears to have been some isolated attacks but I suppose the Toubou tend to wander further down to the east. There's nothing of any interest in the northwest.'

Except the Bardai plant, whatever that is. Maybe Porter actually doesn't know about the operation up there, which seems unlikely. But then I would have thought I'd know about it too, so anything is possible. What was Simon doing?

'Do we watch that area?' enquired Jerry, wondering if he could do some intelligence work of his own.

'No, it's low value. We really only tend to do intelligence-led surveillance now. We don't have the resources to watch everywhere, although interestingly we may be getting some input to a new telecoms satellite being launched by NiCom next year. We should be able to put some surveillance devices on that, but until then we're limited by where our UAVs are tasked to fly. Why? What's interesting about that area?'

Jerry paused for a moment, and then decided to share what he knew with Porter. He told him how he had discovered the file and how the agents had taken it away.

'Well that *is* interesting' said Porter when he had finished. 'Very interesting.'

'Why so interesting?' asked Jerry, his curiosity piqued by Porter's tone.

'Well there was some intelligence from a long time ago, from one of our sources within the Republic...' he began, turning to his screen and tapping on the keyboard, '...about the development of some sort of genetic research facility. Just hang on, it's in this folder somewhere.' He stared at the screen and tapped on the keyboard until he found what he was looking for. "Here it is, come and have a look.'

Jerry leaned over the desk and studied the screen. It contained a standard intelligence form template, which had been submitted by an agent with the codename 'Fisher'. It was dated 4 Aug 2028 and was very brief:

Contact disclosed that a genetic research facility established 2027. Loc unknown.
Aim is to determine genetic code of following groups, potentially more:
Toubou
Marba
Maban
Kanembu
Purpose is to develop genetic weapon. Motive unclear.

'I passed this to Lionel at the time of course, but I had to recommend to him that there was no other intelligence to corroborate this report, and that all other agents in the Republic were reporting perfectly normal routine behaviour. And there's been nothing of note since then either.'

'What do we know about those groups?'

'Those are all ethnic groups from Chad, with the addition of a few others. It is slightly complicated in that several of them are semi-nomadic and so will cross borders according to the seasons, but generally speaking they are Chadian.'

'Is 'Fisher' well connected?'

'Extremely' replied Porter, 'but there was just no other suggestions that weapons development was ongoing, and as I said, there has been nothing on it since. All of Fisher's reports have been routine.'

'So then what was Simon's report referring to? Was he describing a plan for the Republic to attack Chad?'

'Based on what you've told me, it seems plausible, but it would be highly unusual to be collating intelligence without my knowledge. But then I know that Simon enjoyed his research, so you never know.'

'Hmmm, it doesn't explain why Simon never mentioned it to me though. I'd better talk to Lionel about it, just to close it off. Thanks Porter.'

'Cheers Jerry' he replied, and returned to his reading.

Jerry left Porter's office and turned right, heading along the fourth floor to the elevator. He glanced down into the atrium and saw Ananya, the scientist he had met in the elevator. She was coming out of the coffee shop, carrying a takeaway coffee, and looked stunning. Her black hair was tied back in a knot and she wore a short-sleeved white blouse, a fitted black skirt and black heels. *Pretty good for a scientist! I wonder if she's seeing someone. Of course she is, someone that hot can't be single. But then hotness like that can often result in singleness - I should find out. Not now though.*

Right, what to say to Lionel? He must know about the notes or he wouldn't have ordered them to be collected. It doesn't seem possible that Simon was running an operation without anyone else knowing, and he had just come from Lionel's office when I saw him with the file. So Lionel knows about the op. As head of operations I have a right to know about it, so I should just straight up ask him what the hell is going on. Yes, that's the plan.

He knocked on Lionel's door and waited for Lionel's voice before opening the door. Lionel was sitting at his desk, looking at his computer screen. He looked up and smiled.

'Jerry, how was Senegal?'

'Great, all done. Porter has the report. We've got some fixers on the ground and I'm ready to deploy a forward team as soon as we get the green light from Dakar. I think a battalion deployment will be sufficient, with heli insertion and a forward logistic base inside the jungle.'

'Outstanding, good job. Thanks for going short notice, and I'm sorry it had to be that day. Bad timing.'

'No problem, the mission always comes first.'

'Yeah, but that must have been rough for you. I know you guys were close. Simon used to talk about you all the time.'

'Sure, he was a good friend, but that's what I wanted to talk to you about Lionel. About Simon.'

'Oh yeah, what about him?'

'Well I don't quite know where to start, but I found a file in Simon's desk which seemed to refer to an operation involving the Islamic Republic and Chad, but he hadn't said anything about it to me.'

Lionel frowned, and stared into Jerry's eyes. 'What sort of operation?'

'Well it wasn't entirely clear on the notes I saw, but it talked about a plant and that a shipment was delivered. I discussed it with Porter before I came to see you, and he showed me some intelligence reports about a genetic research facility in the Republic. He said he'd shown them to you.'

Lionel sat silent for a moment, looking at Jerry. Eventually he spoke, 'Yes, that's right. Porter showed me some intelligence reports about this, and he recommended no action because it was only one source of intel. As far as I'm aware there has been nothing reported about it since then either.'

'Yes, he said that, and he said you agreed with him.'

'Well yes, I didn't think any further action should be taken.'

'Well what I can't understand is why Simon was writing notes about it, and seemed to have a whole file of documents on it.'

'Did you see any of those documents Jerry?'

'No, only the top page, which seemed to be an operational status report, it mentioned the Republic and Chad, as well as a shipment being delivered, and it talked about our combat effectiveness, and it also mentioned something about a field test. What was he working on Lionel? And why didn't I know about something my deputy had been asked to do?'

'Now Jerry, take it easy, and let me explain this thing' soothed Lionel. 'Take a seat.' He gestured to the leather armchairs and they moved over and sat down. 'Jerry I believe that there is an operation being planned by the Republic, and I believe it is a genetic weapon, designed to massacre a very large percentage of the population of Chad.'

Jerry was stunned. He didn't know what to think. 'Well, why did you agree with Porter that there was no further action required?'

'Shall we have some water?' Lionel called his secretary for some cold water. They waited while she laid it on the table for them and left the office. They took a sip. 'The reason is that I wanted to protect him from it, just like I want to protect you too. This operation is not what we would consider to be the core business of the Task Force.'

'Genetic weapons? No, not at all our core business. I don't even know what a genetic weapon is.'

'No, I didn't either, when the first report came in, maybe two years ago. But I thought it would be worth investigating, partly out of curiosity at what a genetic research facility would be doing, and partly because I couldn't afford to overlook something so potentially significant.' He took another sip of water. 'So I recruited the help of the scientist I introduced you to, Ananya, who is actually a genetic research scientist. She helped me to discover that a weapon of that type was really possible.'

'What sort of weapon?' asked Jerry.

'A genetically engineered weapon, which can target specific ethnicities and not affect others. Her research has proven that specific genes can be identified as being unique to specific ethnicities, and those genes can be worked into a weapon, which attacks those specific genes in the victim.'

'Jeez, who thinks of these things? But why are the Republic doing this? What would they have to gain from killing off Chadian clans? Do you really think they would kill everyone in Chad?'

'Well our agent in the Republic seems to think that is exactly the plan. I have been directly receiving the reports and there is every indication the weapon is developed and ready to deploy. We believe the play is a land grab, which starts with the widespread decimation of the population, particularly in cities, with the weapon which appears to be a new, particularly virulent disease for which there is no known cure. We then believe the Republic will claim the land as its own once the situation has been contained, on account of a large proportion of the Chadian population being muslim, and therefore more comfortable under the command of the Republic anyway.'

'But you can't just walk into a country that has a disease epidemic and say it now belongs to you, whatever your religion' said Jerry.

'Well you can if everyone else is dead. I believe the President intends to extend his borders by whatever means he can, one country at a time. He already did it by bringing together Libya, Egypt and Sudan, and now it makes sense for him to start spreading.'

'Holy fuck' uttered Jerry, unable to believe that something this audacious could actually happen. *I know people can do some pretty fucked up stuff, especially here in Africa, but this is off the scale.*

'I know, it's fucking unthinkable. So I hatched a plan to stop him in his tracks before he can deploy the weapon.'

'Why was Simon involved?'

'Because he had worked with drones previously. And the plan involves a drone strike on the facility, to kill everyone in the facility and destroy the weapon too. According to Dr Ananya the weapon can be destroyed by exposure to fire.'

'Drone strike. You don't want to send in a team to recover the weapon? We could learn from it.'

'No, I don't want it to survive. We don't need to learn from that. And hey, I'm a simple guy! Simple drone strike. Mission accomplished.'

'Okay, seems simple enough. Do you have a definite location for the facility?'

'Oh yes, 100% sure of it.'

'Good, well do you need me to be involved, now that I know about it, and I'm 'unprotected'?'

'Of course, but not until tomorrow. Go home and get some rest before it all begins, there won't be much when it starts.'

'Fine' said Jerry, standing up to leave. 'Well thanks for filling me in on it all.'

'Sure Jerry' said Lionel, ushering Jerry out. 'Good to have you on board. And remember - this is two years in the planning, and is very very sensitive. This operation is so big and so devastating we can't jeopardise our plan, so not a word to anyone.'

As Jerry walked away from Lionel's office, his mind raced with thoughts. *How the hell could the Republic consider something so evil? Why was this kept a secret? Was Lionel trying to get rid of me just then?* He didn't have the answers to any of the questions, but Lionel was right, he did need to rest. He never slept well when he was travelling, and the Gabon mission had taken it out of him too. He should head home, but not until he had caught up on his emails.

Chapter Eleven

Jerry sat in the dark and smoky bar, nursing a beer bottle, which he had absentmindedly peeled the label from. He was lost in thought and didn't see the various customers come and go, or the prostitutes circling the bar at the start of their shift, looking for early marks who had been drinking all afternoon. Sitting at a table in the back corner of the bar he was inconspicuous, except for his white skin.

He shook himself out of his thoughts and took a swig of the beer. He cast his eye around the bar and surveyed the usual crowd of drinkers. Middle aged men in business suits, ties loosened; young men in football shirts laughing loudly; and then the much greater population of men in cheap shirts and jeans, sitting at the bar with no-one to talk to and nowhere to go. The music was a generic african pop tune, heavy on the rhythmic drums, but no-one seemed to be listening to it.

He reflected on the discussion he had had with Lionel and was feeling uneasy. The secrecy of the plot just didn't make sense to him. *Why did Lionel not trust anyone with the plan except Simon? What's the Bardai plant in Chad, and why didn't Lionel mention it? This level of secrecy is totally unprecedented in the Task Force, but then I guess nothing this big has ever been planned. Anyway, I'll get more detail tomorrow.*

Jerry finished his beer and got up, and headed for the door. As he stepped outside, the sound of the music was replaced by the sounds of the street. Cars and scooters sped by, honking horns and shouting. He looked up at the sky and saw that day had turned to night. He turned right and made his way along the sidewalk, weaving between oncoming pedestrians. Hooded youths walked in groups; workers stood around a coffee stand; people emerged from shops; and drinkers spilled from bars, the loud pop music chasing them out. Jerry liked living in this area of Lagos. It was much more alive than the expat compounds most Task Force employees chose, the colours more vivid, the sounds louder, the smells more assaulting to your senses. It felt like living in the true Africa, where trade and enterprise flourished, and people lived fast. He had seen many types of Africa - the poverty, the camps, the farming villages, and the small provincial towns, but he always preferred the energy of the city. There was always something to see, people to watch.

He crossed the street at a traffic lights intersection. Lagos traffic was too heavy to risk jaywalking. It was hot and humid. He began to feel the sweat flow in his armpits as he continued his brisk walk around the corner and past a bakery. The smell of bread reminded him that he hadn't eaten in hours. He spied the nearest street food stall and ordered some jollof rice, extra spicy, his favourite. He ordered a couple of fish moin moin too, they reminded him of samosas, but steamed in banana leaf. As he waited for the food to be served he looked back down the sidewalk, towards the intersection he had just come from.

His eye caught a man looking into an electronics shop window. He was athletic verging on stocky, like Jerry, and he guessed approximately the same age. He looked Nigerian, but equally could have been from Cameroon or CAR. He was wearing dark jeans and a blue hooded top with the hood down. *Have I seen that top before? Was that guy in the bar? He looks too old to be wearing that top.* Jerry's instincts sensed there was something strange about the man, so he decided to stay put and eat his food there at the stall, to see what he did. Jerry stood leaning against a post and tucked into the spicy rice. It burned his mouth and instantly made him sweat. He looked at the street but kept the man in his peripheral vision. He wasn't moving from the window. He had been looking in that window for over two minutes now. And there it was, he glanced over his shoulder directly at Jerry.

Jerry knew the risks of living in the more authentic part of town. Street crime was high in this area, as it tended to fill up with people looking for cash in hand work, or handouts. Desperate people would often do anything to survive on the streets. Muggings and murders were commonplace. In a city of eight million all kinds of horrible crimes went totally unseen on its streets. It was particularly bad since the waves of migrants had started to come from rural Nigeria, seeking a better life in the city because their livelihood had been destroyed by the permanent drought. There were dangerous and desperate people on the street, and you had to stay sharp.

Jerry turned his head and looked directly at his follower, chewing slowly and not taking his gaze from him. After a moment the man looked again and their eyes met. Jerry locked him in a piercing stare and stood still, giving him his very best 'fuck with me and I will fuck you up' look. The guy probably didn't know what he was dealing with, and Jerry would have a far better than average chance of coming out on top, but he would much rather avoid a fight. Sure enough, the man broke his gaze and turned away, heading back towards the intersection. Jerry smiled and took a bite of the moin moin. Excellent.

Jerry finished up his food and bought a bottle of water. He continued his walk home, with his senses slightly heightened now. He walked on the road side of the sidewalk, staying away from the dark passages. A short while later, close to his apartment, where there were fewer shops and the streets were quieter, he heard the sound of running footsteps behind him, approaching fast. He prepared himself for the attack, grateful he could only hear one set of footsteps. When he judged they were a couple of metres away he quickly ducked, simultaneously side-stepping and turning his body to face the attacker, the water bottle ready to be jabbed into his face. The runner, a young man wearing a backpack and with headphones on his head, threw his arms up in surprise and swerved out of Jerry's way. He gave Jerry a look of shock and continued to run, shaking his head.

Jerry smiled and laughed at himself. Today really had been a strange day, he was feeling way too paranoid. He straightened up and span the bottle in his hand. At that moment a large black SUV sharply pulled up beside him and the doors opened at him. He stepped back, ready for the fight, looking to see which of the attackers he should go for first. A man dressed in dark clothes quickly jumped from the back door. He was holding a pistol and pointing it directly at Jerry's chest, Jerry recognised it as a Glock, the same pistol they used in the Task Force - a powerful and reliable weapon, unlikely to jam and therefore not giving Jerry any chance of running. A figure emerged from the front door. Jerry took his eyes off the pistol to glance at him and was stunned. He recognised Victor Amenze, the head of security for the Task Force.

Jerry stared at him in disbelief, waiting for him to speak. He couldn't figure out what the hell was going on. He half expected Victor to smile and explain everything, but Victor was not smiling.

'Get in the car Jerry. I don't want to have to shoot you here in the street.'

'Victor, what the fuck is going on?'

'Just get in the fucking car, or you will die here, right now.'

Jerry didn't like his chances of outrunning the gunman, or the car, and so had little option but to get in the car. He shuffled over the leather seats and sat behind the driver, still holding the water bottle. The gunman and Victor got in and shut the doors as the car pulled out into the road.

'Victor, what is this? What's going on?' said Jerry.

Victor turned in his seat and looked at Jerry. 'Just shut the fuck up Jerry. This is not a situation you can talk your way out of so keep your mouth shut.'

Jerry sat in silence and assessed the situation. This was almost certainly going to end in his death judging by Victor's words, so he would have to get himself out of this car, ideally having incapacitated or killed Victor and his men. He still had the water bottle and he wasn't handcuffed, so that was a distinct advantage. But the gunman sitting beside him was watching him like a hawk and had a Glock pointed at his side. He was likely to shoot at the slightest movement from Jerry, given that not much movement would be required to cause trouble. The doors were not auto-locked. This was routine for the Task Force so they could open them quickly when on ops, and it was a major advantage for Jerry now. Finally Victor didn't appear to have a weapon, at least not one he had revealed so far. The odds were stacked in Jerry's favour, except that the car was now travelling at around 100kph and he was on the driver's side so would jump out in front of traffic.

The car was heading for the road bridge over the lagoon. They were taking him to the port, or perhaps to the swamplands beyond. He would have to do it before they got to the lagoon otherwise he would be limited to where he could run. His only option really would be to jump into the lagoon, and he did not like that option. At two hundred feet that drop would be dangerous, coupled with the potential to land on a passing ship or some floating wood out there, it was best avoided.

Jerry remembered his training on escaping a moving car and knew that it was better to attempt escape sooner rather than later, but the car was now speeding along a three lane highway, headed for the lagoon bridge. They were perhaps one kilometre from the bridge and at this speed would be there in about thirty seconds. He had to act now.

With his left hand he held up the water bottle, as if to take a drink. As predicted, the gunman was alive to any movement and immediately shouted a warning to lower his hand. Jerry looked at him as if to protest, and the gunman raised his pistol from pointing at Jerry's side to his face, just as Jerry wanted. Quick as a flash he whipped up his right hand in a side swipe across the side of the pistol, pushing the gunman's hand to the right. The gunman reacted too slowly and pulled the trigger half a second too late, by which time the barrel of the pistol was pointed at the driver. The pistol exploded less than a foot from the driver's head. It couldn't miss from that range, and there was an instant explosion of blood and bone as the 9mm round barrelled through his skull.

Immediately Jerry followed up the side swipe by hammering his fist downwards into the wrist of the gunman, forcing him to drop the pistol with a cry of pain. Jerry's next movement was a swift elbow up into the nose of the gunman. He felt the bone and gristle crunch with the impact and knew the gunman was done. A quick glance at Victor confirmed that he did indeed have a weapon, which he was now reaching for in his jacket. Jerry lunged at his face with a straight punch, but the headrest of Victor's seat obscured most of his face, meaning Jerry only caught him with a glancing blow to his right cheek. Hopefully enough to slow him down by a second.

Jerry's left hand reached for the door handle and yanked it. He pushed the door hard and didn't wait at all before barrelling himself out of the door head first, rolling his body out to both exit the car quickly, and also to roll as he hit the road. Victor had managed to find his pistol and fired a shot at Jerry's tucked body, just too late, it flashed into the central reservation barrier and Jerry was gone. The driver's head disappearing had slowed the car to about 80kph, which was still too fast for a safe exit. Jerry hit the road hard on his back and continued to roll, his momentum carrying him to the central reservation of the highway. He was on his feet instantly, his back and left shoulder were screaming in pain from the impact, but he ran for his life, not even bothering to look back. He heard the scrape of metal on metal as the big SUV collided with the barrier, and then the screech of rubber as presumably Victor grabbed the wheel to straighten it, but overcompensated and sent the car careering across the highway.

Jerry stopped listening as he ran down the centre of the highway, looking for a spot to cross over. Cars following behind the SUV were slamming their brakes on and honking their horns, but he didn't care. He just ran. He crossed the central reservation with a leap and sprinted through a gap in the traffic, horns honking again. When he reached the sidewalk on the other side he risked a quick look back at the SUV. It had come to a stop across the lanes, and Victor had got out and was watching Jerry as he ran. The back door was opening but Jerry knew that with a mashed up nose the gunman wasn't going to chase him.

He turned and continued to run, getting off the sidewalk into a dark side street and the maze of passages and dark walkways as soon as possible. As he ran he thought of where he should go. This was almost certainly Lionel's doing, why else would the head of security come after him? It also tracked with the secrecy and slight implausibility of Lionel's story. *Fuck! Why didn't I trust my instincts? I should have known it was all wrong.*

Jerry thought of the shortlist of places to go: *Obviously not home; Al's place is a possibility, he's surely not with Lionel; Or maybe Porter...Porter!* Jerry's memory quickly flashed with recollection at the discussion they had had. *Porter will have an idea what's going on...but shit! Lionel knows I spoke to Porter about it. He'll surely be going for Porter too. I have to warn him!*

He pulled out his phone and quickly dialled Porter's cellphone. It rang. 'Come on! Fucking answer!'

'Jerry! How are you?' Porter's voice came through.

'Porter! Where are you? You're in danger!'

'What do you mean old boy? What danger?'

'Listen, Lionel is going to have you killed. He's just tried it with me. Victor got me in a car heading out to the port. I think they were going to dump me in the swamps.'

'Good God! Are you serious? What happened?'

'I managed to escape, but Victor is still out there. I'm on the run in town, in Onikan, in the backstreets.'

'Shit, why is this happening? What did you do?'

'It's the Republic genetic research thing. I guess I've uncovered some sort of secret Lionel doesn't want uncovering. But listen Porter, he knows that you know about it too. I said I'd spoken to you this afternoon. You'd better get out of there man.'

'Oh fuck, right. I'm leaving now. Fuck, what about my family? Is he going to go after them too?'

'I guess he would, but I just don't know what he'll do. I guess anything is possible now.'

'I must call them, thanks Jerry…'

'Wait! Porter? Go to Al's house. Take your family there. He's safe, I'm sure of it.'

'Okay, cheers Jerry.' Porter hung up.

Jerry quickly dialled Al's number. He scanned the streets and the shadows while he waited.

'G'day Jerry, what's going on?'

'Al, I'm in the shit, and I need your help. Can I come to your place?'

'I'm not there mate. We're out for dinner down at the beach. What's up?'

'I can't discuss it over the phone. Will your maid let me in to your place?'

'Sure, I'll give her a call. You okay buddy? D'you need me to come pick you up?'

'No thanks, I'll get a cab. Just skip dessert and meet me at your place as soon as possible.'

'Roger. See you soon.'

He put his phone away and went in search of a cab to take him over onto Victoria Island and to one of the Task Force compounds. He flagged one down and got in, giving him an address. He sat back and closed his eyes and breathed deeply. *Holy shit, this is fucked up. What the hell is going on? What am I supposed to do now?*

His phone rang. He stared at the screen. Lionel. He answered and held it to his ear, saying nothing.

'Hello Jerry. So you managed to escape Victor. I think he underestimated you.'

'What the fuck do you want from me Lionel? Why are you doing this?'

'You mean you don't know? Oh God, that's tragic Jerry. I thought a smart guy like you would have this figured out by now.'

'Have what figured out? What are you planning?'

'Really Jerry? You really don't know? Maybe I shouldn't have you killed after all. You're not nearly as dangerous as I thought you would be.'

'I wouldn't say that Lionel. If I ever see you again I'm gonna fuck you up.'

Lionel laughed. 'Oh Jerry, if only you knew. You'll never see me again. I won't even come and piss on your grave, because you won't have one.'

'Big threats from a guy that sends a hit man to do his dirty work. If you had the balls to face me I'd think about giving a shit what you say.'

Lionel laughed again. 'I admire your spirit Jerry. That's what I always liked about you. You're not just a smart kid, you've got some balls too. But now I'm gonna have to clip those balls off. When my men catch up with you, which they will, they won't waste any time driving you out to the swamps. They'll just shoot you in the face and then feed you to the fish.'

'Not if I find you before they find me.'

'You won't even get close Jerry. Do you think I'm alone in this? You are, but I've got a whole fucking army on my side!'

'How do you know I'm alone? Maybe I'm on my way to the police now.'

Lionel laughed even louder. 'Don't be naive Jerry, you and I both know they'll be no use to you. Who do you think I play poker with? Who do you think I fuck whores with? Come on Jerry, you can't win this. This isn't one of those movies where you take down the big bad guy single-handedly.'

'I'll take you down Lionel. Just watch your back. Whatever shit you're up to won't happen. I'll find out what it is, I'll stop it, and then I'll hunt you down like a dog.'

'Well good luck with that Jerry. Listen, if you get tired of running, just give me a call and I'll make sure you're killed fast - put you out of your misery. Goodbye Jerry. Give my best to Al.' The line went dead.

Give my best to Al? What does that mean? Is Al in on it too? No way, Al is surely clean. 100% clean. How does Lionel know I'm going to see Al? It's probably obvious as he's my only friend. Where else would I go? Or he's listening to my phone calls! Either way it's not good.

He leaned forward to talk to the driver. 'Hey buddy, get there in half the time and I'll double your fare. No, I'll triple it'

'Sure thing boss.' The car lurched forward as the driver put his foot down.

Jerry thought about what to do, and how Lionel knew he was going to Al's. Suddenly it struck him. He quickly searched his phone book and found Al's number.

'Hey buddy, can I use your phone? My battery's dead. I'll pay you for it' he asked the driver.

'Sure boss' the driver handed him his phone.

He dialled Al's number and waited.

'Al, it's me, don't speak. Listen, comms are compromised. Don't go home, go to ERV Charlie and meet me there. I'll make sure your kids are safe, I promise. I'll meet you at ERV Charlie as soon as I can. Got it?'

'Jerry, what the fuck?'

'Al, please trust me. Now take your battery off and throw away your phone and go to ERV Charlie. Sally too. Okay?'

'Okay mate, but my kids...'

'Al, trust me. I've got it covered. See you soon.' He hung up, picked up his phone and removed its battery, opened the window and threw them out. The driver looked in his mirror. 'Sorry buddy, yours is going too. I'll pay you for it I promise.' He did the same with the driver's phone.

"Hey! What the fuck man?' the driver protested. He stopped the car suddenly and got out, walking back up the road to retrieve his phone. Jerry got out of the car and followed the driver, who was now shouting at Jerry, 'What the fuck you doing?'

Jerry held up his hands to calm the driver. It didn't work. He continued to shout at Jerry and push him.

'Please, listen sir' Jerry protested, but the driver wasn't ready to listen. He was ready to fight.

Jerry sighed. He delivered a quick uppercut straight into the man's stomach, driving up into his solarplexus, knocking the wind right out of him and sending him to his knees.

'Look, I'm sorry, I really am, but you have to listen to me. I'm afraid you're in great danger now, probably from the police. They'll be coming for you, and they'll want to know where I am. It's probably best that you get in the trunk and make out that I stole the car from you, okay?'

The driver looked up at Jerry in astonishment, still clutching his stomach and struggling to breathe.

'Okay, that's what we'll do. Up you get, come on.' He helped the driver to his feet, popped the trunk, and turned to help the driver in. But the driver was running up the road as fast as he could manage.

'Oh for fuck sake' sighed Jerry, and set off after him.

Twenty minutes later he pulled up outside Al's house, all was quiet and dark, except for an outside light and the glow of a light inside the house, downstairs. There was no sign of Porter being here yet, or any of Lionel's men either, which was a good thing. He knocked gently on the door and stood back.

After a short delay, the door opened a crack. Al's maid peered out.

'Hi Edith, did Al call you?'

'Yes sir' she replied in her filipino accent. 'Mr Porter is here too.'

'Great, can I come in?' He went in and went straight through to the lounge area, where Porter and his family were waiting nervously.'

'Jerry, what the hell is going on?' asked Porter. 'Are you okay?'

'I've been better, how about you?'

'Well we're alive. What's the plan? Where's Al?'

'He's out to dinner. We're about to go and meet him.' He turned to Porter's wife, 'Hannah, I'm so sorry you're involved in this. It turns out that Lionel is a psychopath and is planning something dreadful, starting with killing all of us.' He glanced down at the children who were looking at him in horror. 'It's okay kids, no-one's getting killed.'

'Stop talking!' interrupted Porter.

'Sure, sorry. Hannah, please take the kids and Al's kids too to a school friend's house. Someone random, not your best friend. Edith, you go too. It'll be a houseful but it's important you stay there and don't leave, under any circumstances. And no phone calls. In fact, give me your phones, everyone.'

A few minutes later Jerry and Porter left the house and climbed into the cab.

'Don't be alarmed at the banging. The driver's in the trunk' said Jerry.

'Oh, fine' replied Porter.

'We'll have to do some misdirection here. We don't want to leave any clues about where we're going.' said Jerry as he pulled the car out into the road. 'Here we go.'

Chapter Twelve

Ayatumbe put on his robe and opened a drawer in a cabinet. In the corner of his eye he watched the two girls get out of his bed and find their clothes. There was silence in the room, except for the hum of the air conditioning. It was amazing what you could make people do for just a little bit of cash he thought, as he threw two hundred dollar bills on the bed. The girls scooped them up and scurried out of the door, going back to whatever slum they had been found in.

He poured a glass of water and walked to the window to look down at the treetops of his garden, stretching away to a distant wall, beyond which lay the sprawling throbbing capital city. He stared out at the dark sky lit by the unseen city and thought of the mass of humanity moving around out there, among its streets, slums and ghettos. For a moment he wondered what those people were doing, and what their lives might be like. He received regular reports on the mood of the population and the potential for civil unrest which gave some clues, but as long as the risk was moderate or below then he generally didn't care very much what the people thought. He took another sip of the water.

He thought of the village he had grown up in after arriving in Chad, where he had the humblest of lifestyles, and thought how far he had come now, right to the very top. If he could pull himself out of the gutter then why couldn't all those people out there? They had become lazy and greedy, he thought. Just looking for handouts when the going got tough. Admittedly the shortage of water was quite extreme now, with the public water system delivering far short of the required volume to sustain the city. The drying up of Lake Chad had badly hurt the city, and the country. All stolen by those thieves from Nigeria, Cameroon and Niger, draining it for their industry and pumping pollution back in its place.

Well now they were all suffering because of it, especially Chad with no coastline. The costs of transporting desalinated water from the Nigerian coast were crippling him, and yet Nigeria continued to increase the cost way beyond what they could pay to support the population, which was resulting in widespread drought, crippling their agriculture and therefore the livelihoods of millions of his people. The shortage of food and water had already killed half a million in the east, but his requests for assistance from other African countries had gone virtually unanswered. Everyone was suffering, but not on the same scale as Chad. But that would all change, and then they would come begging to Chad, and would pay his prices. Not long now. He finished the water and put down the glass, turning away from the window and dropping his robe, heading for the shower.

An hour later, in his office, Ayatumbe reviewed the key points of the evening briefing. He noted with irritation that the Republic had once again refused to back down on the border attacks and were now threatening to patrol the border with drones, meaning they would be attacking his people over the border no doubt. As long as they stayed away from the mountains then that would be tolerable.

He read on, stopped and frowned. He read it again before picking up the phone on his desk.

'I want to talk to the Minister of the Interior, now.' He returned to reading the briefing.

A minute later the phone rang and he pushed a button, activating speakerphone.

'Idris? I have just read in my briefing that there was an attack on the plant? Yesterday.'

'Yes Mr President, a small band of Toubou had been trying to sneak through the mountains to attack it. My men were able to track them by drone and they were destroyed before they could launch their attack.'

113

'Why am I only just hearing about this?'

'I am sorry sir, the reporting from the plant was slow.'

'That is critical infrastructure Idris, I need to be kept informed.'

'Yes sir.'

'Good, now what was their intention? Sabotage?'

'That was the assessment of the commander at the plant sir. They had travelled as a clan in order to disguise their intentions, but then sent a raiding party at night.'

'Do we know who sent them?'

'They came from the north, so perhaps they had come out of the Republic. Regrettably there were no survivors for questioning.'

'Does this mean the plant is no longer secret?'

'I think this indicates that the Republic is aware of the nature of the plant, and are probing to test our defences, as I said in the briefing.'

'This is a disaster! The existence and nature of the plant was supposed to remain a complete secret. How did this get out? Are they watching it by UAV? Do we have spies in the plant? Have everyone killed and a new set of workers found.'

'I do not know how they found out Mr President, but if they already know then new workers will not change that. We should instead focus our energy on repelling the threat from the north.'

'Yes...Wait...' he looked at the briefing again. '...they are starting to patrol the border with UAVs. This must be the precursor to an attack by their land forces. Perhaps they are preparing right now!'

'It is probable Mr President. They will do anything to get their hands on that plant.'

'I knew it! That snake had this planned all along. I want a meeting with you and the chief of the army, tonight. We need to make a plan.'

'Yes sir Mr President. Right away.'

He pressed a button to end the call, and sat staring into space. *The evil bastard has been plotting this the whole time. He no doubt created the attacks just to provoke and distract me. And then sending his secret teams to sabotage my plant. Well he won't find me sleeping. I will move against him before he has the chance to attack!*

Chapter Thirteen

Jerry, Al and Porter sat in a small office, tucked away in the back area of Chez Chay. The sound of the music and customers chatting floated under the door and made the meeting all the more surreal. They were figuring out how to save their lives while people drank and ate next door with no idea what was going on.

'I'm glad you chose ERV Charlie and not Bravo. This bar has much better atmosphere,' said Al with an approving nod.

'Are all your Emergency Rendezvous points in bars?' asked Porter.

'No, one of them is a restaurant' answered Al.

'Right, let's think this through' said Jerry, getting the conversation back on track. 'We need to figure out what the hell to do next.'

'Surely we should have a beer while we're thinking?' said Al. Jerry gave him a withering look.

'Where to start? Well we need to figure out what Lionel is doing before we can make a plan.'

'Just hang on here Jerry, this is all very far-fetched. I just can't believe that Lionel is a murderer, or even potentially a mass murderer. What do you actually know so far?' asked Porter.

'Well I know that he tried to have me killed, and told me as much on the phone too. There's no doubt he's up to something sinister if he's prepared to shoot me and and dump me in the swamps.'

'I just find it so improbable that he could be planning a major operation, involving members of the Task Force, without any of us knowing about it. Particularly me.'

'I know it's hard to swallow buddy, I really do. I'm only just coming to terms with it too. As for who in the Task Force is involved, it's impossible to say, but as I'm sure you'll remember from your MI6 days, you need to be extremely careful who you share information with. He could be paying off anyone.'

'The Service was exceedingly careful about who to use, particularly after the leaking of agent names back in the twenties. The number of our agents that were outed and murdered still casts a dark shadow over the community.' Porter referred to the leaking of the names of hundreds of informants and agents from the international secret intelligence community by a hacking group. The hardest hit had been the CIA, closely followed by the UK's Secret Intelligence Service. 'But paying them off? For what?' asked Porter. 'We don't even know what he's supposed to be doing.'

'We know that he was involved in planning some sort of secret operation with Simon. He told me it was to destroy a genetic weapon facility within the Republic. I have to assume now that he was lying about that.'

'Wait' interjected Al. 'Genetic weapon?'

'Right, you didn't know that. Well according to Lionel the Republic have been developing a genetic weapon at a research facility for three years now. Apparently it has the ability to target specific genes and disregard others. There was an intelligence report about it, right Porter?'

'Yes, it was from two years ago saying the program had started, and was identifying the genetic codes of several Chadian tribes.'

'But could that kind of technology actually exist?' asked Al.

'Well, it's the first example I've come across in Africa. Obviously we've seen biological weapons return in the hands of terrorists, back in the early '30s, but they're still banned according to the Geneva Convention. Of course terrorists don't care about the Geneva Convention, and this is not terrorists we're talking about, and also this is a different kind of idea to straightforward germ warfare.'

'How's that?'

'Well, biological weapons won't discriminate between different types of people, they'll just kill everyone in range. Whereas the principle of a genetically engineered weapon has kind of already been proven by the extensive genetic research into cures for diseases such as tuberculosis, smallpox, and even ebola and SARS. All those millions of deaths back in the '20s sparked a surge in funding for research, as the developed world thought that would be the answer to all of Africa's problems and so pumped all the development budget into that.'

'It's been quite successful though right?' asked Al.

'Sure, disease is down, but that means more people are now surviving, so there are more people to share less water and less food. It was obviously a great thing to fight disease, but talk about unintended consequences…'

'Hmm' mused Jerry, 'so weaponising the genetic cures would just be the next step?'

'Well I'm not a scientist, but it seems perfectly plausible that once you've done all the genetic research then you would just need to introduce something nasty which attacks those specific genes and voila, you've got a hugely destructive weapon. I should say though that in all my time at the Service, I didn't come across anything linked to genetic weapons. It seems incredible that it would come out of nowhere, in our own organisation, in complete secrecy.'

'Well if this kind of weapon did exist then the Geneva Convention would also apply to it right?' said Al.

'Most likely yes, but perhaps the greatest benefit of such a weapon is that it's discreet. It's not like dropping a bomb, or releasing some sarin gas. This could actually look like a disease. It's theoretically completely deniable, and therefore a perfect weapon.'

'Christ on a bike' said Al. 'Surely the Republic can't be doing that? Or Lionel.'

'Well, Lionel told me that he had been in comms with the agent in the Republic, codename Fisher, and had learned that the weapon was now ready for deployment. How much of that is bullshit I can't say, but I do know that in a page of Simon's notes I saw reference to a plant, which is at 40% readiness, but it's in Chad, not the Republic. The page also said that a shipment had been delivered to or from the Republic. No indication of what that shipment is.'

'They did receive some new UAVs recently. Bought from Russia. They have a pretty long range and upgraded weapons platform. They could carry eight missiles the length of the continent' offered Porter.

'That's pretty formidable, but not much to go on, except I suppose it lends credence to the possibility that they really are planning an attack' said Al. 'Anything else?'

'There was a line about a field test which was 100% successful. It said AD is ready, and I think that could be Ananya Devi, who is an Indian genetic scientist recruited by Lionel. She works in the headquarters now.'

'And she's hot too' said Porter.

'She is' agreed Jerry, 'but we also don't know what was tested, or what she's ready for. No jokes!' Al shrugged and un-pursed his lips.

'There was also a section on the readiness of our Div, including the infantry and aircraft,' Jerry went on, 'which suggests that our troops are going to be involved. Given that Lionel said it would only be a drone strike that doesn't track.'

'So perhaps our troops were going to support a Republic strike? He couldn't get away with that,' said Al.

'Of course not' agreed Jerry. 'That is totally against the principle of what we do, unless there is a bloody good reason for it, like in direct retaliation for an attack. And Chad are certainly not intending to attack the Republic, are they?

'There's no evidence from intelligence that they're planning anything at all. No chatter' said Porter.

'Okay, so what's the genetic weapon link?' asked Al. 'Why would he tell you about it if he was just going to have you killed?'

'I can't imagine, unless he's developed one himself?' suggested Jerry.

'Well what has this scientist been doing for Lionel?' asked Al. 'Developing a weapon?'

'Do you have any idea how hard it would be to develop a genetically engineered weapon to target specific ethnicities, using Task Force money and people, in secret? asked Porter.

'No, but she may be the only other person besides Lionel that knows for sure' said Jerry. 'We need to talk to her. Urgently.'

'Right' said Al, 'how do we get to her? We have no idea where she is.'

'We could track her through her phone, assuming she is still using her Task Force phone' suggested Porter.

'But you need to be at work to do that, right?' pointed out Jerry.

'Yes, but I have minions who can do it for me' replied Porter, 'if I can make contact with them.'

'Just choose one - the most reliable' said Jerry. 'Which leads us on to who the hell can we trust? I know that Victor is with Lionel, and so presumably are all the security staff. That's tough if we're looking to gain access to any Task Force facilities.'

'Well we only know that Victor is on his side. It's unlikely that every guy on every door is in league with Lionel' pointed out Al. 'So there may be a way in.'

'Well let's assume that everyone is potentially an enemy, except for us' concluded Jerry. 'It's safer that way. We'll need some weapons and ammunition, so we'll need to bust into the armoury too, unless you know anyone on the underground that has them Al?'

'No-one I'd want to deal with in a pressure situation like this, at night, without backup' Al replied.

'Okay, so we're going to have to break into the lion's den to get what we need. Let's do it tonight. Lionel won't expect us to go there. He'll expect us to be out running for our lives.'

'If this is all true then it's a big risk Jerry. You don't think we should think of another way to bring him down?' said Porter. 'Maybe go to the police or the army?'

'No, he has them both in his pocket I'm sure. He is holding all the aces in this game.'

'But he didn't reckon on there being three jokers in play!' joked Al.

'That's right' said Jerry, 'now let's plan this out from the start...'

Two hours later they wrapped up the planning, just about the time that Chay was closing up the bar. They emerged from the back office after carefully scanning the bar for any potential threats.

'Alright boys' said Chay cheerfully. 'All okay?'

'Yeah, thanks for letting us hole up in there Chay' replied Jerry.

'No problem, how about a quick beer before you go?'

Al raised his hand before Jerry cast him a quick sideways glance. 'No thanks Chay, we're good. And Chay, this is probably obvious, but we were never here, and you don't even know us right?'

'No problem boss'

'Good, because there's something pretty heavy going on, which you don't need to know, but suffice to say if you got involved then you'll most likely end up dead.'

'Then I am not at all interested. My lips are sealed.'

'Good man, thanks again Chay.'

As they left the bar through the back door Jerry stopped and turned to the others, looking them each in the eyes. The tension was obvious in their faces, despite the customary professional demeanour they adopted. His mind raced to think of something inspirational or motivational to say as they departed on their individual missions.

'Guys, I'm sorry you've been caught up in this shit storm. But I'm also pleased it's you. I wouldn't want anyone else on my team through this. Except maybe another fifty or so guys.' They shook hands with grim smiles. 'Take care of yourselves, stay alive, and I'll see you in a few hours. It's time to bring that fucker down.'

Chapter Fourteen

Abu Rashed watched the night-time streets of Khartoum race by through the car window. The black SUV he was travelling in did not look out of place in the capital city, where such cars were commonplace, but his diplomatic car had the advantage of discrete built-in armour and bulletproof windows. Such enhancements meant he could travel around the country with relatively low amounts of security, just as he liked it. It drew less attention to his whereabouts and the meetings he held.

The car crossed the bridge over the White Nile, which was full of barges and small commercial craft, carrying their loads of electronics, food and furniture up the river to the unloading points in the city, and almost looked beautiful at night, poorly lit as it was. He had been told by an imam that the Nile was once a beautiful river, where men fished from small dhows with nets, and the shores were green with parks, agricultural land and forests. That was certainly not the case now - the price of progress, as the shoreline was dominated by high-rise buildings, both commercial and residential, jostling for the best waterfront view. That view was of a dank and polluted waterway, full of dhows night and day, and certainly not home to any edible fish.

The car passed the river and went on past the universities, where the streets throbbed with thousands upon thousands of people, all going about their business, very loudly. The traffic was terrible as too many cars attempted to squeeze into the narrow street system, only to be stopped by the ancient traffic light system which seemed to reduce traffic flow rather than increase it.

He scanned the crowds as he waited, looking at the various forms of life on the streets. A porter pushing a sack barrow loaded with sacks of rice; families out for an evening meal; a motorist paying a bribe to a traffic police officer; a trader selling watches; people sitting at street cafes. All manner of people were found here, except people like Abu Rashed, who most certainly would not normally be found in this part of the city, except tonight.

The car eventually stopped near to the souk. Abu Rashed's security got out first and confirmed it was safe before opening the door. Abu Rashed stepped out, brushed himself down, and stepped off toward the souk. His security led the way, slightly in front, with another a few feet behind, so as not to attract attention. They were carrying weapons, but carefully hidden in order to effect their incognito trip into the souk.

The souk was bustling with life, even more so than during the day. An explosion of sights, sounds and smells greeted the visitor, as every trader attempted to sell their product, which was for the most part exactly the same as their neighbours', but at a fractionally lower cost. They passed a row of barbers, cutting hair and shaving faces in the street, lined up against a wall, next to a small trolley from which a woman sold fresh fruit juices. Abu Rashed passed by without drawing attention, looking like just another shopper walking the souk. The sound of Isha prayer being called by one of the many mosques nearby did not have any effect on the flow of people as they shuffled along together through the narrow walkways.

Eventually they arrived at a door, above which was a small sign indicating that this was the entrance to 'Souk al Bahar', a restaurant. They walked through the open doorway and up the narrow stairs, leaving behind the sounds of the souk, which were replaced by the sound of Arabic music, a bit too loud for comfort in a restaurant, but thematic nonetheless. They saw their table and headed to the back of the restaurant, where two men, also dressed in traditional thobes, sat waiting in silence. They approached the table and greeted each other with handshakes and salutations. The security men took their places and began to scan the room.

'This is an interesting spot you have chosen to meet, Abu Yousef' said Abu Rashed.

'Do you like it? I find it most convenient to meet in the most public of places. It's the very best hiding place if you're looking to not be seen.'

'I can see that' agreed Abu Rashed. 'The traffic is disappointing though, hence I am late.'

'It is challenging these days. Something should be done about it.'

'And insha'allah it will, along with the many other things I will change when I am able.'

'Insha'allah' agreed Abu Yousef.

'The time is approaching Abu Yousef. It will not be long before we can take our opportunity to seize power and make a change.'

'Insha'allah' agreed Abu Yousef. 'Have your plans been working?'

'Very effectively. The attacks have been very successful. As you will have seen, there are a great number of people being displaced. There is confusion around the borderlands; no-one knows who is directing who, and still the attacks keep taking place. We have been so successful that real militia are actually starting to form on both sides, doing our job for us.'

'Ma sha'allah, you have done well Abu Rashed. This is a great success.'

Coffee arrived, and they paused to drink a cup.

'Thank you brother. We have sown the seed and now it is sprouting, which is ironic given the lack of water!'

'May it continue to flourish.'

'Insha'allah. He has been surprisingly easy to control also. I have hardly had to apply any pressure at all. He seems determined to follow his own path into destruction anyway, even without my guidance.'

'Does he truly believe it is the work of Ayatumbe?'

'I believe he does. He is easily flattered by his supremacy, and the arrogance that comes with total command. I believe he thinks he can make decisions independently of their consequences, and has the authority to cross the border at will. This morning I even had to talk him out of deploying troops. He had a great fire in his belly.'

'Excellent news. He is our perfect plaything.'

'Yes. Now what news of the situation in Chad? How is it in N'DJamena?'

'Also good. I have been summoned to the Ministry with increasing frequency this last week. Ayatumbe is becoming more and more agitated. He is even staging a meeting this very night with his Generals, planning a defence of the border. If we do not see a deployment of troops to the border tomorrow then it will surely be the next day.'

'Excellent. He is proving to be just the hot-head we were looking for.'

'Oh, he is too arrogant to see the truth here. He is so busy feathering his own nest, as they all do, that he doesn't even bother to ask the right questions. He forms a judgement and then everything he sees confirms that conclusion.'

'But will we be able to control him? Once the time comes.'

'I am sure of it. He is easily bought, despite his big anti-corruption program. He will name his price when the time comes.'

'And you are perfectly placed to get it from him Abu Yousef. As Ambassador you will be the perfect peace broker once the conflict begins, and then the perfect Foreign Minister to introduce the new relationship in my new Republic.'

'Insha'allah. Are you confident you will get the vote from the shura?'

'Absolutely. Abu Khalid discredits himself with his weakness, without me even needing to try. I am the only choice.'

'Ma sha'allah, ma sha'allah Abu Rashed. You will be a great President.'

'Insha'allah brother. If God wills it.'

Chapter Fifteen

Jerry and Al waited in the dark side street, just a hundred metres from the side entrance to the Task Force headquarters. Jerry watched the building while Al scanned the dark streets for any approaching danger, or for any sign of Porter.

'He's fifteen minutes late' said Al. 'Another fifteen and we'll have to assume he's not coming.'

'He only had to buy some phones and make a phone call.'

'Yeah, seems simple enough, but maybe he ran into some security, or maybe they were listening in to the intelligence phone lines, waiting for him to call in.'

'Like we said, that's all a bit much. Lionel doesn't even know that Porter is working with us. I guess he'd assume Porter is just on the run. They'll be looking outwards rather than inwards tonight.'

'Well I hope so. I don't wanna get my ass shot off when we walk through that gate.'

'Me neither buddy. We just need to hope Lionel doesn't have the whole of the Task Force working against us, because if he does then we're fucked.'

'Proper fucked' agreed Al.

They continued to scan their arcs. It was nearly midnight and Jerry's eyes were feeling grainy and tired. His blinks were lengthening to give his eyes a rest, and some much needed lubrication. The dirty city air dried out and irritated the eyes, even down here near the water.

'D'you think Lionel's in the building still?' asked Al.

'Well his office light was still on when I patrolled by forty five minutes ago, but I couldn't see any signs of movement. Maybe I'll head back out now and have another look, it's only five minutes out to get a good vantage spot by the lagoon.'

'Sure, I'll hold it down here until you're back.'

'Right. If I'm not back within thirty minutes then go ahead without me and this will be the RV point, right back here. And if I'm not back here by first light then assume I'm dead.'

'Roger. Good luck mate.'

'You too' Jerry stepped away from the side street, walking briskly toward the lagoon, over the highway, which was now all but empty of traffic. He turned right when he reached the corniche path, which was dimly lit every fifty metres or so with a lamp post. He walked purposefully, but hands in his pockets so as not to appear too hurried. Even though there appeared to be no-one around, it was always possible there would be someone watching.

After three minutes of walking Jerry had reached a point on the path which gave him a good angle on to Lionel's office window. He looked across the small park area, through the treetops and studied the window, which was still lit. He could not see any movement at all, no silhouettes, no shadows. His was not the only office with lights on, and Jerry was sure there would be no-one else working at this time, so perhaps there were just a few offices where people had forgotten to turn off the lights when they left, and security had not yet patrolled around to turn them off. Or perhaps they were all having a meeting about how to take down Jerry and his team in the conference room, and would be back in their offices in a few minutes, making calls and starting to find them.

He watched the window for ten minutes more before deciding it was unlikely that Lionel was sitting completely still, away from the window for so long. He managed to limit the number of long blinks he took, so as not to miss anything. Satisfied with what he had seen he returned along the path and across the highway, to find Al and Porter waiting for him.

'You made it' he said to Porter.

'Yes, no problem. Here's your phone.' He handed Jerry a new phone with a new card in it. 'It should take them a while to find us with these ones.'

'Thanks' said Jerry, pocketing the phone. 'I still didn't see any sign of movement in Lionel's office, so we can assume he's not there, but of course he could still be in the building. He probably won't be, but it's possible. Did you manage to make contact with someone?' he asked Porter.

'Yes, Francisco is my best man, and also happened to be on duty tonight. He's going to sort out the surveillance kit for us. In fact, he should already have it.'

'Great' said Jerry. 'Well done.'

'Thanks. I just hope she's traceable or we're screwed.'

'Well one problem at a time. Let's get in the building and get what we need first. Happy with the plan?'

Everyone agreed and Porter and Al peeled away, leaving Jerry alone. He watched them disappear in the gloom, heading for the back entrance, before turning around to watch the building again. He looked at his watch, 00:23. He would give them three minutes before starting his approach. As he waited he scanned the gate for any movement in or out. It was quiet. The guard was sitting alone in the guard box, and had been on duty for four hours now. He would be feeling sleepy and less vigilant by this time, Jerry hoped.

The time came and Jerry stepped out of the shadows and walked towards the gate. As he approached the security guard perked up slightly and watched him approach. He didn't reach for a radio or a weapon, so Jerry felt optimistic. When he reached the gate he gave the guard a wave, which was returned with a smile. Another good sign. He put his finger on the scanner and placed his eye on the retinal scanner simultaneously, waiting for a moment for the approving beep. It beeped without delay and the gate unlocked. Clearly Lionel had not anticipated he would return to the headquarters. Jerry pushed it open and let it swing shut. He gave a final wave to the guard and he was away, across the courtyard and into the building.

Jerry stayed on the ground floor when he was in the building, heading for the back entrance. He turned a corner and entered the men's bathroom, where Al and Porter were waiting for him.

'All okay?' he asked. They nodded in response. 'Okay, let's do it. RV back here in thirty minutes.'

They filed out of the bathroom and headed for the stairs. Al went down to the basement, and Jerry and Porter climbed up. At the fourth floor Porter split off and headed for the intelligence cell, Jerry continued up to the fifth floor and emerged from the stairwell after a quick check through the crack of the door. He stepped out and walked purposefully, head slightly down, heading straight for Lionel's office. When he reached it he could see the lights on in the outer office and beyond in Lionel's actual office. Through the frosted glass he still couldn't see any signs of movement, so he tried the handle. It turned and the door opened.

Jerry stepped inside and closed it quietly behind him. He paced quickly across the office and listened for a moment at Lionel's door. Nothing. He tried the handle and again it turned. The door opened noiselessly and he was in, again closing it gently behind him. He cast his eyes around the office, looking for any hidden dangers and seeing none. He knew there was a hidden camera in the corner recording his movement, but hopefully by the time someone watched it he would be long gone with what he needed.

He assessed where he might find any hidden information. The obvious starting point would be the desk, but perhaps there were some other secret spots he might be able to find. A lockable filing cabinet by the desk seemed a good candidate, and to a lesser extent the bookshelf in the corner. Lionel probably was not expecting to have anyone search his office for information on his secret plot, so hopefully he would not have locked it away, so Jerry approached the desk. Its surface was clear so he quickly went to the drawers, starting with the top. Nothing of any intelligence value. The middle one was the same. The bottom drawer had a number of files in, none of which were Simon's file. Jerry spent a few minutes quickly scanning the pages within to find any useful information. Nothing.

He moved over to the filing cabinet and tried every drawer. All locked. Lionel wasn't leaving any clues laying around for him to find. He moved back to the desk and found a note pad. He found a pencil and quickly shaded the page, trying to reveal any impressions made by the pen. Again nothing. He cursed himself for watching too many spy movies and thinking that may actually work. He'd actually just wasted a minute. There was no point trying to hack Lionel's computer as he just didn't have the skills or the time. He then went to the bookshelf and scanned the titles, looking for anything interesting or unusual. On the second shelf his eye was caught by a bound report. He pulled it from the shelf and read the title.

'Identifying genetic immunity to disease in the African Sub-Sahara region by Dr Ananya Devi - Nov 2025'

He opened it and scanned the contents. Nothing leapt out at him but he thought it would certainly be worth taking, just as some background reading. After a quick scan over the rest of the bookshelf he concluded there was nothing of any value to take, and so conducted a quick search of the furniture for hidden pockets or compartments. *Why didn't I join the CIA? This would be a piece of cake then.* He found nothing, and so decided that he had spent enough time in the lion's mouth and had better take his head out now. He made for the door and left quickly. As he passed through the outer office he thought he would quickly check the desk for any clues.

The desk revealed very little. Of course most work was done electronically and so any written notes would be limited. However he took a moment to search through a notebook he found, and on the front page he saw a note relating to travel arrangements for Lionel. Later today, flying Lagos to Khartoum 0900 - 2105, returning next day 1410 - 2150. He would be staying at the Windsor. Finally, something worth knowing! Jerry ripped out the page and folded it, putting it in his pocket. Time to go now. He had used up a lot of good luck. He opened the door a crack and checked the corridor was clear before exiting quickly and heading for the stairs again.

A minute later and he was in the bathroom. He was the first one there. It made him feel nervous to be alone, without any idea what was happening elsewhere in the building. At least it was deathly quiet, which was a good sign.

The door swung open and he quickly turned his head, adopting a ready position. He relaxed when Porter came in carrying two black briefcase-style bags. He smiled and held them up. 'All done, are we good?'

'Not yet. Al's still downstairs.'

'Anything up in Lionel's office?'

'No, except that he's flying to Khartoum today, for one night.'

'Okay, I wonder why? He can't be that worried about you if he's flying anyway.'

'Maybe he'll cancel or at least postpone it now, but if not then that's a good starting point for where to find him.'

'But where do we find Al? It's been a long time now' said Porter.

Almost as if in response to the question the sound of gunshots echoed through the corridors. Jerry groaned.

'Let's go' he said, making for the door. As they left the bathroom he turned his head in the direction of the shots. They were of course coming from downstairs, where the armoury was located. He led the way towards the stairwell, with Porter in tow, lugging the bags.

'I don't suppose you have any weapons in those bags?' asked Jerry.

Porter gave a grim shake of his head as they reached the stairwell door. As Jerry pushed the door open the sound of gunfire grew louder. It was coming in sporadic bursts; which Jerry recognised as the sound of a two-man gun battle, probably from behind cover. He guessed Al must be trapped in or near the armoury, and he would need to get to him as soon as possible, before Al's ammunition ran out, or reinforcements arrived. He turned to Porter.

'I'm going to go down and help Al. Any reinforcements are likely to come through this door, so you stay here and be prepared to smash them in the face with one of your bags as they come through. Hopefully there won't be more than one or two.'

'Right, leave it to me. Go for Al.'

Jerry nodded and raced down the stairs, taking them two at a time whilst also trying to stay light on his feet. He didn't want to attract any attention just yet. As he reached the basement level the gunshots were much louder. The battle was happening right out there in the corridor, just a few metres away. He pulled open the heavy fire door just a crack, to get a view down the corridor. The armoury was at the end he couldn't see, and it was from there that the shots were coming. It was most likely that Al was trying to shoot his way out of the armoury.

He risked a quick look around the door frame, staying as low as possible. His quick glimpse confirmed what he had thought. At the end of the long white corridor he could see a thin sliver of Al in the doorway of the armoury, staying out of view as much as possible. Towards the centre of the corridor, only about five metres from Jerry, a single guard was taking cover in a doorway, changing a magazine. He was only armed with a pistol, but Jerry knew that if he was loading a new magazine then he had at least ten rounds, maybe fifteen. There didn't appear to be any other threats to Al.

Jerry quickly assessed the situation. Al was stuck in the armoury, probably with a huge supply of weapons and ammunition. So why wasn't he shooting his way out with a rifle? Probably to limit the amount of noise made and thereby reduce the danger of reinforcements arriving. Next, the guard was only armed with a pistol and almost certainly had a very limited supply of ammunition. He possibly also had a radio, and would have called for assistance by now if he had. Jerry concluded that a rapid intervention was required, before any extra guards appeared. He quietly closed the fire door and called up to Porter to drop down one of the bags.

Inside the bag was a portable computer and some pieces of delicate surveillance equipment. Not great weapons, and probably quite important to their mission. He couldn't take the chance of damaging them. It would have to be a stealthy approach followed by a manual take-down. It was risky using that approach against an armed man but there were no other options available to him. He eased open the door again and peered round the door frame. The shooting had temporarily abated and Jerry could see why. The guard was out of the doorway and swiftly making his way along the corridor, pistol raised in the aiming position. Al was nowhere to be seen. Perhaps he was changing a magazine, or even hit and lying in a pool of blood. Either way he had to move fast before the guard reached the doorway.

As he pushed through the doorway he estimated that the guard was fifteen metres away. That was a long distance to cover stealthily without a weapon to protect himself. He moved as quickly as he dared, taking long strides and stepping on the outside edge of his boots. Within a few seconds he had closed the gap to seven or eight metres and was still undetected. Two more seconds and he would be on the guard's back. At that moment the fire door closed with a soft hiss behind him. The guard turned his head as he heard the sound and Jerry realised his time was up; he was about to be seen and was exposed in the open with no weapon.

The guard wheeled around as he realised Jerry was behind him, bringing his pistol around in a long arc, due to his arms having been stretched out in front of him. The extra second it took for him to bring his pistol to bear gave Jerry just enough time to dive into a barrel roll, ducking under the guard's line of fire. The pistol flashed and a round split the air above Jerry's head. Before the guard had a chance to change his aim and release a second shot Jerry had bowled into his legs, and at the same time thrust his two fists clenched together, up into the guard's stomach, knocking the wind out of him. He toppled over and rolled onto his back, gasping for breath. Jerry was immediately up and kneeling over him, landing a swift punch on his nose, temporarily blinding him with pain. The guard dropped the pistol and held his nose, which was now erupting blood. Jerry picked up the pistol and in one quick movement pistol-whipped the guard on the side of his head, knocking him out cold. There was no need to kill him unnecessarily; he was after all probably just doing his job and defending the armoury from an attacker.

Jerry got to his feet and raced to the armoury doorway, calling Al's name as he approached. This was not the time to be accidentally shot. Al replied and appeared in the doorway, holding a pistol in each hand. He grinned widely.

'Jeez mate, you took your time. I was about to pull out a rocket launcher.'

'You okay? Have you been hit?'

'No I'm good. Luckily we don't employ marksmen as guards. Is he dead?'

'No, just knocked out for a while. We should get going though, he may have called for backup.'

'He didn't. His radio is here' Al pointed to a handheld radio on the armoury desk. 'But there's a pretty good chance that someone heard all the noise.'

'Yep. Porter's on sentry on the stairwell. Let's get to him now.'

'Sure, just grab this will you?' Al heaved a large duffel bag up and thrust it into Jerry's arms. 'Some toys for us to play with.'

Jerry smiled. 'I'm hoping there won't have to be any more shots fired, but these will be handy just in case things get kinetic. Did you manage to get them all?'

'Yep, Glocks, Z4s, a Mk7 grenade launcher and a whole bunch of grenades, and of course about two thousand rounds.'

'Jeez, how were you going to carry all those? Even with those primate arms of yours!'

'I had steak for dinner! Needed a workout. I loaded a couple of Glocks and a Z4 just in case.' He handed Jerry a Glock and tucked the other in his belt. The Z4 assault rifle stayed in one of the holdalls. Jerry stuffed the pistol into his belt at the back.

'We're good. Let's get out of here' said Jerry.

They left the armoury and headed for the stairwell, pushing open the fire door and calling up to Porter. He replied in a relieved voice and reminded them to bring his bag of equipment. In under a minute they were out of the stairwell and heading for the back door, walking briskly but not running, careful not to draw attention to themselves. Even though the corridors were empty at this time there would still be someone watching the CCTV. Jerry expected reinforcement guards to appear at any moment, roused by the firefight below and running to intervene, but there was no-one. They kept their heads low, negotiated the few short corridors to the exit and then they were out into the open. They quickly checked the car park for any movement. It was about four hundred metres long and wedge-shaped, with the thin end to the right, where Jerry had entered the building. The carpark was surrounded by a high wall, perhaps twelve feet high, with surveillance cameras dotted along it, pointing to the outer side of the wall. Away to the left, at the big end of the car park, the corner was dimly lit. The car park continued around the building at the left-hand end.

All was quiet so they made their way towards the rear gate, where Al and Porter had entered earlier. It was a hundred metres to the gate, so they didn't hurry, just normal walking. At that moment headlights illuminated the left-hand end of the carpark as a vehicle swung around the building and turned towards them. They picked up their pace slightly as they were now only fifty metres from the gate. The headlights of the vehicle, a black security SUV, glared at them and the engine roared as they were spotted. It was a hundred metres away and closing fast.

Jerry knew that the gate was no longer an option for them. They wouldn't be able to make it to the gate and past the guard with security so close behind them. They would have to shoot their way out, which he wanted to avoid, but there was now no choice.

'Go for the gate! Take out the guard!' he shouted to Al and Porter. Al nodded and set off at a pace, lugging the big holdall over his left shoulder as he reached behind him for his pistol. Porter followed on behind, ducking as he ran even though bullets had not yet started flying.

Jerry dropped his holdall, pulled out his pistol, cocked it and checked the safety was off, all in about two seconds. The movements came without conscious thought thanks to his hundreds of hours of training; it was instinct which drove his movements. The vehicle was bearing down on him and it looked like the driver was aiming straight for him. *No intention of taking me alive then!* He took aim at the front grill, not wasting time firing at the bulletproof windscreen. He heard the radiator blow, but still the car kept coming at him, increasing speed. Its headlights blinded him as it neared. They knew as well as he did that he was about to jump aside, but could they guess which way he would go? He fired one more shot and then dived to his left as the driver anticipated him doing the opposite and swerved the other way. It screeched to a halt and the two front doors opened immediately. Jerry was still rolling as the two men leapt from the vehicle. This time they didn't wait to shoot. Their pistols blazed as they opened fire on him.

Jerry had rolled onto his knees and stayed kneeling, keeping his profile as small as possible, gambling that they weren't as good at pistol shooting at night as he was, and that they wouldn't get a lucky hit in. He whipped up his pistol, took aim at the closest man and fired two shots in quick succession - the double tap. The man went down with a grunt, clutching his chest where the bullets had ripped into him. But now the other was closing down on Jerry fast, his barrel still blazing.

Jerry quickly turned his pistol on the man to double tap him too, but a round from the man's erratic firing ricocheted off the car park floor and into his left leg, just below his knee. Jerry felt the fire in his leg as the bullet tore through his skin and exited the leg at the back. He gasped in pain and lost his focus for a moment. A moment too long. His vision returned and there was the gunman, only a few metres from him, pistol pointed and ready.

Jerry roared and pulled the trigger as his adversary did the same. He heard the sound of automatic fire just before he felt the next bullet smash into his hand, throwing him backwards and into blackness.

Chapter Sixteen

Ayatumbe's office was stony silent. Interior Minister Idris Owusu and Chief of the Republican Guard General Yam Yeboah sat side by side on the couch, waiting for the meeting to begin. It was after midnight and they had both been summoned from their beds at short notice to the emergency planning meeting. It was certain that neither of them would have any sleep tonight, and tomorrow was not looking good either.

Ayatumbe swept into the room, not even breaking stride to close the door or bother with greetings.

'We must make a plan tonight for how to counter that snake Al Quraysh!' he began. 'He has been provoking me for too long now, sending his militias into our borderlands, killing our people, threatening our security, and now he is sending his spies to sabotage our infrastructure. I will not stand by and let him bully us into giving up our land and our wealth. I want action! I want to strike the snake, and cut him in half!'

There was silence for a moment, until Owusu spoke up with a suggestion.

'Mr President, I have been monitoring the actions of the Republic and it seems like their militia attacks are increasing in their frequency. Now we are also starting to see the infiltration of special forces teams into the north west, probing our defences and looking for weakness. I have already ordered the guard to be doubled at the Bardai plant.'

'That is good Idris, I do not want any other attacks on the facility. Increase the use of drone patrolling also.'

'Yes Mr President. The eagle drone has been very effective and enabled us to track the special forces team without any detection.'

'Good Idris, but I want even more protection. Now General, what is your plan to counter the Republic attacks?'

Yeboah cleared his throat and sat more upright. He looked nervous.

'Mr President' he began, 'there is no clear evidence from our sources that the attacks are increasing at all. The attacks reported to me seem to be sporadic and happening at about the same rate of one every two days.'

'Are you suggesting my intelligence services are not providing accurate information General?' asked Minister Owusu, as though affronted.

'Well I am saying Minister, that our monitoring stations, as well as the units in the borderlands, are not detecting anything new or unusual. There are still attacks taking place, but they are to be expected.'

'To be expected?!' shouted Ayatumbe. 'I do not expect our neighbour to send his secret troops across our border and conduct attacks on our people and our property. I expect him to respect the border and stop killing. He does it to antagonise me.'

'Yes Mr President, all attacks are an insult to Chad and the legitimacy of its government' chimed Owusu. 'He is insulting our country and our right to live peacefully.'

'I agree with the Minister Mr President' Yeboah quickly corrected himself and getting on board the obviously unstoppable train. 'The Republic is over-stepping its borders and we must take action to push them back. I propose that we deploy our commando troops to repel their attacks, and follow it with a major deployment of armoured infantry to show that we will not tolerate their behaviour.'

'What can our commando troops do, General?' asked Ayatumbe.

'They can deploy by helicopter to the borderlands at short notice, and either carry out defensive operations, or air assault operations over the border. They can take vehicles with them, carried under the helicopter, which will give them much more flexibility. They can operate unsupported for up to forty eight hours, by which time we will have established a logistic base in the region for them to use.'

'Does that achieve my aim though General? I want to punish the President for his lies and strike at his ability to launch attacks against us.'

'We can also deploy our latest generation of UAVs with them, which will provide a powerful surveillance capability as well as some powerful missiles to counter their vehicles and aircraft.'

'Our drones can attack their aircraft?' asked Ayatumbe.

'Oh yes Mr President. We have acquired a new model of drone which can be programmed to track and destroy specific targets, fully automatically, without the need for a pilot or commander. It uses artificial intelligence to predict what a pilot would want it to do, and then does it better than a human could manage.'

'How many of these aircraft do we have?'

'We currently have twelve, with another twelve on order if the trial is successful. They are the very latest technology, bought from Israel.'

'Yes, good' said Ayatumbe. 'They must be programmed to destroy the Republic militias and any of their vehicles.'

'Such a programme will not be able to distinguish between Republic and Chadian militia vehicles, because they are using pickup trucks. There is a risk we will be attacking our own people. It is safer to program it to attack their aircraft Mr President.'

'It is the militias that are the threat General. I want them targeted, whatever the cost!'

'Yes Mr President.'

Captain Hamed Okoro sat on the terrace of the officers' club of the 12th Airborne Regiment of the Armed Forces Republican Guard, in the Chadian town of Am Timan, three hundred kilometres to the west of the Republic border. It was a typically hot night. He was sweating in his heavy combat fatigues as he sat smoking and looking at nothing. He hated being the duty officer, as it always involved carrying out some pointless inspection of an empty warehouse, inspecting the guard on the gate of the camp, and hours of sitting and waiting for nothing to happen. At least he only had to do the duty once every two weeks when it was his turn in the rotation. The rest of the time he would go to visit his family and his friends, as well as the family of his fiancée Arafa.

It was three in the morning and so far nothing had happened except for one soldier failing to return to duty from leave, an unusual occurrence which he could do nothing about until the morning. Desertion was generally not a problem in the armed forces now, as work was so hard to come by. The traditional occupation of Chadian men had been farming, with the remainder split between government service and working in the oil fields in the south. However in recent years the creeping desertification of Chad had decimated the agricultural heart of the country, so more men had flocked to the military, more through desperation than a desire to serve their country. Hence desertion was rare, as the deserter's family would lose the majority of their income. Okoro guessed this particular desertion must be due to a girl.

He took one last long drag on his cigarette and stubbed it out on the side of his chair, flicking the butt into the sand by the terrace. He watched it land and then let his eyes drift away across the grounds of the officers' club towards the distant fence, and the few trees beyond. He thought of Arafa and their wedding, which would be next year, once he had completed three years in the military. Traditionally he would have to work on Arafa's father's farm for three years, but that tradition was thankfully long since dead. His father had been a farmer and it had crippled him, hacking away at the hard dry earth for forty years for an ever diminishing yield as the soil baked it harder and over-farming robbed it of its nutrients. Okoro felt lucky to be a military man, except tonight.

He reflected on how his poor uncle may not have felt quite so lucky to be a military man. He had taken a different path to his brother and had left the family farm to follow a military career. He had served in an armoured battalion of the Chadian Ground Forces during the early twenties. At that time the jihadist movement had been building in intensity and finding support among the population due to the strongarm tactics being employed by the government. The cases of abuse and torture tainted the reputation of the armed forces and drove disenfranchised people into the arms of the various jihadist groups, who increased the boldness and intensity of attacks against the security forces. His uncle had been a driver of a BMP - an ancient Russian-made armoured fighting vehicle, which had been a very effective vehicle during the twentieth century, but had not evolved to match the ever-evolving threats of this century. His uncle's BMP had been blown up during a patrol in the north west of the country. He had lost his legs and suffered major burns to his torso. For the few years he lived after that he didn't seem to feel very lucky to have served in the armed forces, nor very lucky to even be alive.

Okoro had had to work hard to convince his father to let him join the military, and had only really succeeded due to the lack of future in farming. His career so far in the Armed Forces Republican Guard had been eventful. After a three month officer training course at the Republican Guard Academy he had been sent to the 12th Airborne Regiment, where he was appointed commander of a UAV detachment. The detachment contained two Interceptor UAVs and twelve men to operate and maintain them. They had already been deployed twice, to battle rebel forces in the south of the country on the border with the Central African Republic. It was not what he expected from military service, as he had not once seen a rebel, except on a monitor, nor fired his personal weapon in battle. Instead he had watched as his men prepared and launched the UAV, and then as they fired missiles at rebel camps and vehicles from the remote control panel. It all happened many kilometres away, while they never even left the base. However having heard the stories of bombings and shootings that were suffered by the ground forces he had felt very grateful for his distance from the battle.

In recent months though the rebel battles had gone quiet and so had his unit. They had slipped into a routine of training and drill, interspersed with long bouts of sitting and waiting, something all soldiers become very adept at. It had been difficult to keep his men motivated during these long periods of inactivity, as they were prone to misbehave when given too much time off. He had realised that this was the challenge of being an officer in the armed forces. It was relatively easy to command men during war, because there was always a purpose and a mission, but during peacetime there was nothing. All the African Union missions had dried up some time ago for some reason, leaving them purposeless until the next rebel crisis. So he had been proactive in organising extra physical training, and running UAV deployment drills for his men, building them into a well trained and disciplined team.

Tomorrow morning was no exception. He would do physical training with his men at six o'clock before finishing his duty at eight, and then there would be a busy day of a simulated deployment, in which they would practice the call out and set up of the system, flying a mission over the oil fields in the south. He had created a training scenario in which the rebels were attempting to capture the oil fields and his team had been tasked to hunt and destroy small rebel units. Such scenarios were easy to create as there was plenty of historical precedent for it. Civil war had rocked the country persistently for the last fifty years it seemed, so all soldiers would be familiar with the concept. His main challenge of the day would be to get some sleep at some point. He might grab a couple of hours once the drones had launched and were enroute to the oil fields.

His phone rang. He looked at the screen and saw it was the duty clerk at headquarters. Probably some minor admin problem, which couldn't be fixed until morning, but needed to be passed on to him anyway. He answered, and listened. His eyes widened as the clerk spoke, and he sat up in his seat. When the clerk finished he didn't know what to say.

'Right, okay...I'll tell the commanding officer then.'

He hung up and sat staring into space for a moment, not quite believing what he had been told. Slowly he found the number for the commanding officer and reluctantly dialled it. It rang for a long time, before a sleepy voice answered.

'Sir, this is Captain Okoro, the duty officer. I am sorry to wake you Sir, but there has been a call from Republican Guard Headquarters. We are going to war with the Islamic Republic Sir.'

Chapter Seventeen

Jerry woke with a start. The searing pain in his left hand and leg reminded him that it hadn't been a dream, and he really had been shot twice. He tried to sit up but the pain was unbearable as he moved and it made him want to vomit so he stayed down. He gently touched his hand, being careful not to prod it too hard, and found that it was bandaged heavily, all around his hand and wrist, tight and restrictive. He tried to remember what had happened but couldn't recall the details after the car park shoot out.

He turned his head to look around, and discovered that he was back at Chez Chay, laid out on the desk in the same back office they had made the plan. Bright sunlight was flooding in through the window, and he could just make out the sound of reggae music floating under the door from the bar. It all seemed a bit surreal that he had been in a firefight in a dark car park and then the next moment in a beachside bar. He guessed the real transition hadn't been quite so smooth, and he imagined the hard time Al and Porter must have had getting him here, unconscious and wounded.

He wondered where they were. There was no sign of either of them. He looked at the time - 0945. He had been out for nearly nine hours, in which time he he been transported here, treated and bandaged. Maybe they were sleeping after all that action. There were no voices coming from the bar or sounds of movement. He assumed it was Al and Porter that had brought him here, otherwise who else would it have been? He had to find them and find out what happened. He took a moment to take a few deep breaths, to steel himself for the torture about to come, and then with an almighty effort he pushed down on his right hand and slowly lifted his left side off the desk. His kept his arm tucked across his body, to try to minimise the pain from the movement. He swung his legs round and hung them off the desk. He stopped, panting and sweating from the exertion.

He looked down at his left leg and saw that it had been similarly bandaged, below the knee. It was also tight but he could bend the leg freely. He was in a pretty bad state and thought he must be pretty lucky to be alive. *Thank God that guy was a bad shot.*

After a few more moments he prepared himself to move again. He shuffled to the end of the desk in order to minimise the distance to the door, and had another deep breathing break. Again he held his breath and strained himself off the desk, putting all his weight on his right leg, supporting himself on the desk. He reached out for a chair and hopped and shuffled his way to the door. He was glad to note that his leg wasn't as painful as he feared and he was able to walk almost normally after a few steps. He stopped at the door to catch his breath and to stop his head spinning. He tried the door handle and gently eased open the door.

The music was louder now, and he could smell alcohol and smoke, and cleaning products. Slowly he followed the short corridor to the main bar, quietly grunting as he went. The bar was gloomy and cool with the shutters closed, and he adjusted his eyes as he rested at the end of the bar to catch his breath and look around. He saw Al and Porter sitting at a table by the window.

'Hey, who the hell put these bandages on too tight?' he shouted.

Al and Porter looked up and round at him. Their faces beamed.

'Hey old buddy' said Al, quickly rising from his seat and hurrying over to Jerry. 'You didn't sleep for long. We thought you'd be out for the rest of the day.'

'And miss breakfast? Are you kidding?'

Al laughed and gently touched Jerry's arm. 'How are you feeling mate? That must hurt like a bitch.'

'Yep, pretty much'

'It's a pretty nasty wound to your hand, but you were lucky. It somehow passed straight through your knuckles and only nicked a few bones. It took me friggin' ages to stitch you up.'

'Yeah it feels like you stuck a hot poker in there too while you were at it.'

Al laughed. 'Well I could only find one of Chay's corkscrews so that had to do!'

'Don't make me laugh, it hurts.'

Porter joined them, his face smiling, but with a concerned look.

' Hey Jerry, are you okay? We were pretty worried about you for a while there.'

'Well I'm alive, thanks to you guys. What the hell happened?'

'Come and sit down and we'll explain everything.' They helped him to the table and sat him down comfortably, with his leg resting on a chair.

'Well I'm surprised to have even woken up. That wasn't looking good for me for a while there. Thank God that guy wasn't a great shot or I'd be dead for sure.'

'I think you're right' agreed Al. 'You took out the first guy well but the second guy managed to get two shots into you before I slotted him.'

'You did? I thought I had managed to line up on him in time.'

'I think you did, but I made sure of it with the Z4. Him and the driver. It's never cool to shoot a guy in the back but I made an exception for him. I'm sure he would have done the same for me.'

'Christ, it was lucky you got there in time then.'

'Not lucky mate, I always had your back. It just took me a while to get the Z4 out of the friggin' bag! I knew I should have put a sling on it!'

'So what about the guard on the gate?'

'Porter took care of him'

Porter smiled grimly. 'Not really my cup of tea, but it had to be done. I don't think I killed him though, which is good. It was Samuel. I knew him quite well and I didn't want to kill him.'

'It's tough to do buddy, well done. So I guess you had to carry me out of there then?'

'I wasn't gonna carry your heavy ass. We took the car' said Al.

'I thought I'd shot out the radiator.'

'Turns out you didn't do it enough. Luckily it had some life left in it and we were able to smash out through the barrier and get away. It did give up eventually though, but not until we were downtown. I had to carry you the rest of the way, which was fun, trying to move through the city with you on my shoulder and not be seen.'

'So what are the chances of them having tracked us to here?'

'Well we covered our tracks pretty carefully, avoiding most cameras we could.'

'And how about the weapons? Did you manage to bring any?'

'I got them' said Porter. 'My shoulders are still sore now!'

'I think I can beat you when it comes to pain there buddy!' said Jerry with a grimace.

'Fair enough' conceded Porter. 'How about a drink? Water? Coffee?'

'Both, thanks'. Porter got up and headed towards the back of the bar.

'So good old Chay opened his doors for us again then?'

'Yeah no worries. He was cool. Luckily he has a well-stocked first aid kit too. I thought we were gonna have to take you to a hospital and I didn't want to take the risk.'

'Well thanks for patching me up.'

'No worries. I remembered my old team medic training. Although it's been a while, so if you start turning yellow we may need to worry!'

'What was the deal with the leg?'

'Just a graze, with some minor muscle damage again. You lost a bit of blood though, and obviously we don't have any to give you, so you're gonna need to take it easy for quite a while.'

'I'm not sure that's going to be possible is it? What's happening? Do we have a fix on Ananya? Or Lionel?'

'I'll let Porter go through that, but the short answer is yes and no. She must be using a different number, but Porter thinks there's a way to find her. And Lionel must have his encrypted, no sign of him.'

'Oh shit, we're not looking good then.'

'Well there may be some good news. Porter will explain it. Shall I get you some pain relief? Chay doesn't have anything very strong so you're gonna need to keep topped up.'

'Yeah, thanks. Where is Chay anyway?'

'He had to go out for supplies. I've sent him to get some proper drugs, and also some more medical stuff.'

'I don't suppose he's buying some bacon is he? I'm starving.'

Al laughed. 'I'll take a look out back and see what I can find. Hang tight buddy.' He left Jerry alone.

Jerry sat back and moved his wrist slightly, to see if the pain in his hand was abating at all. It wasn't. This was going to be a serious handicap when trying to foil Lionel's plan, whatever it was. He was already on his way to Khartoum, perhaps to initiate the plot, plan, operation or whatever it was. It seemed pretty hopeless now. *Why wouldn't Lionel accelerate the launch now that the surprise is blown and there's a risk of it being exposed? I would. Unless it's not ready yet. We need some more information!*

151

Porter returned with drinks and a handful of painkillers. Jerry popped some of the pills and washed them down with a big gulp of water. It tasted amazing, not like the usual desalinated crap they had to endure.

'Is this real spring water?' he asked.

'Yes. Chay's finest bottle!'

'Thanks. I needed that. So, Al said we can't find Ananya or Lionel, but there's some hope?'

'That's right. I think she must be using a different number to the one we have for her, but there's a good chance we'll be able to track her through surveillance camera facial recognition. It's on the government servers but we can hack those easy enough. I've already got Francisco on it, I'm a bit rusty on the latest techniques.'

'Well that's good news. You've checked she's still in the country first though?'

'That's the first check he's doing. The immigration records are in a different system to the surveillance so he's having to do both. He shouldn't be long now though, he's already been on it for an hour.'

'That's great. Good work man. Is he definitely solid and not going to get busted? We don't want to lose a key asset like him.'

'He should be good. He can work mobile too so he won't arouse suspicion by doing it at work.'

'Okay, so what about Lionel? Can we listen in to his conversations or see his emails?'

'No, he's got it pretty tightly locked up. Either he has been using a different email for the comms or he's doing it by some other means, but there's nothing on the Task Force server about it.'

'How about Simon's account? Have you checked that?'

'Yes. Nothing there either. They took their operational security pretty seriously. I guess they didn't want to leave any trace of what they've been doing. I assume they weren't planning to die on this mission, so they wouldn't want anything incriminating there afterwards.'

'Hmmm, wait a minute…' Jerry thought for a moment. '…if we assume that because they kept their accounts clean then they were planning to come back here, or at least they intended to avoid investigation and prosecution, then does that give us a clue about what they're planning? Something *legal*?'

'Or non-attributable.'

'What could they possibly be doing that is either legal or non-attributable, that needs to be planned with the utmost secrecy and is worth trying to kill me for?'

'And probably involves the use of genetically engineered weapons to kill potentially millions of people.'

'It's tough to keep that on the right side of the law.'

'But it's far more likely that they're not planning to come back to work afterwards. It could just have been good OpSec so they didn't compromise the plan.'

'Yeah, that's more likely I guess. Why would you commit some heinous crime and then just go back to work the next day? They were just being careful.'

'Well we'll see what Francisco turns up about Ananya' said Porter. 'Hopefully we'll be able to find her and then get some more information. I've never worked in such an intelligence vacuum before. Usually any secret in Africa can be paid for, or is abundantly obvious from some surveillance, but this time we don't have a network, there's no-one to pay and we don't have any idea where to surveil.'

Al returned with bacon sandwiches and everyone devoured them in silence, each one thinking of schemes and theories as he chewed. Porter's phone rang. He took the call and after a minute hung up with a sigh.

'Ananya has not left the country, but we're not picking up any traces of her. She must have switched to a different phone, or has some encryption on it. We're not picking up anything on her from our usual channels either - no sightings or flags on the facial recognition system. She's gone off the grid somehow.'

'Well you stay on that. I'd say she's key to this operation and we need to track her down' said Jerry.

'Lionel did fly this morning though. He took off about an hour ago. He must be going to Khartoum to either launch the mission, or for a planning meeting' said Porter.

'Either way, Khartoum is the place to be' said Jerry. 'We need to get there, or get some eyes there. Who do you have in Khartoum?' he asked.

'Only Fisher, who isn't the sort of asset we can just pull out for a surveillance mission, *and* actually may be involved anyway as that must be where Lionel has been getting all his intelligence from, and circumventing me. All other intelligence gathering capability is down in Darfur at the moment. We wouldn't be able to get them to Khartoum in time to see Lionel land, which is in…' he checked his watch, '…nine hours.'

'But we know where he's staying. How soon could we get there?' asked Jerry.

'I'll check flights now' replied Porter, turning to his computer.

'Why not try to get Porter's guys there to Khartoum instead?' suggested Al. 'It's a hell of a journey across nearly the whole of Africa, just to be late to a meeting.'

'I know man, but I just think this is too sensitive to risk with a surveillance crew. I'd rather keep it within us. Also, we don't really know how far Lionel's influence extends. As soon as Porter gets in touch with them that could be us compromised.'

'I guess so, but it's such a long shot too. We don't even know what he's going there for. It could be a total waste of time'

'It's surely our best shot to be there tonight' said Jerry. 'If he's launching then we need to be there to stop him if we can.'

Fair enough, let's go to Khartoum, I hear it's lovely this time of year!' said Al.

Porter spoke as he was typing, 'The next flight to Khartoum, and the *last one today* is at 1145. That's just over two hours.'

'And it puts us three hours behind Lionel' said Jerry. "We'd better hope he doesn't go straight to his meeting or we'll miss him.'

'Hang on a minute' said Al, 'what if Lionel has our names and faces on a watch list? As soon as we walk into the airport we're going to be fucked.'

'Fuck. Yeah, that is definitely possible' agreed Jerry. He turned to Porter. 'Can you have Francisco find out if we're celebrities or not? I'd rather not end this mission before it's even begun.'

'I'll get on to him now' said Porter.

'In fact' said Al, 'without being too paranoid about it, isn't there a chance that all communications are being monitored too? Just us searching for flights to Khartoum might pop up on a screen somewhere.'

'It is most definitely possible, and you're not at all paranoid. It's completely common practice' said Porter. 'Any search done on the net is visible, and if they select some key-words then it'll flag up immediately. It assumes that Lionel is careful enough to have someone watching out for it though, and I would have to say that seems probable. But it just so happens that I am also careful. I'm encrypting all our comms, and I also have a secure link with Francisco, so we're safe. I'll get him searching the immigration database for any flags on you chaps.'

'Thanks buddy' said Jerry. He turned to Al. 'Let's start planning what we're going to do when we get there.'

'Yeah okay, but it's tough to plan in the dark. We don't have a clue what he's up to, or when.'

'No, but we do know where he'll be, and that's a good start. Let's get on it.'

155

Twenty minutes later Porter turned from his computer with a smile. 'So the bad news is that Lionel does have a flag on us all.'

'Which means he has a much wider influence than I'd hoped' said Jerry.

'But the good news is that Francisco has removed them. Unless their man in immigration is constantly checking if the flags are still there then we should be fine.'

'But why wouldn't he check?' asked Al.

'Well once a search criteria has been set, it doesn't drop out or stop working until it's told to. So Lionel's guy, whoever he is, will have just programmed the system and then will be sitting back waiting for it to ping.'

'Let's hope he's not the nervous type who feels a need to check his work' said Al.

'We have to put ourselves out there and trust Porter and Francisco, man' said Jerry. 'We can't just sit here, too afraid to move in case we're seen.'

'I know' sighed Al, 'I just don't want this op to end before it even begins.'

'Get the flights booked' Jerry said to Porter. 'There's no time to lose. If he's launching the plan tonight or tomorrow then we need to be there to stop him.'

Chapter Eighteen

President Al Quraysh emerged from the shower and wrapped himself in a robe, smoothed his black hair and inspected his beard in the mirror.

'Do you have to go, my husband? Won't you spend the afternoon with me?'

'I must go Aishah. I have already been here too long and there are matters I must attend to. I have a Republic to command.' He inspected the hair on his chest and carefully scrutinised his profile in the mirror.

'Will it not wait? You are the President. You may do as you please.'

'Not today my love. There are important matters to discuss.'

'What is more important than what I have for you?' She sidled over behind him and placed her arms around his waist.

He smiled and turned around to look at her. She was so beautiful, he thought. He wanted to be with her all the time, and had been utterly intoxicated by her since they met a year ago. Now six months into their marriage and she still made him feel like a young man.

'There will be plenty of time for that tonight, but today I must discuss important matters of state.'

'Is that pest in Chad still bothering you? You should swat him like a fly as he buzzes around.'

'I would love to, he is indeed irritating, but it is not possible. I do not have such freedom in external matters as I do inside the Republic. There are rules and laws to be followed.'

She sighed. 'I can understand that with important countries like America, or Russia, but not one as minor as Chad.'

'All borders are important' he said. 'And we must officially respect them'

'And unofficially?'

'Well that is what I am discussing today. In such matters there are always other ways to exert your influence and get what you want. Now what will you do this afternoon?'

'Oh nothing, I will stay here all alone...' She fluttered her long eyelashes at him. 'I will go shopping tonight though.'

'I can have anything brought here for you my love. Whatever you desire.'

'No I want to go and look, and see what normal people do again.'

'Yes you're right. I have been keeping you here too much, being selfish with your time. Go out and see the city and do as you please.'

'Thank you. I will buy something for you too. Something we can both enjoy later?'

He smiled and kissed her.

The shura council convened and sat waiting for the President to arrive. Several of the men chatted amiably, but Abu Rashed sat silent and pensive.

'Is everything alright, Abu Rashed?' asked Abu Khalid.

'Oh yes, everything is fine al hamdu lillah. I just have many issues on my mind of late. This situation with Chad is troubling me.'

'Why is that Abu Rashed?'

'Well it seems that there is an increasing number of threats coming out of President Ayatumbe's mouth at the moment. I am concerned that he may be poised to take some sort of drastic action.'

'Why do you suspect this?' asked Abu Khalid.

'Well it has been reported to me that the language he is using is increasingly threatening, and he even convened a late-night meeting with his war council last night. It seems that he may be intending to conduct an invasion of the Darfur region. He apparently views it as the source of the problem and favours a solution in which he can control the fighting parties through oppression. It also has the unique quality of being the only habitable land in the region, due to its few remaining natural water sources. He may be looking to it as a solution to his overpopulation problem.'

'Wallah, has this come from the Ambassador?'

'Yes, he is concerned that the plans are in place right now. He has already been threatened with expulsion and thinks he is being followed everywhere he goes.'

'This is serious. Does the President know yet?'

'No, I will share it with him now. But I fear our reaction may be too late anyway. I think Ayatumbe has been playing games with us this whole time and always intended to take the land as his own.'

'You think he has orchestrated this whole crisis in order to justify taking Darfur?'

'I do. Why else would he escalate the tension so intensely? Why did we not see this coming? He has caught us out I fear.'

'Not yet Abu Rashed. He has not crossed our border yet. Let us see what the President has to say on the matter.'

Abu Rashed leaned closer and lowered his voice. 'Well that is my concern Abu Khalid. I fear he may seek a conciliatory approach and therefore play into Ayatumbe's hands even more. He has been so fixed on a diplomatic solution, perhaps in a bid to avoid using force. He has never yet decided to use force, despite being sidelined and disregarded by so many of our neighbours over these last years.'

'He believes, as I do, that use of force should be a last resort, and is not the way to find lasting solutions to international problems.'

'As do I brother, but we both know that Ayatumbe holds no such view. He is a desperate madman and will do anything he can to further his own aims. Such characters do not respond to reason, only to strength. I fear the President may be unwilling to show such strength.'

'I am not so sure Abu Rashed. I think he may prove more decisive than you think when he discovers what you have to say.'

'I think it is important to support him in this most difficult of decisions. Will you as his deputy advise him as such? I know he looks on you with great respect and values your counsel very much. You have been a great confidante and leader, and he will certainly listen to you.'

'I will Abu Rashed. It is my duty.'

The President entered the room and everyone stood for the usual greetings and salutations.

'Salaam alaykum. Kayf halikhum?' he spoke to everyone. The council replied in kind and they took their seats.

'General Al Buraimi, welcome and how good to see you.' The President gestured to the Head of the Armed Forces and then put his hand on his chest. 'I am grateful to you for coming to offer your counsel at these meetings. I am sure your expertise will be most useful.'

'Insha'allah Ameer' replied the General.

'Now, what news is there today? Have we managed to gather the required aid to provide to the refugees?'

'Not yet Ameer' replied Abu Khalid, 'our agents are coordinating the collection of the aid at the moment. They estimate that it will be another two days until they have completed the collection. However Ameer, I believe there is a development in the situation which may override the importance of this undertaking.' He looked at Abu Rashed as he finished.

Abu Rashed nodded. 'Yes Ameer, I have an update on the situation within Chad which has caused me alarm.' He repeated the information in a grave tone, finishing with '...and the current information we have suggests a much more aggressive approach than previously shown.'

Al Quraysh sat silent and pondered the news for a moment. He turned to General Al Buraimi.

'General, do you have any input on this matter? Is there any reason to believe that such an attack is being planned?'

'Ameer, our surveillance of the Chadian military units indicates that there has been a significant increase in their activity in the last twelve hours. They appear to be mobilising large numbers of troops and equipment from their bases in the south. There has also been an increased level of sorties flown by their Air Force, though their air capability is at present quite limited as we believe they do not have adequate resources to maintain their aircraft at a level of airworthiness.'

'Nonetheless they are mobilising and look to be moving?'

'There has been no significant movement northwards yet, but the levels of activity suggest an imminent movement. They have no planned training exercises so it would seem that they are moving for some other reason. If we assume they are not mobilising an armoured unit to join the humanitarian efforts of the existing troops then I would have to conclude they are intending to move on the border, with the intent to cross it.'

'How long would it be until they could be in a position to cross the border into Darfur?'

'Again, I am assuming the troops already there are not intending to switch to a combat role, which they are not equipped for. So theoretically their armoured units could be in a position to cross the border within the next eight hours if they are fully mobilised within two hours from their bases to the closest border point which is suitable for armour movement.'

'Is armour the most likely option they will use?' asked the President.

'The armoured units have shown the greatest level of activity according to the satellite images. They also have a limited air assault capability, which would involve the use of helicopters to land troops on or across the border. I must stress though that their fleet of helicopters is less than twenty, and are now very old technology. They are Russian transport helicopters and were bought before 2010, so they are very old and will most likely be poorly serviced and I have doubts that they would be able to insert any more than 150 troops in one lift.'

'That sounds like a large force to drop anywhere over the border' said Abu Rashed.

'Yes it is, but they would be unsupported by any other units and could only hope to be a raiding force. I must emphasise though, Ameer, that this is the worst possible scenario and I have doubts that they would be capable of that at the moment, or that they intend to do so.'

'But they are clearly preparing for something' said the President. 'What is the latest news from the borderlands? Have there been any fresh attacks?'

'The loyalist militia attacks are continuing on both sides, Ameer' said Abu Rashed. 'They are now happening with such frequency it is hard to distinguish between them. The number of internally displaced persons and refugees is starting to reach a critical mass which is simply impossible to support. The Chadian troops already deployed there to stabilise the situation are ineffective, and the temporary camps they have established are also becoming targets for further attacks.'

'Are these also the work of Ayatumbe? Is he seeking an excuse to intervene?'

'It is hard to say Ameer, but we have never found any reason for the attacks supposedly by Muslims.'

'It seems clear to me that he is engineering this entire situation in order to justify an invasion of Darfur. What can we do to stop him General?'

'Ameer we have three Divisions of armoured infantry which can be deployed to Darfur, but it will be twenty four hours at least until they would be in place. I have already activated them but they are currently stood down in other areas of Sudan State and need to be mobilised.'

'Twenty four hours is too long General. They will have attacked and consolidated their positions by then.'

'We also have a more immediate solution, in the form of our new integrated UAV system. It is programmed to be fully autonomous, and can track and destroy enemy aircraft or vehicles independently of a human command system. It enables us to deploy it into hard to reach areas, such as the sub-Saharan regions of the country, and it will then provide mobile border defence without the need for significant human involvement.'

'That sounds excellent. How soon can we have it deployed into the Darfur region?'

'It should take around six hours to deploy and program. Currently we have only one system, which contains eight aircraft with the ability to cover two thousand kilometres of border.'

'Our Sudan State border alone is two thousand kilometres. And then there is the Libya State too. How do we protect the whole border?'

'We can choose a deployment point according to the topography of Darfur' explained the General. 'We will cover the land which is most likely to be the enemy's avenue of approach. The rest of the border can be covered by remote surveillance systems, with area defence missile systems and troops waiting to the rear to deploy at short notice once a threat is detected. This is the most pragmatic system we have found to deal with the extremely long border we have. It is not practical to have large numbers of troops patrolling the borders, particularly in such an arid and uninhabitable environment.'

'Tell me more about the area defence missile system'

'It is a smart connected system which uses a series of sensors along the border to detect enemy movement. We can specify what size and type of target we are looking for. Once a target is detected the system then can be set to automatically launch a missile or other type of weapon, or to require human input to authorise the launch. It is accurate down to single vehicle size, should we want that level of detail. However it is still being configured, and we do not have total confidence that it will be one hundred percent accurate. As such it is not currently deployed along the border. However in this situation, if we accept some risk in the targeting profiles then it can be deployed and considered operational.'

'And the time to make the system ready to fire?'

'It can be done within twelve hours, Ameer. We will need to assess the likely targets and program the system, and then get the sensors and missiles in place.'

'These are good systems, and they will protect our borders well, but they are all too far away from where we need them' said the President. 'What can we do to meet the immediate threat from Chad so they are not able to seize Darfur before we can get there?'

General Al Buraimi paused for a moment. 'Ameer, the most effective means of deterring an attack at present would be to conduct a show of force which makes our intentions very clear.'

'What sort of show do you mean?'

'Perhaps a very loud and deliberate display of our capability, in order to deter them from attempting to cross the border?' replied the General.

'Short of shooting down one of their planes, what do you suggest?' asked Al Quraysh.

'Well given that there are no Chadian troops in the borderlands at present, and shooting down a plane would be regarded as an act of war, we could either consider targeting the troops conducting humanitarian relief activities, or the combatants - the Chadian-sponsored militias.'

'Killing non-combatant humanitarian workers, even if in uniform is out of the question. And wouldn't killing Chadian militants on Chadian soil also be regarded as an act of war?'

'Ameer, I would suggest that there is an element of doubt in that area. If they are clearly in Chadian territory then yes, it is war, but if they were actually found in Republic territory then it would be defensible.'

'Do you mean wait until they enter our territory and then destroy them?'

'No Ameer' the General said, looking uncomfortable.

There was silence for a moment as every man in the room thought about the General's implication. It was one thing to defend your borders from an army, but to seize a militant group, on their own side of the border, and execute them as an act of propaganda was another altogether. Abu Khalid and Abu Rashed glanced at each other.

'Ameer,' began Abu Khalid, 'this is a time to show our strength. Both the strength of our capability, and also the strength of our will. Perhaps a strong message now will serve as a strong deterrent to President Ayatumbe and his forces.'

'Perhaps it would' said the President. 'What do you think Abu Rashed?'

'Ameer, I agree that showing your strength in this situation is vitally important. Ayatumbe is an arrogant man and will not be influenced by empty threats. Abu Khalid, do you propose to strike using special forces? Or perhaps a drone strike?'

Abu Khalid cast him a quick look of surprise and faltered for a moment.

'...errr...' he began.

'Perhaps you are right Abu Khalid' said the President. 'This situation has been lingering for too long now, and I have allowed Ayatumbe to shout his rhetoric too much whilst conducting his secret schemes. It has to stop before he endangers us and our security. General, draw up a list of possible options for me. I want to consider them later this afternoon. Abu Khalid, Abu Rashed, you will be there with me to hear the options.'

'Ameer, forgive me but I have to receive a further intelligence briefing this afternoon as the situation is changing so rapidly.'

'Fine, you can report back to me later. Abu Khalid you will be with me.'

'Yes, Ameer' replied Abu Khalid. He fixed Abu Rashed with a hard stare, which was carefully ignored.

'Ameer, I will await your decision before communicating the decision to our ambassador in N'Djamena' said Abu Rashed.

'No, do not wait. Inform him now to begin to withdraw his staff from the embassy. I do not want there to be any risk to them from Ayatumbe's militias.'

'As you wish Ameer.'

Abu Rashed excused himself and left the room, reaching for his phone and dialing the number as he walked.

'Abu Yousef, salaam alaykum. Al hamdu lillah. Yes, all has gone according to plan, he is about to order a pre-emptive strike on Chad. I anticipate it will happen within the next eight hours...Yes, you should withdraw your embassy staff without delay, and you should prepare yourself to become the Foreign Minister. The days of this presidency are now numbered.'

Chapter Nineteen

Jerry and Al studied the African landscape below them and noted its transition during the flight. It had begun over the mountainous tropical jungles of Nigeria and Cameroon, now only a fraction of their former size, replaced instead by vast swathes of deforested wasteland. The wasteland was occasionally interspersed with patches of failing agricultural land and also scarred with the huge open cast bauxite and uranium mines, which had been exploited in the Cameroonian mining rush of the twenties, providing cheap resources to feed the demands of the technology hungry world. The mountains had then given way to the formerly rich agricultural plains of the Chadian Sahel, now arid and depleted and largely empty of life, robbed of its nutrients by over-farming coupled with soaring temperatures.

They had looked down at the landscape and simply could not fathom what made it such a good target for whatever Lionel was planning. As far as they could see there was nothing of any value. All life was now concentrated in and around cities, which would of course make them extremely vulnerable to any mass attack, but what would be the point of attacking such a poor and decrepit country?

The Sahel gave way to desert of the Sahara, which lay out below them as far as they could see as they passed into the Islamic Republic. A vast expanse of nothing, broken only occasionally by isolated spots of civilisation, sometimes for what looked like habitation, and sometimes for some unknown industrial activity - small collections of sand-coloured buildings isolated and alone in a huge sea of sand. Eighty five percent of North Africa was now covered by the Sahara, stretching from the Atlas Mountains in the west to the Red Sea in the east. They marvelled at its enormous size and wondered how anyone could survive in such an environment. They discussed how such survival was becoming increasingly rare, with traditional nomadic lifestyles being threatened by the increasing desertification. Somewhere below them was Darfur, the region of the Republic's Sudan State. Jerry recalled how Porter had told him it was the source of growing tension between Chad and the Republic. Militia attacks were leading to a growing refugee problem, and Jerry wondered with despair about the fate of refugees in such an environment.

Jerry and Al used the time to discuss in detail the plan for the night ahead, focusing on how they would find and track Lionel from his hotel; how they would surveil him as he moved around Khartoum; and when they would go ahead and take him down. They agreed that moving on him as he slept at night would be the best option, partly because that was when he was at his most vulnerable, and also because that was the only time they would know for sure where he was. They couldn't chase him around the city and then set up a hasty ambush with no weapons. Furthermore, Jerry's injuries precluded him from taking part in a protracted pursuit and fight so they needed to conduct this operation on their terms, without a fight if possible. Lionel was in his mid-fifties now, but he was still fit and strong, and they didn't know how much security he had either. They grimly noted how little they still knew about what Lionel was doing.

'A swift grab from his room, followed by some interrogation should get us all the information we need' said Al.

'My concern is that once we take him, will his operation launch anyway without him?' said Jerry. 'He may be making the final arrangements tonight, before we snatch him.'

'We could try to take him sooner. We may be able to catch him if he's at the hotel, before he leaves this evening?'

'But taking him when he's sleeping is the safest time. We're not equipped for a fight with his security team. Let's track him from the hotel this evening if we can, so we can find out what he's doing, and then take him at night. We'll just have to take our chances that he's not launching it tonight and that we'll be able to stop it tomorrow.'

'No weapons, no idea what he's doing, and hoping for the best...not the tightest operation we've ever planned!' said Al.

'No, but it's all we've got for now, unless by the time we land Porter has managed to find Ananya and can tell us everything.' He checked his phone for any new messages, but there was nothing.

'Now we really are scraping the barrel of hope!'

'We sure are, but at least we have the advantage of surprise. He won't know that we're following him now.'

'Unless he connects the dots and figures out that during your search of his office, which he will know about, that you found his flight details.'

'It's possible, but not probable. Anyway, we can't worry about that now. We're landing in an hour and we should get some rest, it's going to be a long night.'

They had both sat in silence for the rest of the flight, thinking about the mission ahead of them. They had both been in much tougher spots before, but had always had the backing of a team, a full intelligence profile, some reconnaissance, and the proper equipment. However shortly before landing a message had come in from Porter, not revealing the details of Lionel's plan, but with an address of where some secret Task Force weapons were cached. So they emerged from the airport into the evening heat of Khartoum feeling optimistic and focused. They hailed a cab and gave him the address.

Jerry watched the city streets go by and noted their difference to the streets of Lagos. Khartoum clearly had a much more Arabic feel to its streets, with many more people wearing the traditional Arabic robes - men in white and women in black. The faces of the people were darker, their noses rounder and wider than in Nigeria. The architecture also had a much more Arabic influence, with high white walls and decorative arches.

The streets were chaotic and were flanked not by sidewalks, but by sandy verges, full of busy workers. The air was thick with dust blowing in from the desert, and gave the dark sky a stormy look despite the searing desert heat.

The cab waited outside the address of the weapons cache - a small industrial unit down a quiet backstreet. They entered through a side door and just a few minutes later were on their way again, with Glock pistols in their belts and Hamner folding stock assault carbines stashed in their bags. They both felt much better and far less exposed to have weapons at hand, particularly as they were heading into a totally unknown situation against a man who had already shown deadly intent towards them. It was also very likely that he would be armed, as would any guards he had with him.

Twenty minutes later they spotted the Windsor Hotel, sitting on the south bank of the Blue Nile, just a few hundred metres from its confluence point with the White Nile coming from the south. They stopped the driver two hundred metres short of the hotel and stepped out into the night. The streets were lit by a dull orange lamp every fifty metres, giving them the chance to discreetly move closer to the hotel entrance and find a suitable observation post. They found a small tea shop across the street and took seats by the window, with a relatively clear line of sight across to the entrance, which was approximately forty metres away. A parked car and the steady stream of traffic obstructed their view, but it was better to have a slightly compromised view than to be exposed on the side of the street. They settled down to wait, sipping glasses of sweet milky karak tea as they watched.

They had not even had time to finish their tea before Lionel emerged from the high doors of the hotel entrance. He was alone, and carrying a brown soft-leather briefcase. Jerry's heart raced and he felt a surge of adrenaline pump into his veins as he realised that a snatch may be possible after all. They rose and swiftly left the shop, being careful not to attract attention to themselves. Lionel stood on the front steps of the hotel, casually observing the street. He checked his watch and looked up the street. Was he waiting for someone? Now was the time to snatch him, before his security or whoever he was meeting got there.

'Al, we've got to move on him now. As we discussed. You go east down the street a hundred metres and then come at him, hugging the buildings, I'll do the same from the west. No fireworks or shouting, just show him the pistols and take him quickly and quietly. We'll head for that side street down there' he gestured. 'Okay? Let's do it.'

Slinging the bags over their shoulders they separated and made their way along the street, staying in the shadows as much as possible in case Lionel happened to see them. There was a steady flow of pedestrians and cars on the street too, which gave them just enough cover to blend in. Jerry crossed the street at a gap in the traffic, keeping his head low and hurrying over, despite his leg aching and making him limp. In his peripheral vision he could see Lionel still standing alone at the entrance, still looking up the street straight past him. He hadn't been spotted. As he reached the buildings on the other side he turned sharply left and began to walk down the line of shops. He quickly glanced up and could see Al coming in the opposite direction, and Lionel still alone. Jerry reached behind him and retrieved the pistol from his belt, under his shirt, holding it at the small of his back. His heart quickened as he paced closer towards the hotel, hoping that Lionel wouldn't turn his head from the street towards him. He was just fifty metres away now.

He dropped his hand and carried the pistol close to his side, ready for action, but then Lionel walked down the steps from the entrance towards the street. His eyes were fixed on a vehicle approaching as he kept walking out into the road. *Fuck! Too late.* An SUV pulled up and Lionel opened the rear door and got in, slamming the door quickly behind him. The SUV immediately pulled away into the stream of traffic.

Shit! He turned to the street and looked for a cab, pushing the pistol back into his belt as he searched. Al ran up to him.

'Fuck, that was close. I'm tracking the car, white SUV, they haven't turned off the street yet.'

A cab pulled up and they jumped in.

'That way, fast' Jerry ordered the driver. The driver gave them a quick look and then pulled away with a screech.

'Where you going boss?'

'Just keep going this way for now' said Jerry, scanning the line of traffic ahead of them for the SUV. he spotted it turning right two hundred metres ahead. 'Take that right, see the SUV? Faster now.'

The driver nodded and put his foot down, undercutting the traffic along the sandy verge. They were fast closing on the turn, Jerry craned his neck to see round the corner to spot the SUV again. There it was, cruising along the road.

'Follow the white SUV, okay?' said Jerry to the driver.

'Okay boss' said the driver, making the right turn. The road was busy, the city was alive with shoppers heading to malls and souks, and was flanked with traders plying their wares from makeshift stalls.

'We'll have to switch to surveillance now' Jerry whispered to Al. 'See what he's up to tonight and then try to hit him in the hotel later.'

'Okay. Fuck that was close!'

'Yeah, that would have been a great grab if we'd had the time. But his security would have been right behind us anyway, so probably best we didn't do it then. Looks like he's heading into town so he's unlikely to be launching any sort of operation tonight. I think we've still got time.'

'Well we don't think he's launching tonight, but what if his operation is a hit here in Khartoum? He could be on his way to do it right now. What was in that briefcase? It could be the weapon, ready to be deployed in a crowded area.'

'Shit I hadn't thought of that. We'd been assuming it was going to be an attack on Chad, but it could be happening right here and now. Are any of those ethnicities listed also present here in the Republic? Specifically in Khartoum?'

'I'm not sure. We could check with Porter.'

'Yeah get on it, I'll find out where we might be going.' He leaned forward to talk to the driver. 'Excuse me, where does this road lead to?' He indicated a road one hundred metres ahead, where the SUV was turning right, joining a busier one-way street. Jerry realised he was sweating, his shirt was sticking to his back and shoulders.

'Government buildings, universities, maybe souk' replied the driver.

'Shit, they're all good targets' he muttered to himself. He turned to Al, 'there are government buildings, universities and a souk on the route we're on.'

Al raised his eyebrows in alarm as he put the phone to his ear. 'Shit' he whispered, then 'Hey Porter, it's Al…'

Jerry sat back and looked out of the window. *Shit, what if this is it? What if the field tests that were done in Chad were on the specific ethnicities that are found in Khartoum? And the shipment delivered to the Republic was actually the weapon being delivered here? Maybe it's just a hit job on one person? It's a bit elaborate for a single target, it must be bigger scale. Maybe we need to take him out right now before he has the chance to deploy it.* He gently rotated his wrist to relieve the throbbing pain.

Al finished up his call with Porter. 'He says there are five ethnicities common to both Chad and Sudan, and they include the Toubou, which Porter said was specifically listed in the initial intelligence report.'

'Fuck, is he planning to deploy a weapon on Toubous in Khartoum tonight?'

'It's a theory. Porter hasn't uncovered anything else yet.'

'God, if only we knew something else, we'd be able to make a more informed decision.' He wiped his brow and took a deep breath. 'Should have got a bottle of water. It's crazy hot here and my hand is sore as hell.'

'Yeah I'm sweating like a horse' said Al. 'Hopefully he's going to a turkish baths, or a swimming pool, or a bar!'

Jerry admired Al's ability to be light-hearted in even the most stressful of situations. He smiled. 'Let's hope so, but I'd settle for just a dark street where we can ambush him.'

The line of cars was having to wait to join the busy road ahead, and the SUV pulled away, merging into the traffic. They were still stuck a hundred metres back. They would lose them if they didn't catch up.

'Hey man, cut down the line' Jerry instructed the driver. He pointed sharply down the road. 'Fast?'

The driver hesitated and looked at Jerry, and then at the traffic behind him in his mirror.

'Can't boss. They'll take my licence boss.'

Jerry looked around. There were no police anywhere, but it was a good point, if they were pulled over now they'd really be in the shit, carrying illegal weapons through the city streets. Jerry quickly weighed up the options. The risk of being caught was far less than the cost of losing Lionel, who had already long since disappeared around the corner. He fished in his pocket and produced a fifty dollar note.

'Fifty dollars? US Dollars!' he handed the note to the driver, who had one final thought before he nodded and turned the wheel, racing down the inside of the line of traffic. At the end he cut in, ignoring the horns of the angry drivers behind him, and pushed his way into the traffic on the busy street. Jerry scanned the traffic ahead for the SUV, but it was nowhere to be seen. He craned his neck to see further down the road, cursing the buses blocking his view, but still nothing. Lionel and the SUV were gone.

'Fuck it!' Jerry slammed the seat in front of him. 'That was our only chance. He could be about to kill hundreds or even thousands of people and we can't even tail him properly.'

Al continued to scan the street ahead, searching for any sign of the SUV. 'He must be up there somewhere. He can't have just disappeared, but he's not on this road. He must have turned off.'

'Are there any side streets?' Jerry asked the driver. 'Can he turn off this road?'

'Yes boss, there on the right' he gestured to a small dark side street two hundred metres ahead. A small van was emerging from it and turning right into the traffic.

Has he switched vehicles? Is he on to us? How could he be? Fuck, we're really clutching at straws now.

'Slow down there' he instructed the driver. The car slowed and they studied the dark street. Only the first hundred metres was visible, in which there were a few cars and motorbikes parked, but no sign of the SUV.

Where is the next turning?' he asked.

'Up there boss. On the left.'

Around five hundred metres ahead was a major intersection with a left turn, controlled by a traffic signal. *Could he have made it through there before we turned the corner? It's our only chance right now.*

'It's possible he made it down there before we saw him' said Al, having the same thought. 'Where else could he be?'

'Go! Fast!' Jerry ordered. He leaned forward anxiously, staring at the intersection in the vain hope of spotting a clue.

'What's down that road mate?' Al asked the driver.

'Souk, mall, hotel' came the reply.

'They'd all make good targets. But unless we catch up with him we have no idea which one he's going to' Jerry sighed.

A few seconds later they turned left at the intersection, tyres screeching as they hit it at speed. Ahead of them another

175

busy street stretched away for a kilometre or more. The street was alive with hundreds of people making their way along and across the road. The shops and buildings alongside the street were lit and bustling with customers coming and going.

'Lots of people, lots of targets' said Al.

'He wouldn't blow it randomly on a street like this. With the care he's been taking to keep it quiet I'd say the target is much bigger.'

After a bit more questioning of the driver, as well as urging him to drive faster, the established that the nearest viable target was a mall just about a kilometre down the road. With no sign of Lionel and no prospect of catching him now, they agreed to quickly check the mall before heading back to the hotel to wait for him to return.

'You know, a mall is a pretty strange venue if he's just targeting Toubou with a chemical weapon. There won't exactly be a concentration of them there, I assume.' said Jerry as they approached it.

'Yeah I could think of better places for sure, but it may be a particular hang-out for Toubou.'

The driver pulled into a side street running alongside what looked like a large office building. He continued to cruise along the street slowly.

'This is shopping mall' he explained, pointing to the building. They looked up doubtfully at its many floors stretching into the sky. 'Also hotel' clarified the driver.

They scanned the vehicles parked outside, searching for the white SUV, by now fearing the worst, but hoping for a lucky break.

'There!' said Jerry, pointing fifty metres down the street. A white SUV was parked facing toward the mall, with its tail lights still on.

'Shit, is that him?' said Al.

'We couldn't be that lucky. It can't be.'

The driver pulled over short of the SUV and they watched as the SUV's occupants got out. Jerry's heart leapt.

'Fuck yes! I can't believe it!' whispered Jerry. 'This is a seriously lucky break Al, so let's not waste it. Let's stay alert and be ready to take him down if we suspect he's going to launch. We'll just have to deal with the political flak afterwards. Now it'll be busy there, which means plenty of cover, but we'll have to be sharp. Use close follow technique so we can take him out more easily, you'll be on point, I'll hang back right. Shoot Lionel first because he's most likely to have the weapon in that briefcase.'

'Roger that' said Al as he discreetly checked his pistol.

'Will they have automatic scanners at the entrances?' asked Jerry. 'It's standard in western malls, but what about here?'

'They must have, it's common technology now' replied Al. 'We should leave the bags with the rifles here in the cab. Maybe I should stay with them and you go?'

'No, we need to follow him in a pair, we'll pay this guy to stick around.'

'What if he looks in the bags?'

'Well then we lose the rifles, but we don't have any other options. We're unsupported. Stash the pistols and let's do a quick comms check.' They tested their devices - flesh-coloured stickers the size of a finger nail which were stuck to the jawbone under the ear, and enabled them to speak to and hear each other through micro-vibrations. It gave them discreet secure communications without having to use a phone, or have a very obvious earpiece in their ear.

Lionel was walking towards the mall with the briefcase in his hand; one security guard was following him. Jerry pushed another note into the driver's hand and told him to wait for them. They got out quickly, eager not to lose him in the crowds. They followed him briskly, without drawing attention to themselves by running. Once they were twenty metres behind him they split into close follow formation. Jerry hung back and to the right as Al walked directly behind Lionel. The crowds entering the mall provided cover for them and they were able to easily follow him. Jerry watched every move Lionel made, looking for the slightest indication that he might be about to take out any sort of weapon. *What the hell does the weapon even look like?*

As they entered the mall Jerry noted the automatic scanning panels above the doorways, designed to hastily scan every person entering the mall for weapon shapes as well as sniffing the air for traces of peroxide and other bomb-making chemicals, which often leaked from explosive devices without being detectable by the human nose. They had stashed their pistols deep down inside their underwear, under their crotches, where the scanners were impeded by the heat and smell. Once through the doors Jerry took a brief moment to survey its interior. The entrance foyer was a cavernous open space three floors high, with three triple-height lanes leading off from it, one directly ahead and one left and right. The mall was brightly lit, and the decor was of smooth white stone, with decorative gold detail on the walls. It was a very contemporary building, and was packed full of Arabic shoppers, some laden with bags, others wandering socially.

Lionel was heading down the right-hand lane. Jerry looked at the signpost which indicated he was heading towards the Shoe Gallery, Restaurants and the Excelsior Hotel. Lionel was striding purposefully down the lane now, past the brightly lit colourful shops, closely followed by his security. His black shirt and silver hair made him easy to follow in the crowds, except for the flow of shoppers coming towards them, which they had to weave between, whilst also keeping the briefcase firmly in focus.

The lane turned sharply to the left. On the corner to the right were some large doors with Excelsior Hotel emblazoned in gold above them. Lionel strode towards the doors and pushed through them. Jerry and Al exchanged a quick glance to acknowledge they should hang back a further ten metres. The hotel foyer would not be as busy as the mall and so would not provide the same amount of cover for them.

'If he's going up in an elevator we'll have to split' said Jerry. 'I'll follow him up to whichever floor he goes to, and you wait in the foyer in case he comes down without me seeing. Stay in comms.'

'Roger, I'll find a spot in cover facing the elevator doors' said Al in Jerry's ear. 'Good luck mate.'

They pushed through the hotel entrance doors and emerged into the lavish foyer of the Excelsior Hotel. It was an explosion of gold, with tall pillars stretching to the high ceiling and ornate chandeliers hanging low. Beyond the reception desks on the left and right was a sitting area that spanned the whole foyer, with luxurious couches interspersed with magnificent flower arrangements. Jerry estimated there were one hundred people in the foyer, which gave them the barest of covers. Busy places were always better, as was a larger surveillance team, but they would have to work with what they had now.

Lionel had strode straight past the check-in desk and turned left without breaking his stride. He clearly knew where he was going and didn't need a key. It made Jerry nervous to be following down a much narrower hotel corridor with twists and turns, where they had no idea of the layout. It had ambush written all over it.

'Let's tread carefully here Al. It looks like he won't be taking the elevator. We don't want to be surprised round the next corner.'

'Roger, I'll lead then' said Al. 'I'll give you the all clear.'

Al stepped around the corner to the right and disappeared from Jerry's view. Jerry waited nervously, waiting for the sound of gunfire if they had been sprung.

'All clear mate, looks like he's heading for the restaurant.'

Jerry turned the corner and followed twenty metres behind Al, who was casually pacing down the corridor and past the restaurant entrance on the left.

'He's heading for private booths at two o'clock' commentated Al. 'There's some heavy security there waiting for him.'

'Roger, I'll stop and take a look.'

Jerry followed behind, looking as casual as possible, smiling at the restaurant staff waiting at the entrance. He stopped to look at the menu and looked over it into the restaurant. It was about half full, and the chatter was relatively quiet. A suited man played piano in the corner. As Al had said, at the back right of the restaurant he could see Lionel entering one of four private booths, separated from the rest of the room by head height screening. Each booth appeared to be a walled room with a smoked glass door, making surveillance inside the room impossible. Al had been right, outside the booth was a security detail much bigger and more formidable than Lionel's guard, who stood beside them. Two men were stood by the door, dressed in traditional arabic robes and headdress, and two men in black shirts, trousers and jackets stood next to them, silently scanning the room. They were not making any attempt to disguise the fact that they were a security detail, which had to mean that there was a VIP or extremely wealthy person in the booth.

Jerry thought fast. *We can't effectively watch them from out in the corridor, so we'll have to take a table, or a booth? No, we wouldn't be able to hear anything and then we're stuck in there. Better to take a table in a vantage point.* He mentally chose the best table and summoned Al. They entered the restaurant and indicated their preferred table to the maitre'd, taking their seats with Al facing the booth and Jerry facing Al.

'What do you see?' asked Jerry.

'Four security, looks like they've got concealed weapons. The arabs under their robes on their right legs, and the westerners on their left hips. Lionel's security isn't carrying.'

'If they got weapons in here then there must be a serious VIP in that booth with Lionel.'

'Yeah, only government would be allowed to have armed security in here.'

'Who the hell is he meeting?' said Jerry. 'A VIP, presumably from the Republic? What is going on?'

'Maybe as those notes said, the Republic really has developed a weapon, and now Lionel is buying it?'

'This is a strange place to buy a biological weapon.'

'It's as good as any. It's probably a bit obvious to travel out to a secret research facility in the desert. A bit too cliched.'

'I guess so, but we need to get our eyes on the inside of that booth. Keep watching it.'

A waitress approached and they ordered a bottle of water.

'I'll take some test photos' said Al. 'In case I can get a shot into the door when it's opened.' He closed his right eye, activating the contact lens in his left eye. As he focused his eye sharply on the door the camera lens followed suit, and took a burst of still images, which were then transferred automatically to his phone. He flicked through them on the phone. 'Yep, camera is working fine. Thank God for Porter and his team of geeks.'

'Yeah, it's good tech, but it's only as good as the operator, so make sure you get that shot. We need to know who is in there with him. Porter will be able to run a scan on the photograph.'

A waiter was approaching the booth. Al again closed his right eye and prepared to focus on the inside of the booth.

'Door opening' he said. 'I see a woman. Focusing now.' The camera did its job and Jerry picked up the phone to look at the images.

'The zoom is good. Clarity is good. You've got some good shots. Get a few sent to Porter straight away so he can start working on them.' Al took the phone and began the upload.

'She does not look like someone that is selling a genetic weapon' said Jerry. 'Let's take another look at the photographs.'

They looked at an image. She appeared to be of arabic origin, and was wearing a black robe, with her hair covered, as was customary. They studied her face. She had large dark eyes with long lashes, a thin nose and full lips. She looked serious, no smiling.

'She's a looker' said Al. 'Maybe Lionel's got himself a girlfriend?'

'They certainly wouldn't be meeting in a private booth in a hotel restaurant if he did' said Jerry. 'She'd be flogged if she was meeting a man in private, especially a western man, so it must be above board. I'm wondering why a woman like that has such heavy security. She must be either a government minister or royalty, which begs the question of why is Lionel meeting a senior female in the Republic that he isn't trying to get into bed?'

'I guess he has to be either buying or selling something then.'

'So when Simon's notes said that the shipment had been delivered, perhaps it meant that the Republic had received a shipment of something from Lionel? Maybe this woman is buying a genetic weapon from Lionel, which has been made by Ananya?' said Jerry.

'Christ on a bike' said Al. 'Maybe that's what the field test was then. Ananya tested it before they made the sale.'

'So that could mean that the weapon is already here somewhere in the Republic, and we have no chance of finding it. Shit! All we can do is take Lionel down and see what we can get from him. At least we know his guard doesn't have a weapon. We won't be able to take out the security to get to her, so we'll never know what she's up to.'

Al's phone buzzed. A message had come in from Porter.

Image is of the President's third wife, named Aishah. Known to us as Agent Fisher.

Chapter Twenty

'Fisher?' said Al. They both sat in shock, stunned by what they had just read.

'Fisher is the President's wife? That is some heavy undercover work. What the hell...?' Jerry couldn't finish his sentence, he was so confused.

'So we've got an agent inside the Republic. It's the President's wife. And Lionel is meeting her pretty much in public?' Al said slowly, thinking out loud.

'I guess they couldn't really meet in private. How would she get away from her security? But what the hell is going on? Is she in with him on his plan then?'

'Beats me. I just can't believe we managed to recruit royalty to be an agent!'

'Let's work this through. We know that Lionel has a secret plan, and it must be illegal because he tried to kill me when I discovered it. The plan involves Chad and the Republic, and something to do with a field test and a shipment to the Republic. We're assuming he has come here as part of that plan, and we can also assume that Fisher is involved too. She was the agent that submitted the intelligence report from two years ago on the genetic research facility, so maybe she and Lionel have been collaborating to monitor the facility's progress and then steal the research?'

'Which she is now handing over to him in that booth?'

'Maybe. But then what is Ananya's role in this?'

'Maybe she will be weaponising the product that he's buying' suggested Al.

'That figures' said Jerry. 'But hang on, how does a President's wife steal genetic research from what is presumably a secret facility?'

'She got it from the President?'

'Hmm, that bit doesn't make sense. She is surely going to be very limited in what she can do as the President's wife. She'll just be collecting pillow talk, gossip from the palace, and maybe influencing him.'

'So maybe she's discovered the location of the facility and is now telling him?'

'That does make sense' agreed Jerry. 'She's just sharing her intelligence. Right under her guards' noses...that's pretty ballsy.'

'Or...the President knows who she is and is communicating with Lionel through her?' posited Al.

'It's possible, but why wouldn't he just set up a meeting himself? It attracts much more attention to send your wife to do it.'

Al's phone buzzed again. Another note from Porter.

Further notes on Fisher:

Syrian born, in 2002. Orphaned during civil war in 2014. No known siblings. Raised in Jordan.

She has been an agent for three years now, all of which under her current pseudonym - Aishah.

Placed in Republic with specific intent of penetrating palace.

Met President Apr 2029, married Nov 2029.
Other than her report 4 Aug 2028 on the establishment of the research facility, her reports have been routine, with no mention of facility.

Also, highly increased security around Task Force locations. Looks like they're searching for us, using police and army too. Look out.

'So she's our spy on the inside of the Republic' said Al. 'When did Lionel corrupt her?'

'I don't know, but we need to get inside that booth now. If we can talk to them both at once then we can beat the truth out of them.'

'Hang on a second buddy' said Al. 'There are five guards out front there, four of them armed, and maybe more in reserve. How do you think we're going to get in that booth?'

'I could pretend to be a waiter' suggested Jerry.

'Yeah, there are probably some perfectly fitting waiter outfits just out back there, right next to a tray of drinks waiting to be delivered to the booth.'

Jerry smiled. 'I guess that's unlikely.'

'We could always shoot our way in. Take them by surprise. We could take out the guards pretty fast and then snatch Lionel and Fisher.'

'The unknown backup concerns me. Any of these customers could be backup, or someone out in the hotel foyer. She is royalty after all' said Jerry.

'Yeah and then we'd have to fight our way out of the building with two hostages. That won't work. Well we'd better think fast, because we don't know how long they'll be in there.'

'Alright, how about we give up being able to get to her. She's too well protected. We'll just grab Lionel later, because it doesn't look like this is the beginning of the operation, so we have some time.'

'That's the smartest idea I think, and the one most likely to keep us alive.'

'Okay then, let's get out of here before we get spotted.'

Forty minutes later they watched out of the rear window of the cab as Lionel and his guard emerged from the mall, got into the SUV and pulled out into traffic. Jerry gave the word and the driver pulled away, ten cars in front of the SUV. They made the rest of the journey back to the hotel checking the SUV was still behind them, preparing themselves for the action to come. As they turned on to the hotel's street they sped up to make some space between them and Lionel, pulling up on the verge fifty metres before the hotel. They exited the cab quickly, bags on shoulders, and hurried through the dark shadows to within ten metres of the hotel entrance, where they turned to pretend to look in through a window and quickly stashed their bags in a corner. Behind them the SUV pulled up, and they watched in the window as a door opened and Lionel emerged alone, just as they had hoped. The car pulled away and they quickly turned, pistols drawn and headed straight for him.

As he began climbing the five short steps to the entrance, they quickly emerged from the shadows. Lionel looked to his left and saw them, pausing with disbelief for the briefest of moments before he ran. He didn't go more than tep steps before Al was on him, crashing down on top of him in a perfect tackle.

'How the fuck…?' said Lionel.

'Hello Lionel, surprised to see us?' said Jerry, bending down to look Lionel in the face. 'Did you think we'd be hiding in some hole back in Lagos?'

'You should be, or better still you should have died' Lionel grunted.

'We didn't want to miss the party.' Al pulled Lionel up from the floor and held his arms behind his back. 'With you and your girlfriend at the Excelsior tonight.'

Lionel looked defiant and gave a sneer. 'So what? You saw me with someone. You don't know anything. You're way out of your depth. If I were you I'd run now.'

'We're done with running. We'll just walk instead. Let's go.'

Al frog-marched Lionel down the steps and began down the street, away from the entrance. Jerry stooped to pick up the weapon bags, grunting with the pain in his hand as he hoisted them up. He indicated to Al that they should cross the street and get away from the hotel as soon as possible. There was still a steady stream of traffic on the road, so they had to wait for a few seconds, leaning against a parked car.

As they waited Jerry thought about how he would get information out of Lionel. They had to work fast and he was going to be tough to crack. He remembered his tactical questioning training and quickly thought through the various techniques he had been taught to extract genuine information without the need for threats, though he suspected that it may have to come to that. This was not a regular operation and they didn't have the luxury of time. First though would be to try and play on Lionel's vanity, and to mock the information out of him.

As they stepped out into the street Lionel thrust his arms downward, releasing Al's grip on him; he started to run. Jerry reacted and quickly caught up with him, swiftly pistol whipping him on the back of the neck and sending him down onto his knees. Al picked him up again before any passing drivers stopped to ask questions. They continued across the street and found a dark passage, which led between some buildings and down to the riverbank. They followed it down until they emerged onto a broken concrete path running along the river, dotted with dim lights. They turned right and walked briskly.

'My men will catch us in a minute. You'd better start saying your prayers boys' said Lionel.

Jerry stopped and faced him. 'You'd better start saying yours Lionel, because the game's up. Your little scheme is over and you're going to go to jail for a very long time. I hear the Republic jails are particularly nasty, especially for traitors and thieves.'

'Traitors?'

'Yes, you think we don't know who Fisher is? You've been using her to subvert the Republic. I expect she's going to be treated to a very lengthy interview, during which she will tell us everything about your little deal.'

'Do you really think I'd tell her anything about the mission? You can ask her all you like, she knows nothing. She's just a small cog in the big machine.'

'She's been stealing state secrets to give to you. I'd say that makes her pretty big, and pretty dangerous to you and your scheme.'

'Stealing state secrets?' Lionel laughed. 'I alway knew you were small-time Jerry. That's why I never brought you on board. You don't have the imagination or the wit to see and do what needs doing.'

'I don't need imagination to see that you're stealing genetic research to make a dirty weapon. What are you going to do? Sell it to the highest bidder? I'd say you're the one lacking imagination Lionel.'

'If it wasn't so sad I'd laugh at you Jerry. Floundering around making up your schoolboy theories while the big boys change the world. You've got no goddam idea how the world works Jerry, where the power lies, and who calls the shots. Whoever controls the resources holds the power. It's always been that way; the rich guys are in charge, not the fucking good guys. They're busy making speeches and writing policy papers while the really powerful people control the world. You still think that good will prevail and bad guys don't win? Look around you Jerry. Bad shit happening everywhere, every day, on a scale you can't even comprehend and you still cling to the pathetic hope that you can change the world by bringing peace and stability to Africa, one hostage rescue at a time? If you had imagination you'd see the real solution to the African problem. It just needs someone to think the unthinkable and have the balls to make it happen.'

'Newsflash Lionel, it takes more than wealth and a chip on your shoulder to change the world. Even if you've managed to get a spy into a government, and you think you have a chance to steal a weapon, do you really think anyone will pay you off?

You know as well as I do that you'll be murdered before you can even make your demands.'

Lionel didn't react. Jerry continued to fish for clues.

'Extortion and blackmail didn't even work thirty years ago when governments were weak and liberal, let alone now. This is the time of action, not fantasy spy plots.'

'You can keep trying to goad me into giving you some information if you like' said Lionel calmly, 'but the longer you waste your time here the closer my men get.'

'It doesn't even matter if you don't tell us now' retorted Jerry. 'You'll talk eventually.'

'I don't think so. I think in a few minutes you'll be dead, and in a few days I'll forget you ever existed. Although I confess that may be tough, because I honestly had high hopes for you once upon a time. I thought you were a smart guy who could see the truth, but it turns out I overestimated you. You're a pussy Jerry; you're not cut out for this kind of thing, so just give it up.'

'I may be a pussy, but you're still nothing more than a thief, and when you're languishing in a cell somewhere in the hot desert you'll be thinking how close you came to changing the world, but then you'll realise that no-one remembers you, and nothing has changed.'

'Do you think it's over? Do you really think that because you've got me that this thing isn't going to happen? Come on Jerry, think big! The wheels are already in motion and you can't stop it now. Why do you think I had to have Simon killed? He didn't share our vision any more, he wanted to get off the train, so I had to push him off.'

Jerry paused and thought for a moment. Had Simon been about to confess to him that evening outside his office? As he thought he didn't see Lionel's foot suddenly lash out and make contact with his left leg, just under the knee. He crumpled as the white pain flooded through his leg and he almost blacked out. As he fell, Lionel viciously threw back his head and butted Al in the nose, at the same time scraping his shoe down Al's shin. He turned and ran as Al bent over and held his face in shock.

'Fuck, come on!' said Jerry, struggling to his feet, helped by Al. They chased him back along the riverbank and up the dark passage. They emerged onto the street, which was still humming with city traffic, despite it being after midnight. They saw Lionel dodging between cars and making for the hotel. They rushed into the road, forcing cars to swerve around them as they ran for the other side, turning right and chasing Lionel down.

Jerry raised his pistol to shoot, but Lionel was already pushing through the entrance doors. They ran after him up the steps and through the doors, bowling into the foyer area noisily, quickly concealing their weapons as the reception staff turned to look at them. Lionel was disappearing round a corner to the right and they quickly followed him, Al leading as Jerry's injured leg held him back.

Lionel was heading down some flights of stairs, into a basement. Jerry guessed he must be trying to get to the SUV, and therefore his security guards. He hoped Al was fast enough to catch him in time. A shot rang out in the stairwell, followed by another. Jerry raced to the top of the stairs as quickly as he could, calling Al's name. He burst into the stairwell, pistol raised, ready to fire, and saw nothing. A quick glance down the stairwell revealed nothing; just three empty flights of stairs and an open door, presumably into the car park. More shots rang out as he descended as quickly as he could, cursing his injured leg.

When he reached the bottom of the stairs there was heavy gunfire coming from the car park. It sounded like Lionel had reached his security guards and they were now engaged in a firefight with Al. He knelt down and glanced around the corner, where he saw Al crouching behind a car just five metres from the door. Lionel's SUV was about twenty metres away to the right. Both guards were behind it, with Lionel nowhere to be seen. Jerry knew he and Al had to win this firefight soon before they ran out of ammunition. He took four hastily aimed shots at the guards, hoping to keep their heads down as he prepared to run.

Al took over the covering fire as Jerry took a deep breath and sprinted as fast as his leg would allow, out of the doorway, firing at the SUV as he ran. He continued past Al, crouching low now behind the cover of cars. He quickly made a plan and decided he had to circle round to the left so he could outflank the guards and attack them from the side. Al's fire from the front would hopefully distract them and give him some freedom of movement. He stopped to take a quick breath, risking a look through a car window towards the SUV. He was almost in line with the car, giving him the angle he needed. He just had to make the dash across the lane and he would be able to fire on them from the side while Al fired from the front, denying them any cover and giving them nowhere to run.

He prepared to make the dash when he saw Lionel creeping around the back of the SUV, with a pistol in his hand. He had had the same idea as Jerry, to outflank Al. Lionel knew that the guards had Al pinned down with fire and just needed to get an angle on him. He was preparing to cross the lane and surprise Al. Now was the time, before Lionel had a chance to move. Abandoning the dash plan, Jerry quickly raised himself up to a squat and lifted his pistol onto the car hood, resting on it for stability. Lionel still hadn't seen him so he took careful aim at Lionel's trunk and fired a double-tap. Lionel crumpled to the ground, dropping his pistol as he gripped his side. Jerry aimed again and fired, just as Lionel dragged himself back behind a car. The bullets ricocheted off the ground by his foot.

Without wasting a moment Jerry dashed across the lane. Lionel was at his most vulnerable now and he had to capitalise on his advantage. Once in cover behind cars on the other side Jerry sank to the floor and laid down on his side, looking under the cars towards the SUV. Only two car widths away he could see Lionel leaning against the front wheel of a car. He saw one of the guards come to his aid and kneel down beside him. Jerry took aim, controlled his breathing and squeezed the trigger. The guard yelled and fell to the right, clutching his thigh, where Jerry's bullet had shattered his bone. Jerry re-aimed and fired twice again, this time at the base of the tyre, hoping to ricochet up into Lionel's leg or back. There was no movement. Either he had missed or Lionel was already dead.

As he prepared to fire more shots he felt a bullet whizz by his head, smashing into the car behind him. He rolled out of the way as another followed it, followed by another in the car protecting him. Al had stopped firing, probably having run out of ammunition, and was lying low, which didn't help him at all. Jerry checked his magazine - only two or three rounds remaining. He had to end this quickly while he still had some firepower..

As Jerry steeled himself to make a charge, Al shouted out that the guards were getting into the car. He looked up from cover. He saw one of the guards piling Lionel into the back of the SUV, before another bullet came whistling past his head as the other fired at him. So they were both alive, and maybe Lionel too. As he thought of what to do next the guard was in the SUV, which then roared into life and immediately screeched away to the left and towards the exit. Jerry was on his feet and pursuing it, firing his last three shots as he ran. They ricocheted off the bulletproof glass and the SUV was gone. Again, they had lost him, and this time it didn't look likely they'd catch up with him.

In the distance he heard the wail of sirens as the police approached; they had perhaps thirty seconds to escape. The hotel staff would have alerted them. The foyer was too risky so they headed for the vehicle exit. As they neared the ramp a police car screeched around the corner and they ducked in cover. It was too risky to use the ramp now, they would certainly be spotted. They looked around for another exit point and saw a fire escape door.

Two minutes later they were out on the street in front of the hotel and had retrieved their bags and were slinking back into the shadows, making their way down the street as hastily as they could.

'Shit. We just blew our main chance of finding out what the hell is going on' said Jerry as they walked.

'If only I'd had more ammo, I'd have been able to fix them for longer' said Al.

'No use worrying about that' Jerry reassured him. 'We weren't planning on a major firefight. We did what we could. Besides, I think I managed to fatally wound Lionel. Two shots in the side, and maybe two in the back. He'll most likely bleed out before they can get him to a doctor.'

'Well let's hope the plan dies with him. I wonder what the plan actually was.'

'What it actually *is*, according to Lionel. He said it was bigger than just him. Though that could have just been hyperbole.'

'Maybe, but he did seem quite confident that it was going to change the world. That does seem like more than a one man operation. What was it he said? "To think the unthinkable"...I can't think what he meant.'

'...and have the balls to make it happen' continued Jerry. 'Maybe he was going to assassinate someone?'

'He also spoke about control, and those in control were the ones with the power.'

'Those in control of *resources* have the power, he said'

'Well the days of oil are numbered, and there are precious few other resources left now, they've all been ripped out of the ground already' said Al.

'Yeah, it's pretty much been hollowed out. But maybe he was talking about a resource like the genetic research. Maybe that is what gives you power now? Holding the power of genetics, to cure or destroy people at will.'

194

'*Or* maybe the people are the resource!...' said Al. 'If you can control them then you have the power.'

'Well it's a hell of a riddle' said Jerry, 'and we haven't solved it yet. And if we believe Lionel, the plan is still out there, with or without him, wheels rolling, unable to be stopped.'

'Well if he's dead then I wonder who's driving now?' said Al.

'Well we don't know for sure he's dead, not until we see a corpse, but like I said, even if his wounds don't kill him, they'll certainly take him out of action for the rest of the op. So there are two more potential drivers we have. One is Fisher, who will most likely be hung out to dry here when Porter tips off the police and they discover her involvement in whatever this is.'

'And the other is Ananya' said Al. 'Or at least she's the only other person whose name we know.'

'Yeah, she must have some answers for us. We need to get back to Lagos and find her.'

Chapter Twenty One

Captain Okoro sat in the passenger seat of his command vehicle, with his seat reclined as far as it would go, trying to get some sleep. It had been a very long day, from alerting the Commanding Officer of their orders, to calling out the Regiment and gathering and checking all equipment. Luckily his detachment were prepared for deployment anyway, thanks to their training, but the rest of the Regiment was not so ready. It had been early afternoon before they were ready to deploy, and they were rolling out of the camp in a long convoy, heading northeast. Military convoys were always fraught with problems, usually lost and broken down trucks, despite there being only one road for them to travel on. He had learned to always expect the unexpected, and never underestimate the capability of the soldier to screw something up.

After four hours of driving, during which he couldn't sleep because he had to command his vehicles and ensure they all stayed in formation and kept working, they reached the site in the desert which had been selected as their operating base. There followed the usual routine of hurrying up, and then waiting, and then hurrying up again, as Senior Non-Commissioned Officers from Regimental Headquarters barked orders and coordinated where each sub-unit would base itself. He had thought that if they really were at war then they would certainly be losing, as this was comical. The Republic could have invaded the country and overrun the capital by the time they had even parked their trucks or pitched a tent. However they eventually were given a position to set up the detachment and had got to work.

While his men were setting up the command station he attended orders at the mobile headquarters. The CO had presented his plan to the Regiment, giving orders to each sub-unit relating to their role in that overall plan. He had told them that the Republic had crossed the international border in a number of places from both Sudan State and Libya State. His Regiment's role was to patrol and protect the Sudan State borderlands, as well as for the Commandos to launch some strikes against militant groups taking refuge across the border in the Darfur region. Okoro's company were tasked to patrol the southern section of the border, looking out for militant vehicles and destroying them on sight. Thy had been ordered 'weapons free, meaning they had free rein to engage any targets they considered legitimate. This was an unusual step, as usually the targeting process was heavily controlled, requiring authentication and then authorisation from a commander before firing. However this was war, and a much more aggressive stance was being taken.

After the orders he had received further instructions from his company commander and had then briefed his men. They had launched the UAVs within an hour, the first of the detachments from the company to do so. The training and drills had paid off and they were operating efficiently, each man knowing his role and conducting it without the need for close monitoring. Okoro had remained in the command station for the first sortie, wanting to be present in case they had come across a target and were to make the first kill of the war. He had watched the live feed from the onboard multi-spectral camera, which combined infra red with thermal imaging to give a picture of the night time landscape almost as clearly as if it were day. It was also equipped with an automatic motion detector and tracker, which zoomed the camera onto any moving object in the field of view out to thirty kilometres, tracking and assessing it against the pre-programmed database of targets. It could classify the target and automatically fire a missile, or be set to manual fire, depending on the mission profile. This mission was manual fire, giving Okoro the decision of what to fire on. He was partially disappointed and partially relieved that they had not spotted any targets yet. As much as he relished the idea of the infamy that would come with making the first kill of the war, he did not want to be the commander that ordered it.

Their first patrol had ended without incident, and so he was trying to sleep at last, but his mind was racing with thoughts of what tomorrow would bring. He had heard the Commando helicopters launching a few hours before, off to make their strikes in the dark of the night. He wondered what the reaction would be tomorrow, or even tonight. Would there be a full-scale retaliation from the Republic? Would the Regiment come under attack? They were less than one hundred kilometres from the border, so any sort of attack would be possible. They could almost fire GPS-guided artillery that far, though the exact range of the Republic's weapons was secret so that was an estimate. He eventually closed his eyes, dreaming of air raid sirens.

It was a siren that woke him, wailing across the operating base, alerting everyone to the impending attack. He opened his eyes and sat up quickly, looking around him and wondering what time it was. It was just before dawn; the light of the sun was starting to glow beyond the horizon, flooding the land in a murky grey light. He must have slept for about three hours he thought.

The siren continued to wail and people were emerging from tents and vehicles, scrambling for their weapons, helmets and body armour and running for cover. The siren signalled an air attack, but it was not known what type of attack it would be. He grabbed his helmet and ran to the company commander's command station, a rectangular iron box, thirty feet long and twelve feet wide. His legs protested at the sudden exertion and his lungs hurt. He burst through the door panting and found the company commander sitting at a planning table. He looked up and beckoned Okoro over.

'Captain Okoro, the Republic has launched five drones against us - perhaps a retaliation for the Commando attacks. Number 4 detachment destroyed one of them shortly after it crossed into our airspace, but the Republic drones can fly much faster than ours. The drones are now within five minutes of being in range, before they can start launching against us. Their drones carry eight missiles each, which would overwhelm our defences. So go now, launch your aircraft and set them for automatic targeting.'

'Yes sir' said Okoro, and bolted from the room. He sprinted the hundred metres to his command station, shouting to his engineer team to get the aircraft ready for immediate launch. He crashed through the door and addressed the pilots and gunners.

'Immediate launch. We are under attack from the Republic drones and have less than five minutes to get out there and engage them before they get into our airspace. Set mission profile to seek and destroy their UAVs, with automatic targeting.'

The crews immediately set to work, performing their run-up checks and programming the mission profile. They worked quickly and efficiently, very familiar with their tasks. Okoro left the command station and went to check on his engineers, who were busily activating the launch systems and checking the weapons.

The two Russian-made Si-50 Interceptor UAVs were fearsome-looking aircraft. They were sandy-coloured aircraft, standing twelve feet tall and thirty feet long, with a wingspan of forty feet. There were four Raptor missiles attached to the underside of the wings, capable of air to air or air to ground attack, guided either by laser, GPS coordinates, or thermal guidance, as well as manual control. The UAV was able to launch two missiles simultaneously, one from each wing, and then again five seconds later, with each missile being independently guided by the aircraft or by the gunner. The engineers were finalising their weapon checks and pre-launch checks, ensuring all straps were released and missiles ready to fire. They reported their readiness to Okoro and stood back as the pilots took command of the aircraft.

The tail-mounted hydrogen jet engines whined into life, and the drones began to taxi away from the station towards the launch area, testing their avionics as they went. Within thirty seconds the drones had turned, begun their short launch run and were airborne, jetting away into the grey sky at full speed. As their engines faded into the distance Okoro went back into the command station and watched the monitors as the pilots monitored the aircraft, and the gunners double-checked the targeting profiles. The monitor showed the scene ahead of and below the drones, being fed from their nose-mounted cameras. The land was racing by, mile after mile of sandy emptiness, as the drones closed in on the approaching Republic drones. Okoro nervously watched the monitor for the first sign of movement ahead, feeling helpless to avert the impending attack.

Suddenly a light flashed on the pilot's control panel and an alarm sounded.

'Missile lock-on, Bird 1 is being engaged Sir' said one of the pilots.

'Range?' asked Okoro.

'Thirty kilometres. Time to impact ten seconds.'

'Lock on to missile and fire defensive Raptor' he ordered the gunner.

'Yes Sir, locking now. Launching. Missile away.'

The alarm continued to chime as they watched the missile roar ahead of the drone at Mach 12, quickly disappearing into the distance. Before it had disappeared the gunner spoke again.

'Target sighted, eighty one degrees, range twenty nine kilometres, speed one thousand knots.' Okoro looked at the monitor and saw the automatic targeting system zoom in on the approaching enemy drone, on the left of the monitor.

'Auto launch active. Missile away.' said the gunner. Again he watched a missile streak away from the drone. There was an explosion on the right of the monitor.

'Enemy missile destroyed Sir. Time to second target, three seconds.'

Another alarm sounded on the other pilot's control panel. The enemy drones were in range and closing fast. The pilots and gunners spoke fast, acknowledging and dealing with each new target as it appeared, but it was too much for Okoro to keep track of on both monitors. Both alarms chimed, the air raid siren wailed outside, and voices filled his ears as he tried to monitor the battle unfolding before him. A sharp voice cut through the noise.

'Bird 2 has been destroyed Sir. Direct missile hit.'

He looked down at the now blank monitor. Its alarm stopped chiming. The pilot and gunner sat back in their seats and looked down.

'It's okay, you fought well' he reassured them.

'Sir, we have three missiles incoming' shouted his command watchkeeper, sat at a different panel. 'Time to impact five seconds!'

'Take cover!' shouted Okoro. But he didn't need to, the crews had already dived beneath the control panels. He threw himself to the ground, under a planning table and rolled into a ball.

The command station was rocked by the shock of three simultaneous explosions, as the missiles found their targets around the base. The iron walls of the command station could withstand the blast waves without being damaged, but everything inside it rattled, rocked or fell over. The noise and vibration was deafening, as if the station was being pummelled by a barrage of giant fists. Okoro was sure the blasts were right outside his station, such was the noise. He tucked himself harder into a ball and waited for it to abate.

Once it had stopped rattling and the sound of the explosions had stopped, he slowly unfurled himself and got out from under the table. The station was a mess, with fallen screens and tables and chairs spilled over.

'Is everyone okay?' he shouted. His ears were ringing.

Everyone confirmed they were okay, and he headed for the door, to conduct a damage assessment. As he emerged from the command station he looked in shock at the devastation that lay before him. Away to the right in the direction of the helicopter park he could see flames and smoke, but the most alarming sight was right in front of him. The company commander's command station had taken a direct hit. Where it had been was now a burning crater, with a small tangle of metal beside it. The station had been ripped apart by the missile, packed with high explosive, travelling at nearly fifteen thousand kilometres per hour. There was no way the company commander or his staff would even have known about their fate; they would have been instantly vaporized. It was no wonder they had felt the blast waves so strongly, the side of his command station was scarred with smoking shrapnel.

He suddenly thought of his team of engineers. *Where are they?* He turned and looked at their vehicles. The six-tonne trucks had been shredded and thrown onto their sides by the impact of the debris from the missile strike, which had been exploding in all directions at two kilometres per second. At this range the vehicles had no chance of survival, or the crews inside them. He ran to the burning trucks and looked inside the first, knowing already what he would find. He shouted in horror as he saw the twisted corpses of two of his four engineers. They had been hit by shrapnel, probably from the missile, the company commander's station, and the shredding truck. He guessed they would have also been killed instantly because their injuries were horrible, their bodies ripped apart.

He felt a sudden urge to vomit. He bent over and retched, but no vomit came, just acidic bile which burned his throat and mouth and made his eyes water. He staggered to the next truck and found the same carnage amongst the burning wreckage. He retched again and fell to his knees sobbing. He felt hands on his shoulders and heard the sound of voices as he closed his eyes.

Chapter Twenty Two

Jerry and Al had been lying low for a few hours, making their plan with Porter and trying to get some sleep. Every siren that blazed by put them on edge and made them think their time was up. The word was out and the hunt was on. They didn't know if the manhunt had been instigated by Lionel, who may have somehow survived and was now exploiting his connections, or just because the police would have looked at the surveillance camera footage by now. Either way they couldn't afford to take any chances by being out in the open. The Task Force safe house was out of the question, in case Lionel was alive; he would have the place covered. Also any public place was too risky, as they didn't know who would be looking out for them. The Republic intelligence network was notorious for its vast size and deep infiltration into society - everyone on every street was a potential surveillance asset. Furthermore the extensive network of facial recognition cameras, based on streets and in key public buildings may now be programmed to find them. As such they had again changed their phones before laying up in a dark corner of a public park, on the eastern side of the city to conduct their planning.

They had agreed with Porter that flying through the main international airport was now far too risky. It would be just too amateurish to walk into an airport and get busted straight away. Instead they were to get to Contonou, in Nigeria's neighbouring country Benin, where Porter had arranged a driver. He had also arranged transport for them with an old colleague from MI6, who as a regular partner in the region was keen to help them clean up the Task Force. Jerry explained that there had been raids on the headquarters, and the whole intelligence department arrested. They had even been named as wanted fugitives.

'It's nice to be wanted' said Al. 'Anything on Ananya?'

'Porter's search capability has all but stopped now that Francisco has been arrested, so we're running out of ideas to find her' said Jerry.

'How can she just disappear? Where could she have gone?'

'Somewhere to prepare for the plan I guess, whatever it is.'

'I can't believe we still don't know what it is' said Al. 'Maybe we *should* have gone to the authorities about Fisher. They'd get the story out of her for sure.'

'It's too risky. If the Republic's involved in it too then we'd be dead. Let's pass it on once we're back in Lagos' said Jerry, checking his watch. 'It's time. Let's head to the RV.'

They emerged from their hide and headed across the park, staying out of the open by pushing through the wide bushy trees. As they brushed past the branches they breathed deeply the sweet scent of the mahogany trees and felt almost relaxed; a temporary diversion from the extreme fatigue and tension that was weighing both of them down.

They reached the edge of the trees and looked out across a large grassed area towards a square seating area; concrete benches overshadowed by a steeply sloping wooden roof. In the dull illumination provided by two street lanterns they could see that it was empty.

'It's a pretty exposed meeting point' grumbled Al. 'There could be a sniper anywhere in these trees.'

'Well that's why we have our extra insurance' said Jerry, pulling out the palm-top. 'I'll scan the area for radio signals and neutralise any threats. Let's radio check now.' They activated their micro-vibration devices and confirmed they could hear each other.

'Radio check' whispered Jerry.

'Roger, strength five. Make sure you shoot straight you bastard.'

'Just get out there you pussy' joked Jerry, 'I only miss half of the time.' Al shot him a dirty look as he reluctantly stepped out of the tree line and strode slowly over to the seats. He kept his head down, hands in pockets, trying to look as inconspicuous as possible for a bear-sized white man in a quiet park in Khartoum in the dark of the night.

Jerry activated the palm-top and initiated a sweep of the area, searching for any digital signal being transmitted within fifty metres. The display indicated two signatures, close together, off to his right. Of course the contact wouldn't come alone; there would always be a back up.

'Two signatures at your three o'clock' he whispered to Al. 'Not moving yet.'

'Roger' came the reply. 'That'll be them. Keep a track on them.'

'Roger that. One minute until the RV.'

Jerry studied the signals on the display. As he looked, a third signature appeared near the others. Not likely a third person, Jerry thought; more likely one of them had activated a secondary device. It had an active signal, unlike his passive sweeper, which made it likely to be either a communications or surveillance device. Any such operation would always include an overwatch element, lurking in the shadows looking out for potential threats. It was probably scanning him now, detecting and analysing his digital signals and assessing his threat level.

The RV time came and Al loitered at the seats. Jerry noted two of the signatures beginning to move on his display. He squinted and looked closer. He had only expected to see one move towards Al, but the new surveillance device instead of staying put in the overwatch position was now moving towards Jerry.

'Al, you have a target inbound, but I've got an unexpected mover in addition to the second guy.'

'So there are three of them now?'

'Yep, so it seems. I'm moving to intercept him now. You'd better stay alert man.' Jerry took out his pistol and stepped silently back into the trees. The signal was about a hundred metres away, and was still moving towards him. The normal routine for a clandestine RV was to leave an overwatch and have just the point man go out. Jerry quickly tried to imagine reasons for the break from protocol, but came up with nothing. This could only be a threat.

'You see anything yet Al?' he whispered.

'Nope...oh hang on, he's coming out of the tree line now. He's black, dressed in jeans and a dark jacket, hands in pockets, walking right at me. What's your status? You found the mover?'

'Not yet' Jerry ducked under a low branch and tried to avoid stepping on dried leaves and twigs. 'I'm moving west, away from you, to see if he follows me away. Then I'll know if he's tracking me.'

'Well, figure it out fast. This guy's nearly on me. Twenty metres.'

Jerry studied the display again; the signal had definitely veered from its course in order to intercept Jerry.

'He's coming at me Al. I'm gonna turn straight for him and challenge him. Take defensive measures.'

'Roger.'

Al had not taken his eyes off the approaching man; he was studying his gait and his body movements, looking for clues of his intentions. He was striding slowly yet stiffly, with a hint of tension in his legs, indicating he may be about to launch an attack. His hands shifted uneasily in his pockets, as though he was handling something; probably a weapon Al guessed. Al stepped back a few paces, putting a concrete pillar between them. He reached back and slowly took his pistol from his belt, keeping it out of sight but ready for action. The approaching man's lips moved and his pace slowed.

'He's looking aggressive here mate. Should I just line him up to be safe?'

Jerry was tucked behind a tree and looked again at the display. His mover was only ten metres away, dead ahead through the trees. He didn't have time to determine their intentions now, but it was clear this was not normal, even in East Africa.

'Roger, line him up; this isn't right' Jerry urged, as he raised his own pistol in the direction of his mover, still unseen in the darkness. There was too much awry for this to be okay, Jerry assessed. There was no time to talk now; violence had to come first.

He quickly pocketed the palm-top and strained his eyes to spot his target. He detected a movement in the shadow of a tree; a dark figure appeared out of the gloom. Jerry quickly adjusted his aim, but before he had time to squeeze the trigger the darkness was split by the burst of an automatic weapon off to his right. The roar of the shots tore apart the black silence of the night and bounced around the trees. The figure grunted and slumped to the ground; a pistol with a silencer fitted fell from his hand. He heard another burst off to the left in the direction of Al.

'Al? Do you copy? What the fuck's going on?'

'I hear you mate, thank fuck' replied Al. 'My guy's suddenly been cut down.'

'Mine too, I'm coming to you now.' He raced through the trees toward the clearing.

As Jerry broke through the trees and neared Al an arabic-sounding voice spoke from the other side of the clearing. 'Put down your weapons and move away from them, out onto the grass. Prepare to authenticate yourselves.'

With no cover to run to and the fair assumption that they were surrounded, Jerry and Al had no choice now but to follow the instructions of the voice. They knelt on the grass with their hands on their heads. A bright flashlight shone into their faces, blinding them and disrupting their senses. The voice spoke again, this time to ask a series of authentication questions to confirm their identities, from first teacher's names to their favourite book, all of which would be known to the questioner. It was reassuring to Jerry that they were following a known Task Force authentication process, but it was by no means guaranteed that these were not Lionel's men on the other end of the flashlight. The questions stopped and there was a long pause. The silence was intense; nothing but the chirp of crickets and noises from a distant road. *Is this the end? Are they preparing to execute us?*

Three men stepped out of the treeline and made for them. They were dressed from head to foot in black, and were carrying short-barrelled automatic rifles with thermal sights attached. They moved quickly across the grass, staying low and scanning the surrounding trees. One man broke away and headed for the body of Al's attacker. The leading man of the other two lowered his weapon as he reached them.

'Mr Vasquez, my name is Faisal, let's get you out of here.' He extended his hand and helped Jerry to his feet. The other man helped Al up.

'Thanks' said Jerry with relief. 'We weren't sure if we were about to get executed.'

'Yes, our alpha team was ambushed on the way in. They're all down. We need to get you away now. Get your weapons and let's go'

As they walked, Faisal quickly explained how the call had come from Porter only an hour ago, and they had not had time to secure the perimeter as they usually would, leaving them exposed to ambush. He explained without emotion how one of alpha team had been killed and the other three badly wounded, and they were already being medevac'd. As they re-entered the treeline two more black-clad men appeared.

'Nothing on them, they're clean' said one of them.

'We have no idea who they were, or how they knew we were coming' said Faisal. 'I'm guessing you know something about it.' It was more rhetorical than an actual question, and Jerry knew better than to say anything. In this line of work, operational security was paramount, and no-one expected to be told the whole story; they just did their job. And so there was very little chat as they hurried out of the park and into waiting cars.

As they moved through the streets of Khartoum it was nearing dawn, and the dark was giving way to gloom. People were walking on the streets, and Jerry could hear the call to prayer being broadcast, beckoning them in. Jerry watched them going about their lives, and reflected on how they had no idea of what horrors may be about to visit them, or some other unsuspecting victim, if Lionel had his way. He closed his eyes and was nudged some time later.

'We're arriving at an executive airport just south of the city' said Faisal. 'There's a private jet waiting for you on the pan.'

'Thanks Faisal' said Jerry. 'I'm sorry about the guy that was killed.'

'Me too' replied Faisal grimly. 'But this op came in as urgent, so I guess you must be on something pretty important; I'm just pleased we were able to get you out. Good luck with whatever comes next for you.'

'Thank you. I think we're gonna need it.'

Seven hours later they landed at a small airstrip near Contonou in southern Benin, and met their driver. He showed them to his car and they set off towards the Nigerian border. As they passed through the town they looked at the streets, the people and the buildings, and they looked very familiar. Neither of them had been to Contonou before and they had expected its french heritage to have left some kind of legacy, other than the French language used in the country, but instead they saw the usual bland concrete buildings, tin shacks and dirty sidewalks so common in African towns. There were bursts of colour whenever they passed a market, but otherwise it was an uninspiring and overpopulated town.

Ten kilometres before the border the driver took a dirt track on the right and headed down towards the coast, passing through a small settlement of concrete block buildings with tin roofs. Small children dressed in rags and playing with dogs, watched as they drove by. Soon they came to the sea, where a small fishing boat was moored. A fisherman was waiting on the shore for them. They thanked the driver and climbed aboard. The fisherman cast off and raised the sails, taking them out to sea and heading east along the coast. They watched the coastline from the boat for a while, before drifting off to sleep.

They were woken by the fisherman, who was pointing to the coast, indicating they were close to Lagos. The sun was getting low in the sky. Jerry checked his watch. It was four in the afternoon. They had been travelling for eleven hours and had made it back without detection so far. They stretched and ate some dried fish that the fisherman gave them, washed down with some horribly desalinated water. As they drank it they looked to the coast and saw the desalination plant which had produced it. That meant they were less than ten kilometres from home.

Jerry hoped their new phones were still safe to use in Nigeria as he dialled Porter's number. It rang and rang and rang, for too long. Jerry began to panic. Had they finally caught up with Porter? Were they going to be waiting for them when they came ashore? Porter answered, breathless.

'We're about ten kilometres away.' said Jerry. 'We should be there in an hour. What's new?'

'Well you're not going to believe this. Fisher has been in touch through the drop box this afternoon. Francisco hooked me up to the system before he was arrested and I've been monitoring it remotely. She said that she wants to come in quickly. She heard about the shootout in the basement and figured it was just a question of time until they dug into it and linked it to her. She's using her Syrian passport to get out of the country today. She should be in the air now and landing tonight.'

'Shit, that's a lucky break, if it's true. Could it just be a trap though?'

'Unlikely. She used the drop box, and she wouldn't know that I'm checking it. It could be just a genuine run she's making. If she'd been caught out in the Republic once they linked her to Lionel then she'd be dead. So I guess she didn't have many choices.'

'I guess so, but do the Task Force know we're monitoring the drop box?'

'It's possible, because of our link to Francisco, the poor guy. So they may be now trying to draw us out of cover by dangling her in front of us.'

'Maybe, so if we're going to grab her, which we must, we need to do it carefully. What have they told her to do?'

'To take the train down to the Lagos Terminus and wait there to be picked up. They've chosen a deliberately weak RV, which makes it much more likely it's a trap.'

'Agreed, but we have to do it anyway. How long do we have to prepare?'

'She should be there by ten.'

'Great. Meet us at ERV Charlie in an hour and we'll get things moving.' He hung up and told Al the news.

'Doesn't this seem a bit risky?' said Al. 'What if they've got the police on it too? We'll be badly outnumbered and seriously exposed.'

''That's possible, but she's the only chance we have. We need to take her discreetly and learn everything she knows as quickly as possible.'

'It's a desperate move buddy, with pretty long odds.'

'I know man, but desperate times…'

'…call for desperate measures. Let's get planning.'

Jerry checked his watch. 21:30. *She should be here soon.* He stood in the shadows at the end of the platform and scanned the entrance, as well as the people stood waiting. The guy sat under the lamp looked like he was undercover, and that was certainly a pistol he was concealing under his jacket. The guy buying cigarettes also looked likely; he was checking over his shoulder towards the entrance too much. Jerry straightened his cap, worn low over his eyes, and focused back on the entrance. Jet engines roared overhead, followed shortly by the screech of tires on the runway. He knew she had already landed an hour ago, and by now she must be close to the station.

He saw her come through the entrance and onto the platform. She was shorter than he imagined, dressed in western clothing, linen trousers and a long sleeved shirt, with her dark hair tied back in a ponytail, revealing her tired-looking face. The two guys Jerry had spotted both moved towards her subtly, without making eye contact or speaking any words. They flanked her as she stood waiting for the train to arrive. Jerry quickly scanned the platform for anyone else behaving oddly, but saw no-one out of the ordinary. Just the two of them then.

The train rolled into the station and they got on. Jerry joined the next carriage and chose a seat facing her carriage, where he could see through the adjoining window as she sat down by the window, one row from the doors. He noticed that her escorts were sitting on the other side of the carriage, lamp guy on the other side of the doors and cigarette guy level with her. He called Al and confirmed that she was being followed, gave him the descriptions of the escorts, and agreed that they would go for Plan A.

He sat back and watched her as the train rocked along the tracks, heading into the city. She was looking nervously out of the window at the dark buildings and streets. Her nerves were natural; she had just spent at least two years deep undercover, posing as the wife of the leader of the Islamic Republic, leaking all kinds of secrets to an international paramilitary force. And now she had fled the country and was about to step into the unknown. Well, she made her choices, Jerry thought, and now she had to live with them. He thought she was even more pretty than when he had seen her in Khartoum. He could really see her face now, her almond eyes, her long nose and her full lips. He could see how she had entranced the President. Those good looks wouldn't be any use to her in jail.

He checked his watch. Three minutes to the station. He felt adrenaline beginning to pump through his veins as he mentally rehearsed what he had to do. A minute later he looked out of the window and watched the mall come into view on the right. It was time. He stood up and straightened his jacket, feeling the pistol in its place, and opened the door to her carriage. A few people looked up as he entered the carriage, but he kept his head down, his cap over his face. He could see the escorts sizing him up as he slowly made his way up the carriage. The train began to brake as it entered the station. The automatic announcement came over the speaker. *This is Yaba Station. Alight for Yaba Mall. Next stop Lagos Terminus.*

The train came to a halt just as he drew level with her. At that moment the window to his right exploded into a thousand pieces and cigarette guy sitting opposite Fisher slumped to his right, his eyes wide open and a hole in his head. *Nice shot Al.* The people around screamed and dropped to the floor. Jerry drew his pistol from his jacket. His eyes met hers and she realised what was happening. She quickly glanced over her shoulder at lamp guy on the other side of the now open doors. He was rising from his seat as he realised it was an ambush. He reached into his jacket for his pistol but was too slow, the open doors provided a perfect window for Al, who from his elevated position on top of the mall could easily pick him out with one shot. As he stepped towards Jerry, his hand in his jacket, his chest exploded in a burst of blood as the bullet ripped through his lungs and heart, sending him to the floor in a heap.

Jerry grabbed Fisher and heaved her up out of her seat. She screamed and begged him not to take her, begging the other panicking passengers to help her, but everyone was too busy taking cover or running from the carriage to listen to her appeals. She was just one more voice in a cacophony of screams and shouts. He dragged her out of her seat and thrust the pistol into her kidneys.

'Let's go, right now. No more noise or I'll shoot you right here.'

He hustled her off the train and down the stairs to the exit. As he did he found her phone in her pocket, took it out and smashed it on the railing, dropping the pieces on the ground. At the foot of the stairs, people were fleeing the station in a wild panic, so Jerry was able to join the crowds unnoticed and melt away. He saw the car waiting and guided her towards it, opening the back door and pushing her in. He climbed in after her and shut the door as Porter pulled away into the traffic.

'Please, don't kill me. They made me do it. I didn't have a choice.'

'Sure sure, save your lies Fisher' said Jerry. 'There's plenty of time for you to talk later.'

The use of her codename seemed to surprise her. 'Fisher? Who is that?'

'We know exactly who you are, Aishah, don't we Porter?' said Jerry.

'Yes we do' Porter replied, turning his head to make eye contact with her. Her eyes widened as she recognised him.

'It's you' she stammered. 'I didn't know you were involved.'

'He's involved alright, but it's your involvement in Lionel's plan that we're interested in, and you're going to start talking right now' said Jerry. 'You can start by telling us who is directing you now, is it still Lionel?'

'I don't know who it was. Someone handed me a phone in the airport and a man spoke to me. He just said he knew what I had been doing for the Task Force, and that I had been working with Lionel. He said I was to get on the train as planned and that there would be two men following me, and that they would have some men waiting to capture you at the Terminus.'

'I wonder if they're curious where the train is yet?' Jerry said, smiling.

The car pulled over and Al got into the front, carrying a sports bag.

'Evening all' he said cheerily.

'Al, great shooting. I couldn't have done better myself' said Jerry.

'I got my marksman badge in Scouts!'

'The drop box communication was a trap like we thought. They knew we would try to grab her. Fisher has told us that she was contacted anonymously and told we would be taken down at the Terminus.'

'...where currently there is a bunch of confused undercover cops, slash bad guys all wondering what the hell is going on' said Al.

'Yep, they'll be waiting for a while yet, which will give us plenty of time to question you' he said as he turned to Fisher. 'You'd better start thinking about how much you value your life because when we start talking you won't have long to convince us you're being honest. This time you do have a choice, and it had better be the right one.'

Chapter Twenty Three

President Al Quraysh paced the room, furrowing his brow and wringing his hands. She had been missing for twelve hours now and he had no idea where she could be. It was impossible that she would leave the palace without security; why would she? She could go shopping any time she liked, anywhere she liked, he gave her no restrictions at all. She couldn't have left him, they were so in love. She must have been grabbed somehow, but it was impossible that an intruder could have penetrated the palace's security. He had ordered a full investigation and no-one unusual had either entered or left the palace. Where could she be?

He walked to the window, looking out at the palace grounds and the city lights beyond. He wondered where she was, and what she was doing. He prayed to Allah that she was safe and would be returned to him soon. If she had been taken, then Allah would judge those who committed that crime when they stood before Him, but not before he had the opportunity to punish them in this life.

An aide entered the room and informed him that his head of security was here. He beckoned him in and offered the man a seat.

'Please, tell me what you know of my wife, where is she?'

The head of security looked uncomfortable, as if he was reluctant to share his news.

'Speak man! Do you know where she is? Is she alive? What has happened to her?'

'Ameer, we have managed to track your wife. She left the palace grounds disguised as a maid around midday. She took a cab from the street outside and travelled to the airport.'

'The airport? Why? Where has she gone?'

'Ameer.' He swallowed. 'She took a flight to Nigeria. She used a passport with a different name - Amena Hussaini. She dressed as a westerner. We saw surveillance footage of her. It was definitely your wife Ameer.'

Al Quraysh was speechless. His mind raced with questions. He grasped the back of a chair to steady himself as he reeled from the shock.

'How can this be? That is not her name. Her name is Aishah.'

'The passport is Syrian. I confirmed it with the Syrian Embassy, she is a Syrian national.'

'Then who is she? A spy? Why has she done this?'

'Ameer, I believe I may know why she has fled the country.'

'Then tell me now. What has she done?'

'She met with a man yesterday, an American man.'

'Wallah! This is not true. Not my Aishah.'

'Ameer, I regret that it is true. She had a meeting with him in the Excelsior hotel, in a restaurant. Later that night the man was involved in a gunfight in a hotel basement. We have identified him as Lionel Caplin. He is a former US Marine, and is the head of the Task Force in Nigeria.'

The President had to sit. He held his head in his hands and tried to process what he was hearing.

'What was she doing with him? What was the meeting about?'

'We don't know what they said Ameer. The security team are always outside the room for the meetings.'

'Meetings? There has been more than one?'

'Yes Ameer, she has met with him every six weeks or so for the last year. The security team has never reported it because there has never been any hint of sexual contact, and because it is not their place to question your wife's meetings, Ameer.'

'When she is meeting an American man every six weeks that is surely cause for concern!'

'We know that now Ameer. I have disciplined the head of her security team. Regrettably he did not inform me of her meetings Ameer.'

'Yes' mumbled the President. He sat in silence, wondering what was happening. This was too much to comprehend. What was she doing? Who was she? Who had he shared his bed with?

'There is something else Ameer' said the head of security, almost apologetically.

He looked up. 'What is it?'

'We found some notes in her belongings relating to a deployment of Task Force troops into Chad after the attack.'

'An attack on Chad? Our attacks?'

'It didn't say who would be attacking. It only included some times.'

'What are the times? When is this attack?'

'It said that the attacks will be happening tomorrow.'

'How could she know the details of our operations? Who is this woman?'

' I am sorry to say, we have to assume that she was a Task Force spy, Ameer. Though what she was spying on I cannot say. Did she show any signs of odd behaviour?'

'No, she was just a loving wife. Or so I thought.' His mind hardened as he thought of all those times they had laid in bed and she had spoken to him in her soft purring voice of his greatness and his power, and how he should teach Ayatumbe a lesson. She must have been spying on him, but was she trying to make him go to war with Chad? He hung his head. It suddenly seemed so clear to him what she was doing. He had invited a spy into his bed and shared his secrets with her. He had told her everything, giving her all the information she needed to carry out her wicked plan.

'No-one can know about this. Do you understand?'

'Yes Ameer. I understand.'

'Do you have anything else to tell me?'

'No Ameer, that is everything we know at the moment.'

'Good. Leave me now. Be sure to tell me immediately when you know anything else.'

The head of security excused himself and the President was left alone. He hung his head and stared at the floor. He wondered what her plan was with him. Why would she spy on him in order to plan an attack on Chad? Had she somehow encouraged him to order the attacks on Chad? She couldn't have. He could never admit to anyone that he had been tricked into attacking Chad by his wife. It would be the end for him.

The aide returned to the room and quietly informed him that his shura council was waiting for him. *The shura!* What was he to say to them? He could not confess to them that he had been tricked. He had gone to war with Chad. It was too late to back out now though, attacks had already taken place and war was inevitable.

He gathered his thoughts and made for the shura, preparing what he would say, and what he would not say. He entered the room and everyone rose from their seats.

'Salaam alyakum' he greeted the council.

'Wa alaykum salaam' they replied in unison.

He took his seat at the head of the table and looked around at his shura council. All good wise men, who had chosen him to lead this great Republic and its muslim community. He owed them much for their trust in him, and he had let them down. But they did not know that. They still believed in him. He must be the strong leader the Republic needed now and steer them through this crisis.

'Thank you all for coming. I know you are all busy. General Buraimi has been keeping me informed of the developing situation in the borderlands. General, please update the council.'

'Yes Ameer. Brothers, there has been fierce fighting in the borderlands today, and I am happy to say that we have taken the upper hand from the start, al hamdu lillah. As we thought, the Chadian armed forces were preparing to move against us, and mobilised their armoured units in the south, as well as their airborne units in central Chad, throughout yesterday. They began patrolling the borderlands with UAVs last night and simultaneously launched attacks across the border using their Commando troops. They destroyed several villages in the Darfur region, including refugees fleeing from the violence. We retaliated with UAV strikes at first light and struck against their airborne units, destroying their helicopters and severely damaging their ability to launch UAVs. We have also targeted their militias in the borderlands, and have destroyed three militia camps.'

'Thank you General' said the President. 'Brothers, we are now at war with the Chadian aggressors. They attacked us but we have repelled their attacks and have demonstrated to them that they cannot harm our people or take our land....'

'Ameer' interrupted Abu Rashed, 'I must stop you. This is not the way of Islam, it is haram. You are acting like a tyrant, attacking innocent civilians and bringing war to our country with no reason.'

Al Quraysh stared in astonishment.

'How dare you! You lie, you snake!' cried Abu Khalid. 'What treachery is this?'

'I am no snake' said Abu Rashed calmly. 'The facts speak the truth. Is it not true brothers?' he turned to the council and gestured. There were muted mumbles and half-nods.

'These are lies' said the President. 'I have acted fairly and decisively in the name of Allah, in order to protect our people from the aggression of the Chadian militias.' *Does Abu Rashed know what has happened?*

'You authorised the attacks on innocent civilians in another country. We all sat here as you did it' said Abu Rashed.

'Such an act is haram. The prophet Muhammad, Praise Be Upon Him, said '*Do not kill women or children or non-combatants*'. That is exactly what you did. You ordered the attacks, knowing those people were innocent.'

'I ordered attacks on the militias. On the combatants attacking our people. I acted to defend our people, in accordance with the law, and with God's will.'

'I have consulted with the council and they are in agreement. What you have done is forbidden. You have overstepped your authority, and you are undermining the reputation of the Republic.'

'You lie Abu Rashed!' said Abu Khalid. 'I have seen what you are doing. You have been trying to divide this shura and giving false counsel to the President. You have lied to us all. I believe you are trying to seize power for yourself.'

'Every man sitting here in this room has heard what I have said. They have all heard me report the facts, and they have all heard this man shout and scream and demand attacks on innocent people. '*A show of force*' was the phrase used. That is not defence, that is attack.'

'We were all here as you reported the build-up of Chadian troops' argued Abu Khalid. 'You told us all that Chad was preparing an attack.'

'I did not say an attack was coming, that was the work of you and the General. You then met alone, without the council, to plan this atrocity.'

'This is treachery!' shouted the President. 'I will not allow you to lie and falsely accuse me of crimes I did not commit. Go from this council! You are dismissed.'

'You cannot dismiss me. You no longer have the authority to commit your tyranny.' He stood and pointed at Al Quraysh 'I am acting as the hand of the council, with the will of Allah, and removing from you the title of President. You will be punished for your crimes and Allah will judge you. You have committed murder in the name of Allah, for your own vanity and megalomania.'

Al Quraysh looked around the room at the assembled council. Everyone except for General Buraimi and Abu Khalid had grave expressions and avoided his gaze. They seemed embarrassed, as if they did not truly believe it.

'Brothers, tell me this is not true, and that this is not your belief. As Allah is my witness, I swear to you that I have acted in accordance with the law. You have all sat and watched me wrestle with this problem. Tell me now that you believe that what I have done is haram.'

The assembled council members shifted uneasily in their seats, but no-one said anything.

'No-one speaks in your defence, *Abu Saif*' said Abu Rashed. 'It is decided.'

'No such thing is decided' said Abu Khalid. 'I have seen you at work Abu Rashed. I have witnessed your deception and your treachery and I have allowed you to incriminate yourself. Brothers, he has been deceiving you in order to seek the throne for himself. He is attempting a coup.'

Al Quraysh's mind raced. Was this her work? Had she been in league with Abu Rashed to undermine him and to force him out of power? Does this mean that Abu Rashed is working with the Task Force? Is the Task Force sponsoring Abu Rashed to remove him from power?

'This is no coup' said Abu Rashed. 'I am merely speaking on behalf of the council, about the failure of Abu Saif to properly lead the Republic. He has defied Allah's will, and the words of the prophet, Praise Be Upon Him, and has killed innocents. I am saying that the council should vote on the fate of Abu Saif. Should he remain as President, or be punished for his crimes?'

'This is all your work' said Al Quraysh slowly, menacingly. He stood and faced Abu Rashed. 'You have conspired against me, to undermine me and manipulate me. You have worked with the Task Force and their spies to engineer this situation. It has been your plan to start this war in order to serve your own ends. You would see me toppled from this post and take it for yourself. But you are the criminal! You act on behalf of the Task Force to undermine the Republic and this council!'

The council members looked in amazement at Al Quraysh, and then at Abu Rashed. No-one could fathom what he meant, or what evidence he had for this accusation.

'The Task Force? I am no agent of the Task Force' said Abu Rashed calmly. 'I am a servant of the Republic alone. You are grabbing any idea that comes into your head to defend yourself. Such wild accusations are the act of a tyrant, seeking to incriminate others in order to protect his own position.'

'I know it is true. You are in league with the Task Force and its spies. You are planning an attack on Chad, as we can see. You have created this war with your cunning words and your deception. You are a servant of the Task Force.'

Abu Rashed was amazed at his desperation. 'These are the ravings of a desperate tyrant, seeking to hold on to power by any means. And it is not true. Brothers...' he addressed the council, 'I say we vote on the suitability of this man to remain as President. I say he has failed in his duty to uphold the law of Islam, to protect his people and to act in accordance with the will of Allah. I say he has murdered innocent civilians with his attacks, and has undermined the international reputation of this peaceful nation, bringing war to our people and our region. He is not fit to be President, and he should be punished for his crimes. Let us vote now. Who agrees that this man should no longer be President?'

'This is treachery!' cried Abu Khalid. 'There will be no vote. This is your work and your deception.'

'The law says we should vote! Who agrees this man should no longer be President?'

In silence, seven hands were raised around the room; all except Abu Khalid and General Buraimi. Al Quraysh hung his head.

'You cannot do this!' shouted Abu Khalid.

'Abu Saif. The shura council has voted. You will be stripped of your title of President, and you will be punished for your crimes against Islam. Abu Khalid, your fervent defence of Abu Saif surely indicates that you are in league with him, or are under his spell and therefore unfit to act in his place. I ask the council to vote again. Brothers of the shura council, who agrees that Abu Khalid has given poor counsel, and has shown bad judgement, and cannot be trusted to continue in his post?'

Again, seven hands were raised around the table.

'The shura council has voted. Abu Khalid, you are to be removed from the shura council and stripped of your title of Interior Minister and Vice President. Which leaves one final matter to be concluded, who will replace Abu Saif as the President? I humbly submit my own name as a candidate. I have shown integrity and leadership throughout this crisis, and I will swiftly resolve it and bring peace back to the Republic. Please brothers, raise your hand if you believe I have the authority to act as President, to defend our nation and our people, and to enact God's will.'

Again, the shura council raised their hands, somewhat slower this time. Such an appointment was unprecedented as Abu Saif had been appointed as the first President of the new Republic. They had never had a leadership challenge, but they had all witnessed the ravings of Abu Saif; his obsession with attacking Chad; his refusal to accept counsel. Based on the law they all accepted and lived by, this seemed legitimate. Yes, Abu Rashed had approached them before this meeting to discuss his concerns and had laid out his case, but he appeared to be correct. Abu Saif had ordered the illegal attacks and they had witnessed it. They had all made a decision, and such was the law, that decision was binding. They had chosen a new President.

Chapter Twenty Four

Porter parked the car in the dark corner of the car park behind Chez Chay. They sat in silence for a while, watching and waiting for any unusual movement or signs of them being compromised. No cars followed them into the car park, there were no strange cars already there, and there were no people hanging around. They hadn't seen any evidence of them being tailed on the drive there, so it seemed they were safe. Movement around Lagos was becoming more difficult as the police were actively on the lookout for them, and concurrently there was now a mystery group of undercover agents also searching for them. Perhaps they were being fed information by whoever in the Task Force had assumed command, and was therefore working with or for Lionel. There was still no clear evidence of who was involved, and who was clean. Jerry was hoping that Fisher's confession would reveal some vital clues.

'Okay, let's go' said Jerry. They got out of the car and made for the rear entrance to Chez Chay, which was open. They slipped inside quickly and closed the door. The bar was in full swing. No-one noticed them enter the rear entrance. Jerry guided Fisher into the rear office, Al and Porter followed.

'Sit down' he ordered her. He sat on the corner of the table, and Al and Porter took seats by the door. 'Now this can go two ways, and I think you know them. If you lie then we'll know it, and things will get difficult for you. But if you tell us everything you know then we'll find a way through this. Understand?'

She nodded. 'I'll tell you everything I know. I swear it.'

'Let's start with what the hell were you and Lionel planning?'

'I wasn't planning anything. I was just put in the Republic to collect intelligence and then later to influence the President, to persuade him to act in a certain way.'

'In what way?'

'I was told by Lionel to flatter him. To appeal to his vanity, and to make him believe that he was invincible. Lionel wanted him to believe that he could do anything he wanted. Then I was to start planting an idea in his head that Chad was an inferior country, and that Ayatumbe was challenging him. I was supposed to make him think that he should invade Chad in order to protect the muslim people there.'

'Well it looks like it worked' said Porter. 'There have been cross-border attacks yesterday and today. You've started a war.'

Fisher looked devastated. 'I never wanted people to be harmed. I really didn't. I was just told to sleep with the President, and to flatter him. To give him everything he wanted and just plant a few ideas in his head. I didn't think it would turn into a war.'

'Were you working with anyone else in the Republic?' asked Jerry.

'No, there's no-one else. I only took my orders from Lionel. He used to contact me every so often and we would meet in a hotel in Khartoum. I would do it in plain sight of the guards, so I never looked like I was hiding anything. I would tell him what was happening and he would give me orders on what to do next.'

'Did he tell you why you were doing this? You must have asked.'

'Yes, he did tell me. He said that he was planning to stage a sort of coup in Chad.'

'A coup? How was he going to do that?'

'He said that once the attacks had begun on Chad then the Task Force would be authorised to intervene, as it would be legitimate, and then once they were in Chad they would seize power.'

'Legitimate? It's not legitimate to seize power, or even to put troops on the ground unless we've been invited into that country to act on their behalf' said Jerry.

'Yes, but he said that the Chadian government would be crippled, and so they would have to intervene. He didn't tell me how they would be crippled though.'

'The genetic weapon' said Porter. 'Maybe he's planning to use the genetic weapon to cripple them?'

'Is he?' Jerry asked her. 'Is he developing a genetic weapon to use against Chad?'

'I honestly don't know. All I know is that he told me to submit an intelligence report a couple of years ago, saying that the Republic was starting to develop a genetic weapons facility. I guessed it was so that he could justify blaming the Republic for the war.'

'That figures' said Porter. 'He generated enough of a trace of evidence so that he could point to it when the war began, to say the Republic were developing a weapon to use.'

'So the Republic is just being used as a tool to justify a deployment. But that doesn't explain how the Chadian government were going to be crippled' said Al.

'It's more likely that he and Ananya had actually developed a genetic weapon, and he was planting evidence in the intelligence cycle to blame it on the Republic when they finally attacked. But what was the weapon?' asked Jerry.

'Have you ever heard him mention a woman called Ananya? Ananya Devi? An Indian genetic scientist?' Porter asked her.

'No, he never said anything about her. He never mentioned that name.'

'What did he tell you would happen to you when he had seized power in Chad?' asked Jerry.

'He said I would be extracted from the Republic and given a new life.'

'A new life where?'

'We never discussed it. He was always reluctant to discuss it because we never had time. We always talked about the mission.'

'Okay, what else did he say about the mission? Who did he say he was working with?'

'He said he had contacts with the Nigerian military, who would be helping with the attack. He also said he had a friendly government in waiting.'

'He was going to install a new government in Chad once he had *crippled* the old one' said Porter.

'But why?' wondered Jerry. 'What did he have to gain from toppling Ayatumbe from power and inserting another guy, who would probably be as tyrannical as Ayatumbe?'

'It's always better to have your tyrant in power than some other tyrant' said Al.

'But I don't get why. Chad has nothing of any value any more. It's more than half desert, and their oil is fast running out too. Most of their mining has stopped and they produce almost nothing. They are one of the poorest and least influential countries in Africa. What is the value in supporting a new government in such a void of wealth and influence?'

'He mentioned something about resources' said Fisher. 'He said they would take control of Chad and its resources, and that would make them wealthy.'

'Resources again' said Al. 'He said that down by the river, just before he head butted me'

'Well Chad doesn't have any natural resources, so he must have been talking about people. How can having control of the people make you rich when you have nothing for the people to do? That's not how economies work as far as I know' said Jerry.

'Hang on, let's back up a minute' said Porter. 'Let's look at the genetic weapon again. Say he has been developing a genetic weapon with Ananya, and he intends to stage this war, assassinate the Chadian government, claiming it's the work of the Republic. Maybe he's then planning to hold the continent to ransom with the weapon. Tell everyone that Chad has the power to commit mass genocide on whoever doesn't pay up. Like the old nuclear threats of North Korea. Maybe he was planning to conduct a demonstration and then start demanding cash, all through the new government of Chad.'

'But why Chad? Why not use the Nigerian government if he was so well connected with them?'

'Maybe it's too terrible for Nigeria to agree to' said Porter. 'You effectively become African Enemy Number One when you take that step. And Chad is such an unstable country anyway. It's always easier to take control of a failing country.'

'Holy shit, he was going to use a government to commit acts of terrorism on his behalf. How did he think he was going to get away with that?' said Al.

'He used to say to me that African leaders were worthless and weak, and could be told what to do' said Jerry. 'And he would talk about the lack of world order now the UN has shut up shop. I guess he was hoping to exploit that.'

'Was?' said Al. 'We don't know it's over or that he's dead. Maybe he or someone else is still running it? After all someone is still monitoring the drop boxes.'

'Yes, it's possible. But we don't know who…' said Jerry. He froze, as did Al and Porter. They had heard a noise from the rear door.

'Chay? Is that you?' called Jerry. No response. He nodded to Porter, who was closest to the door, to open it and have a look. 'Maybe it's a customer looking for the bathroom.'

Porter stood and opened the door a crack. He put his head through to look around the corner at the rear door. There was the sound of a silenced shot and Porter slumped to the ground, his body pushing the door open as he fell. Jerry reacted immediately, knowing he had less than two seconds to save his life. He reached for his pistol and pulled it from his jacket as a black-clad man appeared in the doorway, dressed in black and holding a short barrelled rifle with a silencer fitted to the muzzle. Jerry raised his pistol and fired a double-tap point blank at the assailant's stomach, knowing he would be wearing body armour to protect his chest. Before he could open fire the man was thrown backwards by the bullets ripping through his abdomen. Jerry rolled back off the table and took cover behind it, knowing there would be more gunmen following him.

As the first man hit the ground a second appeared by him. He stepped over his body and sprayed automatic fire around the room, sweeping from left to right. Jerry saw in his peripheral vision as Fisher was hit and fell backwards on her chair. He ducked as the bullets smashed into the walls and furniture above him.

Al had stood and drawn his pistol by this time, and concealed behind the wall was able to raise his pistol and shoot the second man directly in the neck at a range of about two feet. The flash from the pistol merged with an explosion of blood as his carotid artery was ripped open. He fell down, grasping his neck, spasming on the ground.

They both anticipated what would come next, and they were right. A hand tossed a grenade around the door. It rattled to the ground and settled by Fisher's upturned chair, and a second later exploded with a tremendous report. A stun grenade, designed to shock and disorientate the occupants of the room, and make them incapable of fighting. It was always followed immediately by an assault. Jerry and Al had both ducked into a ball, closed their eyes and pressed their fingers into their ears. It wasn't enough to fully protect them, but at least it would mitigate the shock waves that would blast them and they may retain some kind of consciousness.

The blast waves stopped, but the room was full of billowing dust. Jerry opened his eyes and saw the dim shape of the doorway. His ears were ringing and he was dizzy, but he could make out the shape of the third man in the doorway. He saw the flashes of a muzzle as the attacker opened fire. Jerry didn't know or feel where the bullets went. Then another two flashes, this time from below and to the left of the door. It was Al, crunched into a ball on the ground, firing up at the man, who did not see him down low. He fell back as Al's bullets smashed his hip and ripped through his guts. That was three, how many more would come? Usually it would be a four man team, but it may be six. Jerry could hear the dull screams and shouts as the bar cleared out, everyone running for their lives.

The doorway was now crowded with bodies, three attackers, and Porter's at the bottom. Getting in would be a challenge for the next man. But no-one came. Instead a window shattered above Jerry's head as the fourth man sprayed the room with bullets. He had clearly decided the door was a killing area. Jerry and Al both ducked for cover while the initial spray slammed into the walls above them. They knew the shooter would have to change magazines in a few seconds and then they would move. The firing stopped, and they heard the sound of a magazine being ejected as they crouched and ran to the doorway, not having time to check Fisher's body. She had reached the end of her usefulness now anyway.

They ran into the main bar and turned left, following the long wooden bar to the front door. The bar was empty, and when they exited the building they saw people running along the beach and across the car park.

'Let's sweep around and catch him out' said Jerry.

They crouched low and ran around the front of the building, towards the rear car park. As they ran they noted the black SUV in the car park, lights off, engine running and doors open. That told them it was just a four man team, so this was the last attacker. They heard the sound of another grenade and then automatic fire again as the shooter emptied another magazine into the office through the window.

'Non-lethal' Jerry whispered to Al.

As they rounded the corner they saw the man, five metres away, pulling another grenade from his pouch and removing the pin. Jerry waited until he had dropped it through the window and then fired a double-tap at his legs. He fell to the ground with a cry, dropping his rifle and clutching his left leg. Jerry and Al were on him immediately, kicking his weapon away and then kicking him in the stomach. The man groaned in pain and curled into a ball.

'Let's get him out of here' said Jerry.

They dragged the moaning man to the SUV and threw him in the back seat. Jerry climbed in after him. Al ran back to the building and then returned with a large holdall full of weapons and ammunition. He jumped into the driver's seat and slammed his foot on the gas. They raced out of the car park and turned left, heading off Victoria Island and towards the city.

Jerry ripped off the man's face mask and helmet, to reveal a Nigerian man, in his early twenties. He was begging and pleading with Jerry not to kill him. Jerry slammed the butt of his pistol into the man's leg wounds. He cried out in pain and begged some more.

'Shut up' said Jerry. 'I'll ask questions and you'll answer them. Now who sent you?'

'I don't know anything, I swear it.'

'Listen, do you want to survive this and maybe have a family some day?'

'Yes sir'

'Then answer my questions honestly, and we'll drop you off with all your important parts in the right place. Okay?'

'Okay sir.'

'Now, who sent you?'

'I was just ordered to take part in the assault and make sure everyone was killed.'

'Ordered by who?'

'By my team commander. I'm just a soldier! I don't know who the boss is.'

'Who's running the Task Force? Is Lionel Caplin alive?'

'I don't know. Some white guy is in charge. I saw him at the Adeji airbase. He's tall and has a beard. Dressed in black.'

'That doesn't sound like anyone at headquarters' said Al.

'No' said Jerry. 'What are you doing at Adeji airbase?'

'That's where we're based now. We're in one of the hangars there.'

'The Nigerian Air Force base by the airport?'

'Yes, we moved there a couple of days ago.'

'Who moved there?'

'All the Counter-Terrorism teams, a Commando squadron, some engineers I think.'

'Why the airbase?' Jerry thought aloud. 'What aircraft are there next to the hangar?'

'Err, some CH-47s, two C-20 planes, and a bunch of UAVs'

'Sounds like a quick reaction force to me' said Al. 'Ready to launch on command.'

'Yeah, it does' said Jerry. 'What have you been told about the next few days? Have you been told about any missions coming up?'

'We were told we wouldn't be able to leave the airbase for the next week, and we're on thirty minutes notice to move. No specific missions.'

'Definitely a quick reaction force then. Ready to fly into Chad at a moment's notice' said Jerry to Al.

'Sounds like it. The plan is still very much on, with or without Lionel.'

'Well I can only think of one way to find out more' said Jerry.

'I'm reading your mind. I'm heading for the airbase.'

'Time to get in that hangar and find out what your mysterious new boss is doing' said Jerry. 'You're almost done, just one more task for you. You're going to drive us right into the lion's den.'

Chapter Twenty Five

President Ayatumbe pounded his fists on the table, the glass of water jumped and fell over, spilling its contents across the dark mahogany. Interior Minister Idris Owusu and Chief of the Republican Guard General Yam Yeboah looked nervously at the water as it ran down towards them.

'How can this be such a disaster?' shouted Ayatumbe.

'Mr President' began the General, 'we were able to conduct surprise attacks on the Republic during the night, but they retaliated with greater firepower at dawn. They have superior weapons to us.'

'You told me that our UAVs would be able to automatically target their vehicles General. You said we would be able to destroy them remotely without any casualties to our side.'

'Mr President, we were able to target them, and we did manage to inflict some casualties on them. But they have more drones, which have a longer range, and can carry more missiles. We are not able to match them.'

'What are our losses so far?'

'We have lost one hundred and thirty men from the 12th and 14th Airborne Regiments, most of them Commandos involved in the night-time raids. We have also lost four Mi-17 medium transport helicopters and six of our Interceptor drones. Throughout today the fighting has stalled. We have not launched any more attacks yet, and they seem to be sitting waiting for our next move. Perhaps it is time to seek a truce?'

'A truce? Why would I do that General?'

'Because they have a larger force than us Mr President. We are struggling to match them.'

'I will not hear of it. We will show them a fight they never expected. We will fight until every last one of them has fallen.'

'Yes Mr President. They are reinforcing their units with more movements from the north and from the east.'

'And are we reinforcing also?'

'Yes Mr President. I have mobilised two more airborne regiments, one to the eastern border and one in the area of N'Djamena, in case the capital should come under drone attack. We also have our armoured units travelling north and east at the moment. They will be in a position to defend our borders within the next hour.'

'I would say it is too late to defend our borders General. You have already failed to do that. The Republic drones have been able to cross the border as they wish, and destroy our regiments with impunity.'

General Yeboah had nothing to say about that. It had been an embarrassing initial defeat, and had very clearly underlined the difference between their defence budgets. He did not mention that if he had been given more money then he would have been able to buy better UAVs, and more of them.

'Tell me about our tanks General. What do we have and what can they do? And do not tell me how much better the Republic's tanks are.'

Yeboah swallowed. 'Mr President, I have mobilised one hundred tanks, and one hundred armoured infantry vehicles. Each of those armoured vehicles has a cannon, grenade launcher and heavy machine gun fitted to it. The tanks are equipped with a main gun which can fire anti-tank and high explosive rounds. Our tanks are the perfect vehicle for the Sahel and desert environment, where the land is open and flat. If the Republic is planning to use their armoured infantry then they will find themselves seriously outmatched.'

'And do they have tanks also?'

'Yes. They have the T-15 tank, which is an unmanned remotely operated tank. It has a larger main gun than ours, but it does lack manoeuvrability because of there being no driver in the vehicle.'

'How many of these do they have?'

'We don't know exactly how many they have, but it is safe to say they can deploy at least as many regiments as we can, but on both fronts.'

'You mean we will be outnumbered two to one?'

'Yes Mr President. They are a much larger force than us. We should expect them to have more equipment, but our strength is in our tactics. If we can carry out attacks on them before they have the chance to deploy then we can destroy half of their troops before the battle even begins.'

'Good. I want to hear more about that General. Tell me how we will surprise them.'

'Ayatumbe listened intently as the General explained in detail his plan to launch pre-dawn attacks all along the border, neutralising the Republic's forces before they even had a chance to move.

'Excellent General. Ensure you make the most of the surprise this time. I want it to be followed up with a full tank invasion. Head straight for the capital and strike at their heart.'

'Mr President, that is a twelve hundred kilometre drive to Khartoum. We cannot go that far.'

'Do not give me problems! Give me solutions General. Now Idris, tell me about the defence of the plant.'

'Mr President, the plant is secure. As we discussed, the security has been increased, we are using more drones to patrol the area, and we also have a company of Commandos on standby in case there are further attacks.'

'Good. Whatever else is needed must be diverted there. General, you will cooperate with Minister Owusu to ensure the Bardai plant has all the defences it needs. There is nothing more important than protecting our water supply. It is vital to the future prosperity of this country.'

Captain Okoro sat with his head hung as the medical staff rushed around him, attending to emergency patients and installing new equipment just arriving with the reinforcements. His hands were bandaged due to burns received when he ran to the trucks. He had been told he had been clawing at the wreckage, trying to rescue his men, who were already dead anyway. He didn't have much memory of the attacks.

Captain Thomas Adeji, the company second in command, had been promoted to replace the company commander. He had been working hard all day to acquire new aircraft for the company, which had lost three Interceptors. He had been unsuccessful and had to merge three detachments into two. Okoro and his crews had been stood down, due to their manning losses and to deal with the traumatic events of this morning. Okoro felt numb and listless. He guessed that was largely due to the drugs he had been given, but he was also struggling to decide what sort of feelings she should have. Should he feel guilty that he had let his men die? Should he feel anger that they were killed so senselessly? Should he feel grief? His greatest feeling at the moment that maybe there had been a mistake, and maybe they were some other twisted bodies in the burning trucks. Maybe this was all a nightmare and he was about to wake up.

He was roused from his thoughts by a hand on his shoulder. He looked up into the kind face of Thomas, who was his friend and now his superior officer. He sat down beside him, keeping his hand gently on Okoro's shoulder. For a moment they sat in silence, not needing to say anything or to look at each other. Finally Thomas spoke.

'Hamed, I have been speaking to the commanding officer about the new formation of the unit, now we have fewer aircraft and…' he hesitated to say it, '….fewer men.'

Okoro did not react. He didn't feel any emotional pain. He just listened to his friend's words.

'He agreed with me that it would be a good idea if you and your detachment were given some time to recuperate in a less stressful environment. Somewhere that the threat of further attacks is less.'

Okoro looked up now. 'I don't want to be sent on leave Thomas, that's no good for me, or any of us, to sit and have nothing to do.'

'You're not going on leave Hamed, listen to me. We are sending you to the 15th Regiment, to reinforce one of their companies. They've just been deployed to the capital to patrol there and conduct urban defence. It's far back from the front line but you're still operational.'

'Can I go with my team? I want to take them with me.'

'Yes of course. You'll all go together. It's no good to split you all up now, you need each other for support, and most importantly Hamed, they need your leadership.' He squeezed his shoulder encouragingly. 'You need to take command of them and guide them through this. You're all in shock, but that's the role of the officer, to navigate through this setback and keep moving forward.'

Okoro nodded and lifted his head. He looked at Thomas and forced a smile. 'Okay' he said.

'Good. You're on the helicopter at 05:00, so get your team organised and try to get some sleep.' He stood and patted Okoro on the shoulder again, before walking away.

Okoro sat for a while longer and thought about the move. It would certainly get them away from the constant reminder of the deaths; from the crater, the debris, the smell. But it would also feel like they had abandoned their team mates there, like they had turned and run when the going got tough. He didn't like that they were leaving so quickly the place where a third of his team was wiped out in just a few seconds. But that was the nature of the military, he decided; change is inevitable, and you cannot hold onto the past, treasuring it like a prized possession. They had to accept the change and move on. He took a deep breath, stood up, and went to find his team.

Just a few short hours later, after not managing to get any sleep, Okoro stood at the helicopter landing site with his team. They waited in line, Okoro at the front. They were clutching their kit bags, rucksacks on their backs, weapons strapped to their chests and helmets on their heads. They watched as the Mi-26 transport helicopter span up its rotor blades and conducted its pre-flight checks. The ground crew scurried around the aircraft through the billowing dust, removing the chocks from the wheels and checking tyre pressures. Eventually the tailgate lowered and the load master beckoned them forward. They were buffeted by the downdraft of the blades as they neared the aircraft, before filing up the ramp and taking their seats along the sides. It was cavernous inside, with enough room to fit a six tonne truck. In the centre were three large pallets of equipment, covered in netting and strapped down. They placed their equipment where they could, removed their weapons, standing them upright, and put on their seat belts with the load master's help. A couple of minutes later they lifted off, climbing away from the operating base and towards the capital.

Chapter Twenty Six

Adeji airbase entrance gate loomed ahead of them. Powerful floodlights illuminated it, and heavily armed guards stood checking vehicles as they entered. Beyond Jerry could see the large hangars and long low buildings of the Nigerian Air Force, from where their helicopter, UAV and jet fleets were flown and maintained. Jerry had been on the base twice before, for flights around Africa on the military passenger jets operating from here. Usually they flew commercially, or used small chartered aircraft from a private airstrip to the north of the city. This airbase shared the main runway with the international airport and handled a heavier flow of traffic, hence the greater security on the gate.

Jerry and Al had found some spare assault vests in the back of the SUV, and had pulled on some black caps to make them look more authentic. The young attacker drove, his leg heavily strapped to stop him bleeding out before he made it through the gate. Jerry had one of the short-barrelled assault rifles laid across his lap, with the muzzle resting against the driver's side, as a reminder of what would happen if he did anything crazy. They pulled up to the gate, and the driver acknowledged the armed guard with a casual *Hey*.

The guard checked the vehicle pass, and had a careful look at the young man, and then at Jerry and Al. They looked straight at him, challenging him to question them and their right to be there. Jerry's heart pounded, and his hand tightened on the pistol grip of the rifle, ready to lift it and fire through the window at the first sign of trouble. The guard nodded and waved them through. They passed through the floodlit gate area and onto the airbase, turning right towards the airfield and the hangars lined up along the length of the runway. Beyond the hangars Jerry could see many helicopters lined up, rotor blades hanging idle. He recognised them as the latest Russian gunships, the Mi-30. The Nigerian Air Force was well-funded and had an impressive fleet of aircraft, making them without question the strongest armed force in the region. Jerry wondered how many of them were involved in Lionel's plan.

'Which is your hangar?' Jerry asked.

'That one, with the lights at the bottom' he indicated.

'And which one is the accommodation?'.

'Just behind it' he pointed.

'Okay, stop just there, short of the hangar, by that truck' Jerry indicated.

The driver pulled up the SUV by the truck and switched off the engine. He turned his head to see what Jerry wanted him to do next, but didn't make the full turn before Al's hand had chopped down between his neck and shoulder, knocking him out instantly. They dragged him into the back of the car and gagged and tied him up securely. There would be no mistakes, or them being discovered because of a honking horn or a rocking car. They quickly checked their weapons, and stocked up on extra ammunition and grenades, stowing them in their assault vests.

'Okay, first priority is to find Ananya. She'll be the easiest to get information from. There must be some sort of plan of who is sleeping where. Maybe there's an admin office.'

'What about the watchkeeper?' said Al. 'He'll be awake on duty, and also expecting our young friend to check in by the way.'

'Good idea. I'll distract him when we're in, and you knock him out. People are certainly going to recognise us now and know we're wanted, so we'll have to move fast. Also take non-lethal shots where possible. These guys are not necessarily all involved in the plan, they may just be following orders without even knowing what the plan is. I'd feel more comfortable just taking them out of the fight and then finding out later what their level of involvement is.'

'Roger. Let's roll.'

They exited the SUV and made for the hangar, where the lights were on and the watchkeeper was most likely on duty. They sneaked a look through one of the lit windows. It was a long office, with many computer terminals on desks, but no people. Through the door they could see the hangar, which was full of equipment stacked on pallets. Jerry could see pallets of ammunition, as well as heavy duty wooden crates. They moved along to the next lit window. Inside was a watchkeeper. He sat with his back to the window next to the doorway and was watching a TV show on a computer. Next to him were a computer and a radio set. From here he would be the first point of communication for the unit, receiving and sending all messages, logging each one as a record of events and decisions made. It was him who received the call from the unconscious attacker, informing him that the raid had been successful and that Jerry and his team were all dead. The watchkeeper would have passed the message on to the mysterious new Task Force commander and then got back to his TV show. Watchkeepers were rarely curious, and usually sleepy.

'Change of plan. I'll lead and just club him in the head with the butt of my rifle.'

They skirted around the edge of the hangar to the end, where they saw dozens of UAVs and helicopters lined up, silent and still as guards in the night. They found an open door, which they crept through into the hangar, first checking there was no-one around. It looked like everyone was sleeping. They crept up the row of offices lining the length of the hangar, Jerry leading. At the doorway they briefly paused, Jerry switched his grip on the rifle, and stepped into the doorway with the rifle raised. He swung the butt straight down into the side of the watchkeeper's head, knocking him out cold before he could even look up at Jerry.

They quickly entered the office and started searching. Al rummaged through the papers on the desk while Jerry searched the papers pinned and stuck to the wall. He then remembered that this would be the operations room, where the operation would be planned and managed from. That meant they may be able to find some clues about what the operation involves. He looked at the planning board, covered in drawings, diagrams, timings and callsigns, and slowly put together a picture of what was going to happen. He noted that H hour, the time the operation would begin, was 07:00 today. He checked his watch. 03:21. *Shit, not much time to stop this thing.* He turned to Al and whispered.

'Any luck?'

'Not yet, just lots of order forms and dispatch notices. Looks like they're flying a lot of shit out of here today and tomorrow. Into N'Djamena airport according to these manifests.'

'Yeah that figures, check out the planning board' he gestured to the board.

Al stopped his search and joined Jerry by the board. His eyes scanned its contents and widened as he read.

'Holy shit. I see why now. They're planning a full-scale invasion!'

'Starting with a coordinated UAV attack at 07:00' Jerry pointed to the board. 'Out of here, up to N'Djamena, and beyond, to the southern and eastern areas of Chad.'

'Softening up the military units before they invade perhaps?'

'They seem to be heading for the main population centres, so it could be the military units. I'm not sure where they are. But they're certainly going to be flying into the capital, to *cripple the government* as Fisher said.'

'And then shipping in a whole Division of the Task Force the next day to take over the country it seems, including a whole company up in the mountains. I wonder why they're waiting a day to insert the main invasion force?'

'I don't know, but I do know we have to stop this launching, and we have less than four hours. They'll most likely be starting to prepare from five, so we only have an hour and a half.'

'Long enough to sabotage the aircraft so they can't launch' said Al with a smile.

'I like that. Let's find out where Ananya is and then we can knock out a few drones before we go and give her a wake up call. I want to know what the genetic weapon link is.'

They resumed their search, and eventually found a plan of the rooms. They located her room, co-located with the unit officers.

'I don't think we'll be able to take her out of the building silently, so we'll have to make her talk there and then.'

'That's too risky mate, if she screams then we're blown and right in the middle of them. Let's gag her and get her out to the SUV, using this exit.' He indicated on the plan. It passed the fewest rooms but seemed to be the main entry and exit point.

'We'll have to be quick then. Right, let's hit some aircraft before we...' They froze as they heard voices at the accommodation block end of the hangar. They listened carefully, two voices. They quickly dragged the watchkeeper behind the door and positioned themselves ready to step out and knock out the men when they came into the office. They held their rifles ready to butt-strike as the men got closer to the doorway.

'Jeffrey!' one of the men called. Jeffrey must have been the name of the watchkeeper.

'Must be in the can' said the other. 'We'll see him later, come on.' They walked straight past the doorway towards the opposite end of the hangar. Jerry snuck out and watched them. They were dressed in engineer coveralls and carried technician cases, with rifles slung across their backs. They exited the hangar through the door that Jerry and Al had used.

'They look like a couple of UAV engineers off to start preparations, and they're armed. Shit!'

'Yeah, we don't want to risk a fight now and wake everyone up. We'll be blown before we even start.'

'You're right. Let's get the story out of Ananya and then we'll know where specifically to target.'

They left the ops room and made for the end of the hangar. They slipped out of the door and ran across to the accommodation block, hugging the edge of the building as they made for the entrance. It was brightly lit, which would give them real problems if there was anyone around, but they managed to slip into the building and turn right down the main corridor without meeting anyone. The building was silent. They passed the meeting room and counted two more doors. Number 84. Jerry very softly tried the handle, but of course it was locked, she was an attractive woman living in a building with two hundred or so men. Jerry reached into a pouch for a lock-picking tool. As quietly as he could he inserted the tool into the lock and gently massaged the tumblers and springs until they lined up with a click. Al reached over and turned the handle and they swung the door open noiselessly.

Light from the corridor flooded the room and they saw her in bed, eight feet away on the other side of the room. The light shone on her face and woke her. Quick as a flash Jerry crossed the room and clamped his hand over her mouth and wrapped his arm around her torso and arms. She bucked and kicked and tried to scream, but Al was on her, holding her legs. They lifted her and carried her out of the room, down the corridor and out of the door.

They had to go around the building to the SUV on the other side. If anyone saw them now they would be in big trouble. Luckily there was no-one around and they made it to the SUV. They bundled her into the back seat. The driver was still unconscious in the back and lay still. Jerry got in with her, holding his hand over her mouth. Al got into the front. She was breathing heavily and looking at him with terrified eyes.

'No noise and I'll take my hand off okay?' he said.

She nodded. He slowly released his hand and she gasped for breath, rubbing her mouth with the sleeve of her silk nightclothes.

'Who are you and what do you want?' she asked, looking at them in terrified defiance.

'You don't remember me?' said Jerry. 'I'm Jerry and this is Al. We're the guys your friend Lionel tried to have killed. Remember?'

'I remember you' she said to Jerry, "but I don't know anything about him trying to kill anyone.'

Jerry quickly jabbed her in the throat with his left fist. She grabbed her throat with her hands as she fell back against the door and gasped for air. They watched in silence as she clawed at her throat and coughed, heaving for air. She looked at him in terror.

'Something you should know about me Ananya' said Jerry, 'is that I am a true gentleman, I really am.'

'He really is' Al agreed.

'But I don't fall for the innocent pretty girl act for even a second. We know you're in this deep with Lionel. You probably don't know that it was us that chased him down in Khartoum and killed him.' Jerry noted a flicker in her eyes as he said that. *Was Lionel not dead? Or did she not know about the firefight?* 'You should know that I will not hesitate to kill you unless you tell me what's going on. And don't think I won't kill you because I need your information. I'll kill you right here and then go and destroy every one of those drones and helicopters before anyone even manages to get out of bed and find some pants to put on. So get your breath back, stop trying to think of a way out of this, and start talking.'

She stared defiantly at him. 'You have no idea what you're getting into.'

'Yes yes, Lionel gave us that line too. Let's just assume that we're getting into this, however surprisingly dangerous it is. We're not going to leave you alone to continue just because there are some dangerous people out there. Now what is the plan?'

She looked at him. 'Two of you?...' He jabbed her in the throat again. She threw her head back, gasping for air and heaving her chest.

'Ananya, we really don't have a lot of time.' He checked his watch. 'I'd say you have about twenty minutes to make yourself useful before we have to kill you and then get on with destroying all the drones anyway.'

'What makes you so sure that the drones are that important anyway?' she gasped.

'We were in the operations room before we came to see you. We saw Jeffrey. He says hi. We also had a good look at the planning board, all the timings, flight paths, locations. I'd say we've got it pretty close to eighty percent nailed.'

'Maybe eighty five' said Al.

'But we don't get your role. Why did Lionel bring you on board? Have you been developing a genetic weapon for him?'

She studied his face for a moment.

'Well, there's nothing you can do about it anyway so why not. I have developed a genetically engineered weapon to target specific ethnicities within Chad.'

'Within Chad? Its people are the target?' asked Jerry.

'Yes, I identified eleven different ethnicities across the various clans in Chad, from the nomadic clans in the north to the farmers in the Sahel south. Each of them has a unique DNA sequence within their genes, which I was able to classify and develop a mutation for, which can then be inserted into their genes through an editing process.'

'An editing process? Are you going to carry out surgery on all of them?'

'No, it's contained within a virus, which is breathed in. Once the victim breathes it in, it makes its way into their bloodstream and then begins its work. It targets specific strands of DNA and replaces them with the mutated strands, which then replicate and multiply throughout the body.'

'A virus that changes your DNA? Like makes you white? Or tall?'

'Or dead?' said Al.

'The change in the DNA causes a virus to spread throughout the body, which within four hours will cause multiple organ failure.'

'What is it?' asked Jerry.

'We actually haven't given it a name yet. I'm sure someone will soon enough.'

'So you're going to kill everyone in Chad?'

'We will hit all the major population centres and kill around eighty percent of the non-Muslim population.'

'What the fuck?' said Al. 'Does that not strike you as a bit crazy?'

'What's crazy is that the world is overpopulated by three billion people. This continent is overpopulated by a billion, with rapidly diminishing resources. And Chad is particularly hopeless. Half of it is desert, the other half has had all its natural resources stripped out of it leaving it dry and empty. It virtually has no functioning economy, except for its oil, which will be gone soon. It contributes nothing to the continent or to the world, and no-one would be sorry if it just stopped existing.'

'This is genocide. Chad has a population of twenty million' said Jerry.

'But only forty five percent of them are non-Muslim, so very soon we will ease that burden by around seven million. And then there's the rest of the continent.'

'You're crazy. We've seen that sort of genocide before, and the world went to war over it.'

'Yes but that was a different time, in a place where it mattered. This is Africa. Do you really think the world is going to care about seven million deaths from a mystery disease, which only seems to be deadly to certain ethnicities? The rest of the world will see it as a relief, not a crime. After all, if there's nothing to take then the major powers aren't interested. It'll be big news for a few weeks and then forgotten.'

'These sound like Lionel's words' said Jerry. 'I don't think you really believe that, do you?'

Ananya smiled as though patronising a child. 'I know it's difficult to accept initially, but if you're really honest then you'd have to say you agree with the principle' she said. 'There are too many people for the world to support, and the world is trying to tell us that, through the increasing temperatures, the desertification, the disease, the famine. I spent too many years developing cures for diseases, just to sustain the massive population growth. But then working with Lionel I realised my time and energy would be much better spent figuring out not how to eradicate disease, but how to eradicate people. Humankind is a virus to the planet, so it's only fitting that a virus be used to correct it.'

'We all know that the world has some issues with overpopulation and scarce resources, particularly Africa, but the answer is to educate and give people choices, not to eradicate without any choice' said Jerry.

'Very noble coming from a man who is paid to kill people. What sort of education does a mercenary provide?'

Jerry had to admit that working for the Task Force did stretch his principles somewhat. He had never fully resolved the conflict he felt about the Task Force being the bludgeon that countries used to solve their problems. He had always tried to think of himself and the Force to be more of a scalpel, carefully shaping the political landscape, but in his dark moments he lay awake in bed and tortured himself with the truth. Even though they were almost always acting on behalf of legitimate governments, could he honestly say that every target they struck posed a genuine threat to society? Or was it purely a transaction? Now that Lionel had demonstrated his corruption Jerry was even more unsure. What he was sure of though was that committing mass murder in order to overthrow a government was way over the line.

'You're in no position to judge me' he growled. 'This is murder, and the blood of millions of people will be on *your* hands.'

'I can live with that. It's for the greater good.'

'I've had enough of your delusional bullshit.' Jerry looked at his watch. 'Lionel is gone, and we are ending this thing right now.'

'Do you really think that just two of you can stop this? This is bigger than just Lionel.'

'Who else wants this to happen?'

'Start with anyone who has an interest in the preservation of the Nigerian economy. What do you think its future is once all the oil has gone? Sure they have some manufacturing, some limited agriculture, some biotech, but that's not enough to sustain a hungry economy. They need another source of income.'

'International terrorism is not a sustainable source of income.'

She sneered. 'Chad is the unwitting victim in this project because it has an extremely precious resource under its feet, which no-one except the Chadian government and us, knows about yet.'

'And what's that?'

'Water! The resource there is so little of; that countries fight wars over; that is so scarce it is changing landscapes and demographics. Water is the new oil, and Chad has a massive supply of it.'

'How massive?'

'Enough to last for decades, all hidden under the ground where it can't be stolen, or ruined by industry. And what's more, Chad has already put in the infrastructure to start bringing it out of the ground, so we can just take it over and start pumping.'

Jerry connected the dots in his mind. 'The Bardai plant? In the Tibesti Mountains. That's a water pumping plant?'

'Oh so you're not as dumb as you look.'

'You said that Chad has no resources and so it is a burden, but now you're saying it has a huge natural resource. Admit it, this isn't about overpopulation, it's about murdering and stealing.'

'Call it what you want. There are some very powerful people backing this plan. It's an unstoppable train and it's too far down the line now.'

'We'll see about that. Now tell me where this DNA virus is. Is it already loaded onto the UAVs? How does it even disperse?'

'I've told you enough to make you see there's nothing you can do about it. I'm not going to tell you any more. Just blowing up a few drones is not going to prevent this. You should just give up now. '

Her arrogance was starting to piss Jerry off. He pulled out his pistol and turned to Al.

'Do you think we've heard enough from her? I think she's outlived her usefulness.'

'I couldn't agree more. We're just wasting time now.'

Jerry grabbed her by the hair and pushed the muzzle of the pistol up under her chin.

'Wait!' she cried. 'Don't do it! I'll tell you.'

Jerry tightened his grip on her hair. 'This isn't a game. You know we don't have any more time to waste. Tell us now where that weapon is or I swear I will pull the trigger.'

'It's in canisters, which are attached to the drones, where the missiles usually sit. I swear it. I can...''

With no warning Jerry lifted the pistol and clubbed her in the side of her head, knocking her out instantly.

'That's enough for now. And to think I found her attractive once. She's a psycho!'

'Weirdly, I still do! Is that wrong?'

'Let's get her tied up and gagged.'

'We can't take any more prisoners mate, we're running out of gags!'

They trussed her up securely.

'Right, I don't know what we're going to do about the Nigerian government being involved, but I do know that if there's no genetic weapon then it's not going to happen, so let's go for the canisters.'

'Sure, but what are we going to do with the canisters?'

'We'll just release the gas. It's only harmful to Chadians from those eleven clans, and the chances of any of those being on this airbase is tiny. Hopefully it will disperse in the air and no-one will be hurt.'

'And then what?'

'Well then we need to get off this airbase alive. Let's go.'

Chapter Twenty Seven

They pressed themselves against the hangar wall and peered around the corner at the parked UAVs, arranged in two rows. They were floodlit for the technicians, who were now busily working under the nearest aircraft. They could make out two large canisters on each wing of each UAV. They looked just like missiles and Jerry wondered if they were the wrong UAVs, but they must be the ones. There were no other UAVs here.

He nodded to Al and they stepped out and walked confidently towards the technicians, who looked up without suspicion as they approached. Jerry noted that their weapons were propped against the wheel of the UAV, ten feet away from the technicians.

'Hey, can you guys take a look at this?' asked Jerry, pointing his thumb back at the hangar.

'What's up?' asked one of the technicians. They both stepped out from under the aircraft.

'Jeffrey said there's something wrong with his terminal, and could you help him.'

'I'll take a look' said the first technician.

Jerry and Al wasted no more time. With two swift movements they had taken the technicians down and set about dragging them behind the front wheel.

They went to the first canister and studied it. Someone had gone to great lengths to make it look exactly like a regular missile, with the nose cone and fins, as well as the tail fins, but without the usual stamped name and type. The only printed text was 'Compressed Gas'. They studied the nose and the tail to find any point from which the virus gas could be disseminated. In the tail Al found a valve, which looked like it could be undone with a spanner. Jerry fetched an adjustable from the toolkit and handed it over.

'Are we sure about this?' asked Al, as he positioned the spanner on the valve.

'We don't have any other options, so I guess we have to assume she was telling the truth.'

'Okay, here goes nothing.' Al started loosening the valve, one turn at a time, until eventually the gas came rushing out as the pressure inside the canister tried to equalise with the pressure outside. They both held their breath for as long as they could before finally taking a tentative breath. They looked at each other for a moment, looking for signs of impending death.

'Nothing so far, so let's get them all done before it starts to take effect' shouted Jerry over the sound of the escaping gas.

'Sure, but that's as loud as a jet engine' replied Al. 'It's surely going to attract some attention.' They looked around to see if anyone was running towards them.

'All the more reason to get this done quickly. I counted eighteen drones, each with eight canisters, so that's...one hundred and forty four. Let's get on with it. I'll take the other row' said Jerry. He fetched another adjustable, and they set to work. They rushed between canisters, spinning the valves off as quickly as they could, finishing them with their fingers to make it faster. Jerry wondered if this virus did actually affect him, would his increased exposure to it give him less than four hours? He was unscrewing three per minute, with seventy two to get through. There wouldn't be enough time.

The minutes ticked by, and they dashed from canister to canister, from drone to drone. The sound of multiple canisters releasing their gas was incredibly loud now, and Jerry and Al couldn't have heard each other shout. Every time he finished a canister Jerry cast a quick glance over his shoulder, in case they had been discovered. Still nothing. His hands and fingers were aching but he knew that just another ten minutes and they would be done. He glanced over to Al to check his progress and noted that he was a whole wing ahead. *Goddammit, those are some fast fingers!* He put the pain in his fingers to one side and got competitive, twisting and unscrewing for all his worth, each new gush of air like a round of applause that spurred him on. He checked his progress. Three drones to go.

Suddenly above the sound of the rushing gas came the unmistakable sound of gunshots. Jerry took cover behind one of the wheels as bullets ricocheted off the legs of the drone. He reached for his rifle, which was slung across his back. Over the sound of the gas he could hear the shouts of Task Force soldiers, rallying each other and giving orders. He looked up and saw at least ten men approaching through the rows of drones, each moving carefully and using what cover they had. They had stopped firing at the drones and just held their weapons ready. Jerry didn't care about damaging the drones, he lifted his rifle from behind the wheel and fired a short burst of automatic fire at the closest group. They took cover and their advance stalled.

He could hear Al firing from his position too, and saw as he hit one of the guards, sending him crashing to the ground. His colleagues left him, and continued their progress. Jerry again lifted the rifle and fired several short bursts, taking down two of the guards. They were now only about seventy metres away, and Jerry could see that they were western, probably former soldiers just like he and Al were. He really didn't want to kill these men as they were just doing their job, probably not aware of the evil plan they were serving. But it was either him or them now, and he couldn't afford to lose.

The sound of escaping gas had abated, so he shouted to Al to fall back to his row. He laid down covering fire as Al moved, sending the guards scrambling for cover. Al joined him behind the leg of a drone.

'They're not gonna hold off shooting for long' said Al. 'We need an escape plan. I'm pretty sure it's not my destiny to die hiding behind a drone leg.'

Jerry quickly looked around and surveyed their options. The airfield to their left was open with no cover, the hangar to the right would certainly contain more guards. In fact, more were coming out as he looked. Another eight men. That left behind them, which was a hundred metre gap to a row of helicopters.

'Okay, let's get back to those helicopters. We'll lay a blanket of grenades to cover us. Hopefully we'll take out some of these drones too. How many do you have?'

'Four frag and two smoke.'

'Okay, let's do a smoke first and then make a dash for it. You cover to the right.' They each pulled out a smoke grenade, pulled the pin and sent them spinning along the ground. They started to spew smoke as they span, and after a few seconds had provided a curtain of cover. They stood up and ran as fast as they could. As they ran they pulled the pins from the fragmentation grenades and tossed them over their shoulders. In turn they heard them explode, followed by the subsequent explosions of the aircraft, as the compressed gas canisters were fractured and released their gas in a split second, obliterating everything nearby.

Jerry risked a quick look over his shoulder and saw a fantastic scene of carnage behind them. Burning drones surrounded by a field of smoke. The guards had abandoned their no shooting policy though, and were coming fast, firing bursts of automatic from their hips as they ran. Jerry and Al made for the helicopters as fast as they could manage, but suddenly Al let out a cry and fell to his knees. Jerry stopped and looked down at him. He had been hit in the back, just above the left kidney. He was clutching the wound as he tried to lift himself up. Jerry grabbed his arm and hauled him up, putting his arm around his waist to support him. Together they ducked behind the first helicopter and kept staggering along until they had had passed a few more. Jerry looked around desperately. They'd never manage to hide here. They'd be found in ten minutes. He looked over to the nearest hangar, which was about fifty metres away. Where else was there to go.

'Get your smoke out buddy' he said, taking his second smoke grenade from his pouch. 'We're gonna throw the smoke and make for the hangar. See that door? We've got to be fast, can you do it?'

'Sure, let's do it' gasped Al, pulling the pin on his grenade and tossing it under the helicopters, towards the approaching guards. Jerry did the same and they started running. They heard bullets whizzing by them, but managed to make it to the hangar without being hit. They barged in through the door and locked it shut behind them.

They turned to look at the hangar. It was dark, except for the emergency exit lights along the walls. Inside the hundred metre long hangar were hundreds of pallets, stacked with boxes, bags and crates. They stretched the whole way to the opposite end of the hangar.

'Come on, let's find a place to hide in here' said Jerry, guiding Al along. They ran towards the far corner, until Al had to stop. He collapsed on the floor, panting and holding his back. Jerry pulled out a field dressing from one of Al's pouches and unwrapped it.

'Here, press this on it buddy. Push it hard.' He helped Al with the pressure. At that moment the orange ceiling lights glowed dimly and began to warm up. They heard a man's voice calling across the hangar.

'Jerry Vasquez, and Al Van de Berg. Your time is up. Give up now.' The accent was European, perhaps Scandinavian Jerry thought. They heard the sounds of quick footsteps as the guards fanned out around the hangar, searching between the pallets. They would soon be found, the only tactic left, other than a blaze of glory, was to talk their way out.

'This is Jerry Vasquez, head of operations for Task Force Africa' he shouted. 'Any of you Task Force guys out there that know me and Al, you know we're the good guys. Whatever they've told you about us, it's not true.' He sent his voice bouncing off the walls, to conceal their position if possible.

'You cannot talk your way out Mr Vasquez, you are a felon and will be brought to justice…' the voice echoed around the hangar. The lights were a little brighter now.

'Whoever that guy is, he is planning to kill millions of people in Chad,' Jerry continued. 'And then to steal a secret supply of water and sell it. He's using the Task Force to do it' he shouted, hoping someone he knew was listening. He pushed harder on Al's wound as it oozed more blood.

'You are the killer Mr Vasquez. You killed Lionel Caplin.' Jerry could hear the footsteps drawing closer.

'He was in charge of the operation. He was trying to kill us. Listen guys, you have to believe me. If we were guilty we wouldn't come back here, we'd still be running. We came back here to stop this thing. It's genocide!'

'Jerry?' a different voice. 'Jerry, where are you?'

'Yash?' shouted Jerry. 'Yash, you believe me right? You know me. You know that isn't me.'

'I want to Jerry, but they said you went rogue and killed Lionel and Porter.'

'Silence! Stand down!' shouted the voice.

'It's not true Yash, Porter was killed by them. Lionel was heading it up. There's a corrupt streak running through the force.'

A figure appeared around the pallet to Jerry's left. Jerry reacted and quickly raised his rifle, ready for the final battle to begin. Before he squeezed the trigger he recognised Yash, his British team-mate from the Gabon mission. He had his hands up and his weapon down. He put his finger on his lips as he crept forwards. Jerry lowered his weapon and smiled.

'I swear it's true Yash' he whispered. 'It's a huge operation to kill millions and take over the government.'

Yash nodded. 'Of course I believe you. More than I do that wanker' he whispered. He called out to the men around the hangar, 'This is Yash Philips. I know Jerry and I believe him. He's one of us. Stand down.'

'Don't listen to him!' shouted the voice. 'He is one of their accomplices. Shoot them all.'

'I'm not an accomplice. I'm a professional soldier, like all of you' shouted Yash. 'You know me. Do the right thing and stand down now.'

'Don't listen to his bullshit, shoot them!'

'Does that sound like a guy who's doing the right thing?' asked Yash. 'He's using us. Don't let him.'

'Stand down' came the order from various voices around the hangar, as the men made their decision. It echoed around the hangar as more of them agreed. Several of them appeared around pallets and approached Jerry, weapons lowered. There was nothing more from the voice.

'Thanks Yash. This is crazy' said Jerry. 'Who is that guy anyway?'

'His name is Laurence Campbell. He's some senior guy in the Task Force. He showed up yesterday to take over the force, told us Lionel was dead and that some trouble was brewing in Chad. He said we'd be on standby here for the next few days in case it turned bad and we needed to go in a hurry.'

'Well it looks like he's planning to launch the operation this morning.'

'Not since you appeared and blew the place up! You've knocked out a few of those drones.'

'Al got one in the back. Is there a medic here? He's losing blood and needs stabilising immediately.' Al looked weak and close to passing out on the floor. A medic appeared and began working on him.

'We need to get after Campbell' said Jerry. 'Even though his plan is finished we still need to take him down.' He turned to Al and knelt down beside him. 'I'm gonna go and finish this thing buddy, hang tight and this guy will get you fixed up.'

Al nodded and forced a smile. 'Go get 'em!'

Jerry stood and addressed Yash and the team. 'Right, we need to track Campbell down and neutralise him. I don't think taking him into custody is going to be enough, he's too well connected to face any sort of justice. So it will have to be lethal force.'

Yash nodded and gathered his team together to brief them and assign tasks. A few moments later they broke and were on their way out of the exit, heading for the Task Force hangar. As they hit the outside, Jerry noticed that first light had broken, and the morning sun was starting to glow below the horizon. His eyes were heavy and grainy with fatigue, and he had to blink a few times to adjust to the semi-dark outside.

He looked over to the burning drones to assess the damage, and saw that there were several missing. The ones they didn't have the time to clear before the shooting started. Where were they? He ran towards the burning rows, where fire trucks were starting to arrive and fight the fires. He quickly counted the drones he could see, and arrived at fourteen. There were definitely gaps where the final four had been. He looked around, at the helicopter park and past it towards the airstrip. Far in the distance, perhaps a kilometre away he could see the drones taxiing onto the runway and accelerating together down the strip. He watched as they each lifted off the ground and soared into the sky, heading north into the pink morning sky. He checked his watch. 05:43. Campbell had launched the drones early.

He turned back to the burning drones and looked for the technicians they had knocked out earlier. They weren't where they had left them. He scanned around towards the hangar and saw them sitting inside the main hangar door. He ran over to them. When they saw him they scrambled for their weapons, fearing another attack.

'Hey, relax, I'm not here to fight.' He explained what had happened and asked for their help. They cautiously agreed, and explained that the drones had been pre-programmed with routes and weapon release points, and were now flying fully automated. They would reach Lake Chad and cross into Chadian airspace within an hour, and then make their way south to N'Djamena where they would release the weapons.

'Who is controlling them?' asked Jerry.

'No-one now. They have been released on automatic flight. There is no pilot control over them, unless it is overridden from the command station.'

'Where is the command station? There must be a pilot watching them.'

'Those mobile units there.' The technician pointed to a row of units lined up along the side of the next hangar. They looked like shipping containers. 'There's one command station for each pair of UAVs.'

'Which stations are controlling the drones that just took off?'

'No idea. There'll be someone in those stations though.'

Jerry thanked them, apologised about their heads again, and ran to the nearest command station. He drew his pistol and pulled open the door, taking cover behind it in case of any defensive fire. The station was empty and dark. He moved on to the next station and repeated the process, again finding it empty. He continued to check the stations, finding each one in turn empty.

Near the end of the line of stations he finally found one which had lights on, but no-one inside at first glance. He cautiously stepped into the unit, sweeping his pistol round to cover all the corners. The unit was clear. He turned to the command station for the UAVs and found that they had been destroyed; screens smashed and control handles ripped off. Jerry guessed they had been set off on their pre-programmed routes and then the station disabled so they couldn't be recalled. He looked in the next command station and found the same damage. He wondered if these four drones could be taken over by another command station. It seemed possible; he needed a pilot to confirm, but there was no one around.

He stepped out of the command station and looked around. The only people he could see were the firefighters at work, and the guards searching for Campbell in and around the hangars. He saw Yash and called him over.

'Any success with locating him?'

'No, we searched the whole hangar and the accommodation building. How about here?'

'No, but it looks like he's been here. I think he launched the remaining four drones and then destroyed the command units. They're flying on autopilot, on pre-programmed routes. I don't know if a pilot can override them from another command station. Are there any here?'

'I'm sure we can find one.' He turned and shouted to one of the guards to find a UAV pilot and bring him to the command stations.

'How about Campbell?' said Jerry. 'Where else could he be? Maybe he's left the airbase?'

'He arrived by private jet I think. It's parked down at the civilian airport end of the airbase.'

'I guess he'll be making a run for it then' said Jerry. 'He could be long gone by now, and I guess we'll catch up to him eventually with the evidence. The most important thing now is to make sure those drones don't make it to Chad.'

'I'm not sure he's the kind of guy who will be brought to justice' said Yash. 'He's no doubt got friends in high places who will protect him. Who are you going to take the evidence to?'

'What evidence? All we have is a pile of burning drones, and the ops room...and Ananya!' He rushed to the SUV and opened the door. Ananya lay on the back seat, still unable to move. She was now conscious, and looked up at him with fiery eyes. She tried to talk and move her legs, as if to sit up. Jerry closed the door and ran back to Yash.

'She's still there. She's the genetic scientist who developed this weapon.'

A man wearing a pilot's flight suit came running over to them and asked what he needed. Jerry explained about the drones and the command units. He asked the pilot if the drones could be controlled from another command unit.

'Not really, they are each programmed to their own individual unit. Once they established that communication link between the drones and the unit it was impregnable. It's that way so that no-one else can hack a drone and divert it. It's a security precaution.'

'So there's no way of stopping them now?'

'No, they're locked on to their targets. We can't do anything from here.'

Chapter Twenty Eight

Al Quraysh and Abu Khalid sat together in silence sipping arabic coffee, each lost in his own thoughts. It was three in the morning and they were seated in a grand majlis of the royal palace, where they had been kept under house arrest since the leadership challenge the night before. The new President, Abu Rashed, would denounce them in the morning and claim the title of President as his own. Neither had been able to sleep, so they had come to sit together to share their grief. Initially Al Quraysh had indulged in an angry rant about Abu Rashed's treachery and the weakness of the shura in not seeing through his plot. Abu Khalid had given sympathetic nods and grunts; his spirits too low to rouse any anger yet. His dark eyes, hanging jaw and drooping shoulders showed a deep weariness, but his mind was anything but weary. As he half listened to Al Quraysh ranting he was busy running through all of Abu Rashed's comments and intonations that he had witnessed but not previously registered. He was beginning to put together a picture of a man who had systematically laid a trap for the President and then guided him into its jaws.

He had been roused from his musings by a change in Al Quraysh's tone. He had become calmer, more melancholy, and was opening his hands to Abu Khalid as he spoke - exposing his soul. He had revealed his shameful secret about having been duped by a Task Force agent; about having shared his bed and matters of state with the spy. He had hung his head as he confessed his sins to his closest advisor and friend, who had listened with amazement. The revelation left Abu Khalid stunned.

After his confession Al Quraysh had sat deep in thought, trying to recall and work through everything he had ever told her, as well as everything she had said to him. He remembered all the intimate moments they had shared, and winced with pain at the thought that every time she had been only thinking of how to manipulate him further; how to work her way from his bed into his mind. For a while they had sat in silence, unsure of what to say next. The truth they now shared was unthinkable, and neither of them had wanted to confront it.

'What do you think she was trying to achieve? What was her mission?' asked Abu Khalid.

'I assume she was sent to manipulate me into going to war with Chad, because she disappeared as soon as the first attacks happened. Now I think about it she was always very disparaging about President Ayatumbe. She was sowing seeds in my mind.'

'So you would take us to war?'

'Yes, and then lose my Presidency. She must have been in league with Abu Rashed, planning it together and coordinating their attacks on me.'

'You think Abu Rashed is working with the Task Force? That he is a spy also?'

'This is too much of a coincidence for them not to be connected. She flees the country on the same day we go to war, and that Abu Rashed seizes power. That dog is a traitor! He must have been planning to seize power for years now.'

'But why would the Task Force be interested in deposing you and giving the Republic to Abu Rashed? What do they have to gain from that? And why Chad?'

'Perhaps because Chad is so weak. And why? Maybe a proxy operation? Perhaps Abu Rashed is actually a puppet of the superpowers? Maybe Russia wants to have a power base in East Africa? We know they have been tussling with India for the commercial exploitation of Ethiopia and Somalia.'

'Their tentacles are indeed long, and their approaches to us have been extensive' agreed Abu Khalid. 'It is possible that they would use the Task Force to do their dirty work and to get what they want anyway.'

They both silently pondered the possibility for a few moments, reflecting on the approaches that had been made by the super-rich Russian state in recent years. Twenty years ago it had found a way to tap into its mega supply of minerals in Siberia, and had then completed a supply route into China. The resulting trade relationship had catapulted Russia's wealth way ahead of that of its superpower peers. But hand in hand with that wealth came an increasing tendency to meddle in international affairs, even more than it previously had. The African population boom had made its countries increasingly attractive potential customers for Russia, who had been applying enormous economic pressure to extend its influence and wealth; pressure which the Republic had been resisting, preferring instead to establish regional partnerships. It seemed likely that this snub had encouraged Russia to seek alternative means to get their way. Having a new President, who favoured Russian contracts, was a perfect way to bypass the existing impasse.

During his silent pondering an idea had started to form in Abu Khalid's mind, and he had spent a few minutes mentally developing it before proposing his embryonic plan. Al Quraysh had listened silently, and after some initial reticence had then quickly warmed to the idea, attracted by its simple boldness and its enticing promise of redemption. He had sat forward in his seat, his face lighter and alive with excitement at the proposal, and they had quickly developed the plan further before summoning a trusted aide, who had been dispatched with an urgent message.

Several hours later the initial rush of excitement and activity had faded as they waited and wondered. They began to think of problems and pitfalls which would stymie their plan, and the shadow of doubt had crept into their minds, clouding their vision and choking their optimism. What if the American couldn't be found? What if he refused to talk? What if he talked too much? Why would the shura believe them?

They were saved from their anguish by a gentle knock at the door, and an aide giving them a simple nod. They rose excitedly and followed him quickly through the corridors to a service area they had never visited before. It was dark and silent in the dead of the night and made them all the more nervous. They entered a kitchen preparation room; a cold bright room with white walls, metal benches and a hard concrete floor. Al Quraysh's head of security, Mohammed Al Mashra was waiting, standing in front of a chair, on which sagged the broken figure of a man. His head was hung to his chest; only his white hair and the back of his thick neck were visible. His clothes were bloodstained and torn open, revealing the thick torso of a man who had clearly once been very powerful but had now given way to the inevitable decline of middle age. His body was also stained with blood, as well as iodine. A thick bandage was wrapped around his middle. He may have been dead but for the slight rise and fall of his chest.

Al Quraysh nodded to Al Mashra, who stepped forward and slapped the unconscious man hard across his face. He got no response and so tried again. The man grunted and slowly raised his head. His eyes were half open and swollen, his skin was grey. He had lost a lot of blood and looked close to death. His eyes worked slowly upwards to regard the tall figure of Al Quraysh. His expression did not change at all.

'So you are the one. You are the Spymaster. The American. Mr Lionel Caplin.'

He did not expect any acknowledgement or reply. That wasn't yet required in the plan, which was just as well as Lionel Caplin did not look at all ready, or able, to talk.

'You have caused me a great deal of trouble Mr Caplin. You and your spies in my palace, plotting to undermine my authority and overthrow me; creating conflict where there was peace. It surprises me, and almost impresses me that you managed to get someone so close, in such a position as to influence my thinking and actions without me suspecting anything until it was too late. You must have been planning this for some time.'

Again the statement was rhetorical. He was simply laying the foundations of what was to come.

'And now you think you have succeeded. You think that today your plan has been achieved as I am usurped and my country plunges into conflict.'

Still no response.

'But I am afraid you are quite wrong Mr Caplin. Here I am alive and well, and with you at my feet. Now we know what you were planning we will put a stop to the conflict. You will not achieve your sinister ambition.'

For the first time a flicker of recognition registered on Lionel's face. He glanced up at Al Quraysh to read his eyes, unsure if he was bluffing. Al Quraysh saw that he had found his target and continued.

'Your plan has been revealed to me and within the hour not only will you be dead from your wounds, but also all attacks will be halted. The new dawn will not see the carnage you intended. Instead it will see the restoration of peace, and the execution of your accomplices for treason.'

Lionel raised his head slowly to face Al Quraysh.

'Fuck you!' he spat out. 'You know nothing.'

Al Quraysh sighed theatrically.

'Come now Mr Caplin. Do you really think I could know nothing of what you have been doing? This is my country you are meddling with. There is little that happens without me knowing it.'

'Not this time Al Quraysh. I know all of your secrets and you know jack shit.'

Al Quraysh sighed again and nodded to the head of security, who roughly forced Lionel's hands behind his back and began to bind them with rope.

'You are really not in a strong bargaining position Mr Caplin, and it seems there is much you do not know about the country, and the person, you have chosen to screw. Let me demonstrate something you do not know about me; some traditional hospitality. And then we will see how talkative you are.'

Al Mashra lifted Lionel's arms behind his back and tightly bound his two thumbs with the rope. Lionel gasped with pain as his upper body was pushed forward and the gunshot wound in his abdomen was contracted.

'You will find that my head of security, Mr Al Mashra, is quite skilled in extracting information. He does tend to be somewhat old-fashioned in his methods, but they are most effective.'

Al Mashra kicked away Lionel's chair, sending him crashing painfully to the ground. He dragged him backwards using the rope as a leash, to the far wall. There Al Mashra slung the rope over a large metal hook on the wall and proceeded to heave on it, forcing Lionel to scramble to his feet. Lionel was panting with pain, and his already blood-stained bandages were starting to darken with fresh flow. He looked Al Quraysh directly in the eyes now, as if to say *Fuck you again*, though he couldn't manage to actually mouth the words. After a short pause Al Mashra heaved again, pulling Lionel's arms up level with his shoulders. His shoulders were twisted and threatened to pop out of their sockets, causing him to roar with pain. As he was pulled higher the strain on his ligaments intensified as they were stretched beyond their limits. His feet were now clear of the ground, dangling below his hunched and shaking torso. He felt the ligaments rip as they failed to support his weight. The sudden pain was so intense it even exceeded that from the gunshot wound. He let out a guttural scream, unable to control himself. His shoulders and sides were on fire as his muscles now tensed to compensate for the missing ligaments; but in his weakened state they couldn't last for long, and the weight of his body stretched them until they began to rip.

'Stop. Please,' he sobbed. 'I'll talk. I'll tell you...'

Al Mashra immediately slackened the rope, sending Lionel crashing to the ground in a sobbing heap. Al Quraysh stepped forward and looked down at him.

'Good decision Mr Caplin. Now tell me everything of your plan; and do not leave out any details. If you are having trouble with your memory then Mr Al Mashra here can help you to remember.'

Lionel squirmed and wriggled to move his body into a more comfortable position, but couldn't find any relief from the agonising pain. Al Mashra hoisted him by his collar into a sitting position and splashed some water on his face.

'She was supposed to win your trust,' he panted, 'and then convince you to launch attacks on Chad.'

'Why? What is it to you if the Republic is in conflict with Chad? Is it just to undermine me?'

'No,' said Lionel, 'it's just a cover for the main operation. A sort of diversion to make it look like you're really going to war.'

'A diversion from what?'

'From the main attacks we will conduct from Nigeria.'

'On the Republic?'

Lionel looked at him in amazement. He didn't actually know anything about the plan at all.

'No, the attacks are on Chad. There is no attack on the Republic at all.'

'Other than to discredit and depose me!'

'What? No, that's not the plan at all. We intend to seize control of Chad and insert a proxy government. We have no plans for you other than to foment a conflict.'

'Well then what is the role of Abu Rashed in this plan? What is he doing for you?'

'That man is not working with us, or for us at all.'

'This cannot be true. Do you swear it?' Al Quraysh was incredulous. Abu Rashed had to be involved; otherwise what was he doing?

'I swear it. I have had no contact with him at all. My only knowledge of him is through Aishah and what she reported to me.'

The mention of her name made Al Quraysh's blood suddenly run cold.

'Then is he simply a usurper, trying to seize my throne?' he wondered aloud.

Their plan to force a confession from the American, implicating Abu Rashed in his plot, was in trouble. It seemed there was no connection between the two cataclysmic events, which seemed to be too much of a coincidence. Too much for it to be true. The American was clearly lying. Al Quraysh nodded again to Al Mashra, who heaved on the rope, forcing a scream from Lionel.

'I swear it's the truth!' sobbed Lionel. 'I don't know anything about him or what he is doing. He is not part of our plan at all.'

'Then if you are telling the truth, and he is not involved, why are you intending to take control of Chad?'

Lionel hesitated. Even though he was delirious with the pain in his shoulders and chest, he recognised that this was a turning point. It was a big step to give up this part of the plan as it would likely compromise the whole affair.

He didn't have any more time to debate it though as he was wrenched up off his feet by an almighty tug from Al Mashra. Lionel could not stop the over-rotation of his shoulders as his weakened and torn muscles offered no resistance. The weight of his exhausted body was too much for the stressed shoulder joints. His left shoulder slipped agonisingly out of its socket. The pain was white and blinding. Lionel was only half-conscious as the pressure was again released and he fell to the floor. Again water was thrown in his face, followed by a swift slap across his cheek. His half-open eyes struggled to focus on the grim face of Al Quraysh above him.

"Now Mr Caplin. Tell me your plan or Mr Al Mashra will certainly end your life tonight. Talking is your only way to survive this.'

Lionel's eyes spontaneously filled with tears and he sobbed involuntarily. He forced a slow nod and tried to compose himself.

'We intend to seize control of Chad because it has a huge underground reserve of fresh water; under the Tibesti mountains in the north west. It is worth trillions of dollars. The government of Chad thinks it is a secret, but we know. We have a sympathetic new president in waiting, who will work with us and our partners for the pumping rights in exchange for a very generous personal income.'

Al Quraysh stood over Lionel and thought about the audacity of the plan, and its implications. A new fresh water source would make Chad the richest country in the whole continent ....or whoever had control of Chad. It was a great plan, with untold wealth as its objective, and he had fortuitously stumbled upon its architect. Could he steal the plan, and take it for his own? Unlikely as he did not control any of the Task Force assets poised to invade Chad. So it was imperative that he should have control of the American and therefore have a controlling stake in the operation. He now just needed to get rid of Abu Rashed. His course of action was clear: use the American to present evidence to the shura that Abu Rashed conspired against him; have him executed for treason; seize power back; and claim the prize for himself. He sent Al Mashra on an urgent mission to gather the shura council members together before turning to Lionel.

'Mr Caplin you have a new business partner. Now tell me exactly how we are going to seize control of Chad, and then I have a job for you to do.'

Abu Rashed was woken from his light sleep by a knock at the door. He was laid out on a sofa in the private quarters of the palace, where he had retired to in order to reflect on the night's events and what lay before him tomorrow. He had sat for hours thinking about the plans he would make, ministers he would appoint, riches he would amass. He had drifted off into an uncomfortable sleep some time in the early hours. He looked at a clock and saw that it was just after six. Had he been woken for Fajr prayer, the first of the five daily prayers? No, it was too late for that.

The face at the door was that of Abdullah Al Mehlan, Abu Rashed's closest advisor. His face looked grave as he apologised for the interruption.

'What is it Abu Issa?' said Abu Rashed as he sat upright.

'Ameer, there has been a very disturbing occurrence during the night. It seems that Abu Saif and Abu Khalid have brought a man into the palace and they are plotting with him to overthrow you today.'

'Who is this man? How do you know what they are planning?'

'He is an american man who appears to be a commander of Task Force Africa. He is currently speaking about your involvement in a conspiracy to overthrow Abu Saif. We are able to listen to their conversation using a listening device in the kitchen they are using.'

'Wallah, I knew he would try to fight me, but I never imagined he would work so fast. Let me hear what they are saying, right from the start.'

'Ameer, regrettably we only have the last ten minutes of their conversation as the device was not active until a routine patrol saw them in the kitchen and alerted us. They appear to be planning a speech he will give about the alleged treason plot.'

'What treason plot is this? And who is this American? Let me see what they are planning and we will bring it swiftly to an end.'

He rose from the sofa and straightened his robes, before following Abu Issa out of the room. As they walked Abu Issa explained all that had been said so far. They entered a security office, where two men were sitting at a desk looking at computer screens. They stood up and deferentially offered him a seat, which he took without thanks. From the computer screen he could hear the voice of the American, who appeared to be in the closing stages of delivering a monologue.

'...and he wanted the Task Force to infiltrate your government in order to undermine your authority and make you look weak. He said that when he took control of The Republic he would make me commander of the Armed Forces. He also said that he would have the shura council executed and would install his own loyal advisors. I refused to cooperate with him of course and as soon as he took power he tried to have me killed. That is when I contacted you because I knew he was out of control.'

'You were right to come to me. This is a terrible tale of treason and it seems Abu Rashed is quite mad.' The voice of Abu Saif sounded smug and self-satisfied.

Abu Rashed slammed the desk and stood up.

'This is outrageous! These are lies and I will not have it. He is plotting against me in this very palace, and with an international military force no less!' He paced the room, angrily muttering to himself.

One of the security guards nervously looked up from his screen and quietly addressed Abu Issa.

'Sir, it appears that several members of the shura council are starting to arrive at the rear entrance to the palace.'

Abu Rashed turned sharply.

'They are coming now? How did he summon them?'

'Perhaps he has another accomplice. Someone who has free rein to move around the palace' suggested Abu Issa.

'And now he plans to show them this American liar and discredit me, in order to take back power. He is a maniac.'

'Ameer we must also face the possibility that he is about to kill the shura council, perhaps to implicate you and also as revenge for not supporting him. Very neatly serving two purposes.'

'That seems possible. That American must not be seen by anyone. Gather some guards; we must intercept them now. Let's go.'

Abu Issa hurriedly issued some orders to the security men and hastened after Abu Rashed, off to fight for his presidency and perhaps his life.

Chapter Twenty Nine

The helicopter journey to the capital passed in less than an hour. Okoro and his team sat in silence, other than the deafening roar of the twin engines above. Each man thought about the harrowing events of the last thirty six hours, and what might lay ahead of them. Okoro thought about what Arafa would be doing now, and when he would next speak to her. They were not allowed to use phones when on deployment, for fear of the signal being tracked by the enemy, allowing them to identify their precise location. This seemed perverse to him given that the entire operating base was a beacon of internet and radio traffic, but that was one of the quirks of serving in the military, you did as you were told.

They landed and the ramp lowered to reveal a very different scene to that which they had left. Instead of a dusty windy plain they now looked out on a tarmac landing strip, with large hangars beyond. They had come to an airbase on the eastern edge of the capital, where the 15th Regiment were now based. They debarked the aircraft and were directed to a hangar. He dropped off his kit and then met his new company commander, Major Alawesi; a fat man with tired eyes and an unsympathetic expression.

'Welcome to Mtala airbase Captain Okoro. We are based here to conduct urban defence patrols and ensure no enemy aircraft penetrate the air defences and reach the capital. I understand you were involved in an air battle and managed to destroy one of the Republic's Firebirds?'

'Yes sir.'

'I hear you all fought very bravely. Now you're in luck, we have an empty detachment command for you. You have two Interceptors as well as a stand-in engineer crew. You can use your own pilots and gunners. Let me show you your patrol areas on the map.' He spent some time pointing out the areas, which were to the north of the city, along the border with Cameroon, up to the swampland which used to be the site of the magnificent Lake Chad and also formed the border with Nigeria. Okoro looked at the patrol area and noted it was as far away from the action as it was possible to be. They were taking it easy on him and giving his team a risk-free mission. He didn't know whether to be insulted or grateful.

'Happy with your boundaries? Let's go and meet the team.'

Major Alawesi introduced him to his new team of engineers and the two aircraft.

'I'll give you some time to settle in. First mission is 08:00. You had better eat now. It could be a long day ahead of you.'

Jerry and Yash stood in the operations room in the hangar, studying the planning board and all the details of the operation. They had been joined by the drone pilot, who was explaining the capability of the aircraft and the planning figures they could use. They had established that the drones currently in the air were scheduled to fly to the capital N'Djamena and dump their deadly gas all over the city. The distance to N'Djamena was sixteen hundred kilometres, flight time was scheduled to be one hundred and six minutes to the target at cruising speed of nine hundred kilometres an hour, a release run of twenty minutes at four hundred kilometres an hour, followed by one hundred and six minutes home again at cruising speed. Jerry checked his watch again. 06:30. The drones should enter Chadian airspace at 07:23 and reach N'Djamean at 07:29. They would already be halfway across Nigeria by now.

'What if we chased them and shot them down?' he suggested to the pilot.

'If we factor in the scramble time now, a fighter jet flying at Mach 2 would reach the border in…', he did some quick mental arithmetic, 'around forty four minutes, allowing for some time to get up to speed. That's 07:15. And that assumes that the Nigerians have a fighter on standby that we would be able to task immediately, which is unlikely except in emergency.'

'I think this may qualify as an emergency, and there is about to be a war, so who can we talk to?'

'Look, that timing assumes we can scramble the aircraft right now. It will take more than ten minutes to get this authorised by the Nigerians, meaning it could be more like 07:25 before it gets to the border. That's too late, and I just don't think the Nigerians will scramble a fighter for us at short notice.'

Jerry nodded but said nothing. His mind raced with possible solutions.

'One of our helicopter gunships won't make it in time?' said Yash.

'No, they top out at four hundreds kilometres an hour. They couldn't catch a drone at cruising speed, not even by firing a missile which can go supersonic. The drones just have too much of a head start.'

They stood in silence for a few moments, studying the board and thinking of new ideas to stop the drones. Jerry was aware that literally every minute they thought about it was a minute closer to the death of millions of people. Then he had an idea.

'Chad! We should just tell the Chadian Air Force that there are some drones coming for them, and they need to be destroyed. If we tell them why I'm sure they'll agree. How do we contact the Chadian Air Force?'

'We could do it from one of the command stations. They have built-in communication platforms for coordinating between air traffic control centres and Air Force headquarters.'

'Well there's no time to lose. Let's go' said Jerry.

At that moment the windows of the operations room imploded in a thousand pieces, as a heavy machine gun opened up outside. The bullets smashed into the wall, the desks and the planning board. They dove to the floor, putting their hands over their heads to protect from the flying debris. Jerry recognised the high-pitched whine of each burst of fire as coming from a mini gun. It raked across the wall, firing one hundred rounds per second from its six rotating barrels, tearing through the brick and wood.

'Let's get out of here!' shouted Jerry. They crawled along the floor, amongst the broken glass and splinters of wood, to the doorway. Once through they crouched and ran for cover behind one of the pallets in the hangar.

'What the hell is going on?' shouted Yash.

'If I had to guess, I'd say that Campbell isn't done with us yet' said Jerry. 'We know too much now, so he needs to silence us.'

The bullets were now ripping through the wall between the operations room and the hangar, smashing into the pallets and their contents. Jerry noticed that some of the pallets contained boxes of ammunition.

'We'd better get out of here too, if any of that ammunition goes up then this place will turn into a firework show, and we'll be watching it from a couple of feet away.'

They dashed further from the gunfire, putting several more pallets between them and it. The fire was now destroying the next room, moving down the hangar to ensure there was no escape.

'It looks like they're using a vehicle mounted mini gun' said Jerry. 'Pretty soon they'll be coming in the main hangar door. I wouldn't be surprised if there are some troops coming in too, to sweep up any survivors.'

'Campbell must be pretty pissed at us' said Yash.

'Yeah and he clearly has some support still' said Jerry. 'Where are your team? We could use some help here.'

Yash got on his radio and summoned any troops in the hangar.

282

'Only three checked in' he said. 'The others must be somewhere else, out of range.'

'Three will have to be enough. We need to take out that gun, and Campbell too.' He turned to the pilot. 'We need to get you into one of those command stations too, so you can warn the Chadians about the drones.'

'The firing is coming from right next to the stations. It will be impossible for me to get there while the gun is working.'

'All the more reason to get this show on the road right now' said Jerry, as the three Task Force guys arrived. 'What weapons do we have?'

They did a quick weapons check and found they had six pistols and five assault rifles. Jerry sent two of the guys to check what weapons and ammunition they could find in the pallets. He and Yash did a quick recce from the destroyed window and wall of the operations room. There was now a strip of daylight showing where the wall had been ripped apart. It was a wonder that the wall above hadn't yet collapsed.

Through the gap they could see the line of command stations opposite, approximately thirty metres away, running down the side of the neighbouring hangar. They looked down to the left and saw the assault vehicle, an open top all terrain vehicle with the mini gun mounted on top. It was being operated by a gunner, with a loader managing the ammunition cartridges, which were being consumed at a fantastic rate. Patrolling behind the vehicle were a group of troops, waiting for the mini gun to soften the target before conducting their assault. Jerry counted twelve. They were approximately fifty metres away now, moving away from them.

'Here's a good chance to get across to the command stations' said Jerry. 'Go and get the pilot.'

Yash ran to the doorway and called him over. Jerry watched the progress of the assault group. The mini gun was a fearsome weapon, firing up to six thousand rounds per minute. They were more usually mounted on attack helicopters or planes, but this one had been vehicle mounted as a mobile airbase defence platform.

Yash appeared with the pilot. Jerry quickly explained the plan for him to make the dash across while they covered him from here. If the assault troops happened to turn around then Jerry and Yash would open up on them to give him some cover. He nervously agreed and prepared himself to run. Jerry checked he knew all the right information to give and gave him a pat on the back, sending him off.

He climbed out through the gap in the wall, staying low as he began his run across. Jerry and Yash stood ready to provide covering fire. Jerry looked at his watch. The time was 06:45, so he would be able to get the message to them and give them plenty of time to scramble their defences.

Suddenly there was a burst of fire from the right, from the opposite end of the hangar. The pilot fell, hit in the side. He didn't move.

Al Quraysh checked the time. 06:45. The shura would soon be formed in the meeting room, discreetly tucked away in the bowels of the palace, free from interruption. The American had done his job well. His desire to live had proven to be far greater than his stubbornness. Better to be a live millionaire than a dead almost-billionaire. He reflected on how the profits from this plan were going to be fantastical; beyond anything he could have achieved legitimately as President. He hesitated for a moment and thought of the millions of Chadians about to lose their lives in order that he could cash in on the riches they never knew they had. Ah well, they were faceless victims and life was cheap in Africa.

Al Mashra appeared in the doorway. He gave a solemn nod.

'Mohammad Saif Al Awari's car has been destroyed and all passengers killed, as you ordered Ameer. My men used foreign weapons. It will certainly look convincingly like the first of the attacks on the shura.'

'Excellent work brother. I did not want to have to take this action, and Allah will judge me, but it is in the best interests of our country you understand?'

'As you say Ameer, these are dangerous times and there are always casualties.'

'You have prepared the distraction also?'

'Yes Ameer. As the shura begins a team of my men will launch an attack against the rear security gate. It will divert any attention from your meeting and will also give you the ammunition you need to convince the council that drastic action must be taken immediately.'

'Yes, they will certainly feel the danger and will have to make the connection to Abu Rashed seizing control. Once I have their agreement then we can move against Abu Rashed swiftly and regain control. Is the American still alive?'

'Yes, he is being treated now and Abu Khalid is ensuring he is ready. He has had some powerful drugs to treat his pain. The damage to his body will take a very long time to heal though.'

'I am not interested in how he heals. I just need him to stay alive long enough to deliver his speech and activate the plan this morning and to ensure our stake in it. Make sure Abu Khalid knows he is there for the shura to see, but to keep him drugged and get him out quickly; the shura can never learn of the Chad plan.'

Al Mashra nodded and left, leaving Al Quraysh alone in the room. He sat for a moment and darkly regarded his surroundings and his situation. He deeply resented having to hide away in the dark recesses of his own palace, plotting to take back the power that was stolen from him. He reflected grimly that if he had only been more astute he would have seen the treasonous manoeuvring of Abu Rashed and could have stamped on him sooner. Then he would be able to take this golden opportunity being given to him, with ease. Instead he was forced to fight his secret war on two fronts, with only a small group of loyal men to support him. Abu Rashed would pay dearly for his treachery. He had embarrassed him and made him look weak, and that would not happen again. He would also have to catch that spying bitch eventually, but she had fled and would be hard to track down. He wanted to use the American to find her and punish her, but that would have to wait. The first step was to take back power, and then he could apply his stranglehold to the country and stamp his authority on it as he should have done before.

He rose and left the room, turning left down the high-ceilinged corridor toward the meeting room. Two armed guards accompanied him as he strode confidently and purposefully. A window at the far end of the corridor was illuminated by the bright morning sunlight and he allowed himself a half smile as he recognised that with the new day came his chance to create a new beginning; a new start; a new regime. Nothing would stop him taking this chance.

Chapter Thirty

Jerry and Yash craned their heads round to look for the source of the shots and saw a lone figure standing at the end of the line of command stations. He was tall, and dressed in black clothes. He wore a dark beard on his thin face.

'Campbell!' said Yash.

They both swung their rifles round and fired bursts at Campbell, sending him scurrying for cover behind a command station. The fire had attracted the attention of the assault troops, who were now taking fire positions and starting to open up on Jerry and Yash. As they ducked for cover Jerry cursed their bad luck. What were the chances of Campbell being back there with a weapon when the pilot was making the dash? What the hell were they supposed to do now they had lost the element of surprise?

As the rounds smashed into the wall above him he shouted back to the guys searching the pallets to get out and suppress the assault troops. He directed them further down the hangar, to one of the closer offices. They rushed away and a few moments later their fire was fixing the assault troops in place. A couple of troops were hit where they lay on the ground, while the others fell back to escape the fire.

Jerry looked back to the right. He could no longer see Campbell, who must have used the opportunity to escape his cover. Was he coming towards their hangar?

'Let's head inside and see if Campbell comes. The other guys have got those troops pinned down at the end now.'

As they re-entered the hangar from the operations room there was a sudden burst of fire from the mini gun, which had now reached the end of the hangar and drawn up at the main doors. It was now facing down the aisle between the pallets and was blocking them from escaping the room. They took cover behind the doorway again.

'It won't be long until they send the assault troops up this aisle to clear out our guys next door, and then us' said Jerry. 'We have to move or we'll just be pinned down until they come and kill us.'

'Agreed. We need to make the dash across to that first pallet' said Yash. 'We can then work our way around to the main door and take out the gunner from the side.'

'Okay, you go first. I'll cover you with a burst of fire to keep their heads down.'

Jerry knelt down by the doorway and prepared to put his rifle around and fire a burst at the vehicle. It wouldn't deter them for long, but hopefully it would be enough to give Yash half a second to dash across the gap. Jerry counted down and made the burst of fire blindly around the corner as Yash sprinted across the gap. There was almost immediately a flash as hundreds of rounds streamed down the aisle. Jerry squinted through the smoke and dust expecting to see Yash cut to pieces on the ground, but he had made it and was sitting propped against the pallet, his chest heaving from the effort. He then provided cover for Jerry, who ran and rolled across the short gap.

'Okay, we'll find our way round and down to the end. Try to come at it from an eight o'clock position as they'll be expecting us to go all the way to the end, to the nine o'clock. We might just catch them by surprise. Let's go.'

As they prepared to set off across the hangar, there was a sudden burst of fire from their left, from the end of the hangar that Campbell had been hiding. They took cover again as the bullets smashed into the pallets. They were pinned down on both sides now. Jerry guessed it was now Campbell attacking them as it was a lone shooter.

'I think I can work around and take him out, if you go ahead and outflank the gun' he said to Yash.

Yash nodded and once again prepared to move while Jerry provided covering fire, this time at Campbell. Yash was away and running while Jerry blasted the pallets near Campbell to keep his head down. Jerry then stood up and dashed across two aisles too, trying to outflank Campbell without him noticing. He stalked closer as Campbell's fire continued at where they had previously been. They had fooled him. Now Jerry just needed to get a good angle on him and he could finish him off. He quickly checked his magazine and clipped in a full one. This was not the time to be caught without rounds.

He glanced around the corner of the pallet and caught a glimpse of Campbell's position. He was firing from a window at the end of the hangar, which gave him a good view of most of the aisles between pallets, but not of Jerry's. Rather than risk being spotted during another movement, Jerry decided to take a shot from here. He switched the rifle to single shot, rested the barrel on a box on the pallet and took aim, calming his breathing rate and focusing his eye through the weapon sight. As Campbell popped up to make a burst of fire, Jerry squeezed the trigger and sent a round spinning straight into the chest of Campbell's, who dropped his rifle and fell to the floor. Jerry quickly ran towards the window, to finish him off. As he ran he could hear a loud burst of fire as Yash attacked the mini gun vehicle, followed by silence.

Jerry reached the window and leapt through it, landing next to Campbell, who lay clutching his chest, wheezing and coughing. Jerry kicked away his weapon and stood over him. As Campbell lay panting on the ground they looked at each other, finally face to face, and sizing up their foe.

'You still won't win this Vasquez' said Campbell.

'Did you really think you could get away with it?' said Jerry. 'You can't just kill millions of people and keep it a secret.'

'Come on, this is Africa. We can get away with whatever we want. We always have.' He coughed and spat bright red as his ruptured lungs filled with blood.

'Not this time. Whoever you and your friends are, and whatever kind of privileges you enjoy, you have to be held accountable to the rule of law.'

'My friends make the rules and the laws, and they sure as hell won't hang for this. As far as the world is concerned this will be another mystery virus.' He gasped and coughed again. 'It will get a few weeks of airtime before the next headline. Owusu will be sworn in as the next President and then everyone will continue to not give a shit about Chad. It's the way of the world.'

'Well I stopped Lionel in Khartoum, and now I've stopped you; and we're about to stop those drones too. If you live long enough you'll get to see that; how you and Lionel failed.'

Campbell coughed again. Blood bubbled out of his mouth and ran down his cheek. His chest heaved and whistled as he tried to breathe. He stared at Jerry for a long moment as he began to convulse and drown in his own blood.

'Fuck it' he gasped. His head lolled back and hit the ground, his chest stopped heaving and he lay still.

Jerry looked at him for a moment longer, wondering who this mystery figure was and who his powerful benefactors may be. At that moment he didn't care. It gave him no pleasure to kill Campbell. He felt nothing.

A quick check of his watch. 06:56. He turned and ran towards the corner of the hangar, peering around the corner towards the far end where the troops had been suppressed. There were numerous bodies sprawled on the floor. He studied them closely in case any were still laying in wait. The shots had all but stopped now, so he guessed that Yash and the team had been successful in destroying the mini gun and the troops. He checked his watch.

06:57. He had less than ten minutes to get the message to the Chadian Air Force, and he had no idea how to convince them it was a genuine warning, or how to operate the radio. He hoped that the technology would be intuitive. Surely it would be just like using a computer. He ran across the gap and burst into the first command station in the line, and quickly searched for lights and power switches. He eventually found a switch for the lights.

06:58. The array of controls and monitors was baffling and he didn't know where to begin. He just needed to find one power button. He started to press every button he could see, until finally he got lucky and the system started. As it came online he located the monitor most likely to be the communication centre, the one with the keyboard under it. There was a headset resting by the keyboard. He picked it up and put it on.

06:59. The system interface was very similar to the cockpit view of an aircraft, with dials and readouts on the screen, as well as a blue section at the top, which he guessed represented the sky. He tapped a few keys on the keyboard, but nothing happened. There was no obvious way of navigating around the screen, or any obvious menus through which to search. So much for it being intuitive he thought.

07:00. He had an idea that it may be touch-screen, and so touched one of the simulated dials. A menu screen appeared in the sky blue section at the top of the screen, offering mission specific data such as waypoints, altitude settings, vectors, target coordinates. He quickly yet thoroughly checked that none were what he needed and touched another dial, continuing his search through another menu subset.

07:01. Finally he touched a dial which launched a list of airspace management centres, listed alphabetically by name and also by code, neither of which he was familiar with. He could not see a way to search by country name, or city, and so began to scroll through the list, scrutinising each one to check if it was in Chad. Eventually he came to Mtala Airbase in N'Djamena, Chad. At last!

07:02. He touched the name on the screen and a dialogue box opened up in the sky blue section. He selected 'Open Channel' and the headset came to life. He could hear a man's voice, which sounded like an air traffic controller at work. As the man spoke, his words appeared in text in the dialogue box. Jerry wasted no more time, he cut in on the speaker.

'Hello Mtala Airbase, this is Jerry Vasquez of Task Force Africa, calling from Adeji Airbase in Lagos, Nigeria. Do you read me? Over' He saw that his words had appeared in the dialogue box. He waited for a response. He repeated his message and waited.

07:03. 'Hello Adeji Airbase, this is Mtala Airbase. We read you. Over'

'Mtala Airbase, I am calling to warn you of an imminent attack on your city by four incoming UAVs, currently in Nigerian airspace, due to enter Chadian airspace around 07:20 above Lake Chad. They will then turn and head for N'Djamena where they will commence a lethal attack on the government and people of Chad. Over.'

'This is a channel for aviation control. Misuse of this channel is an offence. Please desist and leave the channel free for operational traffic. Out.'

'No wait! I am absolutely serious. Four UAVs are enroute to Chadian airspace, and are carrying a biological weapon to deploy over N'Djamena, which will kill millions of people. The UAVs are uncontrollable from this end and so must be shot down. Do you understand? Over.'

There was more silence from the controller.

07:04. 'Mr Vasquez, can you verify your claim? Over.'

'Verify? What do you want me to do? It is a secret plot to murder millions of Chadians, and then form a new government to steal a secret supply of water in the mountains.

How can I verify that? Look, connect me to the commander of the airbase immediately. This is not a drill, it is live.'

'Please wait Mr Vasquez.' There was another silence as the controller presumably passed the message up his chain of command. 'Mr Vasquez, I am connecting you to Brigadier Maaluf, he is the base commander.' There was another short pause.

'Hello, Mr Vasquez? This is Brigadier Joseph Maaluf. I am the commander of Mtala Airbase. Who are you and what are these claims you are making?'

'Brigadier, my name is Jerry Vasquez, I am the head of operations for Task Force Africa, based in Lagos. I have undercovered a secret plot to overthrow the government of Chad following the murder of millions of Chadians by a biological weapon, which is currently aboard four UAVs that will enter Chadian airspace from Nigerian airspace in less than twenty minutes from now. I implore you to deploy defensive countermeasures to repel those UAVs. They will bring certain death to millions of Chadians.'

'Can you substantiate these claims? How do I know you are not lying?'

'Have the Nigerian Air Force logged a border crossing by UAVs for this morning? It is not an official mission. You will not find it on any log, but those drones are coming Brigadier. You must destroy them.'

'I will verify that. Please wait.'

07:05. The Brigadier's voice came back on the channel, this time with more of a sense of urgency than before.

'Mr Vasquez, this is Brigadier Maaluf. We are scanning for any aircraft approaching the international border, but there are none displaying on our radar.'

'They must be using stealth technology. They have been set on autopilot, on pre-programmed routes via Lake Chad, and will deploy their weapons at 07:29. Please scramble any aircraft you have to defend against them now. Over.'

'Thank you Mr Vasquez. We will monitor the situation. Out.'

'Monitor? No, you need to deploy aircraft right now. This is serious. Someone called Owusu is due to become the next President.'

'Minister Owusu? The Minister of the Interior?'

'I don't know who he is, but he is due to become the next President when the government is killed. The man behind it is called Laurence Campbell, a senior Task Force officer. They were fomenting a war between Chad and the Republic to cover the attacks. Isn't it true that there is a major deployment going on right now? It is the work of this plot to create a cover story for the attacks. Millions of Chadians will be killed under the pretense that it is an attack by the Republic. You must destroy those drones now. Can you afford to take that chance?'

'How did you know about the deployments Mr Vasquez?'

'Look Brigadier, we can talk all morning if you like, but you are running out of time. In...seventeen minutes those drones will be crossing into Chadian airspace, and then they're set for the capital and millions will die. What do you have to lose?'

'Fine, thank you Mr Vasquez. We will see to it. Out.'

Jerry sat back. He had done all he could. Now it was up to Chad, if it wanted to save itself.

Chapter Thirty One

Captain Okoro sat with his team and new engineers enjoying a coffee after their breakfast. They were getting to know each other in the traditional military style akin to dogs sniffing bums. He had relayed their experience at the border yesterday, and in turn had learned about each of their deployments to previous rebel uprisings over the years. They had also discovered that they had several colleagues in common, such was the small size of the UAV community. He looked at his watch and turned the conversation to their first mission of the morning, to conduct a four hour patrol to the north of the capital. He confirmed with the engineers that the aircraft were ready.

'Yes sir, both birds ready to deploy, fully fuelled and loaded with Raptors.'

This was the kind of easy reintroduction his team needed. He felt grateful to his old friend for arranging it.

'Captain Okoro! The company commander needs to see you immediately!' a runner from company headquarters reported. 'You are to prepare the aircraft for immediate launch' he told the engineers. Okoro nodded to the engineers and then stood up and followed the runner to the company commander's command station. He entered to a scene of urgent activity, with all control terminals occupied and the buzz of barked orders and radio communications. The company commander turned to him and smiled grimly.

'Well Captain, there is to be no easy introduction for you I am afraid. I need you to launch your aircraft immediately. The whole regiment is on alert. There is a threat of four UAVs approaching from Nigeria, which are entering our airspace with the intention of attacking N'Djamena and killing millions. There is a mission profile already being uploaded to your station. You are to seek the UAVs and destroy them before they have a chance to deploy their weapons. Any questions?'

'Do we know anything about the capability of these drones? Are they similar to those of the Republic? What is their cruising speed? What is the range of their missiles? When can we engage them?'

'We suspect they are using stealth technology because we cannot trace them by radar, so we don't know anything about them or their weapons, other than that they are biological. They should be destroyed as far away from the capital as possible, once in our airspace.'

'Okay sir. I'm on it.' He ran from the station to his own, noting the two UAVs were already running, and the engineers conducting their final checks. He wondered if they would both come back from this mission, or if any of them would even still be alive. Biological weapons? He had only ever heard of their use many years ago and didn't think humanity could stoop so low again. He was constantly surprised by the cruelty men could inflict on each other.

Chapter Thirty Two

Al Quraysh swung open the door to the meeting room with an almost theatrical gesture, as if a fanfare were playing to mark his reappearance. He dominated the doorway for a moment, allowing the room's occupants to turn and regard him. The gathered members of the shura council looked up suddenly from their hushed conversations; their faces were almost as dramatic as his entrance. The mysterious secret summons they had each received had aroused feelings of trepidation and fear in equal measure. The unprecedented events of the past twenty four hours had shaken them all, and had left them with a deep sense of unease. As they realised it was actually Al Quraysh that had summoned them, he saw the looks of surprise give way to those of relief. Al Quraysh may have even detected a trace of joy in some of those usually solemn faces.

'Welcome brothers' he announced grandly. 'Thank you for coming at such short notice, and I appreciate your discretion. I realise I must have interrupted your morning prayers, for which I am sorry, but as I am sure you will agree these are desperate times, and I have had to resort to desperate measures.'

The shura council collectively looked at him in astonishment. They were starting to grow nervous again as it dawned on them that Al Quraysh was acting under his own authority, and this was no official shura meeting.

'I must begin with terrible news brothers' said Al Quraysh, entering the room and proceeding to the head of the long table. 'Brother Saif's car has been attacked and destroyed while travelling here to this meeting. Regrettably it appears that he and his aides have all been murdered.'

There were nervous mumblings from the gathered men. They looked at each other in alarm, and back to Al Quraysh with questioning expressions. The presence of armed guards behind him in the doorway added to the tension that was now gripping the room.

'Who would commit such a horrendous crime, I am sure you are asking yourselves; and I am again sorry to have to bear such tidings. Since the emergence of Abu Rashed's treasonous plot yesterday I have received many visits and offers of support from friends and believers in my rightful claim to the presidency.'

The assembled men again shifted uneasily in their seats, as they all knew thât none of them had approached him to offer such support.

'One such visitor was a great surprise to me, as he was not known to me at all. Nor was he a citizen of our country or a foreign politician. He came to me with some most disturbing news of a devious and sinister plot being hatched within this very palace. A plot to overthrow me through false accusations and misdirection. And you brothers, I am afraid, were also victim to this deception.'

There was no response from anyone seated around the table. They each waited nervously to see in which direction this monologue would turn.

'And I must also tell you brothers, that Abu Rashed had an equally gruesome fate in store for each of you. Brother Saif's murder was the first of a planned series of executions, intended to wipe out the shura council. This is why I had to summon you all at such short notice, for your protection, and also to urge you to act now to save the legitimacy of this country's government.'

As he paused and the assembled men looked at each other, the sound of distant gunfire broke the silence. The harsh rattle of multiple automatic weapons seemed to punctuate his sentence. Without hesitation, Al Quraysh continued.

'You see brothers, the wolves are already at the door. That is no doubt his killing squads seeking us out, to continue his terrible plot.'

He gestured to Al Mashra, who turned and made a beckoning signal down the corridor.

'The visitor who revealed this terrible plot to me was an American. The head of the Task Force in Africa, who had been asked by Abu Rashed to take part and support the coup with his troops. He refused, and instead wanted to support my legitimacy. He was very badly tortured by Abu Rashed's men, but we have managed to keep him alive. He is here now to deliver the news to you himself. But we must act quickly brothers, as you can hear, Abu Rashed's assassins are approaching.'

The shura council members shifted uneasily in their seats and exchanged concerned looks. They felt trapped and helpless in this small meeting room, with a deposed president speaking of murderous plots and the sound of a gun battle outside. Their fears would only have worsened when they beheld the sight of Abu Khalid pushing in a wheelchair containing the slumped figure of a man. His head was hung low on his chest, which was entirely wrapped in bandages, as were his arms, which were held in slings across his chest. His face had clearly been beaten, but they could not see the full extent of it as his head was drooped so low.

'Gentlemen, this is Mr Lionel Caplin, an American citizen who leads the Task Force in Africa. He was asked by Abu Rashed to commit his considerable resources to help overthrow me, and what you see before you is the price he has paid for his respect for international law and order. He is very badly hurt and has had extensive medication, but he wanted to share with you his story before he receives the full recuperation he deserves. Mr Caplin...'

All heads turned expectantly to Lionel, who did not move at all. Abu Khalid lifted Lionel's head to reveal a bruised and swollen face, with dried blood at his nose, lips and brow. His eyes were half open and clearly not registering where he was or who he was with. Abu Khalid beckoned for water and lifted Lionel's eyelids, repeatedly calling his name.

Before Lionel had a chance to respond there was the sudden sound of gunfire in the building. The guards at the door turned to face it, but as they turned the nearest guard was thrown back in the doorway, blood spurting from his back as a volley of bullets smashed through him. His body lay twisted on the floor. The crowd regarded it with horror as blood began to pool around him.

'Return fire!' screamed Al Quraysh to the other guard, retreating from the doorway further into the room. The terrified guard raised his rifle and unleashed a blind burst of automatic fire around the doorway, not even bothering to look where he was firing. He exhausted his magazine in one burst and then hesitated slightly before reaching for another. As he fumbled for the clip the shots came again from down the corridor, sending all occupants of the room diving for cover under the table. Lionel even managed to raise his head and look around at the commotion but was powerless to act, even if he had wanted to.

The guard eventually fitted the clip to the rifle and cocked it for action again, but he was too late. The attackers had quickly made their way up the corridor and were at the doorway, dispatching him with a single short burst. A hand appeared and issued a single grenade into the room, which rolled under the table before exploding with a tremendous boom. The stun grenade sent shock waves through the room, disorientating all within and leaving them senseless. The attackers quickly entered and ordered everyone to put their hands behind their heads. As they slowly complied Abu Rashed entered and surveyed the scene. He sneered.

'Well, Abu Saif, it appears I have interrupted your war council. Did you really think you could plot against me in my own palace?'

'The palace is rightfully mine!' shouted Al Quraysh angrily. 'It is you that has been plotting. I have already explained your treachery to the council. I will take back what is rightfully mine.'

'I don't think so brother. It appears I have the upper hand, and these good men here agreed with me just yesterday that you are no longer fit to lead. I can only assume that you are here to plan some terrorist action and are trying to convince them to act with you.'

Al Quraysh realised that he was in a very weak position. His only chance now was to talk his way out using the American as his only equity, and convince the shura to believe him.

'Wait, this is not what it seems' he urged as he rose to his feet, standing defiantly before his usurper. 'Brothers, what I have told you already is the truth. This man before us is the aggressor. See how he comes in with guns blazing? He cannot be trusted to be the president of our fine country. He is nothing more than a thug - a villain with an army, and he will lead this country in the wrong direction. The American will tell you...'

'Enough!' barked Abu Rashed. 'I know the lies you have prepared with the American. I know that you are in league with him to convince the shura of my guilt. But let me tell you brother, you should have slipped away without any noise and enjoyed the comfortable retirement I would have handed you. Instead you chose bitterness and revenge, which will only lead to pain and suffering.' He looked to Abu Issa beside him, who gave him a pistol. He paused for a moment and weighed it in his hand before looking back to Al Quraysh.

'It is a shame for you that you did not know when you had had enough. You were right actually, I did plot against you, because you are weak. You do not have the courage to lead this country to the greatness it deserves and is capable of. So I created the skirmishes around the border between the so-called Chadian militias and our people. I made it appear that we were on our way to war in order to expose your weakness. I do not know who this American stooge you have found is, but he has nothing to do with me. I am far too clever to rely on an outsider like him to do my dirty work. I do things my own way.'

He raised the pistol and pointed it at the centre of Al Quraysh's chest.

'You should have had the courage to exert the power this country needs.'

'Wait!' begged Al Quraysh, holding up his hands. 'I have to…'

The pistol barked and Al Quraysh was thrown back against the wall, a hole gaping in his chest. He was dead before his corpse has slipped to the floor. As the echoes of the shot reverberated around the small room, the hunched figures of the shura council held their breath and wondered if they would be next.

'Rise brothers' called Abu Rashed. 'All is well. His evil plotting is over and you are safe.'

Slowly the shura members rose to their feet and dusted themselves off, looking in disbelief at the death that surrounded them. The public servants and clerics had never seen violence such as this at such close range. They lowered their eyes so as not to see the carnage before them.

Abu Rashed regarded the men as they rose. The poor creatures were virtually wimpering as they beheld the scene. It was to be expected from such good honest men, who use words as their weapons. He noticed Abu Khalid rising from his knees too.

'Ah Abu Khalid, so you are here too. As you are no longer a shura member you have no right to be here. I also know that you would not wish to be part of my government going forwards. You have always resisted me and my ideas. I also know that you were there in the room, plotting with the American. There is no doubt where your allegiances lie, and now you shall lie with him.'

He raised the pistol again, and pulled the trigger before Abu Khalid had the chance to say anything. Without hesitation he turned the pistol to Lionel, who was quite unable to do anything but give Abu Rashed a last bitter look. Abu Rashed looked deep into Lionel's eyes and thought he saw a flicker of...was it fear? No, it really seemed to be something like contempt. How wasteful to carry such an emotion into death, but how very typically arrogant. The pistol spoke again and Lionel slumped where he sat.

Abu Rashed turned to the shura members, who were now in total shock at what had unfolded in the last few seconds. He could see them shrink before him, fearing that they would be next in this ruthless killing spree.

'Brothers, it seems Abu Saif and his accomplices were hell bent on taking revenge today. He was clearly disgruntled at having been legitimately deposed and was starting to make wild accusations with no evidence whatsoever. It seems obvious to me that he lured you here to murder you, just as he intended to murder me, as revenge for your roles in his downfall. I am relieved that I managed to get here in time to stop him. He will no longer be a threat to you.'

The shura members seemed to loosen slightly as they realised that the pistol was not to be turned on them next. His conciliatory words were a welcome surprise to them and they began to relax somewhat.

'However, I fear you have seen too much and so you cannot continue as my council.' He paused and regarded them with an expressionless gaze, before turning toward the guards at the door. 'Use their rifles and make sure their fingerprints are on them.'

With one last look over his shoulder he addressed the panicking men.

'It appears gentlemen that we did not arrive in time to save you. Abu Saif's terrible legacy will also include your deaths. I have no doubt that Allah will reward you for your sacrifice.'

He left the room and strode down the corridor. He heard the pleas for mercy, the deafening roar of the rifles cutting down the shura council members, followed by silence. It seemed appropriate that they should die with Abu Saif; a very neat conclusion to an untidy morning.

Chapter Thirty Three

As Okoro entered his command station it was alive with activity. The pilots and gunners were hastily running through their pre-flight checks, and establishing communications with company headquarters as well as air traffic control. He could see the mission profile on the screens of the pilots, and on the gunners' screens the radar picture of the land out to the north of the capital. He could already see several shapes making their way north. The regiment had scrambled quickly, this was clearly a very real threat. It was an extra challenge that they were facing drones invisible to radar, as they would have to rely entirely on their onboard cameras.

He explained the situation to his crew as they taxied for takeoff. There were no rousing speeches required for this mission, everyone understood the cost of failure and the sense of importance of this mission was as never before. The crew got to work, getting airborne and up to speed quickly and smoothly. They moved onto their allocated vector and proceeded north. The airspace had been divided equally between each squadron in order to cover all possible approaches and keep a wide defensive line. His was just about as far to the east as it was possible to get and still stay in the N'Djamena area, meaning he was much less likely to encounter any action. He wasn't sure if he was upset or pleased about that now. The thought of being the detachment that let the killer drone through did not appeal to him at all, just as the thought of being a hero did not entertain him either. He just had a duty to stop the attack and save his country.

He looked at his watch. 07:21. His drones were still fifty kilometres from the border but their cameras were scanning out thirty kilometres. The enemy drones could be anywhere, but they would be most likely to meet in the swampland area of Lake Chad. He wondered if there were still any people living around the lake, which had previously provided life to so many, but was now no more than a sad reminder of the excesses and greed of humankind. If there was anyone still there then he thought they would be about to see an amazing aerial spectacle, possibly followed by an agonising death if the weapon were to affect them. He hoped this battle would only be watched on screens.

At 07:23 they were entering the Lake Chad area, where they should be engaging the drones, as early as possible. He turned up the open communication channel to listen to the battle unfold across the rest of the companies. There were already some aircraft engaging the enemy drones as they came across the border. He felt a tinge of disappointment as he was confronted with the possibility that his team may not get to engage any drones at all. The battle could be concluded before they even came within his range.

Across the channel came the news that the enemy drones were deploying effective defensive countermeasures, such as electromagnetic bursts to disrupt missiles, and evasive flying patterns. These were the new generation of Artificial Intelligence UAVs, built to operate independently as well as, if not better than when piloted. These drones did not have measurable reaction times and did not make human errors. Okoro gulped. This was not going to be the duck shoot they had hoped for.

'Target sighted. Bearing 320 degrees. Thirty kilometres. Speed five hundred knots. Heading 110. Altitude fifteen thousand feet' one of the gunners reported.

'Roger, altering heading to 030 to intercept' said the pilot.

'Roger, preparing to engage.'

'Stay together' Okoro instructed the other UAV crew. 'Hunt as a team.'

'Roger sir, altering heading to 030.'

Across the communication channel they heard that one of the enemy drones had been destroyed. The crew reported an explosion bigger than usual. Okoro assumed this was the effect of a biological weapon being destroyed.

'Tracking for missile lock...target locked. Launching missile. 3,2,1. Missile away.'

They watched the missile streak away on the monitor, speeding towards its target. A missile from the other UAV sped alongside it. Okoro hoped that the enemy drone would not be able to counter two missiles at once. He was disappointed, as both of the heat seeking missiles were fooled by the drone's decoys and exploded in mid-air. The drone span left of the debris and continued on its path as Okoro swore. He thought fast about how to defeat the intelligent drone's defences, and came up with a plan.

'Attack it from the front and the rear at the same time. Its active defence radar may have a problem focusing on two targets one hundred and eighty degrees apart, especially on its tail.'

'Roger sir, changing course to 355 degrees to fall in behind it' said one of the pilots. A minute later they were in position, the other drone having looped around to stay in front of the enemy.

'We're only fifty kilometres from the capital now. This may be our last chance to defeat it' said Okoro. 'Launch two missiles each.'

'Roger sir' the gunners confirmed. They began their targeting process, acquiring and locking the target, before counting down and launching.

'Missiles away'. Two streaks of fire scratched across each monitor. The whole team watched with bated breath as they neared the target. One missile was defeated by the drone's countermeasures, two, then the third missile, coming from the rear, hit its target. The high explosive packed into the body of the missile was detonated by the proximity fuse, creating a huge ball of energy and shrapnel. The shock waves and shards of metal ripped through the drone's fuselage and fuel tanks, igniting the stored hydrogen. At the same time the shrapnel hitting the gas canisters penetrated them, releasing the compressed gas with violent force. The resulting blast was bigger than any of them had seen before, blinding the camera for several seconds.

The crew cheered and released their nervous energy. They had never faced such a sophisticated adversary in their time operating UAVs, and the relief at having overcome it was enormous.

The gunners reported the destruction of the target. Their celebration was short-lived though as they learned from the communication channel that there was still one enemy drone active, having punched through the defensive line. Its coordinates, heading and speed were reported.

'Set vectors to intercept' ordered Okoro. 'Maximum speed.'

The two crews quickly altered their headings and speeds and began speeding back towards the capital. Okoro could see from the radar screen that several other UAVs were doing the same. Those late to scramble were in the fortunate position of being closer to the capital and therefore had a chance to chase the drone and intercept it. Okoro's UAVs were approaching from the northeast close to Mach 1, ten kilometres out from the city. He thought that the enemy drone must be well within missile range and wondered why it hadn't fired yet. Perhaps it wasn't due to fire missiles, but to drop bombs instead. But there was no time to think about that, catching and destroying that drone was all that mattered.

He informed the chasing crews of the recommended attack strategy, though it looked like this was just going to be a classic mass attack strategy as all the chasing drones would be firing at one target.

'Target sighted, fifty degrees, five kilometres, heading 160 degrees.'

He heard other detachments on the channel declaring their sighting of it too. It looked like there would be a simultaneous launch of missiles, more by luck than design.

'Target locked, launching missile, 3,2,1, missile away'

Several streaks of fire filled the monitor. The enemy drone suddenly changed course, conducting its defensive measures. The missiles changed course also and continued the chase. They watched two of them explode in mid-air again, confused by the defensive pulse, before they saw the incredible sight of a successful hit. The drone exploded in a huge fireball. The crews cheered, channeling the intense feelings of fear into an emotional outburst of joy and relief. They patted each other on the back, wiping their brows and calming their heartbeats.

Okoro was overwhelmingly relieved. He gripped his crews' shoulders and congratulated them, trying hard not to cry. After all that time he had just remembered Arafa, and his family, and how they would be totally unaware of how close they had just come to annihilation. He steadied himself, and fought back the emotion.

'All units, return to base.'

Chapter Thirty Four

President Ayatumbe sat at his desk reading the report. His brow was furrowed, his face fixed in a look of disgusted disbelief, which eventually gave way to anger and resolve. General Yeboah stood watching his face, unsure of what was to come next, either punishment or praise. He would be the first to admit, privately, that this was an embarrassment for the military, having been fooled so convincingly of the threat posed by the Republic. He would be keen to make the point that it highlighted the lack of investment in their intelligence gathering capability as well as military hardware, but this did not seem like a good time to raise the issue. Instead he would simply be content to keep his job, as well as grateful to still have his life.

Ayatumbe lowered the paper and thought for a moment. This was incredible reading, and he was having difficulty comprehending the range of alarming issues raised in it.

'General, thank you for bringing this to me. You are a trusted colleague and I value your loyalty.'

'Thank you Mr President. I regret that it took such drastic action to eventually discover the full truth.'

'I also regret that we were unable to detect this treachery sooner. I have placed too much trust in the political system. It is clear to me that there is a need for tighter control of security in this country. I want you to ensure there is no more chance of threats to us.'

'Yes Mr President. Did you have anything in mind?'

'Yes. We will have fewer politicians and more soldiers in government, more people I can trust. I want a full review of all non-ethnic Chadians. It is most alarming that Minister Owusu was not Chadian but Nigerian. There should not be any non Chadians in government or the military.'

'Yes Mr President.'

'You will have Minster Owusu executed as a traitor of course. Publicly. All must see the price of treachery in the new order.'

'Of course Mr President. I will arrange that immediately.'

'I knew we could not trust the Task Force. Did I not say that General?'

'You did Mr President.'

'And they were in league with Nigeria. Have I not always said that Nigeria could not be trusted?'

'You have Mr President.'

'It was a treacherous scheme, but foolish! Did they really think they could defeat us? I should punish them. They will not receive our water, except at a much higher price.'

'Yes Mr President. Would you like to review the security arrangements at the water source?'

'Yes, it is not good enough. We have not kept it secret enough. Now it is known it has become a target. I want a garrison there to protect our interest, with full capability.'

'Yes Mr President.'

'We must also reach out to the new President of the Islamic Republic and establish a trade agreement. Perhaps to ship our water through the Republic to the coast. He has already show great wisdom in pulling back troops from the borderlands and ending this war. I think we will be able to work with him in future. More than his war-hungry predecessor.'

'I agree Mr President. He was instrumental in swiftly ending the war.'

'Yes, but there must be no mention of that in the media of course. I want there to be one very clear message, that we forced them back across the border and ended their invasion. He will do the same in the Republic I am sure.'

'Furthermore, I think a victory parade is required. To show our strength and that we cannot be broken.'

'Yes Mr President. And what weaponry would you like on display? We have taken a number of casualties in terms of our equipment, but the UAV has been the hero of the hour.'

'Yes, UAVs at the front. Perhaps we need some new equipment General. Prepare a list of what you think we need.'

'Yes Mr President.'

President Muhammad Abdullah Al Hamoodi, ruler of the Islamic Republic of North Africa, sat at his desk in his Khartoum palace. He surveyed his surroundings and did not approve.

'I want new furniture here. This is old and worn. It is not befitting of me.'

'Yes Ameer.'

'I also want a new mosque to be constructed in each of the state capitals. They should be the biggest the Muslim world has ever seen, with the one here in Khartoum as the biggest.'

'Yes Ameer.'

'Al Quraysh has been laid to rest?'

'Yes Ameer, he and the shura members have been accorded full state honours.'

'Excellent. We must publicly honour his name and protect the reputation of the office of President. He ruled with wisdom for much of his time, but was overtaken by greed and megalomania. He will now seek forgiveness for his crimes at Allah's feet.'

'Insha'allah you will have the strength needed to bear the responsibility of your new title.'

'Insha'allah. Has Minister Al Rasmid settled into his new office?'

'He has Ameer, he will attend your first shura council this morning.'

'Insha'allah. The new shura council will reflect the new Republic much better. A stronger, but more open country. We must trade better with our neighbours.'

'Yes Ameer.'

'Chad will become a good trading partner now the war has ended. We must extend our hand to President Ayatumbe and strengthen our ties. We must capitalise on the goodwill that I have created by bringing the war to a close.'

'Your leadership was inspirational to our people Ameer.'

'Yes, it was very timely that I was able to move so swiftly to seek a peaceful solution to the conflict. The attacks by the Chadian militias were beyond control and created such terrible problems for our people. The refugees will now start to go back to their homes.'

'Yes Ameer. The militias have instantly dispersed without any trace. The people can return to their homes without fear of attack or persecution.'

'Yes. Ensure the media continues to report that. Our victory must be clear.'

'Yes Ameer.'

Okoro strode down the dusty street with a spring in his step, despite the great fatigue which swamped him. He hadn't slept in days and was as tired as a dog, but the adrenaline of battle was still coursing through his veins, as well as the thrill of what was about to come. He and his team had been given a week of immediate leave, in recognition of their brave and meaningful contribution to the war effort. He was due to be further recognised on his return from leave with promotion to Major, and his own company command. His father would be very impressed, and so would Arafa's father. Arafa herself would just be delighted to see him.

He skipped over a trench by the side of the road and regarded the buildings of the small village in a warm satisfied light he had not previously seen. The ramshackle huts, swept by wind and dust certainly presented no romantic vista, but Okoro couldn't help but grin at them as they told him how close he was to his love. He crossed the empty street and turned down a long track, flanked on either side by fields of red-headed sorghum, swaying in the hot wind. It would soon be time to harvest them, and another year of worrying about the yield would be over. Spirits would be high at the house of Arafa's father. They would certainly slaughter an animal tonight to celebrate his return, and while he would not be permitted to talk about the details of his missions, he would certainly be able to talk about the glorious Chadian victory.

The house of Arafa's father came into view as he crested a small rise in the track. A small single-storey dwelling, surrounded by his modest farming plot, with a few goats and scrawny chickens loitering around the open area to the front of the house. He should have gone home to his mother first, but he so desperately wanted to see Arafa that he had decided to take the scolding when it finally came. His heart was racing as he thought of the joyful reunion he was about to enjoy with his fiance.

He wondered if there may even be a suggestion of bringing forward the date of their marriage, in light of the special circumstances. As a Major he would be entitled to married living quarters at his base, meaning Arafa could come to live there too and they could start a family right away. His short military tour now looked like more of a long career, which promised modest wealth and prosperity for his family, and perhaps even an end to the back-breaking life of farming for Arafa's father; now he would be able to support everyone on his Major's salary.

As he neared the house, there was a stirring from within. He could see movement through one of the small windows. It was five o'clock and the women would be preparing the family's dinner now. Hopefully they would have enough for an extra person tonight!

The door opened and in the dark opening he saw the shape of Arafa's mother. He smiled and waved, quickening his pace. She disappeared inside the house and he could hear quick chatter between her and Arafa. And then in the doorway appeared the sight he had been waiting so long for. His beautiful Arafa, dressed in a long drab dress, but looking as perfect as he had ever seen her. She held her hands to her mouth in shock, not believing that her mother had been right. She lowered her hands and revealed a wide white welcoming smile.

Jerry gently knocked on the door and opened it quietly, peering round it to check Al was awake. Al was propped up in the hospital bed, looking out of the window at the trees. He turned his head and smiled.

'Hey mate, come on in.'

'How're you holding up buddy?' Jerry walked in and perched on the edge of the bed.

'Definitely been better, but making a good recovery. The doc says there's no lasting damage and I should be back to full mission readiness in under a month.'

'Take your time. There's no rush, and as my second in command you're going to have to take on more of a planning role now anyway.'

'So you can still get out there and dole out the justice?'

'Someone's gotta do it! How about Sally and the family? How are they?

'They're good. They were pretty shaken up but they're tough. She said Porter's family are shipping out?

'Yeah, heading back to the UK. His body is being repatriated tomorrow.'

'I guess the Task Force is taking care of them?'

'The very best. It won't bring him back of course but it's the least they deserve.'

'How about you?' asked Al. 'Are you healing okay? Those were some nasty wounds.'

'Yeah I'll live too. That'll be the end of my leg-modelling career, but I'm good.'

'How's the new boss?'

'Very European! Got lots of ideas about transparency and accountability, and sharing data. Looks like there's a new world coming to Africa.'

'A lot better than the world there would have been.'

'Yeah, that was a frightening prospect. I still think about how they would have gotten away with it if I'd just gone into Simon's office a few minutes later. It's scary.'

'Yep, I guess that would have made us accessories to genocide. Tough to explain that to the International Criminal Court.'

Jerry laughed. 'Well we'll see how Ananya goes with that. Her reputation in the genetic research world will take a bit of a knock from serving twenty years for war crimes.'

'Ironically she may have actually gained some positive notoriety. I saw on the TV that her research has sparked a debate about new methods of mass vaccination. She may be an unlikely heroine in this story.'

'Very unlikely I'd say. But if it moves on human understanding then it wasn't all bad I guess. There has been a pretty cold response from Chad of course, condemning the Task Force collectively. Our reputation has certainly suffered.'

'I'm sure it will pass. There'll always be a new crisis.'

'Well as it happens…' said Jerry with a smile, '...Senegal is still waiting.' He placed a file on Al's bed. 'How about some light operational planning to relieve the tedium of healing?'

Later Jerry sat on the beach, looking south over the Gulf of Guinea to the distant shimmering horizon. He squinted under the blazing sun; it was shaping up to be a hot summer which would at least keep away many of the tourists he usually had to share his favourite drinking spot with. He regarded the few holidaymakers currently enjoying the gentle surf, blissfully unaware of the heinous crime that had been planned just a few kilometres away. Maybe the holidaymakers were wealthy Chadians who had come terrifyingly close to never again seeing their friends and family back home. He smiled grimly as he thought of the many tragedies that must be averted each day without ever making it into the public consciousness, and even worse the non-averted tragedies that remained unknown. In this post-information age it seemed so easy to manipulate the masses through government disinformation; it was never totally clear what was really happening at all.

He took a long pull on his beer. It was warming up; time to get a fresh one. He looked over to Chez Chay, which sat dark and empty, closed for refurbishment. Beyond it he caught sight of some beachcombers, searching the sand for anything of worth to sell. Probably refugees from the west he thought, come to seek better fortunes in the big city. Just like the millions of others, searching for a better future for their families and instead meeting the usual mix of fear and suspicion, which evolved into rejection and hostility. There were just too many people trying to access the limited resources. Jerry reflected on Lionel's scornful words about his beliefs and wondered if in some way Lionel had been right, and there really wasn't any hope for the continent. It was certainly a grim situation, with no prospect of improvement any time soon. If Lionel was dead, Jerry was quite sure his hateful ideas had not died with him, and there were many more like him with narrow minds and cold hearts. There was certainly much more human suffering to come in Africa, and the other continents.

He finished the beer and took another from the small cool box. There would be plenty more work for the Task Force for sure, but it could wait just another hour.

15151011R00188

Printed in Germany
by Amazon Distribution
GmbH, Leipzig